A Summer Affair

Also by Susan Wiggs
in Large Print:

Halfway to Heaven
The Lightkeeper
Passing Through Paradise
The You I Never Knew
Enchanted Afternoon
Home Before Dark

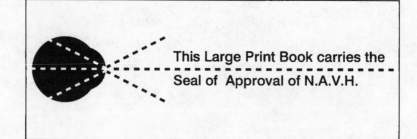

This Large Print Book carries the
Seal of Approval of N.A.V.H.

A Summer Affair

Susan Wiggs

WHEELER
PUBLISHING

Published in 2003 by arrangement with Harlequin Books S.A.

Wheeler Large Print Romance.

The text of this Large Print edition is unabridged.
Other aspects of the book may vary from the original edition.

Set in 16 pt. Plantin by Ramona Watson.

Printed in the United States on permanent paper.

Library of Congress Cataloging-in-Publication Data

Wiggs, Susan.
    A summer affair
        p. cm.
    ISBN 1-58724-523-X (lg. print : hc : alk. paper)
    1. San Francisco (Calif.) — Fiction.   2. Fugitives from justice — Fiction.   3. Female offenders — Fiction.
4. Single fathers — Fiction.   5. Physicians — Fiction.
6. Widowers — Fiction.   7. Large type books.   I. Title.
PS3573.I38616S86 2003
    813´.54—dc22   2003057581

Dedicated with love to Mary Hyatt —
"Mensch" a reader who became
a true friend.

National Association for Visually Handicapped
---------------------- *serving the partially seeing*

As the Founder/CEO of NAVH, the only national health agency solely devoted to those who, although not totally blind, have an eye disease which could lead to serious visual impairment, I am pleased to recognize Thorndike Press★ as one of the leading publishers in the large print field.

Founded in 1954 in San Francisco to prepare large print textbooks for partially seeing children, NAVH became the pioneer and standard setting agency in the preparation of large type.

Today, those publishers who meet our standards carry the prestigious "Seal of Approval" indicating high quality large print. We are delighted that Thorndike Press is one of the publishers whose titles meet these standards. We are also pleased to recognize the significant contribution Thorndike Press is making in this important and growing field.

Lorraine H. Marchi, L.H.D.
Founder/CEO
NAVH

★ Thorndike Press encompasses the following imprints: Thorndike, Wheeler, Walker and Large Print Press.

Acknowledgments

Thanks to my first readers, whose insights and observations always keep me going: Lois, Kate, Anjali, Rose Marie, Susan, Sheila, P.J., Joyce, Barb and Alice. As always, thanks to Martha Keenan of MIRA Books for her editorial eye. Grateful acknowledgment also belongs to the Daniel E. Koshland San Francisco History Center of the San Francisco Library, which directed me to the primary source material that inspired this story. Other primary source material came from Indiana University's machine-readable transcriptions of the Victorian Women Writers Project, including the works of Isabella Bird, the "Englishwoman in America." The Schaeffer Library of Drug Policy and the Library of Congress provided fascinating and factual information through their collections about opium legislation and the history of the opium trade.

Part One

Mad City

"San Francisco is a mad city, inhabited for the most part by perfectly insane people whose women are of remarkable beauty."

— Rudyard Kipling

One

He never even knew her name. Not her age,
nor her favorite color, nor what she looked
like when she smiled. All he knew for certain
was that she had been a prostitute, and she
had ingested too much black drop opium.

As though searching for some rationale for
the tragedy, he made a final study of her
gaunt, bony face, her frizzy hair the color of
a brass spittoon. One arm was permanently
disfigured from a poorly-healed break; it
must have ached for years. Yet in spite of all
that, she was oddly beautiful, almost defiantly
so in the face of the grotesque indignities
heaped upon her by life, and now by death.

Strange that he would be the last to look
upon her.

In a ritual he'd performed far too many
times, he tucked her into a bleached canvas
shroud. The garment had been hand sewn
and donated by the Ladies Aid Guild, whose
members gossiped and drank imported tea as
they performed good works for the betterment of society.

He pulled the drawstring tight. Then he

rolled the creaking wheeled cot out through the back of the building and stepped into the thick, cool air. San Francisco was a different place at the hollow hour between dark and dawn.

Night still haunted the city, darkness clinging in corners and crevices of the waterfront district, lingering under the bows of ships in the harbor and trailing down crooked stairways that led to dank-smelling basements. He checked his pocket watch. The colorless limbo would linger for another hour before first light smeared the foggy sky over the bay.

Travelers often remarked that San Francisco had grown into one of the world's great places, but he wouldn't know about that. These days he rarely left the city, anyway.

A rescue wagon, serving double duty as a morgue transport, backed up to the raised bay jutting out into the alley. "Let me give you a hand with that, Dr. Calhoun." Willie Bean, his orderly, jumped down from the driver's bench.

Together, with as much reverence as they could manage, they loaded the nameless woman into the wicker morgue casket on the flatbed cart.

Blue Calhoun tucked a stray corner of the shroud down into the casket, lowered the lid, then buckled the fastener to hold it shut. The ancient leather strap, cracked from frequent use, practically crumbled in his hand as he cinched it tight. The lid sprang upward several inches.

He stared at the broken curl of leather. "This is useless," he said.

"She won't notice," Willie pointed out.

"I will." The idea of the woman being driven through the city streets, her casket lid flapping open at every bump in the road, made him want to growl with frustration. He unbuckled the belt at his waist and yanked it through the trouser loops. Then he passed the supple Italian leather through the lid closure and fastened it securely. Feeling Willie's stare, Blue became conscious of the jerky, repressed violence of his movements.

He took a deep breath and stepped away from the wagon. Working half the night to save a woman beyond saving had left him exhausted and emptied out. "Ready," he said, signaling for Willie to go.

"You can't save them all, Doc." Willie took the reins. He clicked his tongue and drove off, the wagon disappearing into the weightless veil of fog until only the hollow clop of the horse's hooves could be heard. By this time tomorrow, the dead woman would be loaded into a contract box and buried among the sagebrush and sand dunes of Lime Kiln Point at a cost of $2.60 to the City and County of San Francisco.

Blue heard a few muffled pops — fireworks,

or more likely, gunshot, coming from the waterfront district. He was so hardened to the sound that he felt no alarm.

He rotated his aching shoulders, feeling knots and twinges of tension in every fiber of his body. His meddlesome friends and well-meaning family liked to remind him that he was a vigorous man in his prime, but he didn't feel that way at all. Each patient tore off a little piece of his heart, yet he carried on. This was his entire life now. He didn't know what else to do.

Long ago, he'd stopped questioning himself. It didn't matter why he was compelled to go down to the seamy underbelly of the city, night after night, to find the sickest, most hopeless souls, to gather them in like a blighted harvest, to nurture and heal, or to comfort and then let go. It took a certain measure of arrogance to practice medicine with such doggedness, but it was more than arrogance that drove him. He was like a miner who kept sifting and searching through the detritus of humanity for a glint of redemption. No matter how many people he rescued, dozens or hundreds or more, all his heroics would never make up for the one he'd failed to save.

He had spent the past ten years trying to reclaim that moment.

The distant *bong* of the clock in Montgomery Square signaled five o'clock. It was as good a time as any to head home, catch a few hours' sleep, then see his regular patients. The medical wing of the Mission Rescue League would be served during the day by his associates. The league was staffed by nuns and volunteers whose chief qualification was the only one that really mattered — compassion.

He collected his heavy satchel, jammed on a hard felt Homburg hat that had seen better days and climbed into his one-horse phaeton, a sporting vehicle he favored for the speed of getting through the city streets. Few horses had the strength and stamina to climb the undulating hills of San Francisco, and people generally made use of the cable cars whose steel ropes connected the commercial area like thick webs.

Blue rarely used cable cars. His horses came from his family's own breeding farm. He'd left behind a haunted childhood and grew up there, racing along the seaside cliffs on light-boned, muscular horses that quickly became famous throughout the region. Life had been unimaginably sweet there, at the ranch his parents called Cielito, so sweet it had left him ill-prepared for the harshness of the world.

He'd learned the easy lessons of life but not the hard ones. He used to believe life was made for joy and that love lasted forever. He joined the Union Army, and he actually believed at the outset that he fought for a just cause. Only later did he discover that even justice had its horrors. And the war was not even the worst thing that had happened to him.

He drove through the damp miasma rolling in off the bay. His route took him past filthy-looking hells with signs advertising Steam Beer, Five Cents. He passed the occasional reeling drunk, busy hod carrier, scurrying woman or furtive child fleeing with stolen goods.

In Keeler's Alley, a pair of Barbary Coast crimps headed toward the waterfront, supporting their human cargo between them — a half-conscious man whom they'd drugged, probably with a Micky Finn.

With no real hope of success, Blue pulled alongside the crimps and slowed the horse. "Looks like your friend's in a bad way," he said. He recognized this pair. The younger of the two wore a jaunty hat with a distinctive pheasant feather in the brim. They were Charles Pisco and Abner Punch, two of the most successful and shameless crimps in the area. For the right fee, they were known to do the sorts of things even bad men shunned.

"Aye, that's a fact," said Pisco.

The victim made a sound, something between a whistle and a snort. His face was obscured beneath the brim of a battered hat.

Blue knew better than to challenge the

16

crimps. For some years, he had maintained an uneasy territorial truce with men like Pisco and Punch. He didn't interfere with their business, and they didn't interfere with his. But tonight, still haunted by the nameless woman's death, he felt compelled to save the boy.

"I'm in no hurry. I could give him a lift," he offered.

"That won't be necessary, sir. We're nearly there."

They didn't say where, but he guessed they were headed for a bar pilot's Whitehall skiff, to be ferried out to a ship bound for the high seas. The shipmaster would pay the crimps a cut of the seaman's wages, and the victim would awaken to forced labor for untold months at sea.

"The boy's too young to raise a beard," Blue said as his head lolled back, showing a smooth, tender cheek.

"Old enough to run up a tab he can't pay at the Sailor's Home." The famous establishment, run by the Ladies Seaman's Friends Society, was the biggest and most corrupt crimp agency in town. Pisco offered a patently insincere grin. "Nice try, Dr. Blue, but the fact is, a sailor's life'll be a step up for this one. He's a little too fond of the Shanghai smoke."

"So you're in the business of curing addicts now?" Blue asked.

Punch laughed as though Blue had made a joke. Then he tipped his peaked hat. "Good day to ye, sir. We must be going." The men hurried with their burden out of range of the misty globe of light cast by a street lamp on the corner. Blue watched them for a moment, the lad small and slight between his two burly abductors.

This happened every night, Blue told himself. As Willie said, he couldn't save them all. It was absurd to even try.

He had no idea why he put his fingers to his lips and let out a sharp whistle, freezing the crimps in their tracks as they turned the corner toward the wharf area. He tapped the horse into a trot and caught up with them.

"How much?" he demanded.

Pisco and Punch exchanged a look. "Well, now, Doc, we're looking at a strong youngster here, a hard worker. I imagine he'll fetch at least eighty dollars."

"That's twice what you'd get, and you know it." Blue dug in his pocket and counted out five ten-dollar gold pieces. "It's a bird in the hand," he said. "Take it or leave it."

The transaction was finished in minutes. The boy lay in an unmoving heap on the floor of the open cart. For all Blue knew, he'd purchased a corpse.

As he headed away from the damp and seamy waterfront area, he drove past a block of densely-packed warehouses. Even at this

18

hour of the morning, the narrow street was jammed with drunks and thieves, laughing and fighting, disrupting traffic. Blue's carriage creaked and sagged, and the horse was skittish for several blocks, until the waterfront lay far behind.

Morning light tracked across the bay. The first ferries of the day glided between Alameda, Oakland and the city. The chill air was softened by a fine haze that would soon yield to hard summer sun.

Blue urged the horse to pick up the pace, for he was anxious to get some food and water into the greenhorn. He lived in a hilltop neighborhood of grand houses and broad gardens, where bellies were full of food instead of beer, young boys attended school rather than crimp joints and women were never sent nameless to paupers' graves.

His passenger, however, seemed to have other ideas. When Blue slowed for the turn into the service alley behind his house, the boy stirred. Clasping his hat down over his head and clutching a filthy, oversized coat around him, he jumped out and staggered away, into the rabbit warren of servants' quarters and stables that lined the alley.

"Hey," Blue yelled after him, but he already knew it was too late. The greenhorn would go sleep it off somewhere, and probably find himself in the same trouble tonight.

He shook his head over his expensive mistake and slid open the livery door himself, not wanting to awaken Efrena, who presided over the best stables in the district, with a half dozen stalls, three buggies and her own snug quarters aloft.

Muttering soft nonsense to the Cleveland Bay horse, a favorite from his parents' coastal breeding ranch, he removed the traces, rubbed down the damp hide and led him to his stall. After checking the water trough, he poured sweet oats. The horse jerked up his head and sidled back.

"Easy, Ferdinand," said Blue, latching the stall door. "We both need the same thing — breakfast and a nap."

Uncharacteristically, the horse didn't bury his muzzle in the grain, but grunted and flattened his ears.

"Please yourself, then," Blue said, and headed for the door, satchel in hand. He followed the gravel walkway to the back door of the house and stepped into the quiet kitchen. He helped himself to two of Mrs. Li's oat muffins, prepared last night and left in the larder for his early-morning meal. It was his favorite time of day, the empty, uneventful lull between the chaos of night at the Rescue League and the quiet order of his Nob Hill day practice. He took the muffins and a crock of butter into the dining room.

The moment he sat down, the back of his

neck prickled with the sense that he was not alone.

Then the unmistakable metal prod of a gun barrel pressed between his shoulder blades.

Two

The faint scent of burned powder stole through the air. The gun had been fired recently.

Violence erupted inside Blue, the reaction invisible to the sneak thief with the gun. He had a nearly uncontrollable urge to turn on the intruder and flatten him. But he resisted, forcing himself to breathe out slowly, to let go of the impulse. A scuffle was too risky right here, right now, considering what was at stake. *Lucas.* If he heard gunfire, the boy might try something rash.

Blue set down his butter knife and gingerly raised his hands. "Look," he said, speaking in a low voice so as not to awaken his son upstairs, "no need to hurt anyone. Take whatever it is you came for and be on your way."

"I require the immediate services of a physician," said a faint voice in an unexpected British accent.

For a split second he considered lying, then thought better of it. No need to send the intruder marauding through the household. "I'm Dr. Calhoun," he said.

"I know. You gave me a lift."

So this was the thanks he got for being a good Samaritan. He wondered why Pisco and Punch had failed to check for a gun. "You cost me fifty dollars."

"I didn't ask you to do that."

"If I hadn't, you'd be slave labor on a ship somewhere."

"No. I'd be dead." The boy's respiration was accelerating.

Blue flicked a glance at the clock above the dining room mantel. It was still early yet. Lucas wouldn't be up for another hour. Mrs. Riordan, the housekeeper, slept like the dead at the other end of the house. Delta, his assistant, rarely appeared before nine o'clock. Mrs. Li, who lived in a bungalow in the service alley with her daughter, would not report for duty until she had finished the day's shopping down at the farmer's market and at wharves where the fishing boats docked.

"I can't be of much help in this position," he pointed out, his hands still in the air.

The jab of the gun barrel was the only reply. The terrible silence was broken by the steady ticking of the mantel clock, and by a heavy *drip, drip* of some viscous substance hitting the oak parquet floor. Even before he glanced down to check, Blue knew it was blood. He could smell it, as familiar to him as brine to a seaman. He wondered why the

23

crimps had shot the boy. Or had someone else done the shooting?

"Put the gun away," he ordered, "and I'll have a look at that wound." He started to lower his hands. The gun pushed aggressively into the nape of his neck until his hands went back up. "I'm a physician by choice." He let irritation penetrate his voice. "I don't have to be forced at gunpoint to do my job."

"I've no money to pay." The intruder sounded incredibly young.

"I promise to waive my fee," he offered. Half of San Francisco knew that about him, or so it seemed.

"I was counting on that."

"I'm going to lower my hands and turn around," he said. "I'll take you to the surgery and we'll get you fixed up. You'll need to put away the gun."

"I'm keeping the gun."

"I'm worried about it going off," Blue said.

"I'm worried about dying," stated the gunman.

"Put it away, or I won't be able to treat you."

"Yes, you will. . . ." The voice trailed off into woozy silence. The gun barrel wavered. The floor squeaked and crystal clinked as the outlaw staggered back against the glass-fronted china cabinet. When the gun barrel wavered again, Blue stood and spun around, going for the weapon. Before he could disarm the intruder, the gun was aimed again, trained steadily at his chest. It was a well-oiled Colt's cavalry pistol, held in a child's curiously delicate hand.

Anger flashed, quick and hot. Child or not, this person had brought violence into his house. Still, despite the things he'd seen in his years of practicing medicine, Blue was shocked by the boy's appearance. Shadowed by the brim of a battered hat, narrowed eyes peered at him through a veil of pain and suspicion. Younger than Lucas, the intruder had rounded cheeks, now gray from traumatic blood loss and shock, lips bluish and trembling. The threadbare coat all but swallowed the slight form. The back hem of the old coat was stained scarlet. Blood dripped steadily on the parquet.

Blue wondered how he had fallen into the hands of Pisco and Punch. Homeless boys who managed to escape the crimps often turned to violence when they ran out of options. What shocked Blue about this lad was the youngster's stamina. He'd apparently followed Blue into the house and was still standing. He expected the outlaw to collapse at any moment. Then Blue would disarm the young fool and, more out of habit than compassion, try to save his life.

"Follow me to the surgery." Hands still in the air, he led the way to the foyer, through a door and under a breezeway. Purple clusters of wisteria dripped from the pergola vines that grew up from sturdy, wrist-thick trunks; he'd planted them a lifetime ago, for Sancha.

A trail of round, livid drops marked their route to the annex adjacent to the main house. At this hour of the morning, it was deserted. Blue stepped through a gleaming white enameled door and held it open for his unexpected patient. He had built this place for healing, but through the years it had grown to something more. Here, women confided their most intimate secrets and men confessed their deepest fears. His duties as a physician gave him access to the private lives of strangers, and he kept his patients' confidences with a reverence that was almost sacred.

"Put the gun away and I'll examine you in here," he said to the gunman.

"Stop complaining about the gun," said the boy. "It stays with me. For protection."

That accent, Blue reflected, would not be out of place at an English tea party. "From me?" he asked.

The narrowed eyes measured him. "Perhaps."

"You came here for help. Let me help you."

The desperado's breathing became more labored by the moment. With instincts he had never really lost, Blue grabbed the gun. He disarmed the outlaw the way he had learned in thousands of army drills, angling his opponent's arm skyward while gripping the wrist. He looped his thumb behind the trigger to keep it from firing. In a matter of seconds, he had possession of the pistol.

A familiar wave of revulsion lurched through him. Even holding a firearm he had no intention of using nauseated him with old horrors. With quick efficiency, he unloaded the gun, tossed it into a metal cabinet and locked the door. Pocketing the key, he turned back to his patient only to find himself staring at emptiness.

The outlaw had collapsed on the floor. A ghastly bloodstain bloomed at the back of the threadbare coat. Working quickly, he lifted the slight form to the cloth-draped table and lay the lad in a prone position, facedown. Grabbing a pair of surgical scissors, Blue cut the back of the coat up the middle from hem to neck. Under that was a linen shirt, gray with age, saturated with blood. He cut the shirt away and applied the scissors to a frayed undervest, exposing a messy wound.

Blue rolled up his sleeves, his narrowed gaze never leaving the scarlet ooze. He would have to proceed without Delta's assistance. Not impossible, he reminded himself. In his days at the army post in Wyoming, he'd operated under far worse conditions.

Seeping blood obscured his view of the surgical field. He dipped a sponge in a basin of boric acid solution and cleaned away the blood until he could view the wound.

It was a good thing the boy had passed out. Because removing the bullet was going to be excruciating.

Inserting a finger into the entry site, Blue determined that a single ball had penetrated below the inferior angle of the right scapula.

"How did you manage to get this far?" he asked, talking to himself as was sometimes his habit when he operated. "A wound like this would fell a two-hundred-pound man."

The bullet had burrowed across the narrow back, and Blue's sensitive fingers discovered that the lead ball was still lodged inside, setting the patient up for a raging infection. So he went on a hunt, probing delicately and consistently, until at last he found the slug. Wasting no time, he used a pair of locking pincers to remove the bullet.

He debrided the ragged tissue with precise cuts, removing gritty adhesions and lacerations from the site of the injury. Threads of powder-burned fiber from the dirty shirt polluted the torn muscle and flesh. Blue set his jaw, hoping the patient would not regain consciousness in the midst of the excruciating process of cleaning, closing and dressing the wound. At medical college, he had studied under Gordon Black, a gifted Scottish surgeon who believed with unwavering conviction in the importance of maintaining a sterile surgical field. Not all doctors embraced the concept, but Blue's service as an army surgeon had provided plenty of support for the idea. At least ninety percent of bullet wounds treated in the field resulted in lethal infections, and contamination was surely the key factor.

For a second, rage flashed through him, quick and sure as a lightning strike. Someone had gunned the lad down like a fleeing animal.

Except this one had not been down for long.

Admitting to a grudging admiration for the patient, Blue asked, "Who shot you?" No answer, of course. "You were running away when it happened. That much is clear."

The likely scenario involved some variety of mischief on the Barbary Coast, the place where all such troubles started in the city. The shadowy district of shabby bars and bawdy houses provided Blue and his colleagues at the Mission Rescue League with a steady supply of victims. Most suffered the fractures and contusions of assault, however, as they were rolled for their valuables. The unfortunate on the table here didn't seem likely to possess anything of value save the well-maintained pistol Blue had seized.

Perhaps this lad had managed to escape Pisco and Punch and stagger away, still under the influence of the heavily-drugged beer known as Mickey Finn. Perhaps he'd taken a bullet in the back during the flight from his captors.

But the crimps favored blackjacks and knives over guns. It was not to their advantage to cause permanent damage to their stock-in-trade.

Unless the youth was damaged when the crimps got their hands on him. In that case, maybe they weren't taking him to a ship's captain at all. No wonder they'd parted with the victim so readily — they'd already been paid to dispose of him.

Blue used surgical silk and a curved needle to close the wound. Then he applied a bandage treated with herbal salve and mustard plaster. It was a healing poultice no one in medical school had ever heard of. The remedy was the invention of his talented nurse, and over the years he'd come to the conclusion that nothing worked better than Delta's preparation. He laid the patch over the wound and found a roll of gauze to wrap around the gunman's torso.

A quiet moan drifted from the surgery table. The patient would be howling in agony soon. Without Delta's help, Blue knew he'd have an awkward time binding the wound. He spread the cut edges of the bandage across the narrow back. He used his surgical shears to cut the fabric of the coat and shirtsleeves down each slender arm. Then he gently held a bony shoulder, turning the patient on one side and winding the bandage around the torso.

He dropped the ball of gauze. He nearly dropped the patient as well.

He had seen plenty in his years as a physician, but on this particular summer morning, he wasn't quite ready for the unexpected. The outlaw on his surgical table was a woman.

As confounded as he was mortified, he quickly finished bandaging her. Then he snatched a gray cotton gown from a folded stack in the cabinet and threaded it on to the woman's arms. The bedjacket was standard army issue; he'd kept a dozen or so of the garments. After being cashiered in disgrace ten years earlier, Blue had felt disinclined to return the government's property. In light of all that had happened back then, appropriating a few bedjackets seemed a minor infraction.

After he tied the jacket at the nape of her neck, he laid her on her side. The woman was small and lean; no wonder he'd mistaken her for a boy. The swath of gauze around her chest accentuated her thinness. There was a certain delicacy in her features and hands that fit well with the few words she'd uttered in her British accent. Her deep brown hair might have been glossy at one time, he supposed, gingerly lifting a dark lock away from the neckline of the garment. Despite her youthful appearance, he noted a certain quality in her sharp features and callused hands that hinted at hard experience.

She had been remarkably quick with the gun. And quick to threaten violence. Who knew what life had done to the creature in his care? A bright spark of interest took him by surprise. He considered himself a compassionate man, but his newest patient affected him in a peculiar way.

Time to alert the authorities. As one of the city's original subscribers to the American Speaking Telephone Company, he could normally count on fast service when he needed it.

The woman moaned again and drew up her legs, a reflex response to extreme pain. Agony and defiance mingled in a soft, almost musical voice uttering a wordless plea. He glanced at the locked metal cabinet containing syringes and morphine. Perhaps he should give her something for the pain. No, he thought, best to get help without delay.

An ominous metallic click stopped him halfway to the door.

The patient had awakened. Blue turned to find her sitting up and pointing a black-handled Derringer straight at him.

Although needles of panic iced his veins, he regarded her calmly — a young, desperate woman with hacked-off hair and eyes full of secrets.

"Again, miss?" he asked, allowing a note of exasperation to creep into his voice. She truly was remarkable, he admitted to himself. Her resilience was impressive.

Yet her entire appearance had an unexpected effect on him. Because in the middle of his cold fury, he felt something else. Something rare. Not just interest, but a fascination, almost.

"You should have checked for an ankle holster," she pointed out. Seated with her legs dangling over the side of the table, she kept the cocked gun and her unsettling gaze aimed at him.

Blue weighed his options. Despite her size and the gravity of her wound, she had admirable stamina and an impressive threshold for pain. She spoke in an educated manner and was damnably clearheaded and focused for someone who had just been shot and then operated on.

"That's not the only thing I should have checked," he said.

"I should like a glass of water," the woman said. "Please."

Blue felt a prickle of irritation — at himself. He was the physician here. It was his job to ease her suffering. Not for the first time he realized that grief, time and loneliness had eroded his soul, hardened him to the pain of others. That was why he labored at the Rescue League, why he employed trou-

bled or homeless women in his own household. It was a penance for him. The trouble was, his self-imposed penance failed to work. He was no closer to redemption than this gun-toting Englishwoman.

He offered her water from a porcelain cup, which she managed to drink without lowering the gun or taking her eyes off Blue. He knew that if she discharged the weapon, she was unlikely to hit him, even at close range. But he couldn't afford to take a chance, not with Lucas in the house.

"Thank you for saving my life," she said, setting down the empty cup.

"Another jewel in the Redeemer's crown," he said.

"Ouch. Your sarcasm's sharper than your surgeon's knife."

He didn't bother to apologize as he sat down on a swivel stool and regarded his patient. She was as alert as ever, but the bright hardness of her eyes, coupled with the ashen pallor of her face, told a deeper story. An infection was already building. He'd learned to recognize the subtle symptoms.

"I can offer you ether or morphine for the pain," he said.

"No, thank you. I need to keep my wits about me."

So she was familiar with the effects of the drugs he had in his medicine locker, or at least she pretended to be. Refusing to allow

himself to weigh the risk, he stood and placed his hands at her waist, thumbs drawing inward circles over the rough cotton duck fabric of her pants. She was a soft wisp of a woman, one he'd term fragile if he didn't know better. She gasped and shoved the small handgun hard at his chest. "What the devil do you think you're doing?"

He continued his examination, pressing his hands over her midsection and then down each thigh, into the dusty leather of each boot. "Checking for more concealed weapons." A curious throb of awareness disturbed his concentration. He was reacting in the most unguarded and basest way to the soft, female form his hands were exploring. It was insane, he told himself. He really ought to get more sleep. "You'll forgive me for not trusting you."

"I'll do nothing of the sort." She kicked at him, narrowly missing his groin. "You're impudent. What sort of man would debauch a woman who came to him in need?"

"The sort who's a doctor. And I assure you, I'm not in the habit of debauching my patients. If I need to debauch someone, I imagine I'd choose a woman who doesn't share your affinity for mayhem."

"I'm actually not a violent person. I've had a difficult night."

"That makes two of us, Miss . . . ?"

Not surprisingly, she didn't fill in the blank

for him. Continuing to ignore the gun, he picked up the old coat he'd cut from her bleeding body and patted it down. A crinkling of paper in one of the pockets drew his attention.

She dropped the porcelain cup. It shattered on the floor. "Don't you —"

"Too late." He took out a printed first-class parlor car billet from the Great Western Railroad Company. "Miss Isabel Fish-Wooten," he read from the ticket. "I'm guessing that would be you. Traveled from Denver to San Francisco, I see." He checked the date. "Been here less than a fortnight, and you've already managed to get yourself shot."

Their gazes locked, and he felt a heated stab of resentment. She had brought violence into his home and his place of work. He deserved some answers. "Tell me, Miss Fish-Wooten," he said. "What are you doing in disguise, with a bullet in your back?"

She regarded him with a steadiness he knew must be hard-won. "If I answered that, Doctor, would it change the way you treat me?"

"Of course not. On my oath as a physician, I serve humanity without prejudice."

"Then why ask?"

For a traumatically wounded woman, she was annoyingly logical, he thought, making no effort to hide his resentment. After all these years, he should know better than to ask. Some stories spoke for themselves: the coal miner with wheezing lungs, the upcountry greenhorn with a private itch, an immigrant girl bleeding to death from a self-induced abortion, the elderly war veteran with defeated yellow eyes and years of whiskey on his breath.

"I concede your point," he said. "In fact, you don't need a gun to make it."

"Nevertheless," she said in a soft whisper.

Isabel Fish-Wooten. What the devil sort of name was that? A name for a dainty society fribble, plucking lace hankies from her sleeve and crooking out one finger as she sipped tea from a bone china cup. Not impersonating a boy and getting involved in Barbary Coast shoot-outs.

She studied his diplomas, framed and hanging on the wall. "Theodore B. Calhoun. Your medical degree —" she squinted at an ornate certificate "— is from Toland Medical College. I have never heard of that."

"It has a different name now. The University of California."

"I'm sure that's a fine institution."

Blue could tell she was weak from blood loss and was likely to drift off. Then he could appropriate the pistol and bring in the authorities. He didn't much care for authority, but he despised guns even more. He regarded the Derringer with loathing. It was no bigger than a child's toy, yet he knew well the havoc it could wreak. He was certainly no stranger to guns, and even now the sight of one dredged up memories that had haunted him for years.

"You have a beautiful home," said Miss Fish-Wooten. "Are you a millionaire?"

The question startled a brusque laugh from him. She was an absurd woman, but keeping her engaged in conversation seemed safer than letting her wave a gun around the surgery. "I beg your pardon."

"I was wondering if you're a millionaire." She offered a vague, rather startlingly beautiful smile, and just for a moment, he could see the woman she might be if she weren't an outlaw and half-dead on his table.

She put away the smile like a cherished keepsake and added, "I came to America to marry one."

He eyed the ragged remains of her clothing, lying in a shredded heap on the floor. "I take it you didn't succeed."

"I abandoned the plan after meeting a few truly ghastly prospects. All the candidates I encountered were either decrepit, lecherous or both. So I changed my plans."

"You don't want to marry a millionaire after all?"

"I intend to become one on my own."

"And have you succeeded?" he inquired.

She dismissed the question with a wave of her hand. Even so, the gun held steady. "Not yet. But I'm in no hurry. There's too much of this country to see. Too much of the world. My vocation in life is to travel. I like to describe myself as a lady adventurer."

"You should be more careful about the sort of adventures you pursue."

"And how would you describe yourself?" she inquired. "As the famous Dr. Calhoun, medical director of the Mission Rescue League?"

He didn't bother to reply, nor to ask her how she knew of him. People in need tended to find him quickly. People who lacked money found him even quicker than that. Still, she was the first to demand his services at gunpoint. Despite that unique situation, he held his tongue. All his life, he had been a man of few words, but that didn't mean he didn't have plenty on his mind.

Miss Isabel Fish-Wooten had no interest in him anyway, he told himself. She neither cared for nor understood his passion for healing. She was probably only making conversation in order to keep herself awake. She blinked her increasingly heavy eyelids, which kept trying to flutter shut. She fought delirium with a certain grim determination that was at odds with her cultivated manner of speaking. She held on to consciousness for much longer than he would have predicted.

"May I have more water, please?" she asked.

He found an unbroken cup in the cabinet, keeping his eyes on the gun. "You don't have to demand anything from me at gunpoint," he said.

"That's what I was told by the last man I shot."

He turned to refill the cup from an ewer under the pump. "Do you make a habit of shooting people?"

"Certainly not." She sniffed in an injured fashion. "But this is the wild West. I read all about it in Mr. Mark Twain's newspaper column. People live and die by the gun here."

"Fools live and die by the gun here."

His bitterness seemed to startle her. "You are half-right, at least."

He handed her the water and watched her drink. She inspired in him an unsettling mixture of interest, annoyance, compassion and revulsion. She was not beautiful, nor even conventionally pretty, yet he found he could not take his eyes off that intense, piquant face. Her storm-colored eyes were set off by thick lashes and shadowed by secrets. She had a small nose, pointed chin and the dewy pale skin that characterized English girls. Not that he'd known many English girls, but aside from the gunshot wound and the terrible haircut, this one seemed fairly typical.

"You'll want to send word of your mishap," he said. "Whom shall I contact?"

She frowned. "Contact?"

Gathering patience, he said, "About your injury. You'll need serious bed rest and plenty of help during your recovery. Can we send a wire to your parents or . . . ?"

"No."

"Any family? A traveling companion?"

"No." With each "no," she sagged a little more on the cushioned table.

"Look, instead of playing this guessing game, just tell me whom to contact."

"No one. As a matter of fact, I must be on my way."

"I'm afraid not, Miss Fish."

"Fish-Wooten, if you please. And I certainly shall be on my way."

"You're injured. You've undergone a serious surgical procedure. The risk of infection is high. In my professional opinion, you must keep still and rest."

"Did I ask for your professional opinion?"

"No."

"Then I shall —"

"You demanded it. At gunpoint," he reminded her.

"Oh. I did, didn't I? Well, you've rendered your opinion, and I am grateful. But I must be going."

Exasperated by the woman and by the absurd conversation, he said, "Let me help you lie down."

"No, thank you." She propped her shoulder against the wall. He could see her battling shock and fatigue — and winning the fight.

He stole a glance at the clock. In perhaps another fifteen minutes, Delta would be coming to work and Lucas would be getting up. He didn't relish the prospect of either of them encountering the first patient of the day.

He stayed quiet, hoping she would drop off to sleep. As expected, she started to nod, her eyelids sliding to half mast and her head lolling to one side. His gaze slipped to her gun hand. She still kept her index finger curved around the trigger.

He leaned forward, preparing to make his move, when she dragged herself alert, her eyes opening wide, eyebrows lifting. He froze, hoping she couldn't tell from his stance that he'd been going for the gun.

"Just because I've stopped talking," she told him, "doesn't mean you've won the argument."

He couldn't even recall what the argument was about. But he simply nodded and maintained his silence. She seemed satisfied and relaxed against the wall. A moment later, her chin sagged to her chest. Her hand, still holding the gun, lay in her lap but she was truly asleep, her breathing slow and even through slightly parted lips.

Finally, Blue thought. She had lasted longer than many a grown man with lesser injuries than a bullet in the back. His window of opportunity was closing fast.

He could hear the distant, buttery voice of Delta Beasley, singing as she came up the walk. He set his jaw and scowled. It was a fact that all women were born noisemakers. Delta was the finest nurse he knew, but she had an annoying penchant for singing spirituals, a habit Blue found depressing. His very earliest years of life had been spent on a Virginia plantation, and the singing reminded him of those days. Given what had happened there, before his father brought the family to California, he didn't relish reminders.

Focusing on his mysterious patient, he knew he had only seconds to take possession of the gun. As a young soldier facing the chaos of battle, Blue had learned to be quick and decisive. Later, as a physician stationed at a fort in Wyoming, he'd learned the value of stealth and precision.

One thing he'd never learned to appreciate was the unending treachery of a female. He practically owned the weapon when, in one swift movement, she straightened up, pointing the pistol at his chest.

"I only ever give a man one warning," she said through gritted teeth. "You just used yours up."

"That won't stop me from trying," he said, as furious with himself as with her.

"What's the matter?" scolded Delta. Like a well-stoked locomotive, she marched into the

43

surgery and eyed the bloody bullet lying in an enameled surgical tray. "Don't you get enough patients on your own, you got to go dragging gunshot victims in from the Lord and his apostles know where?" She placed her hands on her hips and looked from Blue to the gun to the patient. "I declare, you probably go down to the waterfront and pry up rocks better left alone." The whole time she spoke, Delta moved toward Miss Fish-Wooten. "Hold out your hand, girl, and let me check your pulse."

The edgy patient, gun in hand, shook her head. "My pulse is fine, I'm sure."

Delta sniffed disdainfully. "I bet you got a fever."

"No fever," Miss Fish-Wooten said with a stubborn lift of her chin.

"You sure know how to pick them," Delta said to Blue.

"You keep nagging me about finding a new woman," he said.

"That ain't funny, boy. Where'd you get this one, anyway?"

"She found me." He caught Delta's expression. "I swear, she did. One minute I was eating a muffin, and the next thing I knew, she had a gun to my head."

"And blood on your floor. I saw the trail. A fine mess, too. Bernadette's going to have a fit of apoplexy. You know how fussy she is about her floors. I swear, you need to sleep some nights, 'stead of prowling around digging up trouble. You won't do anyone a lick of good if you don't get some rest. The world needs rescuing but no law says you got to see to all of it personally." The whole time she spoke, she kept her attention on the patient. "Honey, let me get you another pillow."

"I'm not lying down," said Miss Fish-Wooten.

"Just to lean on, baby," Delta said in her soothing lullaby of a voice. "I'll fetch one from the linen cabinet here."

Blue motioned with his eyes for Delta to grab the gun. Over the years, he and his assistant had learned to communicate without words, sending silent messages across the surgical table.

They'd known each other since their army days. How a young slave girl had become a surgical nurse for the Union Army was the stuff of legend. She had served at the hospital of the Union Second Corps at Gettysburg. The survival rate in her command was the highest of the battle. Because she was a female and a Negro, she did not win any medals for her fearless service, patching up Union soldiers and sending them back onto the field of combat. As ham-fisted stubborn as any morally righteous woman could be, Delta Beasley didn't need medals. She won something far more precious — the hearts of the men whose lives she saved.

To this day, a few retired soldiers still remembered her with a letter or small gift at Christmas.

Blue was one of those privileged few. As a wounded and terrified sixteen-year-old horse soldier, he had been put into her care. When she'd saved his life, he had promised her he would study medicine. More than two decades later, he'd not only kept that promise, he'd made Delta an integral part of his practice.

They continued, in silence, to weigh their chances against the lady adventurer. Too risky, Delta indicated with a flickering glance at the gun.

He noted the steadiness of the stranger's trigger finger and the steely look in her eyes. It was an expression he remembered from his days of treating battle wounds in the Indian wars after he earned his medical credentials.

This woman possessed a warrior's angry will to live. She must be suffering unimaginable agony, yet she showed only disdainful superiority as she said, "I know what you're thinking, both of you. And your assistant is correct, Dr. Calhoun. It's best to avoid provoking me. I confess to having an occasionally volatile temper." She caressed the trigger with her finger, yet all the while, she never stopped staring at Blue. "Pray don't try anything. I would hate to have to hurt anyone. But you understand, that wouldn't stop me."

Delta nodded. "Honey, I only try what I

know I can get away with. You want to hang on to that gun, you go right ahead. I never had much use for a gun myself. But you go on and keep yours. I won't pay it no mind."

She'd be as good as her word, Blue knew. Delta always was.

"I reckon you'll be late on your rounds," she said to him. "And I guess we'd best report this shooting to the police."

Miss Fish-Wooten scrambled from the table, swaying a little as she jammed on the battered hat. "I'm afraid I must be going. I'll need my Colt's back, please." She underscored her request with the Derringer.

As he unlocked the cabinet, Blue wished he'd left the damned thing loaded. Since his departure from army service, he hadn't turned a gun on anyone, but he'd never been invaded in quite this manner, either.

"And the bullets," she added, helping herself to a laboratory smock hanging from the back of the door. Wincing with pain, she donned the bleached cotton coat and put the pistol and bullets in the pocket. Then she backed toward the door, wobbling a little.

Go, thought Blue. Fast and far.

But as quickly as the thought crossed his mind, he said, "You shouldn't be up and about yet. You're weak from trauma and blood loss, and you're bound to get a deadly infection."

"Are you asking me to stay?"

"I'm telling you the hazards of leaving."

"That answers my question, then."

She took two more steps backward, then turned and hurried toward the exit. She stumbled out, letting the spring-hinged door swish shut behind her.

By the time he realized he'd never see the woman again, Blue was shaking. The reaction was wholly unexpected. After all he'd seen and done, nothing should surprise him, nor move him to any emotion except the steely sense of duty that had ruled his heart for the past decade. He thought, after such a long time, that he'd found a way to live his life. It was not joyful, but at least useful, and he had taught himself to neither want nor expect more. Deep down, he knew he didn't deserve more. His fatal mistake had been in succumbing to restlessness and ambition rather than settling down to a quiet life. If he'd learned to be content rather than rejoining the army in search of adventure, Sancha would still be with him.

Yet while he was tending Isabel Fish-Wooten, something had flickered to life inside him, a rare energy he'd never felt before. He quickly ground out the spark.

He turned to find Delta studying him. Her face resembled a fresh-baked currant bun, plump and shining.

"What?" he asked.

"Mmm-hmm," was all she said. Then she turned and set about cleaning up the surgery.

Three

Blue's only son came bumbling, bleary-eyed and surly, down to the kitchen a few minutes later, in search of food. At fifteen, Lucas Montgomery Calhoun was as handsome and sulky as a Lake District poet, and had the disposition of a bear disturbed from hibernation.

He acknowledged his father with a growl and jerked open the pantry door. "We're out of graham gems," he said, ambling through the arched doorway to the dining room.

"I'll send a news wire to the *San Francisco Examiner.*" Blue lightly touched the samovar on the sideboard to see if there was the slightest hope of warm coffee left in the urn. But, of course, the flame under the samovar had burned out while he was cleaning up the surgery after treating his mysterious gunshot victim.

With the air of a starving martyr, Lucas flung himself into a chair. "I don't see why we're always running out of things to eat."

"Because you eat everything in sight," Blue said. "You've been doing it for years." He drew a sludgelike substance from the samovar and took an experimental sip. Cold and bitter. Truth be told, he hadn't had a decent cup of coffee in ten years. Mrs. Li was a brilliant cook, but had never mastered the science of making coffee. Mrs. Riordan, the housekeeper, probably made excellent coffee, but Mrs. Li protected her turf, right down to the flame beneath the coffee urn.

Lucas clunked his elbows on the table. "I wake up starving and there's nothing to eat —"

To shut him up, Blue stuffed the abandoned, half-eaten muffin in the boy's mouth. "You know, in some aboriginal cultures, the eldest son goes out into the bush and hunts for the family's food every day."

Chewing and swallowing, Lucas nodded at the scene outside the big picture window. Huge houses with formal gardens stretched as far as the eye could see, and the roadway was jammed with hacks and a straining cable car. "I'll get right on that," he said. "Afterward, we can start on the ritual scarring."

Blue watched his son with equal measures of exasperation and affection as he followed Lucas to the kitchen. The boy grabbed a steel milk can from the icebox and washed down the muffin, drinking straight from the can.

"Where did you learn that?" Blue asked.

Lucas found another muffin and consumed the whole thing in one bite. "Mrph," he said.

Blue marveled at his capacity to consume

food at a furious rate, like a wild creature preparing for winter.

He had Byronic good looks, with wavy dark hair spilling over a noble brow. The shining hair framed an olive-toned face so like his mother's that sometimes Blue found it hard to look at him. Every reminder of Sancha was a stab at his heart.

Today, the boy was wearing rugged dungarees and a threadbare shirt with the sleeves rolled back. He looked more like a ragpicker than the son of a doctor.

"I hope you're not planning on going out in public like that," said Blue.

Lucas threw him a long-suffering look. "I'm working on the grounds of St. Mary's today. Father Jock needs help with the mowing and pruning." He took another drink from the milk can.

Blue immediately felt guilty. He had a bad habit of assuming the worst about his son. It was true that Lucas always seemed to be in trouble, though. During the school term, his teachers complained that he cared more for mischief and pranks than study and books. Over the course of the summer, he and his gang of rowdy friends trolled the city hills like sailors on shore leave.

This streak of altruism was as welcome as it was unexpected. "Oh. I didn't realize you'd volunteered for the church," Blue said. "In that case —"

"Do not drink straight from the can." Mrs. Li's sharp-toned voice cut through the kitchen as she came bustling in through the back door, her arms laden with parcels and her daughter June in tow. "Use a glass."

"Can't." He tipped the can, showing her. "We're out of milk."

"There is no delivery until tomorrow," she scolded. The cook's lacquered hair was done up in a rudderlike arrangement that bobbed in agitation as she spoke. Blue wondered idly if she slept with her hair in that complicated coiffure. It must be damnably uncomfortable.

Lucas wiped his sleeve across his mouth and grinned, but not at Mrs. Li. All his attention was focused on the cook's daughter.

Seeming to shrink into the shapeless broadcloth sacque she wore, June averted her gaze as rose-tinted blotches bloomed on her face. At sixteen, she had reached that peculiar stage of almost unbelievable beauty, when the sweetness of girlhood collided with the frank, sensual appetite of womanhood. There was, of course, a physiological explanation for this transition, but Lucas didn't know that. He thought it was magic.

If Blue tried to tell him otherwise, the lad would never believe it. Of course, he didn't believe anything his father said these days.

Look at our boy, Sancha, Blue thought with a sudden bright pang of regret. He's falling in love. Is there something I'm supposed to do about that, some advice I should be giving him? How the devil do I handle this on my own?

"You go now, shoo." Mrs. Li made a whisking motion toward the door with her hands. Like Blue, she had detected the crackle that charged the air lately between their children. Lucas and June had grown up together, practically brother and sister, but a few months ago all that had changed. The change coincided with a certain lush ripeness that had come over June in her fifteenth springtime.

"I'll be home by suppertime," said Lucas, snatching another muffin and rushing out the door.

"Maybe there's hope for the boy yet," Blue mused, watching the lanky, loping adolescent hurry toward St. Mary's with one suspender dangling and the sunlight flashing in his glossy hair. "He's working in the churchyard today."

"Maybe he learn his lesson this time."

"How's that?" Blue frowned.

June said something in Mandarin to her mother.

Mrs. Li waved her silent, then pressed the palms of her hands together. "Oh, he did not tell you. This is punishment, not good works."

Blue's pride congealed to disappointment. "What did he do this time?"

53

June spoke again in Chinese, an urgent protest. Mrs. Li ignored her daughter. "Steal communion wine from church storeroom. He and his friends, they drink until they get sick. Father Jock found Lucas sleeping in church."

"Then the boy had a better evening than I did," declared Rory McKnight, letting himself into the kitchen without knocking.

Blue's best friend was a ball of energy, in constant motion as he greeted the ladies, affording them the same respect and charm he'd offer to a gold-rush heiress. Then he went into the sunny adjacent dining room in search of coffee. McKnight had flame-red hair and an infectious sense of humor. The purpose of his visit was to discuss the Rescue League, which he served as chairman of the board of directors. But thanks to Miss Isabel Fish-Wooten, Blue was running behind, had not slept a wink and would have to reschedule.

"What am I going to do about Lucas this time?" Blue asked, plowing a weary hand through his hair.

"Thumbscrews?" Rory asked, sipping his coffee, then wincing. "The rack?"

Blue folded his arms across his chest and faced the window, scowling in the direction of St. Mary's. From here, he could see the slender Gothic spire and one side of the church, skirted by a broad swath of greensward bordered by flowers. In one corner, by a stone fence, there was an outbuilding or gardening shed of sorts. There, Father Jock supervised a work crew of ne'er-do-wells, outfitting them with rakes, scythes and a wheelbarrow.

"Maybe I should send him to finish his schooling with the Jesuits of Santa Clara," Blue said.

"What about military school?" Rory suggested.

"Good plan," he said. "That way he'll be not just an angry, rebellious youth, but an angry, rebellious youth with a gun." Given his history with the military, Blue wasn't about to entrust his son to an institution that taught blind obedience through pointless drills and endless marches, run by cruel officers who cloaked themselves in lies.

Rory studied his manicure, then took out a handkerchief to buff one fingernail with the precise attention to detail he gave all aspects of grooming. "Why is he angry? Why is he rebellious?"

"Because he's breathing?" Blue suggested.

"Because he's fifteen."

"That's not helpful." But Blue grinned as he said it, his heart lightening for the first time since black drop opium had killed one of his patients. Rory always managed to lift his mood. They'd met as soldiers in the War Between the States. Blue had been shot and left for dead. Then, risking death himself, a young infantryman named Rory McKnight had carried him off the field of battle and rafted him a mile down the river to a hospital tent that more properly resembled a slaughterhouse, where dying men placed bets on the speed with which the barbers could amputate limbs. But there, his luck had held. Rory had taken him not to a field surgeon armed with charriere saw and brass tourniquet, but to the formidable nurse called Delta Beasley.

After the war, Rory and Blue had shared quarters as each finished his schooling. Did Lucas have a friend like this? Blue wondered. Did he have someone he could count on, no matter what?

Rory folded the handkerchief in measured lines and tucked it into the pocket of his frockcoat, leaving exactly a half-inch margin showing. When they'd shared quarters as university students, Blue used to tease McKnight about his fastidious habits, but Rory clung to them without apology. He was a man of humble background and remarkable accomplishments. Given the boyhood he'd endured, he felt entitled to treat himself well.

As a child, he'd been rescued from the ghetto known as Five Points in New York City. The Children's Aid Society had sent him west aboard one of the famous so-called orphan trains to a family in Nebraska. Having no taste for farm life, McKnight had headed for San Francisco. He'd made the most of every opportunity offered, from being a charity student at the Pacifica Latin School to a full-tuition scholar at Yarmouth College. He was now a skilled criminal lawyer in the city.

"Remind me never to have children," Rory said.

"And you're so good at taking my advice."

"I am when you're right. But you're rarely right." Rory set a case of legal briefs on the table. "I, on the other hand, am frequently right. You should've remarried long ago, my friend. Raising Lucas with the help of a wife would have been far easier than going it alone."

"You sound like my stepmother," said Blue. "Eliza's a big believer in rescuing widowers with troubled offspring."

"I rest my case," said Rory. "Eliza changed your father's life. His heart. His whole world —"

"I don't need to change my life or my heart or my world. Just my son." To avoid the never-to-be-resolved topic, he said, "You mentioned having a rougher night than my wine-stealing son."

"I certainly did. One of my clients dragged me out of bed in the wee hours. There was a shooting down at the waterfront, and he was called in for questioning."

Blue felt a hum of awareness, as though he

already knew what he couldn't possibly know. "Was he involved in the shooting?"

"Not this time," Rory said, "but he's always been a favorite of the police."

"So what happened?"

"It was a shoot-out of some sort. Over an opium shipment, of course. After all, what would the opium trade be without violence? I've never known importers to be so reluctant to pay their duty fees. For a perfectly legal substance, it certainly does cause a lot of trouble."

Blue knew why that was so, and it wasn't just the money.

Rory made another attempt with the coffee but abandoned it in disgust. "A police officer was shot," he said. "The gunman, too, but he escaped."

Blue felt a chill that quickly escalated to icy apprehension. "Did — Is the policeman dead?"

"No, but I understand he could be, soon. He's at Mercy Heights Hospital. Let's hope they keep him alive long enough to identify the scoundrel who shot him."

Four

Sometimes when she first awakened, she made herself lie very still, with her eyes closed. For a few precious minutes, she would try to remember who she was. Then she would decide who she would be this day.

She had so many different masks, she sometimes forgot which one she was wearing. Like now.

The burning sun cleaved through the vision, splintering it into bright shards. She became aware of dry, earthy smells and distant sounds of traffic. Some object rough with rust leaned against her. She sensed a confined space, cluttered with cobwebby equipment.

She drifted, watching harsh slants of light through the planks in the wall of a . . . She couldn't quite recall what sort of abandoned building she'd staggered into. Some kind of storage shed.

A fecund aroma hung in the warm air. Through the dimness, she could make out the iron skeletons of tools — a rake, perhaps, and some type of bladed, long-handled scythe. She watched a spider spinning her web, patient and noiseless in the unmoving hot air.

Then she remembered. She had not been able to put much distance between herself and the doctor's house. She recalled seeing a vast greensward that reminded her of the grassy expanse of Windsor Castle's Home Park, surrounded by cut stone and shadowed by a slender steeple. A garden in a churchyard seemed as safe a place as any, and she'd holed up in a little outbuilding in order to rest, perhaps regain her strength. But, uncounted hours later, she didn't feel stronger in the least.

Her eyes were closed, but she was spinning. Time passed, and she was lost again. Was she on the deck of the ship? The tea company clerk called Mr. Leland had promised her a first-class billet. Seven beautiful days at sea, her destination the Sandwich Islands, a paradise she'd seen only in dreams, but one she'd always longed to visit. She smiled, envisioning white sugar sand and deep turquoise water, orchid forests and native feasts and ceremonies.

Outside, the sounds of the city rushed past — shouts in a variety of languages, the clop of hooves on brick pavement, whistles and shouts from drivers and draymen, clanging bells and the grind of commerce. Seagulls squabbled and dogs barked.

Slowly, through a mind made sluggish by fever and pain and reluctance to face facts, realization broke through the airy fantasy.

There was no ship, no billet, no civilized and prosperous tea company. There was only an opportunistic thief, her own gullibility and someone who was an even better liar than she.

How had everything gone so wrong, so quickly?

The answers spun away like clouds in a windstorm. She dragged her mind back to ponder the more immediate problem. She needed to remember where she was, and she needed to find a way to stay alive.

She had been doing so ever since the day her mother had abandoned her at a London workhouse. Escaping horrors she refused to think about, she'd pulled a new identity out of thin air and created a life for herself. She was Isabel Fish-Wooten, lady adventurer. With the speech and manners of an aristocrat, a convenient talent for gambling and a deadly accurate aim with any firearm, she traveled in grand style, from Europe to the Middle East to North America. She'd seen four of the seven wonders of the world. She'd sailed three of the seven seas. For the past year, she'd been touring the vast United States of America. The rollicking, high-rolling spirit of the wild land and ambitious people suited her perfectly — until last night.

After so many years on her own, she was supposed to be good at survival. Yet only this morning, she'd nearly thrown herself into the jaws of the enemy. Dr. Calhoun had patched her up beautifully, and she had actually begun to feel safe, up until the moment the nurse had sent her fleeing for her life.

I guess we'd best report this shooting to the police.

She tried to put together what had happened last night. Fragments of memory swirled around her. She snatched at them as they drifted past: the sizzle of danger in the night air, a drunken man calling out.

She had gone to the shadowy waterfront district in order to reclaim her stolen fortune. Instead, she'd encountered a worse crime in progress. A police officer was being shot at like a wharf rat. Some inexplicable, latent sense of decency had compelled her to intervene. She'd deliberately drawn fire to herself and nearly got herself killed.

That wasn't like her. She was supposed to be a survivor, not a hero. She was only good at saving herself, not other people.

She was also supposed to be good at disappearing without a trace. The talent had saved her skin more than once. Of course, it was troublesome to disappear unobtrusively when you were shot in the back.

She'd never imagined being shot would hurt so damnably bad. After the life she'd led, one would think she'd be prepared to endure every sort of hurt, but a gunshot wound was a new and ghastly revelation. It had felt like the blow of a sledgehammer, slamming into her back. Her lungs had emptied and stayed that way for several horrifying moments as she'd lain facedown, blood pulsing from the wound in surges she could actually feel as she pondered an increasingly bleak fate.

As she lay bleeding on the wet brick pavement, she remembered hearing an argument — had it been a lovers' quarrel? She recalled a woman's pleading followed by a man's voice: *Dear God, what have you done?* And a chase or scuffle, perhaps. She couldn't be sure. Then a brief firestorm and a surprisingly cultured male voice slipping like a shroud over her. *Leave that one. Have him taken to a place he won't be found.*

Her valise containing all her worldly possessions had been ripped from her hand. She didn't know who had taken it or why, but she did know the valise contained a world of secrets that could ruin her if they ever came to light.

Remembered fear caused her head to pound as she recalled the rough grip of a pair of low criminals. Someone had paid them to dispose of her. Thank God Dr. Calhoun had happened upon them and paid them again — this time for her freedom.

They probably thought they were selling the good doctor a corpse.

Perhaps they had.

She'd always had an unerring instinct for self-preservation. But also, it seemed, for trouble. Calhoun had repaired the damage, yet an offhand comment from the nurse had shattered her illusion of security. She was in terrible trouble, and even the truth wouldn't save her.

She felt her consciousness beginning to fade. Her vision shimmered and danced. In his stern, emotionless voice, Dr. Calhoun had read her name from the train billet: Isabel Fish-Wooten.

The doctor's hands had been so gentle with her that she'd nearly wept, unaccustomed as she was to compassion. But she'd held in the tears. She'd had so much practice at that. He would have thought her weeping was due to pain, of course, so she didn't bother. He'd warned her of weakness from blood loss, followed by an opportunistic infection, a potentially fatal fever. She'd taken her chances rather than lie there in his surgery, waiting to be arrested or worse.

Not that she'd done anything wrong, of course, but one of many hard-learned lessons her travels had taught her was that innocence had less validity than the word of a powerful man or the threat of bodily harm.

It occurred to her that she might be dying.

She was too exhausted to be alarmed by the notion, but regrets tiptoed across her consciousness. Not for the life she had lived but for the life she had missed. She did not regret the things she had done. Well, perhaps one or two, but they were minor infractions. No, her regrets were for the things she had failed to do.

She would die never having learned to ride a horse. She'd never held a baby in her arms — not that the notion had any appeal whatsoever, but what woman didn't think of such things? She had never worn a real diamond ring or kept a friend longer than a few months. She had never seen the islands of the South Pacific or eaten fish roasted on a native fire. She had never heard someone play a ukelele. She'd never kissed a man just for the pure sensual joy of it, she had never got blind, stinking drunk, had never felt the strong, clean power of pure faith. She had never seen a whale, and she had never celebrated her birthday.

She was dying a failure, an incomplete woman. And there was no one to mourn her. She tried to do the mourning herself, but could summon no more than a ragged sigh of discontent. Anything more required too much energy and didn't seem worth the bother.

Pain and heat weighted her eyes and muffled her hearing. She hurt so much that it really wasn't like pain at all, but something huge and all-consuming, a mystical force. A burning, pulsing state of grace.

An angel came to see her. She was quite certain it was an angel because when he wrenched open the door, he was surrounded by a nimbus of golden light. He was a heavenly vision, with his abundant wavy hair, broad shoulders, perfect cleft in his chin, narrow hips.

With the last of her strength, she pointed the gun at the angel.

"There you are." The angel had a wonderful tenor voice and spoke in an educated manner, with proper diction. "I've been waiting for you all day."

I'll just bet you have. She tried to answer but her throat was dry as ash, her tongue thick and her lips parched.

She took aim, seeing two of him for a moment. Which was the real angel and which was the illusion? Then the images fused into one glittering vision. He was looking off to the side, displaying a flawless profile. It was a shame to have to shoot something so beautiful.

"You knew I would come as soon as I could, Lucas." This new speaker sounded decidedly feminine, a young woman's voice brushed with a note of exotic music. She sounded timid and excited all at once.

"Help me put these tools away," said the

angel called Lucas. "What time does your mother expect you home?"

"At seven o'clock."

She took something from him — a crook-neck gardening hoe — and hung it on a peg. "So we have half an hour."

"Aw, June." Lucas slammed a shovel into the corner. "Why can't I just come courting?"

"You know very well why."

These two were charming, thought Isabel, but her consciousness was fading fast. Her own personal angels. She was amazed they hadn't noticed her, slumped against a pile of musty burlap sacks, pointing the Derringer at them.

"Tell me," he said, leaning toward her, capturing her small, fluttering hand. "Tell me why."

"For one thing, it's forbidden." She ducked away, stifling a giggle. "There are laws against intermarriage."

He laughed. "I don't want to marry you. I don't want to marry anyone just yet. I only want —"

She squealed and ducked again, stepping inside the shed, bumping against a wheelbarrow in her haste.

"Besides," Lucas continued, pursuing her, "I'll marry whom I please. You should see my grandmother."

"Is she Chinese, too?"

Don't come any nearer. Isabel tried to bark

the order but something had happened to her voice. It came out a gravelly rasp.

"Almighty Jesus." Even as he spoke, the boy called Lucas shoved himself in front of the girl.

"Don't swear." A shiny head peered around his shoulder.

He thrust her behind him again. "Hush. Be still."

He gaped at Isabel with a look on his two faces she wished she had never seen. She really needed to shoot him, but which one? No matter how hard she tried, she could not fuse both images into one. Could he see that her head was on fire? Did he know she was dying?

With lightning swiftness, he leaned down and snatched the gun, holding it by the fat little curved barrel. Fool, she thought, squinting at the small Sharp's double Derringer. Didn't he know how to handle a gun safely? Apparently not. He shoved it away somewhere.

"Got it," he said, his voice trembling a little.

The greenhorn. He ought to search the shed for her other weapon. The much more accurate, much more deadly Colt's pistol. She'd stowed it under a stack of empty burlap sacks.

"Who could it be?" asked June. "What do you suppose we ought to do?"

"Stay back. He could still be armed." Lucas bent closer. He was no angel but a young, pagan god. He was not simply handsome, but beautiful in a way that, in a few years, would make him a true danger to women.

"He's hurt or sick or something." A surprisingly gentle hand brushed at her cheek. "It's fever." His fingers brushed something else. "And this gunman is a woman," he whispered. "Jesus Christ."

"Don't swear," the girl said again.

"Clear out that wheelbarrow. We'll put her in that."

A wheelbarrow? Isabel attempted an indignant protest but managed only an aspirated croak. The boy and girl were clumsy but clearly trying to be gentle as they jostled, then lifted her into the creaky wooden receptacle.

"We're taking her to your father, aren't we?" said June.

"Yeah." The muscles in Lucas's arms corded taut as he lifted the handles of the wheelbarrow. "Maybe for once he'll think I did something right."

Five

Blue was only a few minutes late for his meeting with Dr. Vickery, dean of the Regis College of Medicine. After an exhausting day, Blue had managed to steal a nap before leaving for his appointment at the San Francisco Club. He wished he could reschedule and catch up on his sleep, but this meeting was critical. Rory and Blue had chosen Fremont Vickery after careful deliberation.

They needed more medically trained personnel to work at the Rescue League, and Dr. Vickery could provide just that. Presiding over a sizable medical college, he could authorize students to work there as part of their training. Blue hoped he'd be amenable to an agreement.

The moment he stepped into the hushed, understated opulence of the venerable San Francisco Club, Blue felt an unearned sense of privilege. The requirements for membership to the exclusive brotherhood had nothing to do with factors in his control. In order to be admitted to these hallowed halls, one had to be a white gentleman of good family, nominated by a presumably older, wiser white gentleman of similarly good family. The wives met in a salon on the ground floor, taking tea and exchanging gossip, but the second-story parlor was exclusively a man's domain.

Despite his cynicism about the membership requirements, Blue couldn't deny the appeal of the place. Simply walking into the walnut-paneled foyer and surrendering his hat and umbrella to an attendant gave him the sense that he was entering a different world. A quiet world of gently-aged liqueurs and hand-rolled cigars, of learned conversation and high-minded discourse.

Fremont Vickery was there already, seated in a thronelike wingback chair upholstered in polished leather and studded with round-headed brass tacks. In person, he looked every bit as distinguished as he did in the portrait that hung in the main hall of Regis College. He had abundant silver hair, full sideburns, a close-cropped beard and an air of unimpeachable authority.

He was one of the wealthiest men in the city, no small designation given the concentration of gold rush millionaires, railroad magnates and successful entrepreneurs. The source of his immense wealth was a matter of speculation. Some said his wife, Alma, who suffered from delicate health, had brought him a vast dowry. Others cited his busy private practice and his affiliation with Mercy Heights Hospital. Blue suspected that Regis itself was a gold mine. As a financial enterprise, a medical school tended to be quite rewarding. With the proper funding, any physician could obtain a charter for a school, establish himself and chosen colleagues as the faculty. Student fees provided a healthy source of funds.

But according to Rory, the source of the Vickery millions was his position as the state's public health officer. His chief duty was to inspect and collect fees from every vessel that entered port, and he was paid well for the service.

Blue guessed that he was paid even better with bribe money from importers eager to avoid scrutiny from the customs service, but that was none of his affair. His business with Vickery had to do with medicine, not commerce.

"Dr. Vickery," said Blue, shaking hands as the older man rose to greet him, "thank you for meeting with me. Mr. McKnight should be along shortly." He hid his irritation at Rory, always late, always certain he'd be forgiven.

Vickery motioned for him to take a seat. "It's a pleasure to see you, Dr. Calhoun." The genteel drawl of his native Georgia drew out the words.

"So," said Vickery, "you want my help with

your clinic for the indigent."

The league was more than a charity clinic. It was a place of hope. Women who were alone in the world, who sold their bodies in order to survive, were given a second chance at the waterfront compound, staffed with nuns and other compassionate people from area churches. The office functioned in cooperation with an agency on the fringes of the Barbary Coast district, and through the efforts of the Rescue League, many desperate women found work as domestic help or laborers.

A discreet waiter arrived with a decanter of amber-colored whiskey and filled two crystal glasses. "We need to expand our medical services. I've long believed the city's problems of crime and epidemic are related," said Blue. "One exacerbates the other."

"We already have a plan for removing the indigent from the streets. There's a smallpox isolation ward at Laguna Honda."

Blue gritted his teeth. He was not talking about removing people from sight, but healing them and pointing the way to a better life. "There's no facility in the most blighted areas of town," he pointed out. "The Barbary Coast and Chinatown. The docks are rife with disease, and construction on the new Embarcadero is not even finished. Once it's in place, the need will be even greater. The sickest people of all aren't able to drag themselves from their beds, much less enter a hospital miles away."

Blue could feel Vickery's attention sharpen, and he was quick to explain himself. "I'm not proposing a rival project or anything of the sort. We simply need more doctors, and I hope to get some by forming an affiliation with a medical school."

Vickery leaned forward and selected a cigar from the tooled leather humidor on the low table between their chairs. He stroked his long, pale fingers down the length of a fresh cigar. A waiter hurried forward to light it for him. Vickery enjoyed a few puffs before he replied. "But you understand, charities are for churches. We are physicians, my friend, not missionaries."

"And the people who come to the Rescue League are ill," countered Blue. "Not heathen."

Vickery settled back in his chair and crossed his ankle over his knee. A twist of bluish smoke drifted lazily from the tip of his cigar. "You're an interesting man, Dr. Calhoun. You've had an interesting career."

"If you say so, sir." Blue decided he had no choice but to let Vickery patronize him.

"You come from one of the best families on the west coast, yet as a youth you joined the Union Army at the height of the war. Why would you do that?"

Blue tried not to look too incredulous. "Sir, I had a duty."

So Vickery knew more about him than he'd

realized. Why? he wondered. Out of a sense of curiosity, competition or both?

"And what was it," Vickery asked slyly, "luck or guile, that prompted you to marry a Montgomery?"

Blue gripped the arms of his chair to keep himself from taking a swing at him. The Montgomery family was descended from Spanish royalty, and the first Montgomery had taken possession of vast territories along the coast a hundred years earlier. Their collective wealth rivaled that of a small European nation.

"It was neither, sir," Blue said, though he knew Vickery would never believe him. "Sancha and I were childhood sweethearts, and our marriage was a love match."

"I see. You'll forgive me for asking, but why, after setting up one of the most prosperous practices in the city, did you abandon it and rejoin the army?"

"The army needed doctors at the frontier. Just because there wasn't a war on didn't mean people were not getting sick — or killed." Yet if Blue had known what that tour of duty was going to cost him, he would have stayed in San Francisco, treating cases of the gout and ladies' vapors and pretending it fulfilled him.

"You were widowed while serving in the army, were you not?" inquired Vickery.

Even now, a decade later, the old rage and

grief gouged at him. His loss. His failure. "My wife was killed while we were posted at Fort Carrington, Wyoming."

"I'm very sorry. The loss of one's wife is a blow from which a man never recovers. If I lost my Alma, I'd be done for," Vickery said. "Was it an accident?"

Of course it wasn't an accident. But Blue saw no point in trying to explain the inexplicable. Attempting to place the blame where it belonged had landed him in enough trouble years ago. "Look, I understand you have questions about my departure from the military."

"I like to know who I'm dealing with."

"I was cashiered and sent home in dishonor. Does that factor into your decision about the Rescue League?"

"That depends. Does it factor into your performance and commitment to your vocation?"

Blue didn't answer. The past didn't simply melt away like the winter snow on the slopes of the mountains. Although invisible to the eye, the past resided in a man's heart, a dark, slow poison with no antidote.

Still . . . that could not stop him from trying to improve life for others. With a slight shake of his head, he declined the offer of a cigar. "Not in the least. My hope is that you'll lend your support to our present enterprise on its own merits, not my reputation," he said. "It's an opportunity to improve the public health, and to train medical students in the field."

Rory McKnight finally joined them, fashionably late and fashionably dressed as always. He made no effort to hide his delight at being in the company of one of most prominent men in the city. He took full advantage of the whiskey and cigars, but quickly got down to business, handing Vickery a folio of papers related to the proposal.

"You've come up with an admirable and detailed plan," Vickery said, flipping through the pages. "I shall read this carefully and give it due consideration."

"Dr. Vickery," Blue said, "I'm not looking for consideration, but approval, as quickly as possible."

"That's not possible."

"Why not?"

"You can't simply dive headlong into the underworld and rescue people from ailments of their own making."

"That's precisely what we've been doing since the Mission Rescue League was founded." Blue exchanged a glance with Rory. They were both thinking the same thing. Vickery was going to reject the idea. "Sir," he said, "we're proposing to improve the general health of the city. Isn't making San Francisco a better place good for us all?"

"Of course. But you understand, the presence of a medical facility in the vicinity will mean nothing but trouble."

"I believe Dr. Vickery is concerned that a licensed physician is bound to be the target of addicts seeking morphine and ether," Rory said, interceding before Blue lost his temper. "And unfortunately, he might be right."

"This happens to me constantly, whether I'm working at my private surgery or at the Rescue League," Blue admitted, thinking of the hissing wrecks who frequently approached him, demanding opium. Their persistence was matched only by that of his well-heeled patients, pleading for laudanum or paregoric. "I'm certain you encounter that as well, Dr. Vickery."

He hesitated. "Such blights of humanity are a fact of a doctor's life." When he leaned back and re-lit his cigar, Blue noticed two things about him. Vickery had a slight tremor in his hands. And the skin of his right hand was scraped raw, like a bare-knuckle boxer's.

"Sir, we'd like your answer as soon as possible," Blue said, trying to bring the conversation back to the original topic. "The practical experience for your students would be invaluable, and the service to the neediest of the city immeasurable."

"I know that." He patted the folio Rory had presented. "I intend to give this my approval, and I'll announce the opportunity to my advanced students first thing in the morning."

Blue was stunned, but didn't want to say anything, in case he'd heard wrong.

"To the public health, then," Rory declared, lifting his glass and draining it. Unlike Blue, he seemed unsurprised by the ease with which they'd achieved their purpose. Steepling his fingers and resting his elbows on his knees, Rory leaned forward to inquire, "How did you get so blessed rich, Dr. Vickery?"

Blue ground his teeth in frustration, but Vickery merely grinned, lifting his glass to the light and studying the amber liquid through the crystal facets. "I've never been afraid to take a risk," he stated. "And I've never shrunk from doing what has to be done, even if a sworn duty is distasteful to me." He rose hastily. "Although I would enjoy a lengthier visit, I must be going, gentlemen. My wife gets agitated when I'm late."

Rory watched him go. "Lord preserve us from agitated women."

Blue studied his untouched whiskey glass. All day long, he'd been edgy and distracted, and that made him annoyed at himself. But he was more than simply annoyed, and he knew better than to blame it on lack of sleep. He was troubled. He had treated a woman wounded by a bullet. And last night a policeman had been shot. He carried the knowledge around like an unwanted weight in his surgical kit.

Something had to be done. A violent outlaw was on the loose, and Blue knew who she was. Perhaps. Thus far, he'd said nothing, as though his silence would make the incident go away. This morning she'd walked out of his house and his life. He wanted to believe she was no longer his responsibility. But he couldn't shake loose his suspicion that she had shot a man. Or the knowledge that she was armed and dangerous. If she shot another person, the fault would be Blue's.

"I need your advice," he said to Rory. He explained about the woman disguised as a boy — wounded, armed and endowed with a baffling and unexpected charm. "She walked away and I don't know where she went," Blue concluded. "So now what?"

"Now you give her description to the police and let them try to find her. Would that all females were so easily dealt with." A born womanizer, Rory often encountered problems when his many liaisons intersected. He dispensed with them with a panache Blue admired but did not envy.

His suggestion made perfect sense. Yet Blue resisted it nonetheless. His experience in the army had taught him to distrust authority. "She didn't explain what happened to her," he said. "Perhaps she's innocent."

"You want her to be," Rory stated. "Why,

Dr. Calhoun, I'm intrigued."

"I want her well," Blue insisted. "Healed. It's what I want for all my patients. And I want to be certain she doesn't harm anyone." He drummed his fingers on the table. "I should try to find her. She can't have gone far. She was too weak."

"A person who is in trouble and armed with a gun is capable of getting very far indeed," Rory pointed out. "Look, Blue, it's not up to you to save every street Arab in the city."

"I'm a doctor. I don't concern myself with the soul. Just the body."

"Your work is done for this person. Let the police —" Rory stopped. "You're not going to do that, are you?"

Blue was thinking about a woman he'd treated last year, a petty thief who had been brought to him after being arrested and taken to the Josten Street jail. The following day, none of the officers in charge could explain how the bruises and lacerations of a brutal rape had appeared on her, seemingly overnight, nor why the initially calm woman was hysterical at her arraignment.

"I need to see the man who was shot," said Blue, heading for the door.

Rory stood, surveying the San Francisco Club with genuine regret. "Wait," he said. "Allow me to savor this for one minute more." Then, realizing Blue was not persuaded, he finished his glass of whiskey and joined Blue outside. "You're not riding that infernal beast of yours, are you?"

"No. It's just three blocks to the hospital."

"Good. I can't stand horses." Rory made no secret of his dislike for animals. Raised by an adoptive family in Omaha, he'd had his fill of rural life. He preferred the city with its noise, indoor plumbing, electrical lighting and imported foods.

Mercy Heights Hospital was filled with the noise and smells of the sick and injured: grave, low-toned conversations, moans of pain, open weeping. Although Rory turned markedly pale, Blue barely noticed the reek of putrid wounds, body fluids and cleaning solutions as he approached the charge nurse. The realm of the sick and dying had been his world for so long that he barely noticed the rank smells and terrible wails.

A nurse in a crisp wimple brought them to an iron-framed bed at the end of a ward. A plain wooden crucifix hung on the white plaster wall above each bed. "Here he is, poor man," she said in a thick Irish brogue. "Hasn't stirred a blessed eyelash since they brought him here in the wee hours."

"Head wounds will do that," said Rory, then shut up when both the nun and Blue glared at him.

The wounded man had a plain face like a potato harvested from freshly-turned earth.

Large ears, heavy jowls, a swath of bandage like a turban around his head.

He had a name — Patrick Brolin — and he wore a wedding band, the gleaming warm gold faintly scratched and dimpled by time and wear. Blue hadn't worn his own wedding band long enough to earn those scratches and dents.

The nurse saw him studying Brolin's thick-fingered hands. "A lovely wife he has, and four children, all grown. His wife tells me the grandchildren are every joy of his life, bless him."

Only one man lay dying in this hospital bed, but he was not the only victim. The outlaw's bullet had felled the man's wife. It had ripped through the living flesh of children and grandchildren.

She had done this, Blue told himself. She had gunned down a good man in cold blood.

Blue took his pulse, then used his stethoscope to listen to the man's lungs. He thumbed open one eye, then the other.

"He's dehydrated," he told the nurse.

"He hasn't had a moment's consciousness, sir."

"Use the Bering tube, then. Get some water in him." Blue tested the tonic reflexes. "Who is the physician in charge of this patient?"

The nun squared her shoulders as though prompted to straighten up. "Why, Dr. Vickery himself, sir."

Blue and Rory exchanged a look, both finding this fact interesting, though neither mentioned it as they left the hospital. Both knew Brolin's furious comrades were tearing the city apart, seeking the shooter. One of their own had fallen, and they were hungry for revenge. "And it's more than likely," Rory pointed out, "that whoever did it won't live to be arrested."

Blue nodded. There was his dilemma, then. Overzealous peace officers were sure to seize the power to accuse, hunt down, convict and execute without consulting judge or jury.

"It's the wild west," said Rory, stepping up to the cable car that would take him to his lodgings. "Vigilante justice still prevails."

Six

"We're in for a world of trouble," June Li said to Lucas as he parked the wheelbarrow at the surgery entrance. It was late in the day, and Lucas felt fairly confident Delta had gone home. His father's adjacent office and surgery provided a possible way for them to enter the house unnoticed by Mrs. Li or Mrs. Riordan.

"Don't be a ninny. This woman needs help, and we're helping her."

"Then why are we sneaking like this?"

He didn't answer, and knew she didn't expect one. The proper thing to do, of course, would be to summon help and wait for an adult to take over. But Lucas was fighting for his independence, and doing things on his own was a way to wage the battle. "Get the door for me," he said. "I'm going to have to carry her."

The woman was slight, nearly as small as June, but in her unconscious state, she was as limp and ungainly as a large sack of turnips. Straightening the soiled jacket she wore, he slid one arm behind her and the other beneath her knees. He felt the bulk of a bandage, surmising that she was injured in the chest or back. She moaned but did not open her eyes. He straightened, staggering a little, then headed for the door. June led the way through the quiet surgery and across the breezeway to the main house.

The woman's head hung limply to one side, and as he moved into the vestibule, he was overcome by a powerful wave of protectiveness. She seemed so helpless.

As he walked with her, he smelled the distinct sulphurous odor of burned gunpowder wafting from her hair. A memory flashed through his mind. It came and went so swiftly that he couldn't quite grasp its meaning, but it had to do with his mother. He had been only five years old when she died. He didn't remember that day, not clearly. On some nights he dreamed of it. But the memory was elusive, like a dream floating away upon waking. He had no idea why bringing this wounded woman home should evoke thoughts of his mother, but he knew he was doing the right thing. And he knew the perfect place to take her in this too-large, too-quiet house.

"Master Lucas, is that you?" Mrs. Riordan called from the back of the house, toward the kitchen.

"Yes, I'm off to get cleaned up for supper," he said. He jerked his head toward the broad curve of the staircase, indicating to June that they were going upstairs. She shot him a dubious look, but complied.

"We're going to my mother's room," he whispered.

June stood still. "Your father doesn't like anyone going in that room."

"It's the best place for her," he said. "The other rooms are too small and poky."

"Your father will —"

"Just help me," Lucas said, his arms trembling with his burden. She was on fire with fever. "Quickly."

Looking more dubious than ever, June opened the door to a perfectly neat, light-filled bedroom. It had been in this state for as long as Lucas could remember — spotless, decked in white, his mother's possessions still in evidence. There was a comb and brush set on a vanity table, a writing desk with paper and pen at the ready, a dresser with hatpins and atomizers and dozens of other feminine things whose purposes eluded him. A set of double doors with polished brass handles separated the room from his father's private lodgings. As far as Lucas knew, his father never opened those doors.

With aching, arm-shaking slowness, he lowered the woman to the bed. Her dusty boots smudged the white counterpane, and the battered hat fell to the floor, revealing dark hair, badly cut. June arranged the embroidered pillows. Then they stepped back, at a loss.

He could not tell the woman's precise age. He couldn't even tell if she was pretty. She had a wide mouth with cracked lips, smooth skin that blazed an unhealthy, angry pink. She didn't move, though her breathing was shallow and quick.

"Why here?" June whispered, challenging him again. She had always questioned him, ever since they were small and fought over every possible thing. "Why didn't we wait in the surgery? He'll probably want her transported to a hospital. Or to her home, wherever that might be."

"She's bad off," Lucas said. "Her best chance is to be here, where my father can tend to her."

"So you say. I still think we're in a world of trouble."

"Listen, the one thing I know for certain about my father is that saving lives is the reason for his existence. That's what we're doing. Saving a life. He won't argue with that."

Lucas spoke with more conviction than he felt. The fact was, lately all he and his father ever did was argue.

"He's not going to be happy with you," June warned.

"Nothing can make my father happy," said Lucas. He went and checked the ewer and basin. The large white china pitcher was empty but clean. More vague memories drifted past and evaporated.

"That's a strange thing to say."

"I think I remember a time when he was happy, but it might just be a dream. When I was small, he used to laugh and toss me up into the air. We were on the beach, I think."

"He might toss you somewhere when he learns what we've done," June said. "Are you going to tell him she pointed a gun at you?"

Lucas set his jaw. It was one of many bones of contention between him and his father. All his friends had guns and practiced shooting at the range down at Hayes Park. Sometimes he sneaked down to practice with them, and he always envied the boys whose fathers stood behind them, teaching them accuracy and judgment. "Maybe I'll tell him," said Lucas. "Maybe then he'll realize it's time for me to have a gun of my own."

"What is so important about shooting a gun, anyway?" she asked.

"All men know how to handle a firearm."

June sent a look at the woman on the bed. "Just men?"

"Women, too, I suppose. You should learn."

"Why?"

"What if some crimp tries to shanghai you?"

"Silly, they don't shanghai women."

"They kidnap them. Sell them to the tongs." He wished he hadn't said that. It was too close to what had actually befallen her mother. "Anyway," he said, "if I had a gun, I'd become the sharpest shooter in the city, and if anyone tried to kidnap you, I'd save you."

"What, by shooting me?"

"No, goose, by shooting — ah, never mind." He grew serious. "But if anyone ever tried to harm a hair on your head —" he dared to reach out, to touch the shining obsidian silk of her hair "— I would save you, June Li. You know I would."

"I do know that, Lucas." Her blush deepened to the color of a ripe persimmon.

He was pretty sure he was blushing, too. His ears felt on fire.

"But I don't want you to have to defy your father for my sake," she added.

"I do that enough on my own," he admitted. "I swear, there is nothing worse than a stern father."

June took the pitcher and headed for the door. "A stern father. I have no idea what it is like to have any father at all."

She left to fill the pitcher with water.

"Sometimes I don't think I do, either," said Lucas.

Seven

Blue rode home on Gonzalo, a glossy, athletic saddle horse. Like all of his horses, the gelding had been bred and trained at Cielito. Horses from the sprawling seaside ranch were famous, not so much for their bloodlines as for their flawless training, usually at the hands of his stepmother, Eliza, or his young half sister, Amanda. Both women had a gift for training horses, and every one of the Calhouns loved to ride. Gonzalo was one of life's few pleasures for Blue. The horse displayed a special swiftness and snap, and his sole focus was on obeying and serving his master.

Blue had often thought of sending Lucas to the ranch for training.

As he made his way to the house, he tried to shake off the cares and tribulations he carried around like invisible baggage. As always, it was impossible. A doctor's duties didn't end with the closing of the day. He didn't get to enjoy the farmer's satisfaction of looking back over freshly turned furrows in the earth, or the mason's pride in the perfectly tessellated rocks in a wall he'd built. He couldn't point to a banker's balanced ledger and say he'd accomplished his goal that day.

Instead, he dragged home a burden of worry and tension. On most evenings, those silent companions accompanied him through supper, and eventually to bed.

That was the father Lucas encountered each night. Blue wanted to be different for his son. He wanted to be jolly and light-hearted, and he used to try hard, for Lucas's sake. But Lucas, for all his faults, was no fool. He could see through the facade, could detect the worry behind the smile. And as the boy got older, Blue let the false mask of cheerfulness slide away, revealing the somber man he'd become.

As always, the house was fragrant with the smells of supper kept warm on the cast iron kitchen range. When Blue came home late — or often not at all, due to his work at the Rescue League — Lucas took supper in the kitchen with Mrs. Riordan.

But today, the kitchen was bright and busy. The cook and housekeeper, who disliked each other and rarely spoke, were engaged in a loud conversation that stopped the moment Blue stepped into the room.

"Is something the matter?" he asked, looking from Mrs. Li to Mrs. Riordan.

"Is not my fault," said Mrs. Li.

"I told him it was a terrible, desperate idea," said Mrs. Riordan, tucking a lock of ginger hair into her cap. She was uncommonly beautiful, too young to have endured what she'd suffered until Blue had offered her employment keeping house for him.

"Told who? What?" he asked.

"Lucas, sir."

He wasn't surprised. Trouble in this house generally answered to that name. But a familiar icy fear clutched his gut as he imagined the endless possibilities for disaster. No, he told himself. These women wouldn't be in here arguing if Lucas had come to some physical harm. "Where is he?"

Bernadette Riordan knit her fingers together. "He insisted on settling her in Mrs. Calhoun's chamber, sir. He wouldn't listen to a word we said. I swear on the saints, I told him —"

He broke away and went to the foyer, taking the stairs two at a time. Sancha's room was off-limits. Lucas knew that. No one went there, no one touched her things or used the furniture. Only Bernadette and the day maid went there to keep the room spotless, as though waiting for her to return. "For the resurrection," he'd overheard Bernadette say to the maid when she hadn't known he was listening.

He burst inside and stopped short. Twin gas jets above the bed hissed softly into a taut, charged silence. Their ghostly, colorless glow settled over the scene.

Lucas sat by the bed, leaning forward as though in prayer. An oversized shadow on the wall outlined his profile. And in the bed that had once belonged to Blue's wife lay the outlaw, Isabel Fish-Wooten.

Eight

While Blue tried to hide his shock, Lucas stood quickly. "Where have you been?" he demanded. No greeting, no explanation, no apology for putting a stranger into his dead mother's bed. Yet there wasn't a trace of anger in his voice, only desperation. "Hurry," Lucas continued, motioning with his hand. "You have to save her."

Blue was seized by a swift memory he didn't know he had — Lucas at age five, running across the stockade at Fort Carrington with his hands cupped around some delicate, precious treasure. He barged into Blue's dispensary and opened his little hands to reveal a tiny unfledged baby bird, its skin the color of bruised flesh, its beak grotesquely large, its head too big to be supported by its skinny neck. "Daddy," Lucas had said, "you have to save it."

That had been back when everything was different. When Lucas had believed his father could do anything.

Blue crossed the room, his feet soundless on the French carpet he and Sancha had

95

picked out together. Ghosts rose from the ivy design twining through the rug, threatening to trip him up.

But old ghosts and a defiant son faded as a sense of mission rose up in him. He gave his full attention to the woman on the bed, and curiously, it was a relief to see her. At least if she was here, she couldn't be out committing murder.

No, she could be in his home committing murder. Scowling, he took Miss Fish-Wooten's hand and pressed three fingers to the inside of her wrist. Her pulse raced. Fever raged through her. Heat rolled off her in waves, as though she was a loaf of bread fresh from the oven.

Her English rose cheeks were on fire, and her dark hair lay plastered to her brow. She still wore the white smock over the gray jacket he'd given her this morning.

He thumbed open one eye, then the other, his fingers warmed by her fevered brow. Her pupils responded to the light. The irises were as clear as a spring creek. But she was completely insensate. Reaching behind her, he drew her up. She lolled forward, and for an awkward moment they were embracing. A peculiar and unexpected feeling took hold of him. In the most fundamental way, he was aware of her as a woman. The rare flicker of intimacy startled him, and he pulled back. Setting his jaw, he lifted her to check for bleeding; the bandage he'd applied this morning was stained with dried blood the color of earth. He settled her back against the pillows again. His gaze lingered on her mouth, and he found himself remembering the charm of her smile, even when she was pointing a gun at him.

"Has Delta seen her?"

"No. She'd gone home for the day by the time I got here."

"Where'd you find her?"

"In the gardening shed at the churchyard."

"And she was like this when you found her? Did she speak?"

Lucas glanced away. A furtive hand drifted to the pocket of his dungarees.

Blue straightened up in a rush of anger and panic. "She was armed, wasn't she?"

Lucas stuck his hand into his pocket and brought out the small Derringer. Blue regarded the obscenity in the palm of his son's hand.

He grabbed the pistol. "Christ, it's loaded. Never carry a loaded weapon," he said. "Don't you know any better than to —"

"How would I know?" Resentment threaded through Lucas's words. "You've never allowed me anywhere near a firearm."

Lucas had always been fascinated by firearms of all sorts. He constantly sneaked off to Wild West shows and shooting competitions, and each year for his birthday, he pleaded for a gun.

Blue had no idea what to make of his son's fascination. He didn't understand how Lucas could be so enamored of something that had destroyed his family. Yet logic told Blue the boy remembered nothing of the horrors wreaked on the Wyoming prairie. When Blue found them after the battle — or *incident,* as the army had termed it in the official documents that had followed — Lucas had been gently cradled in his dead mother's arms, protected by her to the end.

A little boy with large brown eyes, Lucas put his finger to his lips and said, "Shh. Mama's sleeping. She said I must be very quiet so she can sleep." But even at such a tender age, Lucas must have known the unnatural sleep was the beginning of an unimaginable grief. For when Blue had plunged to his knees in the dust and ash, the boy had said, "Save her, Daddy. You have to save her."

Blue emptied the chamber of the Derringer. He shoved the bullets into one pocket and the gun into another. "Where's the pistol?" he demanded.

"I just gave it to you."

"The other one. The Colt's."

"There was just the one."

"She had another."

"Well, I didn't see it. She's in a bad way," Lucas reminded him. "Shouldn't you be tending her?"

98

He was right, of course. Blue pushed his son farther away from the bedside, then bent and folded back the coverlet. It was edged in heavy Belgian lace, a wedding gift from Blue's uncle Ryan and aunt Dora.

He bent over the bed where he used to make love to his wife. Now he examined a murderer.

He knew even before he checked her that the wound had become infected. Despite his precautions, the poison was spreading through her. He couldn't think straight, and it wasn't like him. Ordinarily he had no trouble giving his total absorption to a patient. Yet this stranger, here in this bed, had an unsettling effect on him. The past lived in this room, and that was why Blue could never come here.

Every object held a piece of his heart. Even the smallest detail — a hairpin left on the vanity table, a half-finished letter in her handwriting — stabbed him with a reminder that he used to know how to be happy. He used to know what it felt like to greet each new day with pleasure, to smile from the heart and to feel glad he was alive. He used to know what it was like to love a woman. Being here reminded him of all that. No wonder he never came to this room.

He turned to his son, making no attempt to hide the fury in his face. "Why the devil would you bring her here?"

Lucas stared at him in disbelief. "Oh, sorry. I thought you were the doctor in the family."

"Generally when one is threatened by a gun, one goes for the police." He put up a hand to forestall further sarcasm from his son. He sent him down to the surgery for supplies, and the boy hurried out, more obedient and unquestioning than he'd been in ages.

After Lucas left, Blue eyed Miss Fish-Wooten with resentment. "So I'm to start and end my day with you," he muttered.

Her eyelids fluttered but didn't stay open. There was such delicacy about her. It was hard to believe she had survived the day.

"Give me one reason I should save you," he said. "Because I'm a doctor who took an oath? Because my son brought you to me like a bird fallen from the nest?"

Scowling with fury, he took off his frock-coat, rolled back his sleeves and poured water into a basin.

He thought with fading wistfulness of his plans for the evening — a quiet supper with his son. He'd actually hoped Lucas would be too exhausted from the churchyard gardening to pick a fight with him. On some evenings, Blue paid a visit to his longtime mistress, Clarice Hatcher. Elegant, accomplished and undemanding, she had been a small yet diverting part of his life for years.

But alas, tonight would belong to Miss Isabel Fish-Wooten.

Nine

Isabel was glad she hadn't shot the angel after all. At least, she didn't think she had. Her memory of the dusty shed was still a blur of images as her senses whirled with pain and fever. But she was quite certain she hadn't gunned down her savior. It was a good thing, because by the looks of things, the angel had brought her to heaven.

And heaven was exactly as she had imagined it. She lay upon a cloud of soft eiderdown while golden light streamed in soft slanting bars through an open window, bathing her in warmth. Gauzy curtains blew inward on the gentlest of breezes. A rare sense of safety and security enveloped her. Somewhere not so far away, seraphim sang in a velvety voice.

Swing low, sweet chariot . . .

Interesting, thought Isabel. The angel sounded nothing like those fussy chorales that performed in churches, rolling their Rs and singing in Latin as though they knew the meaning of the incomprehensible prayers. These words were clear and sweet, ringing with honest emotion, as a proper hymn should be.

Coming for to carry me home . . .

She realized the song was a Negro spiritual. In the slow slide of its melody, the soulful notes held all the sorrow in the world, yet hope and joy echoed through the words and hovered in the silences between them.

A dark shadow slipped over her. The golden light outlined a formidable shape. This angel had nut-colored skin and shining hair pulled away from a serene face. Her appearance stirred a vague memory in Isabel, but thinking too hard caused her head to throb in a way that should be disallowed in the hereafter. Isabel felt vaguely miffed. What was the point of dying if you could still feel pain?

"Mercy, you're awake," said the dark angel. "It's about time. You had us worried." She rested the back of her hand on Isabel's forehead. A motherly touch, thought Isabel, though she had no idea how she would know what that was. "I'll just be fetching Dr. Calhoun," the angel added.

Dr. Calhoun. A swift memory swept over Isabel — broad shoulders, gentle hands, accusing eyes. A decidedly earthbound sort.

When the angel went away, Isabel pushed herself gingerly to a sitting position. Her wound burned like hellfire and damnation. And it struck her then, a knife twist of revelation, that she wasn't in heaven after all. That should be no cause for surprise. Certainly she'd never expected to find herself in paradise, given the way she'd lived.

Very well, then. She wasn't dead in the least, but alive and hurting.

The movement of her head caused her to see stars. Whirling images flitted in and out of her consciousness — light, lace, scrolled woodwork. The wobbling room wavered in and out of focus, its beauty blurred but undiminished by her imperfect vision. Sunlight and fringe, white linen and ruffles. The walls were painted a lemony yellow, and crystal sconces crowned the gas jets. A white marble fireplace dominated one wall. There were doors leading to adjoining rooms, French windows framing a balcony decked with alabaster crocks. In one corner was a draped vanity table with a round mirror. The bed itself was a wonder, its soaring posters carved with sheaves of rice, topped with pineapple-shaped finials. Draped in sheer white tulle, the canopy formed a graceful arch over the softest of mattresses.

Everything was clean and light, right down to the white cotton bed gown she wore. Someone had taken her clothes, such as they were. She frowned, thinking that there was something important about that, but the thought fluttered away before she could capture it.

The door to the light-filled room opened and in walked a tall man, his imposing form limned by sunshine as he passed in front of the French windows and approached the bed. The air pulsed and lurched around him.

Dr. Calhoun. Theodore Calhoun, she realized, seeing him through a thick haze. He'd worked so hard to save her. It was the one thing she recalled with crystal clarity. She had threatened him at gunpoint, yet he'd treated her with more tenderness than any man ever had.

But she'd sabotaged his efforts to heal her. She could still hear his warnings and protests echoing in her ears. She'd left despite his admonitions, of course. What else could she have done? And now look where it had brought her — right back to him. Amazing. In all her travels, she had never come back to anyone before. Perhaps that meant something.

If her head would stop whirling, if her mouth weren't so dry, she would ask where she was. And then she would tell him not to look so concerned. She thought she detected shades of guilt in his stern face. This wasn't his fault, she wanted to tell him. He probably saved lives every day and shouldn't regard her as a failure. Holing up in a filthy shed and coming down with a raging fever had been her fault entirely. She was beyond saving, and had been for a long time.

He paused by the bed to study her while she regarded him with curiosity and mounting confusion. His wide shoulders balanced nicely with his impressive height, and unlike many men of fashion, he was clean-shaven. He was dressed in a suit of dark, crisp superfine. The white boiled collar and cuffs were professional-looking rather than fussy. He had abundant hair the color of the wheat fields she had passed on her journey by train across the heart of America.

His most arresting feature by far was his eyes. They trapped the light. They were as blue as shattered sapphires and filled with unspoken thoughts she wished he would share. He had the sort of face every girl pictured when she was young and hopeful enough to dream of marriage.

He was not merely handsome but . . . protective. She wasn't sure what made him seem that way. The set of his jaw, perhaps? His aggressive posture?

"So you're awake," he said, his voice harsh with contempt.

Despite his obvious animosity, Isabel felt glad she had not been taken to heaven after all. This was much more interesting.

"Good morning," she said. Her voice creaked like a rusty, unused gate hinge. She cleared her throat and tried again. "Good morning, Doctor."

"A better morning than yesterday," he said,

angling a spindle-legged chair to face the bed and taking a seat.

So she'd only lost a day and a night to the murky oblivion of fever. Then she remembered the disquieting reason that had prompted her to flee in the first place. He and his nurse — the woman she'd mistaken for a singing angel earlier — were going to set the police on Isabel. Regardless of what had really happened at the waterfront that night, she was bound to be in big trouble.

"Where am I?"

"This is my private home. You belong in a hospital but you're too ill to be moved."

"I'm not going to any hospital."

"Not today. You're too ill."

She tried to work out a plan in her head, but the fever burned away her thoughts like coals in a hungry fire. Bright ideas glowed only to turn to ash a second later. Clearly she was in no condition to flee again. For the time being, she would be forced to lie here, imprisoned in a strange house by a man who clearly resented every breath she took. She despised her imprisonment with a clarity that shone through the heat shimmers of fever. She never, ever wanted to surrender control of her life to someone else.

Yet she would have to regain her strength before she could take back her freedom. That being the case, she was determined to make the best of the situation. Despite the searing pain in her back, she summoned what she hoped looked like a grateful smile.

"You saved my life twice," she said. "I wish I had two lifetimes to repay you."

He took her wrist in one hand and pressed his fingers to her pulse. Though she told herself he was a physician who was obliged to treat her, his tenderness nearly made her weep. She'd never been touched in this way, ever. Until now. Until him.

An odd notion occurred to her while he held her hand in his. She wanted to let this moment stretch out into eternity. Perhaps it was a bizarre side effect of her raging fever, but for now, at least, it was the dearest wish in her heart.

When he caught her expression, he looked taken aback. "I'd best give you a powder for that dyspepsia," he said. "You look as though you're taking a turn for the worse."

"I'm not getting worse," she assured him. "And I'm not dyspeptic."

He leaned toward her, putting his face so close she could feel the warmth of his breath. She could smell his scent of soap and bay rum, could see the perfect shape of his lips, the strong cut of his jaw and the intriguing facets of his eyes. An unexpected sense of anticipation rose in her chest. Another out-of-the-blue notion swept over her. For the first time since she was a young, idiot girl, she yearned for a man to kiss her. And it was not just any kiss she craved, but a swift, hard crushing-together of mouths, a deep sharing and tasting, an intimate and delicious communion. She had no idea where that peculiar desire had come from. The fever, surely.

With infinite gentleness, he rested his hand on her brow and closely studied her eyes. She lost herself in his gaze, seeing depths within depths there and finally, reflecting back at her, a tiny image of herself. Gaunt cheeks and large eyes. Her hair hastily cut by her own hand. Could he see her thoughts? Could he feel the yearning in the pulsing rhythm of her heart? Could he sense the beginnings of true adoration?

"You're not suffering from digestive upset?" he asked. "Headache, nausea?"

"No." She frowned at him. Perhaps he was not as wise and wonderful as she'd thought if he mistook the look for dyspepsia. So much for yearning and desire.

The chair creaked as he shifted, leaning forward. "Look, Miss Fish-Wooten, or whatever your name is —"

"You may call me Isabel," she said expansively. Her voice seemed to emanate, disembodied, from another part of the room. She was quite drunk with fever, but long ago she had schooled herself to speak with perfect diction, and her aristocratic accent still rang true. "I know it's quite early in our acquaintanceship, but under the circumstances, I feel as though we enjoy a rare level of intimacy."

"What you mistake for intimacy is simply the duty of a physician toward a patient."

"So I am nothing but a bag of bones to you." She waited for him to protest, but he didn't.

Instead, he glared at her. Even glaring, he was uncommonly appealing. A pity they had met under such disastrous circumstances. It would not be the first time Isabel found herself in the right place at the wrong time. But as so often happened to her, the disaster came with an interesting opportunity. He was sitting at her bedside, not three feet away.

Dr. Calhoun. Theodore Calhoun. A man whose physical appeal was surpassed only by his capacity for gentleness. Whose foul temper masked a humanity she had never before encountered in a man. He stirred her heart. His very nearness caused goose bumps to race over her skin. She wondered if she might be falling in love with him, quickly and passionately. She was, after all, a lady adventurer. And being in love was one adventure she'd never enjoyed. So far, it felt exhilarating, as though she were no longer earthbound, but floating in some happy warm state.

Or perhaps that too was the fever.

"Are you married, Dr. Calhoun?" she

asked, getting right to the heart of the matter. Of necessity, Isabel had few scruples, but stealing other women's husbands was something even she would never allow herself to do.

It wasn't a difficult question, yet he gaped at her as though she'd spoken gibberish. His face paled and then reddened in quick succession. And finally turned so cold that she stopped floating for several moments.

"He's a widower," said a new voice. A lanky boy walked across the room and stopped at the end of the bed. "I'm his son, Lucas. My mother died ten years ago."

The first angel. The one who had brought her here in a wheelbarrow. And now he brought her a pitcher of fresh water and tidings of great . . . well, if not joy, then possibility. So. Dr. Calhoun was a widower.

"Please excuse yourself, Lucas," said Dr. Calhoun. "This is a private consultation with a patient and it's not proper for you —"

"Nonsense, he rescued me from certain death. Heaven forbid that I'm too ill to thank him properly." Struggling to concentrate through the vague laziness of fever, Isabel smiled at Lucas. She sensed an ally in him. In her precarious position, with the possibility of arrest looming over her, she needed all the allies she could get.

Lucas Calhoun was an uncommonly handsome young man, which was not surprising given the father's appearance. But where Dr. Calhoun was fair, Lucas was dark. He'd inherited his coloring, she supposed, from his mother. His late mother.

"I am Isabel Fish-Wooten," she said. "And I am so terribly sorry for your loss. How awful that you've been motherless these ten years." She wondered why a vigorous man like Dr. Calhoun had never remarried. Could it be that his late wife was his one true love and he couldn't bear to have another? Or had she been a vile harridan who had put him off wives for a decade?

"Thank you, ma'am," Lucas said, shuffling a pair of endearingly large feet.

"I lost both my parents at a young age," she admitted, which was the truth. She, too, had grown up without a mother, and that fact had shaped her every bit as much as the liberally-applied cane of the workhouse master who had raised her. "But they live on, here in my heart," she added, which was a bold-faced lie. She paused, surprised to feel genuine empathy for the boy.

"I appreciate your concern, ma'am."

"Oh, heavens, you needn't thank me in the least. I am deeply indebted to you, Lucas," she went on. "You truly did save my life." She shifted her gaze from the son to the father and back again. Tension crackled between them, and she knew it was not just the fever at work. Her mind began to tackle the

111

problem in front of her. Who would she be today? Who would she be for this fine young man and his enigmatic father?

She often liked to fashion her character specifically to satisfy people's expectations. She studied the pair of them a moment longer, and her heartbeat sped up. Who did they need in their lives? And why did she want so badly to be that person for them?

Lucas blushed under her scrutiny. Oh, she did enjoy young men. They were so easy to read and entertain. Yet her deepest interest was for the father, whom she could scarcely read at all and who didn't seem to be the least bit entertained by her.

"Yes, well, I believe you have work to do, Lucas," said Dr. Calhoun. "You'd best be on your way to St. Mary's."

The blush turned to the dull red of resentment. "Yes, sir."

"You're employed by the church, then," she prompted, hoping to override the father's obvious dismissal.

"For the time being," he said. "I'm working on the garden." He glanced at his father, then his large brown eyes softened as he regarded Isabel. "May I pour you a glass of water?"

"Yes, please. I'm dying of thirst." She had apparently consumed a pitcher of water upon waking at some point in the night but she didn't remember drinking it. She eyed him gratefully as she took dainty sips from the glass.

The fragile English rose, she decided. That was what Lucas wanted her to be. Someone easy to care for, someone who would neither challenge nor judge him. The father, of course, had different needs, and she wasn't quite sure what those were. She sensed that he was a complicated man, and that his needs would not be easily met. She would start with the basics, then. He was a doctor. Quite likely, he needed someone to heal. To rescue, perhaps. Well, she could satisfy him on both counts. Maybe he could rescue her from her own stupidity.

"I shall never be able to repay either of you for saving me. First you, Dr. Calhoun, for treating my injury, and you, Master Lucas, for finding me in the throes of delirium and bringing me into your home. Truly, fortune has blessed me."

Lucas offered a slight bow of politeness. "I'm glad you're better. If you need any—"

"Son, it's time for you to go."

The youth glared at him. "I'm glad you're better," he repeated to Isabel. Then he left quickly.

"You forgot to tell him goodbye," she pointed out to Dr. Calhoun.

He frowned. "He forgot, too."

Ah, she thought. Things were indeed strained between them. A pity, that. They were two fine men who ought to share a close bond, particularly in light of being without a wife and mother.

"Is Lucas your only child?"

"Yes."

"You must be very proud of him."

He didn't answer but refilled her water glass.

She took another drink, enjoying the soothing trickle of cool water down her throat. "When I woke up, there was a woman —"

"My assistant, Miss Delta Beasley. She was here the morning you were shot." Dr. Calhoun sat back and regarded her inscrutably.

A chill scuttled across her skin. "Then I owe her my thanks," she said. His expression didn't change. "Why do you look at me so?"

"I'm trying to decide what to do with you."

"You're a doctor. Your job is to heal me."

"And so I shall."

She relaxed a little. For the time being, perhaps, he would forget about setting the police on her. "I have every faith in you, Doctor."

"And I have none in you," he stated.

"I beg your pardon." Her consciousness began to waver. The delirium pulsed, dark and shapeless, at the edges of her vision.

"I see no point in pretending there is anything normal about these circumstances. You don't belong here, and yet here you are. I don't know you, and you haven't exactly been a fount of information about yourself. But I do know you're quick to draw a gun on an innocent man —"

"To protect myself."

"— and you're the victim of a shooting —"

"Oh, and that's my fault?"

"And your injuries coincide a little too neatly with the attempted murder of a police officer."

Relief blossomed in her heart. "You mean he's alive?"

"Ah, so you admit you know something about the shooting of Officer Brolin?"

"Know about it?" she said. "Heavens, I was there."

"Then I prove my point. Or rather, you prove it."

"Just because I was there doesn't mean I shot him." Her voice kept breaking, and she hoped she was not getting sicker.

His features turned hard with skepticism. Isabel's heart sank. She realized, at last, that the event that had brought her together with Dr. Calhoun imprisoned her as surely as a barred concrete cell in the military reservation on the isle of Alcatraz. Suspicion was bound to poison his opinion of her. She had to do something about that.

Shutting her eyes, she lay very still, reconstructing the events leading up to the shooting. Everything had happened so fast that night. Some of the moments were a frantic blur. But she was perfectly clear on one matter.

"I didn't shoot anyone," she stated. "I didn't do what you think I did."

"And I should believe that because . . . ?"

"Because it's the truth."

"I found you shot in the back and armed with two guns, one of which had been recently fired," he said. "A few hours later I learned an officer of the law had been shot. The logical conclusion is that you were involved in the shoot-out."

"There's a flaw in your logic, Doctor."

"And what might that be?"

"If I had shot at someone, I would not have missed. He'd be dead." She leveled her gaze at him, but he wavered anyway, as though the wind rippled through him. "I never miss. Ever."

"I'm also not familiar with your shooting skills."

"I'd be happy to prove my claim, day or night. I'm certain that in a city of this size, there's a shooting range."

"There are several, but no, thank you. In fact, if you're indeed as innocent as you claim, then I'll send for the police right now and you can explain how you came to be shot and taken into the custody of two known criminals."

"No." It came out as a bark of desperation.

He subjected her to a frank stare. Despite his accusations and skepticism, he drew her in. It was uncanny, the affinity she felt for this man who never smiled. She almost wanted to get shot a second time just so he'd touch her again, touch her with that aching tenderness.

"No?" he echoed. "But you just said you can prove your innocence."

"I know exactly what I said. But I suspect you're not a stupid man. You know the circumstances alone will convict me." She fixed him with a look that she hoped would make him uncomfortable. The truth was, she felt weak as a willow. Her eyes burned and her thoughts kept trying to drift away before she could snatch them back. "I don't suppose a fine upstanding citizen like yourself has ever found himself in circumstances where things were not quite as they seem."

Maybe she only imagined it, but he seemed to hesitate. Perhaps some of the anger melted. She hastened to press her advantage. "What will it take to convince you of my innocence?"

"I'll send for the police. Innocent people are usually eager to get to the truth."

"Innocent people sometimes become victims of circumstance."

She watched his face change, become taut with unhealed emotion. Somehow she had struck a nerve. "The unfortunate thing is that often while pursuing a false lead, the police are distracted from finding the true culprit."

He lifted one eyebrow, an expression that made him look even more handsome than ever. "Perhaps you should make that statement to the police, then."

"They'd be even less inclined than you to believe me. Dr. Calhoun, I am a traveler, a foreigner just passing through. The fallen man is one of the city's own. On top of that, he was working to keep the peace. Sympathy will be with him. And of course, the police will be desperate to capture a suspect — even the wrong one. If you hand me over, I doubt I'll even get the benefit of a proper hearing. They will show no mercy, not even to a woman."

He leaned back in the chair, folding his arms across his chest. "For an Englishwoman —"

"How do you know I'm English?"

"I can tell by your accent."

She was English, to be sure. But she was not the sort welcomed into polite society. She'd spent most of her life running away from that fact.

"For an Englishwoman, you seem well-versed in the subtleties of criminal justice."

"Is that a compliment or a criticism?"

He surprised her with the barest flicker of a smile, just a quirk of his lips. "I'm not sure."

That miserly hint of a smile all but melted her. She wished she didn't feel so limp-willed and scatterbrained. She'd survived plenty of disasters in her life, and she must survive this. But getting shot and being accused of attempted bloody murder were serious indeed.

She regarded him with a sinking heart. "You're not convinced, are you? You still believe I shot that poor man."

"You fled when you believed I was sending for the police. Hardly the behavior of an innocent woman."

"But quite consistent with the behavior of a frightened woman. A frightened and wounded woman. But even wounded, I realized I was in trouble. A shooting is not a crime that can be easily traced."

"So if, as you claim, you didn't fire upon the officer, whom did you shoot?"

"No one. I fired my pistol into the air, deliberately. To distract the murderer."

"And the murderer would be . . . ?"

"I can't be certain. It was too dark to see." She shut her eyes and tried to recreate the scene in her mind. Had she missed something, a clue, a flicker in the shadows that would clarify the terrible events?

All was a shattered puzzle, the pieces lying meaningless on the ground. While hiding out in the churchyard, she had thought the bits of memory were part of a dream, or more accurately, a nightmare. Now she realized that not only had something terrible happened — she had witnessed it. Yet precisely what she had witnessed was unclear, as frightening as an unseen threat in the darkness.

She shut her eyes to stop the spinning, but that only made things worse. In the pulsing glow of fever, she saw it again — a menacing figure whirled in her direction and fired four shots in quick succession. "There was someone in a cloak or long coat of some sort. That was the person who shot me," she said. "But not just then. The first shots . . ."

"Yes?"

"A man was fleeing — your policeman, I presume."

"Perhaps. He can't verify any of this," Dr. Calhoun explained. "He hasn't regained consciousness. If he was running, and the other man was shooting, how did you manage to get involved?"

"I told you, I fired into the air. Then I ran, too, looking for cover. I stumbled over . . . I thought it was a heap of rags, but it was a man, lying drunk. He shouted something and scuttled away, I think. I got up right away, but that was a mistake. That was when —" She opened her eyes and looked directly at Dr. Calhoun. The sight of him steadied her. "I've never felt anything quite like it."

"A bullet wound, you mean."

"It was like being hit by a cannonball. It struck me flat to the ground. I couldn't breathe. Everything blurs together after that. I heard voices calling, feet running along wet pavement." *Dear God, what have you done? Leave that one. . . .* "I remember nothing else until I awoke in your carriage." She still wasn't sure how she'd been dragged through the confusing rabbit warren of the Embarcadero, half-constructed and littered with building refuse.

The effort to relate the incident exhausted her. She felt as though she'd run for miles, and the sickness welled up, reared like a hot wave. "Please, I need to . . ."

Bless him, he didn't need any more prompting than that. "Let me help you," he said.

She didn't just let him. She gave herself to him, completely and utterly, all but sinking into his arms as he helped her to stand. The simple act of walking seemed beyond her. She thought her feet were touching the floor, but could not feel them.

Dr. Calhoun murmured to her in a soothing fashion. "Don't hurry. You'll feel light-headed from the fever. I won't let you fall. . . ." Step-by-step, holding and encouraging her, he showed the way to the water closet, then closed the door behind her. As she was washing up, she caught a glimpse of her image in the gleaming oval mirror that hung over the lavatory basin.

"Dear heaven," she whispered. She could

121

scarcely distinguish dirt from dried blood. Her eyes appeared bruised and bloodshot, her lips cracked, her cheeks sunken in. In her haste to contrive some disguise, she'd used a man's straight razor on her hair, and the resulting dark spiky locks were unfortunate indeed. Vanity aside, she looked like a very sick woman. It seemed a miracle that she'd been given a chance to survive.

Still swaying, she staggered back to the white lace bedroom. Though she reminded herself that his touch was impersonal, his supporting arm around her felt like an embrace. His slow, patient steps and his painstaking gentleness as he helped her back to bed nearly shattered her. It was such a simple thing, one person helping another. Yet it was complicated by emotions so intense she didn't quite have a name for them.

She was out of breath by the time she lay against the pillows again. He handed her a cup of water, tipping it as she drank. Some impulse she didn't understand caused her to reach up and touch his hand.

He set aside the cup and stepped back from the bed. She tried to read his expression, but she didn't know him. Ah, but she wanted to. He was by far one of the most interesting people she'd ever met.

"I look an absolute fright," she said. Fatigue broke over her, and she struggled to stay conscious.

He didn't deny her statement. Instead, he said, "I'll send Miss Beasley to change your dressing and help you clean up."

She drifted on a raft of fever and panic, and her protest came out in a stream of disjointed and desperate nonsense. She was not the sort to swoon, but she did just that, and it was a most interesting sensation. Images jerked past in a series of frozen frames, like the pictures in a magic lantern show at the theater. Then everything burst in a white light, and she was back where she'd been when she'd awakened, in the misty white netherland between consciousness and sleep. She called out to him, reached for him, and she had no idea whether or not she was dreaming when she felt him reach for her and gather her in his arms.

It was a dream, surely. Nothing so wonderful could actually happen to her.

She never did find out the truth about that moment. Her fever ebbed and flowed like an unpredictable tide, and she lost track of the passage of time. Days passed uncounted. Eventually she was able to sit up, to drink water — and to argue with Dr. Calhoun.

"You promised you wouldn't call in the authorities."

"I made no such promise. I said we would pursue the matter when you're better."

"I'll never get better if you keep threatening me."

"It's not a threat. You claim you're innocent, so we must seek justice for you."

She gaped at him in disbelief.

"What your assailant did to you is illegal," he stated.

"I know," she snapped. Then she cut her gaze away. "But I'm not that naive."

"You might be surprised."

"I simply cannot believe someone could be punished for hurting me."

"In this country, they say justice is blind."

"They also say all men are created equal, but in my travels across America, I've seen no evidence of that." She waved a hand in exasperation. "I can see my word has no value to you."

"But mine does," said a tall, good-looking man, immaculately groomed and dressed. He stood in the doorway regarding Isabel with blatant curiosity and, if she was not mistaken, a small measure of flirtatiousness.

She knew she was not mistaken when Dr. Calhoun scowled at him. "You're accosting a wounded woman in a private chamber," he pointed out.

"It makes them so much easier to seduce that way," said the stranger, striding toward the bed. He performed a perfect bow. "How do you do, Miss Fish-Wooten? I am Rory McKnight, an extremely clever lawyer and quite possibly the only friend of Blue Calhoun."

Blue. Blue Calhoun. Somehow, the nickname suited him. "His only friend?" she asked Mr. McKnight.

"With a disposition like that, he's lucky to have even me."

"Your presence in a lady's chamber is offensive. What are you doing here?" asked Dr. Calhoun. His manner was long-suffering, and Isabel knew without asking that these two had sparred many times. They were an odd match, the solemn physician and the devil-may-care lawyer, yet she sensed their almost brotherly affinity for one another. Side by side, they made a striking pair, light and shadow, the sun and the moon.

"I've come to see your lovely visitor. You invited me, remember?" He turned to Isabel and sent her a dazzling smile. "I'm guessing he didn't explain that he gave me your firearms in order to investigate the crime."

Shock muted her, but only for a moment. "He did what?"

"He took the entire gardening shed apart until he found the Colt's. It was a favor to you," McKnight said hastily. "You see, I am something of an expert in crime investigation."

A headache pulsed madly behind her eyes. "I'm ill, Mr. McKnight. You'll have to explain all this to me."

"I'm not ill in the least," said Dr. Calhoun, "but I'd like an explanation, too."

Holding the gun between thumb and forefinger, he said, "I used the French method of determining the origin of the bullet. You see, each weapon puts a particular mark on the bullets it fires, because its compression is unique." McKnight reached into the watch pocket of his waistcoat and pulled out a misshapen bullet. "You removed this from Miss Fish-Wooten, and I took it to an expert gunsmith. Judging by the caliber, lands and grooves, we determined the weapon of origin."

Isabel's heart sped up — with hope or dread, she couldn't be certain. It was a struggle to keep up with the conversation, but she sensed this debonair stranger was helping her case.

"This is a sixty-seven caliber ball. It's from a Confederate weapon imported from England during the War Between the States," he explained to Isabel. Then he placed the ball in the palm of Dr. Calhoun's hand. "And what you'll really find interesting is that the bullet taken from Officer Brolin appears to be from the same gun that shot your houseguest."

"Are you certain?" asked Dr. Calhoun. "Did you compare the two?"

"Indeed I did. I have friends in the police department who don't mind sharing certain details of their investigation. So now it's a matter of finding the gun and then finding its owner."

"And have the police done so?"

"Not yet. The weapon might be difficult to find since it's not in common use. It might belong to a veteran of the war or to a collector."

Isabel watched Dr. Calhoun's face. She wished she knew him better, wished she knew whether she was seeing relief or rage.

"So it's good news," McKnight said. "Miss Fish-Wooten is quite likely to be deemed innocent."

"But that means a murderer is still at large and still armed with a deadly weapon."

Hiding her fear, she sent Dr. Calhoun — Blue — a smug look. "That's what I've been telling you."

"You could have used the pistol in question and then discarded it," he pointed out.

"Your accusations get more far-fetched by the moment," she snapped.

He glared at her. "Then tell me something I can believe."

She glared back. "That's an impossible task."

"Why, because you're a habitual liar?"

"Because you're an untrusting, autocratic, humorless —"

"I see you're getting along swimmingly," Rory McKnight interrupted, gathering up his things. "This might be a good time to make myself scarce." He stepped outside. Dr. Calhoun followed him, but she could hear their conversation through the half-open door.

". . . detain her now, she'll die from lack of medical care," McKnight pointed out.

Dr. Calhoun murmured something indistinct.

"Turning her in now is a death sentence, Blue, and you know it," the lawyer persisted.

Dear God. Her savior was going to hand her over to the police. She looked wildly around the room for a way to escape.

McKnight spoke up again. ". . . never know for certain. Even if she survives her injury . . ."

Isabel caught her breath. For the first time, it occurred to her that she could die. Dying was yet another adventure she had not experienced, though she was certainly in no hurry for that one. She waited, praying Dr. Calhoun would agree with Mr. McKnight that she was too unwell to be turned over to the authorities.

Dr. Calhoun came back into the room, scowling deeply. Bit by bit, she let out the breath she was holding. A floating sensation lifted her up, and vaguely she recognized the sensation as fear. She wanted to beg him as she had never begged anyone before, to exhort him to let her stay, to make her better. Yet the idea of pleading with him was such a foreign notion that she didn't even know where to begin.

"Dr. Calhoun —"

"Miss Fish-Wooten —"

They both spoke at once and both interrupted themselves. For a few seconds, they stared at one another. Then, a moment later, a Chinese woman in an oversized apron hurried into the room. The unexpected moment of intimacy passed.

"Dr. Blue," said the woman, "you must come. Mr. Peterson is waiting downstairs. The midwife says his wife needs a doctor bad. Needs a doctor quick."

Ten

The moment the news was delivered, Isabel saw a distinct change take hold of Dr. Calhoun. The anger and suspicion he'd subjected her to vanished. It was as though a new mask dropped over his face. His eyes were sharp and clear, and instantly shifted focus. He reacted immediately, heading for the door, issuing instructions to unseen persons as he went. "I'll need my surgical kit. Don't bother with the rig. I'll go with Peterson." Almost as an afterthought, he added, "See that Miss Fish-Wooten keeps to her bed at all times. And give her something to eat."

Then he was gone, leaving a curious vacuum of emptiness. Isabel had never known a man who had the ability to fill an entire house with the power of his energy. She stared at the place on her wrist where he had touched her to find the rhythm of her heart. A phantom warmth lingered there, and no matter how hard she tried, she could not stop thinking about him. Just what had she gotten herself into this time? This was nothing like her other adventures. Ordinarily she went sightseeing and dined in elegant hotels, and the people she met were no more important to her than the wines she tasted. Yet now she found herself in the home of a man who suddenly seemed very important to her indeed.

His suspicion plagued her like a rash. He didn't trust her. Even with a fine, upstanding citizen like Mr. McKnight offering all sorts of proof of her innocence, Calhoun seemed determined to believe the worst of her. She was used to skepticism, but in this case, she was telling the truth, and she was desperate for him to believe her.

The woman spoke in Chinese to a younger woman who had come into the room, bearing a breakfast tray. It was a girl, actually. In a modest muslin smock, her eyes downcast, she appeared to be a younger, softer version of the elder.

"I am Mrs. Li," said the woman. "This is my daughter, June Li." Apparently satisfied that she had done her duty, she rattled off a series of what sounded like marching orders in Chinese. Finally, she turned and left the room, motioning for June to follow her.

But like most young people Isabel had observed, the girl had a mind of her own. Once the mother was gone, June Li returned. She stepped soundlessly through the doorway, then edged close to the bed, more apprehensive than shy. Isabel was delighted to see that the girl was back. She hated to frighten people. She disliked intimidating anyone. As a child, she had been frightened and intimidated more than she cared to remember. She was loath to inflict that on anyone, even those who deserved it.

"Do you like to be called June Li, or June, or Miss Li?" she asked in her most polite fashion.

The girl dipped into a curtsy. "June is my American name. That's the name I prefer."

"And you must call me Isabel."

"Yes, ma'am. My mother's true name is Li Mei, but that only confuses people."

She could see this line of questioning was fast becoming tedious to the poor girl. "June, I have a feeling your mother wouldn't approve of you visiting me."

"My mother approves of very little," she said ruefully, offering a conspiratorial smile.

Excellent, thought Isabel. Here was a chance to learn more about her circumstances, and about the inscrutable man who had rescued her. "I see. In that case, I have a confession to make."

"Ma'am?"

"I've suffered an unfortunate injury and it's left me quite weak. I wish I could tell you all about my adventures but I'm afraid I would wear myself out. So I was wondering if you could tell me about yourself."

"Myself, ma'am?"

The girl was so polite and reserved, Isabel knew it would take some work to draw her out. "That's right. One of the chief pleasures of traveling the world is learning about other people. Where were you born? What do you dream about?"

June's eyes sparkled as she considered the question with obvious pleasure. Most people loved to talk about themselves; it was a fundamental fact of human behavior.

"I was born right here in San Francisco," she said. "In a house on a street called Tuck Wo Gai — that means Virtue and Harmony Street. It's Washington Place in Chinatown." Her bright, dark eyes turned somber as she lowered her voice. "My mother says the house is no longer there."

"And where do you live now?"

"In a service alley flat behind the hill. It's just in the next block. My mother cooks for Dr. Calhoun."

"And your father?"

She stared steadily at Isabel. "I have no father."

Isabel stared back. "Then we have something in common."

For some reason, that released a flood. June was suddenly as talkative as a nesting magpie. She was sixteen years old and had lived in the neighborhood since she was seven. She knew how to cook shoo-fly pie and duck a l'orange. She could read, write and speak both Mandarin and English. Her passion and greatest talent was sewing — not ordinary things, but fine dresses and luxurious accessories for ladies. "Dr. Blue let me study drawing with the tutor he hired for Lucas," she explained. "I've created dress designs all on my own."

"Why do you call him Dr. Blue?"

The girl shrugged. "You must ask him."

"I shall, of course. I want to know everything about him."

June was only too happy to oblige. Over the next hour, Isabel learned that although the beloved "Dr. Blue" was regarded as a local hero, it was not a reputation he cultivated.

In the San Francisco underworld, his name was spoken with reverence. To the sick and desperate of the waterfront alleys, he was simply Dr. Blue, who treated patients without judgment and often for no pay. He didn't ask questions beyond those involved in his diagnosis and treatment. He was as likely to accept a fresh-caught salmon as cash for payment. Neighbor told neighbor, shopkeeper whispered to customer, and his fame spread. Sometimes in the night, when a young mother was distraught over her feverish baby, and nothing she did made a difference, a friend might tell her, "I know someone who can help." Everyone seemed to know that the bell next to the surgery door could be turned at any hour of the day, and Dr. Blue would come. Surgical kit in hand, he headed out into the night on a swift horse and often didn't return until dawn.

By the end of the story, Isabel was seeing double again. Two Junes, two faces as perfect as newly-open flowers. She frowned. "You were there when Master Lucas found me, weren't you?"

The wavering twin Junes fused into a single image. "Oh, yes. I was with Lucas." A world of youthful hope reverberated through the words.

Isabel sent her a smile of delight. "So he's your beau, then."

"No," she whispered, casting her eyes down.

"But you adore him. I can tell."

"Sometimes I dream of being sweethearts with Lucas, yes. But it can never be."

"Why not?"

"There are prohibitions against it."

"That's the most preposterous thing I've ever heard. Laws against loving?"

"This was not my idea."

"My advice would be to ignore them and love him anyway."

She shook her head. "That would only cause hurt."

"Forcing yourself not to love him — now, that would hurt." Isabel shut her eyes and pictured Dr. Calhoun's son, with his wavy dark hair and intense brown eyes. "He's a young god, June. I don't see how you can resist. Or why you would bother. Don't turn away from love. Heavens, it's the only thing that makes sense in this world." Isabel offered a vague, drifting smile as a wave of weakness rolled over her. She was ill-equipped to offer such advice, but suddenly she believed her own words with all her heart.

"My mother says hard work and sacrifice are the only virtues that make sense for a girl like me."

Isabel winced, hearing echoes of St. Anselm's workhouse in the girl's words. "You understand, falling in love is an amazing gift. It doesn't happen often."

"Has it happened to you?"

"No. Never. I've never let it. And look at me, alone in the world, not a soul to care if I live or die."

"Dr. Blue cares. Lucas cares."

Something inside Isabel grew warm. The girl's words were breath blowing new life into a dying ember. "Lucas told me his father is a widower. What was his wife's name?"

"Sancha Montgomery." June whispered the name like a secret.

"Sancha Montgomery." Isabel repeated it. "It's a lovely name, different and interesting."

"I never knew her. There are pictures of her in the front parlor. She was very beautiful."

"Of course she was." What other kind of wife would the incomparable Dr. Calhoun have?

"This was her room," June said. "Did you know that?"

Isabel thought she had heard wrong over the pulse pounding in her ears. "He's put me in his dead wife's room?"

"Not . . . exactly. Lucas brought you here."

"Why would he do that?"

"It's the best room in the house. He was very worried about you, Miss Isabel."

She plucked at the white gown. "And this?"

"I think it was probably hers."

Isabel shut her eyes. Colors whirled across her mind. "I am going to burn in hell." She made herself smile and open her eyes again. "How did Mrs. Calhoun die?"

"No one speaks of it. The family was stationed far away in a place where soldiers fight the Indians. Lucas was very small."

"So she was killed by Indians?"

"Lucas says there was a battle and she died. Nurse Beasley says Dr. Blue has never been the same since it happened."

A tragic hero, Isabel thought. No wonder I'm half in love with him.

She didn't realize she had spoken aloud until June flashed a grin, as bright and fleeting as a passing hummingbird. "All women are," she confessed.

"All women. You mean his patients."

137

"I mean everyone. Ever since he and Mr. McKnight founded the Rescue League —"

"He started it?" Isabel was astonished.

"He and Mr. McKnight, yes. Mr. McKnight was a rescued orphan who made good. He has known Dr. Blue since the war."

Isabel absorbed the information. The San Francisco Mission Rescue League was famous throughout the city, bringing hope to hopeless cases. Isabel made her way in the world on her own, and she always had. Yet now she wondered, if such an agency had existed when she was in desperate circumstances, would things have turned out differently for her?

She forbade herself to speculate. It was futile, and she was in enough pain already. Yet she wondered why Dr. Calhoun seemed so reluctant to rescue her. Was she not desperate enough, not fragile enough for him?

June's butterfly hands fluttered over the breakfast tray as she gathered dishes and napkins.

"Why do you suppose he started the agency?" Isabel repeated, in case the girl hadn't heard.

June stopped what she was doing and folded her hands in front of her. Eyes downcast, she said, "Nine years ago, my mother was his first . . . client." Without looking up, she explained that her mother — bossy, dignified Mrs. Li — had been sold by her own uncle to a merchant in Shanghai. She had

138

grown old and bitter before she reached the age of twenty.

Because of her own past, Isabel heard all the things June Li was not saying. She understood the complete horror of such an existence, the loss of everything — freedom, pride, identity, innocence — that made a person human.

"I have two brothers and two sisters," June went on. "I never knew any of them. Some died. Some were sold. I was the youngest. That's when my mother found Dr. Blue."

"That's a remarkable story."

"Yes. All the women who work here were rescued by Dr. Blue."

"All the women who work here?"

She nodded. "There's Bernadette Riordan, the housekeeper, an Indian woman named Efrena who looks after the horses and rigs. And Delta Beasley, of course. But he didn't rescue her."

"He didn't?"

"No. She rescued him, to hear her tell it."

"I think I'd like to hear her tell it." What a strange and wondrous place this was, Isabel thought. The home of a man who devoted his life to healing people and rescuing women.

What a shame, she thought, that she was in such trouble locally. Otherwise, she wouldn't mind staying for a while.

Eleven

So she wasn't a murderer, thought Blue. Rory McKnight had never been wrong before, and he knew better than to encourage his best friend to leave a dangerous criminal in the house. Rory had been adamant about letting her stay. "A woman with her looks might suffer worse than fever if she's incarcerated," he'd warned. "She'll haunt you."

Rory knew him as well as he knew the inner workings of the city's police department. They were as vengeful as he stated, and might not stop at rape, either. The idea of sending a patient away to die was beyond repugnant to Blue. It was unthinkable. At any rate, he had to trust his friend and his gut, and both were telling him that Isabel Fish-Wooten would do no harm.

Yet even so, she unsettled him. There was something he saw in her, something that was going to throw him. He wasn't certain why he got that feeling from her, but it was undeniable. For years he had dedicated himself to rescuing women in need, women who were sick or frightened or fleeing a troubled past.

He wanted this one to be no different from all the others who passed through the Rescue League.

But she was entirely different in ways he could barely explain to himself.

For now, though, he had to let the matter go and give his attention to the emergency at hand. The frantic Mr. Peterson brought him to a neatly furnished house and directed him to a room that reeked of birth smells — blood and sweat, terror and hope. Mrs. Peterson lay abed, damp sheets twisted around her ungainly form while Leafy Bonner, the midwife, sat at her side, mopping her brow with a cloth. An older woman — probably Mrs. Peterson's mother — sat in a window seat, stiff and pale with terror.

Blue removed his frockcoat, then set his surgical kit on the table. Within moments of examining Mrs. Peterson, he understood why the midwife had sent for him. He, of course, was the last resort for the frantic young mother. Like most women, she was a modest, God-fearing lady who tolerated a physician only as an extreme measure.

He tried to be respectful of her modesty while still doing his job for the unborn baby. Or, in this case, babies.

"Twins, Mrs. Peterson," he said, his voice neutral but encouraging as he reached beneath the sheets. "They're going to need some help making their way into the world."

"I tried everything in my birthing kit," Leafy said, indicating an open wooden box on the bedside table. It contained a medieval-looking array of clamps and tongs, vials of herbs, apothecary jars and a cloth parcel stamped Far East Tea Company. The midwife shut the lid of the box with a snap. "I gave her morphine drops, but it's not helping. Do you have a syringe, Doctor?"

"I'll use some ether if it's needed," he said.

"Morphine's better. Quiets 'em right down. I hear it's three times stronger than opium. Is that true?"

"You ought to ascertain that before you administer it," he pointed out.

"Should've given her more drops," Mrs. Bonner said, ignoring his cutting tone. She shifted the stem of her pipe from one side of her mouth to the other. Blue liked and respected most of the midwives he encountered in his practice, though this one was different. She was more experienced as an abortionist than a baby-catcher. He wondered how she acquired morphine. It was supposed to be dispensed only by a licensed physician.

At least she had the sense to know when to send for help, he conceded. For the time being, he set aside his suspicions. And she was a helpful assistant, though clearly skeptical of his insistence on a sterile field. She proved to be a calming influence on the exhausted mother, urging her to marshal her strength for the labors ahead.

Mrs. Peterson's mother, on the other hand, was paralyzed by terror. She could not even pray and, indeed, had difficulty breathing. She simply slumped in the window seat with the curtains drawn, her face frozen into an expression Blue wished he didn't recognize. It was the look of someone whose world was falling away, whose future was a well of darkness.

"Get yourself a glass of sherry," he said to the older woman. It wouldn't make the fear go away but might momentarily dull the edges of the torture. That was what loving someone did to you, he reflected, eyeing the woman with both pity and understanding. It took you apart, piece by piece.

Blue considered himself fortunate to have been raised in a fine family and educated well. But no one had ever taught him the most fundamental truth of all — that love was a form of exquisite torment from which there was no release but death. Of course, no one had to teach him that. He'd learned that lesson on his own as a gunshot wound had drained the life from Sancha ten years ago. The only way around it was to die together, and that generally only happened in tragic fiction.

Clearing his head of thoughts that had no proper place at a birthing, he summoned an encouraging smile for the laboring mother.

"Twin birth is less a matter of medicine than mechanics, but I'm glad you sent for me."

She didn't smile, yet the firm set of her jaw indicated that she was prepared to face the ordeal. Blue had seen that steely determination before. It was something he respected and believed in, though no medical text had ever given a logical explanation for the phenomenon. Yet any physician attending a birth knew it to be so. A laboring mother possessed a special reserve of strength that gave her the power to move mountains.

Within an hour the exhausted, frightened creature on the bed became a goddess as she pushed forth a smallish but healthy baby boy. Forty minutes later she brought forth his brother, who was even smaller and not quite so lusty with his cries. The midwife took a towel and rubbed the little arms and legs, and gradually the color of life bloomed over him, a gorgeous red flush radiating out to his extremities.

Blue shut his eyes, momentarily savoring a sense of triumph that didn't rightly belong to him. Yet it was impossible not to feel brushed by the sheer wonder of the event he'd witnessed. He knew his role in the birth had been vital, and a deep gratitude settled over him. Sometimes, even for the briefest of moments, he could admit that life was good indeed.

Opening his eyes, he busied himself with

the mother, inspecting the afterbirth to make sure there was no abnormal bleeding and checking her pulse and temperature. He spared a glance for the young woman's mother. The older lady turned into a different creature, cooing and swaddling the infants as she prepared them to meet their father. Tears poured down her face and a profound joy radiated from her, as palpable as heat from a well-stoked stove.

Finally, when the room was put back in order, the drowsy but triumphant mother propped in bed and holding an infant in the crook of each arm, the husband was brought in. Abject dread was replaced by the same radiance that possessed his mother-in-law. He bounded rather than walked to the bedside and fell to his knees beside his wife.

"My darling," he said, "look at you and our beautiful sons. We are better blessed than the angels in heaven."

Blue caught the mother-in-law's eye. They both knew through bitter experience that more than joys and blessings lay ahead for the new family. Hell, everyone knew that, but people still carried on, still loved each other and hurt each other and got their hearts broken again and again. The only protection from the pain of loving was the knowledge that it was going to happen. The smart ones kept their guard up.

Blue had learned to be smart.

The new father gave him a generous fee. His eyes were bright as he said, "You saved them. You saved them all. Praise God. How can we ever thank you?"

Blue let his gaze settle on the beaming mother and the two sweetly sleeping infants. "You have," he said. Motioning to Mrs. Bonner, he stepped outside the room.

"You did a fine job for a sawbones," she said. "I'll finish up here, look after the mother."

"I'm curious, Mrs. Bonner. Where do you get your supply of morphine drops?"

She gave a rasp of laughter. "You think doctors is the only ones who can get it? It's down at the docks, or in Chinatown, any night you want. Just because I'm no sawbones doesn't mean my patients have to suffer."

On his way back home, he decided to take a shortcut through Woodward's Gardens, a large public resort where traders set out their wares on summer afternoons. Walrus tusks, wampum and whalebone etched with designs decked the draped tables. Silk scarves, brooches and tiny paintings on canvas drew tourists and natives alike. He slowed his strides at a display of hair combs.

I look an absolute fright.

He certainly didn't owe the woman any-thing, yet he found himself picking up a shiny pair of celluloid combs. Then he put them back down. Good God. What was he thinking?

"A perfect choice, sir," said the woman selling the combs, pushing them toward him. "Handsome without being gaudy."

As he reached into his pocket for change, he told himself he was making the purchase simply to help out the vendor, who was thin and whose dress was threadbare. She took great care folding the combs in tissue paper and handing them over. He thanked her briefly, cursed himself for a fool and walked down a row of other displays.

A familiar-looking hat caught his eye — it belonged to Abner Punch, half of the notorious team of crimps. Punch seemed more interested in the strolling shoppers than in the wares for sale. Scouting for his next victim, perhaps, Blue thought, raising his hand to get Punch's attention. Perhaps he would shed some light on the night of the shooting. He might explain how an injured woman had fallen into his hands. But as soon as he spotted Blue, Abner Punch hurried away.

He probably wouldn't have told the truth, Blue concluded. With an unsettled air, he approached a draped table bearing a selection of firearms.

"What can I show you?" the merchant asked, leaning forward over the table.

"Have you any Confederate pistols?" Blue asked.

"I'm afraid not, sir. Those are rare enough these days. Are you a collector, then?"

Blue shook his head and moved on. It was a long shot, anyway.

Down the block from the garden resort, he recognized a stately woman in a hat constructed of peacock feathers. It was Clarice Hatcher, making her usual rounds in the city's fashionable district. She was shopping, which seemed to be her second-favorite pastime. Like attendants to a princess, her maid and two footmen followed at a respectful distance, laden with hatboxes and parcels tied with twine. The footmen made an odd pair — an Irishman of prodigious height and a Chinese man with a mustache so long he tucked it into a sash around his waist.

As he approached her, Blue slipped the parcel with the hair combs into his pocket. He did not want to have to explain Isabel Fish-Wooten to anyone, but most particularly to Clarice.

"Theodore, you cruel piece," she said, pausing in her regal stroll. "Why haven't you been to see me?"

"My duties have kept me busy," he explained, bringing her gloved hand nearly to his lips and bowing over it.

The glare she shot him conveyed the silent message that he was an idiot for neglecting her. And he was, perhaps. Clarice Hatcher was every man's dream of the perfect mistress. She was beautiful, widowed and wealthy. But Blue cared little for those attributes. She possessed a singular trait he valued above all others. She had absolutely no expectation that he would fall in love with her. All that existed between them was an agreeable sexual heat, coupled with a few shared interests including golf, horse racing and light opera.

Neither of them yearned for more depth in their relationship, she because she enjoyed a lazy, feline contentment in her own life, and he because he had closed off that part of his heart after losing Sancha.

There was something melancholy and disquieting in the thought. At times when Blue allowed a moment of self-examination and reflection, he wondered if he had lost the ability to feel anything deeply anymore. Then he had only to consider his son and the reminder clutched at his heart. Oh, yes, he could love. He could hurt and fall apart. That was why he was so careful not to look for true intimacy with a woman. The unprotected heart was nothing short of folly, a disaster waiting to happen.

"Stroll with me," she said, slipping her arm through his. At the height of summer, San Francisco pulsed with a festive atmosphere. Foreign merchants and travelers thronged the streets, and local tradesmen loudly vied for their trade. The strong, rich aroma of fish wafted up from the wharf area. Horns sounded from the steamers and ferries criss-crossing the bay, and the squabbling gulls and barking harbor seals added their voices to the shouts from the waterfront.

"Is there anything so fine as San Francisco in the summer?" said Clarice.

She didn't seem to expect an answer, so he didn't offer one. He both loved and hated the city. He loved its vitality, its rousing politics and the earnest promise of its citizens to create a world capital. He liked the hills and valleys of its neighborhoods and the misty beauty of the weather, even when the fog clung for days on end. Yet he hated the blights of crime and poverty, the staggering contrast between the wealth and ostentation of high society and the corruption of the under-world, the violent world that came alive each night, then left its victims to the dawn.

Knowing Clarice, he was fairly confident she wasn't interested in his views on the matter.

She chattered on, flitting from one topic to the next — the weather, the new merchant block going up in Sutter Street, the scandalous behavior of someone he didn't know at a soiree he hadn't attended. She struck him three times on the arm with her fan. "You aren't listening, Theodore."

"Of course I am," he lied.

"I wanted to know who chose the theme of this year's charity benefit for the Rescue League."

"My stepmother and sisters," he said. "They always do."

"And you let them?"

"Why wouldn't I? Without the benefit, the league would go bankrupt and cease to exist."

"But, Theodore, Arabian Nights? It's so barbaric. Why couldn't they have chosen the Roundtable of Camelot, something romantic and chivalrous? Honestly, dreaming up some sort of veiled costume is simply too taxing."

"Then you won't be attending?" he asked, though he knew the answer.

"I'd never disappoint you like that, Theodore."

He patted her gloved hand. "I'm afraid I must head straight back to my surgery," he said. "I've a critical patient." Ordinarily he would offer a detail or two to amuse her, but he stayed circumspect about Miss Fish-Wooten. He had no idea on what he was going to do about her.

"You are a most exasperating man." She tapped him on the arm again with her closed fan. "But I will forgive you if you promise to accompany me to the Shooting Club ice cream social this Friday. It's going to be well-attended."

"I shall make every attempt —"

"You will not make every attempt," she cut in. "You will attend, Theodore." As always, her temper flashed like a stiletto blade. "The mayor will be in attendance, as well as Senator Butler from Washington, D.C. And Mr. Hopkins, and Dr. Vickery —"

"Fremont Vickery?" he asked, suddenly interested.

"Yes. That is, if his wife doesn't take sick again. She's always been sickly, as I hear it." Clarice Hatcher was a vicious gossip but, unfortunately, much of her information was correct. Blue felt a new empathy for Fremont Vickery. Like all public figures, he had a private life, too, and apparently Vickery had his troubles. *If I lost my Alma, I'd be done for.* Those had been his exact words. Now Blue wished he'd listened better.

"Let's hope she's better in time for the gala," he said to Clarice. He banished her pout with a whispered suggestion in her ear, which made her purr like a cat. Then he took his leave. He had one more stop to make before he went home, and he was in a hurry.

Twelve

Blue walked a few blocks to St. Mary's. The dim nave smelled of old stone and moldering masonry. He heard the steady *drip, drip* of the holy water font and found himself awash in memories. He had married Sancha in this church, amid booming music from the two-storey pipe organ. Together, he and his bride had navigated a sea of fresh flowers flooding them from a host of well-wishers. What a long time ago that was, and not just in years. He had been a different person back then. Happy and full of hope.

He found Father Giacomo Sean Collins, known as Father Jock, in his office, alternately staring at the ceiling and fiddling with the ink pump on his fountain pen.

"Working hard, I see," Blue said, stepping into the office.

Father Jock jumped up, all smiles. His towering height, along with a dramatic cloud of snow-white hair, made him seem larger-than-life. More than one young Sunday school student had mistaken Father Jock for the Almighty himself.

"Heavenly saints, I need a sermon. I ask the Lord above for the proper words, and he sends me nothing but a blank page."

"Welcome to the human race," said Blue. "I'm looking for the fruit of my loins."

"Ah, young Lucas. No finer lad in the city," the priest declared.

"The wine-stealing incident aside."

Father Jock waved his hand. "Harmless mischief, to be sure. I'm in need of help this summer, and I'm happy enough to enlist Lucas rather than that ee-jit O'Halloran boy who pruned the rosebushes to nubs last year." His thick eyebrows descended. "But Lucas is home this afternoon. I'm certain the lad said he was needed at home."

Blue felt no alarm but a twinge of annoyance. Lucas had told him expressly that he'd be working in the church gardens today. "He's not at home."

"Let's have a look around, then. Perhaps I misunderstood."

As they walked through the gardens of St. Mary's, more memories assailed Blue. The Montgomery family had funded a pergola in memory of their beloved daughter, and in summer, it bloomed with bright white stars of jasmine. Father Jock paused respectfully as they passed it. "May her dear soul rest in peace," he murmured. Then he sent a knowing look at Blue. "But of course, she's not at all at peace now, is she?"

154

Blue scowled. "What?"

"Your late wife. She's not at peace, because you won't let her go."

"I shouldn't have come to see you. Each time I do, you seem compelled to counsel me in my grief. After all these years, it's become boring."

"Aye, grief is a tedious matter," said Father Jock, deliberately misunderstanding. "Best to put it behind you. Some men live lives filled with many loves. Others love but once. But of course, that's their choice."

Blue strode away. "I don't know what you're talking about."

"Ah, you do."

It was not the first time they'd had this discussion, and Blue knew it would not be the last. He told himself not to take the bait, but the priest had a way of goading him. Lately, everyone in his life wanted to counsel him in the matter. He was damned tired of defending his decision to remain a widower.

They found no trace of Lucas. He had compounded his infractions by lying to both Blue and Father Jock. The priest seemed unperturbed, even amused. "In the matter of his punishment, I'll let you do the honors this time." As he headed back to his office, he turned and called across the yard. "Why the devil do you think your boy steals wine and gets into mischief? It's a bid for attention, man."

"It works, then," Blue said ruefully.

★ ★ ★

He walked swiftly homeward, wondering what his son was up to this time. With Lucas, he could never be sure, and with Isabel Fish-Wooten as a temporary resident, it was anyone's guess.

The house looked fine, though, as solid as a marble mausoleum. It was a far bigger house then he had ever needed, but it had been a wedding gift from Sancha's family, who had spared no expense when it came to their only daughter.

He and Sancha had spent four perfect years here. Then he'd decided to serve in the army again. She insisted upon accompanying him to Fort Carrington, viewing it as a grand adventure. The adventure ended when she was gunned down in front of her tiny son's eyes.

Blue went straight to Sancha's room. He found the door ajar, and from the hallway, he could see Lucas sitting with Isabel Fish-Wooten.

Multiple protests leaped to his lips. She was a stranger, a lady abed, and it was hardly proper for his son to be in her presence. But he knew what Lucas's reaction would be if he sent the boy away. It wasn't that he feared his son's resentment. That would be like fearing the sunrise; it was going to occur no matter what. But he was weary of Lucas's constant defiance.

For several moments, he watched unnoticed from the doorway. His patient looked quite a bit improved. Apparently Delta had seen to tidying her up, and perhaps she'd had a nap, for she looked rested. On a table beside the bed, she and Lucas were playing a hand of poker, something he'd forbidden his son to do. To Blue's astonishment, Lucas played with the consummate skill and assurance of a seasoned cardsharp, lacking only a cheroot and glass of whiskey to complete the picture.

But the look on Lucas's face as he smiled and spoke with the houseguest was anything but cynical. Amazing, thought Blue with a not-altogether-pleasant jolt.

"I've never actually played for money before, Miss Fish-Wooten," Lucas said, pushing a stack of coins across the green tablecloth.

"Dear boy," she said in her oh-so-haughty accent, "a gentleman never plays for money. He plays *with* it." Reaching out with a dainty hand, she lifted the stack of coppers and let them scatter.

Lucas's dark eyes danced with enchantment. "Is that so?"

"Absolutely. Remember that, and you will never feel desperate about money."

Lucas grinned at her.

She frowned, more in confusion than disapproval. "What is it?"

"Nothing. It's just . . . You're not like most ladies I've met."

"And what are all those other ladies like?" She plucked ruefully at her hair. "I suspect they are better groomed."

The boy blushed and shrugged his shoulders. "Most girls talk all the time —"

"I've been accused of doing my share of talking."

"But you're straightforward and matter-of-fact. You talk about things besides fashion and gossip. You're much more interested in other people than yourself."

Blue stood amazed for half a minute more. Who was this lively young man, so eagerly soaking in the dubious advice of an uninvited guest? The change in Lucas was dramatic. His son, who seemed to care about nothing, had finally found something to care about.

The trouble was, he'd allowed himself to be charmed by a person of shady character, despite Rory's claim of her innocence.

He strode into the room. "I take it you're feeling better, Miss Fish-Wooten."

She regarded him calmly from the bed. She looked like a princess, propped against lace-edged pillows and wearing a modest, expensive-looking gown he could have sworn once belonged to Sancha.

Each time he looked at Miss Fish-Wooten, he found his gaze drawn to her uncommon eyes. Large and thickly-lashed, they resembled something out of a pre-Raphaelite portrait. A man could drown in those eyes if he wasn't careful.

"Much better indeed," she told him, smiling up at him from the bed.

He had such an unexpected reaction to the smile that, for a moment, words failed him. His mouth felt dry, his chest warm, as though he'd caught the fever that afflicted her.

"I'm off, then," Lucas said suddenly, folding his fan of cards. "I'm going back to St. Mary's. I've more work to do." He bade a polite farewell to Miss Fish-Wooten.

"You told Father Jock you were needed at home," Blue said.

A dull red flush stained Lucas's cheeks and the tips of his ears. "And he told me to return at my convenience."

"We'll talk about this later," Blue promised and clenched his jaw in frustration. Why couldn't the boy simply do as he was told?

"Yes, sir." Stiff-backed with resentment, Lucas left the room.

For some reason, it bothered Blue that the stranger had witnessed the awkwardness between him and Lucas. And it wasn't the first time she'd seen them like this. His troubles with his son were private, and her scrutiny intruded into tender places he preferred to keep shrouded in darkness.

"Perhaps you should go after him," she suggested.

"He has work to do."

"Pruning box hedge at the church. It's not the most urgent of errands."

He sent her a quelling look as he moved the tray full of cards aside and took out his stethoscope. "Lucas is fifteen. A bit of rebelliousness is normal at that age." As soon as the words escaped him, Blue regretted the moment of candor. She had the oddest effect on him. He tended to blurt things out to her.

"Oh, he's more than a bit rebellious," she declared. "We had a long, honest talk about it. He's deeply resentful of you and angry at the world at large."

He glared at her as he fitted the earpieces of the stethoscope in place, then pressed the monaural to her chest. A reassuring rhythm pulsed in his ears. "Ah. So while I was out today, you obtained competence in the science of psychology."

She sniffed. "I wouldn't know about that, but I know plenty about the human mind and behavior."

He felt a singular urge to laugh, but suppressed it. "Psychology is a field of study of the human mind and behavior."

"Well, I have something the science clearly lacks."

"What's that?"

"Common sense, obviously."

"And what does your common sense tell you?"

160

"That he's deeply resentful of you and angry at the world at large," she repeated with an excess of patience.

"Thank you, Dr. Freud," he said.

"Dr. who?"

"The alienist who is doing pioneering work in the field of psychology."

She waved a hand to indicate disinterest. "Just because you refuse to see the trouble doesn't mean it isn't there."

"Miss Fish-Wooten, whatever troubles I may or may not have in my life are none of your affair."

"That still doesn't mean they don't exist."

The stronger she got, he reflected, the more annoying she became. Perhaps he should stop feeding her.

Clearly he needed to establish some rules. That image of her, so companionably playing cards with Lucas, simply would not leave him alone. "I'd like you to limit your contact with my son," he said.

"I'm sure you would," she replied breezily. "He really is a fine young man. What a joy he must have been for you to raise."

"Indeed." It occurred to him that he was envious of her ease with Lucas, the naturalness of their rapport. He was also suspicious of it. He was not about to confess that the boy had been a trial from the moment Blue had explained that his mama was dead and gone and would not be coming back.

161

"So you agree, then? During your stay here, you'll keep to yourself and not have any visits with Lucas. I shall inform him, too, of course."

"Dr. Calhoun?"

"Yes?"

"Do you know what a horse's ass you sound like?"

"You have experience with horses' asses?" he shot back.

She sent him a soft and lovely smile. "I do now."

He pushed the table away, scattering playing cards. "You are here at my pleasure —"

"And you seem so very pleased with me," she pointed out, unfazed. "All vulgar joking aside, Doctor, I believe it's only fair to let you know that I welcome and encourage visits from Lucas. Your son is a wonderful boy. When I first saw him, I mistook him for an angel. But just because he's wonderful doesn't mean he's going to stay out of trouble. He has questions he needs answered. And pretending you don't know what those questions are is simply a display of willful ignorance."

"What the hell is that supposed to mean?"

"It means, dear doctor, that at a heart-breakingly young age he lost his mother under mysterious and violent circumstances he doesn't understand. And no one will talk about it with him. He was raised by a de-

162

manding perfectionist of a father who is trying to rescue the whole world while ignoring his son."

How, he wondered, had the conversation deteriorated to this? To her unsolicited and wildly erroneous opinion of his personal affairs? If she were a man, she'd be spitting teeth from a broken jaw, Blue thought. Instead, he shielded himself from the words she'd spoken and said, "So you've been gossiping with the help."

"As a matter of fact, I have. I adore gossip."

"She surely does," said Delta, coming into the room with a tray of dressings and salves. "I bet you're plumb worn out, aren't you, honey?"

"Not at all," Isabel assured her. She aimed a glare at Blue. "Nearly everyone has been so very kind. I'm getting excellent care."

Her coloring was poor, Blue observed, revising his earlier idea that she was on the mend. "Be very still now. I need to listen to your heart."

He concentrated on doing what he did best — being a doctor. Her heartbeat was normal, though her temperature and respiration were both elevated. Despite his brusque order, she kept trying to chatter with good-natured earnestness. He suspected she was fighting hard to get better, but her appetite was off. The hollows in her cheeks seemed more pronounced.

"How did you sleep today?" he asked her.

"Perfectly well, thank you."

He frowned, wondering why she would lie. "I need to examine the wound," he said to Delta.

The injury concerned him. It was suppurating and in need of further cleansing. He and Delta performed the painful procedure quickly, expecting her to weep and scream in protest. But she lay perfectly still. He could see her face in profile against the crisp white covering of the pillow. Her expression was blank, as though she'd gone away somewhere.

This self-distancing was a reaction he had observed on rare occasions. It was a way to cope with horrific pain and was generally used by those who lived with a chronic illness — or those frequently subjected to agony.

He wondered who had hurt her before.

He felt Delta watching him, but ignored her. He knew what she was thinking, anyway. This woman was trouble. Innocent or guilty, she was bad news. In naval terms, she would be known as a loose cannon, rolling uncontrolled on deck. The only thing more foolish than setting her free was keeping her close.

By the time he finished, she seemed exhausted by the ordeal and perfectly willing to indulge in a long rest. Before he could allow her to drift away, however, he had a number of questions for her.

He waited while Delta straightened the area and gathered the soiled bandages and dressings. He never came into this room. When he was first married, he had been reluctant to leave it, because this was where he and Sancha used to retreat from society, where they entered the safe haven of their love for each other, where the outside world could not intrude or interrupt. In this room — in this very bed — they had made Lucas, and in this same bed Sancha had birthed their son in a burst of pain and joy. They'd tried to have others, but had not succeeded. Maybe, thought Blue, having just the one child was part of some grand and terrible plan that was bigger than either of them. Because the only thing harder than raising Lucas without Sancha would have been raising Lucas and other children.

"Miss Fish-Wooten," he said once Delta had departed, "I'd like to transfer you to a hospital."

She said nothing but held him in a steady regard that made him feel vaguely foolish and defensive.

"It's your best chance for a full recovery," he said.

She seemed quite calm as she folded her hands in her lap. "I don't see why you're so keen on making me leave. Other women

165

you've rescued have stayed on."

She'd wasted no time prying into his affairs. It was true that the women here had come to him in a state of need, and stayed for the situation he could offer them. Yet the idea of keeping this particular woman in his life was uniquely unsettling. "Many more have recovered and moved on."

"I have skills, you know. I can be useful."

"Oh?"

"I speak French and Russian. I am a crack shot with a rifle, a pistol or a shotgun."

"I have no need of a Russian-speaking game hunter."

"You never know."

"Why do you wish to stay?"

"I never said I wanted to stay. I simply asked you why you didn't want me to."

"I never said I didn't want —" He stopped short of saying something he'd come to regret. "I don't enjoy pointless debate," he stated.

"Then you never should have rescued me in the first place."

"God save me from this conversation," he said through gritted teeth.

"It's a perfectly good conversation."

He took a deep breath, determined to wrest control back from her. "What were you doing abroad so late at night, disguised as a boy and armed to the teeth?"

"Well. It's about time you asked me that."

Actually, he had asked for an explanation the morning she'd stowed away in his carriage, but she seemed to have forgotten the exchange. Interesting. "Were you waiting for an invitation?"

"I was waiting for you to use your common sense."

Damn, but she was an irksome bit of baggage. "All right. Let me allow you the opportunity to explain so I'm not tempted to turn you over to the authorities."

"You won't turn me over to the authorities."

"What makes you so certain?"

"I heard you discussing the matter with Mr. McKnight. I'm too ill. I'll sicken and die if you give me over to the police. You don't want me to die. I'm too important to you."

"All my patients are important."

"Not in the way I am."

He tried to deny the impact of those words, but she seemed somehow to sense the undercurrents between them. As was so often the case with Miss Fish-Wooten, her words took him by surprise. She moved him in ways he'd never felt before. He tried his best to maintain a professional distance, but he kept looking at her as a woman, not a patient. He couldn't stop himself from wondering how her cheek would feel, cupped in the palm of his hand, or what her full, soft lips would taste like if he kissed her.

It felt like a physical effort to shake himself free of the thought. "You're talking nonsense," he said.

"You're pretending you have no idea what I'm talking about."

The hell of it was, he knew exactly what she was talking about. That unnatural electric spark of attraction hummed in the air, here of all places, in the room he'd once shared with the only woman he'd ever loved. It was obscene, he told himself. But undeniable.

He watched her carefully. There was something compelling about her face, its small angular features softened by the uncommon delicacy of her skin, and shadowed by those enormous, dark-lashed eyes. It occurred to him that the fascination he felt toward her was not only reckless but inappropriate. He had no business entertaining these feelings for her, of all women.

Though he scarcely knew her at all, he believed she was completely unsuitable. She was unacceptably young. There were those, of course, who would term him a man in his prime, vigorous and active. But he felt old. The richest part of his life was over, the cream skimmed off the top and spent with impunity. What remained was duty. To expect anything more would be sheer foolishness.

But at the moment, he must concentrate only on her recovery. "You need to rest," he said.

She dismissed the statement with a graceful wave of her hand and looked around the room. "You have a beautiful home. I think you truly are a millionaire."

He didn't reply. She was probably right. Sancha's family was descended from the original settlers of California, a long line of fiercely aristocratic hidalgos who worked the land and, over generations, amassed a fortune. As the only surviving Montgomery of her line, Sancha had come to their marriage dowered with an embarrassment of wealth. Blue did what he did best — he took care of it. He invested and ultimately managed to preserve her fortune because it was important to Sancha. Now he preserved it not for his own sake, but for Lucas.

His lack of response didn't stop Miss Fish-Wooten from talking. Nothing, not even a bullet wound, stopped her from talking. "I used to dream of living in a beautiful house on a hill, with a perfect garden and nannies pushing prams and servants doing the least little thing." She waited. He was intrigued, but he didn't want to encourage her. "Then I realized the truth. It takes more than servants and art treasures to make one happy. A person's happiness is not found in fine things. Do you want to know where it's found? Of course you do, though you might pretend you don't." She paused to draw breath. "I don't know, either," she admitted.

169

"Then why are you still talking?"

"Because I'm still trying to determine the answer. Unlike you, I haven't given up. And unlike you, I believe I'm on the verge of finding the solution. I think it's in the journey."

"This discussion lost its point long ago. I'm leaving. Delta and I have other patients to see." Blue took the wrapped hair combs from his pocket and tossed them ungraciously on the bed. "Here."

"A gift?" Slowly, as though to prolong her anticipation, she unwrapped the parcel. "Oh, Dr. Calhoun —"

"I thought you might be able to put them to some use."

Her face was suffused by happiness. Her eyes were luminous and filled with an emotion he wanted to share. Instead, he stepped away from the bed. Christ, it was just a pair of combs. But her smile as she carefully tucked them into her hair told him what he'd known the moment he'd bought them. It was much more than that.

Thirteen

Lucas sat stiffly in a straight-backed chair in his father's study. Several days had passed since the forbidden card game, and he had dared to think perhaps he would escape punishment. A vain and foolish hope, of course. He'd merely enjoyed a reprieve. Between his private practice and his service to the Rescue League, Father was constantly busy. Lucas used to long for more time with his father, but lately, he counted the absences as a boon. He never missed an opportunity to make the most of his freedom.

The door to the study opened, then shut with a quiet click. Lucas stood and turned, his posture perfect. "Good afternoon, sir," he said.

"Good afternoon. I'll get right to the point, Lucas —"

"Sir, I meant no harm. I was merely entertaining a guest."

Father sat down at the desk, steepled his fingers and regarded Lucas over the top of them. All his life, Father had seemed like a god to him, huge and blond, overwhelmingly powerful, those clear blue eyes filled with a world of feeling — anger, frustration, sadness — but never contentment. How often had they sat in this posture, Lucas thought, as though locked in silent combat?

"May I be seated, sir?"

"Please do. Now, as to the gambling, I don't believe I need to remind you of my views on the subject. Suffice it to say that I've forbidden —"

"Why?" Lucas couldn't help himself. His father had a habit of forbidding everything that made life interesting and adventurous. He wanted Lucas to be as controlled and serious as he was.

"Because it erodes a man's character. Gambling is driven by greed, and it preys on the vulnerable."

"It's a game. A diversion."

"Fine. Then you won't mind manning the gaming tables at the charity gala for the Rescue League."

Lucas was horrified. The prospect of attending a fund-raiser was dreary enough. Dealing cards to perfumed old rich ladies would be a special torture. His friends would never let him hear the end of it. But he took one look at his father's face and knew it was pointless to argue. Lucas had been hoist by his own petard. "Yes, sir." Defeated, he gripped the arms of the chair. "May I be excused?"

His father almost smiled. Almost. But there was something icy and forbidding in that almost-smile. "Son, gambling is not the point of this meeting."

Lucas blinked, confused. "Sir?"

"I have to know . . . what I mean is, what the devil possessed you to bring that woman here?" Father almost never showed his temper. It was contrary to his nature to exhibit any sort of passion at all. The dark flashes of emotion in his eyes startled Lucas. Yet somehow, Lucas sensed the anger was not directed at him.

"You raised me to show compassion to the wounded and sick. Should I have left her to die in a gardening shed?"

"Of course not. But good God, Lucas. To bring her into this house, put her in your mother's room, her bed —"

"It always comes back to my mother, doesn't it?" Lucas snapped, finally understanding.

"It does when you put a stranger in her bed," his father shot back.

"My mother doesn't have a bed." Lucas knew his reckless honesty might get him in trouble, but he was past caring. "She doesn't need anything 'in that room. Yet you keep everything just as it was when she was alive."

Father was quiet and still, and a curious distance glazed his blue eyes. "Because I cherish the memory of her," he said softly.

"Then remember her in your heart." Even though his brain knew it was a bad idea, his mouth wouldn't quit talking. "I'm sorry she died. But she isn't real to me, Father. How could she be, when I scarcely remember her?" He saw his father wince as though someone had stabbed him between the shoulder blades. Lowering his voice, Lucas added, "I can't make myself remember her, no matter how much you might want me to. Sir, I meant no disrespect, bringing Miss Isabel to that room."

He'd acted out of instinct, at first. Then, when June had questioned him, he'd realized he had a deeper purpose. He had little hope of making his father understand, but oh, how he wanted to. All his life, he'd felt obligated to assure his father that the life they'd made together after his mother died was fine. Yet now that he was older, he was sick of trying — and failing — to bring the light back into his father's eyes.

A clean, fierce defiance took hold of Lucas. "I know little about our life with my mother, but I do remember one thing. When she was alive, you were happy. If she were still alive, you'd still be happy. I'm sorry she's the one who died that day instead of me."

For a moment, his father appeared to be drowning in plain air. He seemed unable to take a breath. He went white around the lips, a sign of controlled fury. Then, finally, he summoned up his voice. "By God, don't you ever say that. Don't even think it."

Lucas stood and paced to the window, looking out through the parted draperies at the distant bay, alive with local ferries and ships bound for ports all over the world. He didn't acknowledge his father's agonized command. "I'm nearly grown, Father. I'll be leaving home in the fall. And so I hoped . . ." He turned back to face his father. Now the idea sounded silly, but he tried to put it into words anyway. "I thought helping Miss Isabel would . . ." He gave up, letting his voice trail off. His chest ached. He ached all over. Nothing he said ever came out right.

His father's eyes blazed so bright that Lucas nearly flinched. "You can't simply replace your mother, not in this house, and not in my heart."

"I wasn't trying to replace her," Lucas snapped. "I was trying to help someone. And I did help her, and now she's here with us. If you want to punish me again, fine. Punish me. But don't hurt her by throwing her out." He couldn't stand it any more. He glared at his father. "I'll do as you ask at the charity event. Good day, sir."

His son was either a gifted liar or wiser than Blue gave him credit for. The quarrel preoccupied Blue all through the day. Lucas had pointed out something Blue rarely considered — the boy had known his mother only in the simple, concrete manner of a five-year-old child. He couldn't miss her the way Blue did.

It was a shock to realize his son was worried about what would become of Blue in the fall, when Lucas went away to complete his education. However, installing a foreigner in Sancha's room was not the answer. Surely Lucas knew that.

As to the uninvited guest, Blue felt equally preoccupied with her. He caught himself hurrying through his afternoon duties just to get home early. Once there, he rushed halfway up the stairs, then paused at the landing. Good God. He hadn't raced home from work since —

A commotion inside Sancha's room startled him, and he hurried the rest of the way up the stairs.

Bernadette Riordan opened the door. She was known to be the prettiest housekeeper on the hill, with deep auburn hair and creamy skin, and eyes that danced with humor despite the abuse she'd endured at the hands of the late, unlamented Mr. Riordan. "You're just in time for the birthday party, Doctor."

"What birthday party?" He struggled to appear calm and professional, yet he was breathing hard from rushing.

"Come in and you'll see."

He stepped into a room he scarcely recognized. Brightly-colored crepe ribbons festooned the ceiling from corner to corner, and the drapes were open to the sunshine. The entire household was assembled around the bed — Mrs. Li and June, Bernadette and Delta, even Efrena, who ordinarily kept to herself.

"Welcome to my birthday party," said Miss Fish-Wooten, smiling at him from the bed. "I hope you've come to wish me many happy returns of the day."

"I've come to irrigate your wound," he said.

She pantomimed a swoon, fluttering an invisible fan in front of her face. "Is he always this romantic?"

The others laughed with her. The sound of women laughing was unfamiliar to his ears, and like an ancient and beloved memory, it touched a hidden place inside him.

He regarded his patient, gamin and bright-eyed, the center of attention. Delta and the others had taken good care of her. She simply shone, from her scrubbed face to her manicured hands to the clean white coverlet that lay across her. Someone had fixed her hair, and the two shiny combs he'd given her held the short locks in place. She wore a proper lady's bedjacket, its lace collar forming a gossamer scroll across her delicate white throat.

He knew where the garment had come from. Sancha's dressing room.

He waited to feel a blaze of fury. Who the

hell did she think she was, sitting like a queen in his wife's bed, wearing her clothes and surrounding herself with servants?

But the fury never came, and he wasn't sure why.

"We'd best be changing that bandage now," Delta said, breaking the tense silence that spun out between Blue and his patient.

The women took their leave of her, each pausing to say goodbye as they cleared away the tea service. Efrena, who had once been Sancha's best friend and who had traveled home with him from Wyoming, gently patted Miss Fish-Wooten's hand. "I am honored to meet you," she said.

"Thank you for coming," said Miss Fish-Wooten. She hesitated, then seemed to come to a decision. "I've never had a birthday celebration before."

"Never?" June looked shocked.

"This is my first." Miss Fish-Wooten beamed. "I feel like a brand-new woman."

What sort of person, Blue wondered, never had a birthday? She'd offered few clues about her background, though he recalled her admission that she'd lost her parents at a young age. Then what? he wondered. What had her life been like after that? What had brought her, wounded, into his world?

This urge to know her confounded him. She was a patient, nothing more, regardless of what his son and the women in his household wanted to make of her.

She was still smiling after everyone save Delta had left. That smile affected him in such strange and unexpected ways that he stepped away from the bed. He needed to escape the sticky pull of her attraction, needed to clear his mind so that cold reason could prevail.

With a serene expression on her face, she submitted with her customary stoicism to Delta's removal of the bandage. He wished the wound looked better than it did. But that was a bullet wound for you. They always became infected. If she'd been hit in an arm or leg, amputation would have been indicated.

He and Delta held one of their silent conversations about the problem. Other than constant vigilance and a good dose of luck, there was no specific remedy. They cleansed the site with carbolic acid. Miss Fish-Wooten kept talking, though the treatment must have been excruciating. "Everyone has been so wonderful here," she said. "I feel quite lucky indeed."

"Oh, that's the truth, honey. This whole house is a lucky place," Delta assured her as she and Blue replaced the bandaging. Although Delta was adept at adhering to conventions of modesty, she did manage to indicate several faint, horizontal marks on the patient's back.

"You've been hurt before," Blue said to her.

She laughed. "Goodness, is there anyone who hasn't?"

"There are marks on your back that resemble scars from a whipping."

"You must be an excellent physician," she said. "You're very observant."

"What happened to you, Miss Fish-Wooten?"

"I've had my share of adventures."

Delta sent him one of her silent messages: Don't pry. Then she finished with the bandaging and left the room, leaving Blue alone with Miss Fish-Wooten.

Despite Delta's warning, he couldn't stop thinking about those obscene whitish furrows across his patient's delicate skin. "Perhaps you were severely disciplined as a child."

She was silent for a few seconds. "Perhaps I was."

Holding her by the shoulders, he helped her to sit against the pillows. Her silky hair brushed against his cheek. Filling his arms with this woman was a danger to his heart. He knew this, yet still he held her for long moments after he should have let her go and left the room. She smelled of soap and the dried sachets women liked to put amid their bed linens. Her skin glowed with a low-grade fever, but the sparkle in her eyes came from another source. There was a fullness to her lips that drew him, reminding him that he was not nearly so controlled and jaded as the face he presented to the world. He almost

180

kissed her, almost tasted those lips, almost trusted the promise in her smile. Then a cold reminder surfaced.

"You don't like surrendering information about yourself," he commented, stepping back, finally in control of the mad impulse that had nearly seized him.

"That makes two of us, Doctor."

She had him there.

"The fact is," she said, "I don't find myself very interesting. There's a whole world to explore — that's what fascinates me. I am happiest when I travel. When I stop, I get in trouble."

"Now that I can believe."

"I love the idea of constantly seeking something. And so long as I am seeking, I am content."

Though he would never admit it, he not only understood but agreed with her. He, too, was a seeker, though not in the sense of Isabel Fish-Wooten, wandering the world, looking for adventure, or happiness, as she implied. He sought answers to problems, cures for his patients, healing for the wounded. The constant quest kept him too busy to bother with contentment.

"Do you want to know what I'm looking for?" she inquired. "I'd wager you do, although you are loath to admit it. I'm looking for my next destination. I had hoped to go to the Hawaiian Islands, to see what the South

Pacific is like. Have you ever been there?"

"No," he said. "Some of my seafaring patients have traveled there." They'd brought back wondrous reports of the tropical islands, with lava mountains draped in lush greenery and wild orchids, home to natives as mysterious as the stars in the sky. But he couldn't imagine going all the way to the South Pacific to see it for himself.

"Have you ever been anywhere? Do you never feel the urge to travel and see the world?" she asked.

"I've seen plenty." Turning away from her, he glared at the window. There was no need to travel in order to see what the world had to offer. He'd seen battlefields strewn with the bodies of young men, babies being born, sick people getting well. He didn't have to go far to know the things the world offered. "Other than a yearly trip to my family's home on the coast, I haven't left the city in a decade. My life is here, and here it stays."

"A decade. That's ten years."

He turned back to face her. "Ah, you're clever, as well."

"Don't be sarcastic to a bedridden woman. I might have a relapse."

The idea of her extending her stay here bothered him more than he wanted to admit. "I forbid you to have a relapse."

She laughed. *Laughed.* Since he'd returned from Wyoming, there had not been such laughter in his house.

"How could you possibly stay in one place for ten years?" she asked, her mirth subsiding gradually, like a fading melody.

"I have a son to raise, a medical practice to maintain. I am medical director of an extremely busy charity league. I've no time to do anything else."

"You could find the time."

"I don't choose to. There are those who live their entire lives never venturing beyond the radius of a single town or farm, and they are perfectly content. It's more common than you think."

"What, contentment?" She sniffed. "Not around here." She took a small, leather-bound book from the drawer of the bedside table. "Lucas brought me this. He thought it would ease my boredom."

The thought of Lucas constantly visiting Miss Fish-Wooten unsettled Blue. However, forbidding the boy to see their guest would only make Lucas more determined to visit her.

Blue picked up the book. *From the Earth to the Moon*, by Jules Verne. Abigail Calhoun, his cousin-by-marriage, had sent it as a gift to Lucas. The story was a fanciful adventure, with no value that Blue could see.

"I've heard it said that there is a whole world inside a book," Miss Fish-Wooten declared. "But reading doesn't satisfy my curiosity at all. It only piques it."

She was so easy to disagree with, he thought. "On the contrary, an excellent book makes the actual experience superfluous," he stated. "It's possible to go to Timbuktu and back, never leaving the comfort of one's chair by the fire."

"That is absurd. Reading about a place is not the same as going there."

"It's a more convenient mode of travel. That's why books are so useful."

"But mere words, even those of the most gifted writer, cannot do justice to the experience. The islands in the Hawaiian archipelago, for instance. I've read descriptions by the finest writers of our age, but I simply must go there and see for myself. I must feel the air on my skin, smell the scent of orchids and fruit, ride the surf as the natives do."

"And risk contracting leprosy or malaria, getting bitten by poisonous flies —"

"There is always a risk in anything worth doing."

He had no idea why he was so entertained by this conversation. "I have never been so philosophically opposed to someone as I am to you."

"I don't know about that. I'd venture to suggest that you oppose your son in a number of things."

He bristled, but could not deny it. "Lucas makes it a point to know my views on everything so that he can take the opposite stance."

"No wonder I find him so agreeable." She beamed with an expression so bright that he momentarily forgot his animosity toward her. "I've enjoyed our talk immensely, Dr. Calhoun."

So have I. He astonished himself with the thought.

"I expect you'll be feeling quite a bit improved in the near future," he declared, mystified by his attraction to her. She was a disaster in the making, and the sooner he sped her on her way, the better. "Then we'll see about reporting the attack against you to the police."

He left her sputtering in protest. The moment he stepped out of the room, he breathed a sigh of relief. She would not need his attention until tomorrow at least. Surely the most difficult part of his day was over.

Or so he thought, right up until the moment June Li came running, to hand him a telegram.

Fourteen

"It's not that I don't love my family," Blue explained to Rory the next day as they departed a meeting with the senior staff of the Rescue League. "I do, but their timing couldn't be worse. I'd nearly forgotten they were coming to town."

"All of them?" Rory asked. "Even that infernal sister of yours?"

"Which infernal sister?" he asked, even though he knew the answer. He liked putting his friend on the spot.

"Belinda, of course." Rory gave a mock shudder. "The little one, Amanda, is as sweet as the day is long. But Belinda . . ." He gave another shudder. "It must have been hell growing up with her, sheer hell."

They walked amid shoppers, tourists and tradesmen crowding the boardwalks and sidewalks. The roadway roared with a constant stream of traffic — hansoms and drays, horse cars and swaying omnibuses, cable cars straining up the hills. Here in the bustle of the city, his childhood in Virginia seemed a distant dream, or something that had happened to someone else. He and his sister had spent their earliest years on a Tidewater plantation.

"I know you'll find this hard to believe," he said, "but Belinda was like a fairy child. Her nature was as light and tender as a breeze in springtime."

"You're right. I don't believe you. A fairy child? That harridan?"

Blue reminded himself that Rory knew her only as an ambitious, hardworking woman and heir apparent to the family ranch. Of all four Calhoun offspring, she alone had bound herself to the land called Cielito. It was an unexpected bond for a girl who had been raised a Southern belle.

Time and fortune had changed her for the better, Blue thought. Rather than concerning herself with fashions and balls and attracting a rich husband, she worked side by side with their father, managing the business with consummate skill. Neither he nor his sister had ended up with the sort of life that was expected of them, Blue reflected. Many years ago, his widowed father had remarried, and he and Eliza had two more children. Perhaps Blue's half siblings, Hank and Amanda, would find the sort of settled contentment that seemed to elude Blue and Belinda.

"You should be grateful to Belinda. She is in charge of this year's charity ball for the Rescue League."

187

"All right, I'm grateful, but that doesn't mean I have to like her." Rory lifted one eyebrow. "She's the one who chose the theme of Arabian Nights, isn't she? Do you suppose she has inappropriate fantasies about being abducted by a sheik?"

"I don't doubt it in the least. I assume your burnoose is on order from the costumer."

Rory squared his shoulders, strutting a little. "It is now."

Another concern shadowed Blue's thoughts. "How the devil am I going to explain Miss Fish-Wooten?"

"Just say she's a lady outlaw who got shot in the back, and now you're falling in love with her."

The suggestion made his stomach drop like a ball of lead. He broke out in a sweat and hoped Rory didn't notice. "You're insane."

"Ha. I'm right and you know it. I've never seen you behave this way over a woman."

"I've never had a woman order me around at gunpoint," Blue snapped.

"She's had an interesting effect on you. When I think of all the ways women have tried to attract your attention over the years, I am amazed at their ingenuity. Yet all it took was a lethal threat, and you're putty in her hands."

"And you're imagining things."

"I would love to see how your family reacts to this paragon of virtue," Rory said, unaffected by his temper.

"Of course you would. Come to supper this evening and make a fool of yourself." He knew Rory would be there with or without an invitation. For all his complaints about Belinda, he was oddly fascinated by her, and practically a member of the family anyway. Lacking a family of his own, Rory found the boisterous Calhoun clan irresistible.

They parted ways in the business district, in front of the granite monolith of the Montgomery block, four storeys tall, where Rory kept his offices. Blue sent for his horse and rode up to Mercy Heights Hospital to check on Officer Brolin. He had done so each day since the shooting, even though Brolin was not his patient. He did not want this man to die. He didn't want any man to die but there was more at stake than a life here. He needed for Brolin to live. He needed for Isabel Fish-Wooten not to be accused of murder.

In the hospital foyer, he encountered Mrs. Alma Vickery. The wife of Fremont Vickery was one of the city's most famous hostesses, and she took her role seriously. She dressed in high style, with every hair in place, her posture flawless as she glided across the foyer to greet him.

"Dr. Calhoun," she said, extending a slender hand.

He touched her fingers — even through the glove they were ice-cold — and bowed. "Mrs. Vickery. I'm flattered you remember me."

"Don't be. You are not the sort of man a woman easily forgets."

He had no idea what to make of her comment. She was older, and attractive in her way, with a pretty Southern drawl and soft, light hair. But they had never had more than a passing acquaintance at social events.

A heavy musk of perfume surrounded her. She was tiny and elegant, her eyes slumbrous and shiny black. He studied her for a moment before catching himself, and surrendered her hand. But not before noticing the erratic cadence of her pulse. He remembered the worrisome gossip Clarice had shared about her.

"I trust you are well," he said, resisting the impulse to see if she was feverish.

"Indeed I am. And looking forward to the Benevolent Aid Society Ball. Surely the most worthy of events. I understand the entire Calhoun family is involved."

"Yes, ma'am, we are."

"How very admirable." Her chin trembled as though she were genuinely moved. "It is wonderfully idealistic to suppose the poor wretches cast off by society can be saved."

"It's quite possible, Mrs. Vickery. The Rescue League has been doing it for years."

"But I imagine some cannot be reformed

regardless of your striving," she said.

"That doesn't mean we shouldn't make the effort."

A smile flitted across her lips. "Of course you're right." Her gaze slid around the perimeter of the foyer.

"Are you looking for someone?" asked Blue.

"Fremont and I have a supper engagement this evening, and he is running late as usual." She sighed delicately. "Saving lives takes precedence over social affairs, doesn't it, Dr. Calhoun?"

He didn't suppose she really needed a response. He was trying to choose a way to politely excuse himself when Dr. Vickery arrived, a footman in tow, holding a top hat and opera cloak at the ready while Vickery surrendered his laboratory coat and rubber-backed surgical apron.

The moment he spied his wife, his manner swiftly changed. He focused on her with the intense absorption of a bridegroom waiting at the altar. Perfectly-barbered sideburns framed a genuinely adoring smile. The affection in his look was returned with true sincerity by Mrs. Vickery. The two of them had been married a good twenty years, Blue supposed with a pang of envy. Their obvious regard for one another hinted at a richness his own life lacked.

"Hello, my dear," Vickery said. "Please forgive me for being late."

"There is nothing to forgive. It is just as I was saying to Dr. Calhoun. There is no need to apologize for being a hero. The saving of lives takes precedence over all else."

With military bearing, Fremont Vickery turned to greet Blue. "I wasn't expecting you. Did we have an appointment?"

"No. I stopped in to see how Officer Brolin was doing."

"You're taking quite an interest in my patient."

"The entire city is." Since the incident, the press had gotten involved, avidly reporting every detail to a hungry reading public. Dramatic accounts of the officer's bravery in the face of a phantom shooter plastered the pages of the *Register*, the *Evening News*, the *Examiner* and daily broadsheets.

"It's a tragic and fascinating case," Blue said. "The imagination of the public is always captured by the mystery of a comatose patient. There is always the hope and possibility that he'll awaken and solve the puzzle for us."

"I assume your interest is not so prurient," Vickery said.

"Of course not."

"It's a grim business," Vickery said with an offended air. "A man's life hangs in the balance, yet the scandal sheets report the shooting as though it were a sporting event."

"Poor Fremont," said Alma Vickery. "We must all pray for Officer Brolin to survive. In fact, we should all go to him right now."

"But my dear —"

"Come along, Fremont, it's a perfect idea." She headed toward the ward. "I can't think why I haven't been to visit him yet. I should have done so days ago."

Vickery hurried after her and Blue fell in step. Vickery took his wife's elbow. "You've been away since Wednesday," he reminded her. "You've had no time to go visiting."

"Since before the shooting," she said. "I had a ticket to Monterrey. I know that, Fremont. Don't you think I know that? I'm not a child." Her irritation melted into compassion when she reached the ward where Officer Brolin lay. At present, a woman who appeared to be his wife sat beside a priest on a bench by the bed.

Vickery made brief introductions. Blue acknowledged them but his attention stayed with Brolin. Alma Vickery occupied herself with Mrs. Brolin, murmuring words of comfort. The wife was speechless with despondence and the priest's lips moved constantly in prayer, his fingers worrying the beads of an onyx rosary.

Brolin's head was swathed in bandages, binding a thick patch to the right temporal region, presumably where the bullet had entered. The gauze bore rusty stains but, surprisingly, was also damp from the seepage of fluids.

"When did you perform the debridement surgery, Doctor?" asked Blue.

Vickery noted the man's pulse. "I didn't operate."

"Who did?"

"No one. The bullet was not embedded." Like most physicians, Vickery held surgeons in low esteem, and apparently avoided surgical procedures.

Blue couldn't help himself. Vickery surpassed him in eminence and experience, but that didn't make him infallible. "Clearing the wound to prevent infection is always indicated in the case of a gunshot wound, is it not?"

Vickery squared his shoulders, the opera cloak swinging with the motion. "Sir, are you suggesting my patient is not receiving the very best of my care and attention?"

"I'm suggesting a standard surgical procedure —"

"Which, if you must know, is scheduled for the morning, Doctor."

Blue bit back the obvious question, Why would treatment be delayed? The tension drew taut between them and did not slacken until Alma turned from her conversation with Mrs. Brolin and the priest.

"The monster who did this must be found and punished," Alma declared. Spots of color stood out on her cheeks. Her eyes gleamed and her hands fluttered in agitation.

"My dear, you mustn't work yourself into a state." Vickery steered his wife to the door.

"I'm not in any state, Fremont. Why would you suggest such a thing?"

"We must be going," he said, nodding respectfully to Mrs. Brolin. "Until morning then, madam."

They took their leave, heading back through the ward once again. Blue accompanied them, saying no more about the Brolin case. Not at the moment, anyway.

The Vickerys departed like royalty on parade in a polished white coach-and-four, Alma's ostrich feather bobbing in the breeze. Blue lingered at the hospital, turning over the problem of Officer Brolin in his mind.

Fremont Vickery was a famous clinician with an enormous success rate. Yet he'd made no progress with Brolin. True, a brain injury was the most baffling a physician could encounter, but to delay the most rudimentary of measures was a questionable decision. In a case involving an officer of the law, a case so closely scrutinized by the local press, Vickery would not willfully endanger a patient.

Blue reminded himself that physicians often disagreed on courses of treatment. What seemed obvious to one man might be considered outrageous to another.

As he returned to the ward, he encountered a young woman he thought he recognized. She wasn't a nurse. A laboratory assistant, perhaps. In a crisp white smock and sturdy brogans, her brown hair scraped back into a bun and a stack of case records clutched to her chest, she resembled an earnest schoolgirl.

"Dr. Calhoun?" she said, "I'm Leah Mundy."

"Miss Mundy." He nodded in her direction.

She tilted her head to one side. "You don't remember me, do you?"

He slowed his pace down the corridor. "I'm afraid not, Miss Mundy."

"Sir, I'm a medical student from Philadelphia, studying here on a fellowship."

"Welcome to San Francisco," he said, trying to figure out where he'd seen her before. In a lecture, perhaps? The medical colleges of the city were famous for training women as well as men, a radical concept that had brought a good deal of fame and even some notoriety to the institution.

"Dr. Vickery advised me to visit the Mission Rescue League, and I did so last week," she added.

He nodded distractedly. Perhaps he had seen her there. But he was more intrigued by the idea that Vickery was sending medical students to the clinic to observe.

196

"The work you are doing there is so commendable," she added, apparently unnerved by his silence.

Hoping to put her at ease, he let a very slight smile unfurl on his lips. "What can I do for you, Miss Mundy?"

"Sir, I'm interested in your public health project. Dr. Vickery presented the opportunity of working there to his advanced students."

Blue felt guilty for thinking ill of Vickery earlier. The man had clearly made good on his promise. "I'm pleased by your interest, Miss Mundy."

She released the sigh she'd obviously been holding. Her look of relief nearly made him smile. "Dr. Calhoun," she said, "if possible, I would like to offer my services." She took a nervous breath. "I don't have my physician's credentials yet, but I could assist you, or . . ." Her voice trailed off and she looked up at him as though he were a dog that might snap at her.

"You want to work at the Rescue League."

"I'd ask for no compensation. Dr. Vickery made it clear that it's supported solely by private funds and by a charity administered by the Benevolent Aid Society."

"How long have you been in the city, Miss Mundy?"

"Less than three months," she said.

She seemed earnest enough, but Blue had

his doubts. Some of the city's training institutions made for dubious medical practitioners. A student could graduate from some of the local proprietary schools after only one semester of lectures. Too many "doctors" began their careers without any practical experience, but with a diploma and license to practice.

"I assume Dr. Vickery will provide a recommendation," he said.

"Oh, yes, sir. He's a marvelous teacher. Some students complain that he's too exacting. It's common to spend a full day after a dissection writing up a report."

"And is he too exacting?" asked Blue, intrigued.

"I don't believe so, sir, but —" She bit her lip.

"But what?" Blue asked.

She darted a worried glance down the hall and lowered her voice. "He has no tolerance for a dissenting point of view. The truth is, sir, I've learned not to challenge him."

He liked her candor and trusted the keen intelligence that shone from her. "We'd be honored to have you, Miss Mundy."

She regarded him with shining eyes.

He frowned slightly. "Is something the matter, Miss Mundy?"

"Why, you're not nearly as —" She broke off, clasping the charts closer to her chest. "I beg your pardon, Doctor. What I meant to say is that you are very accommodating."

"And you thought I would not be?"

"To be honest, sir, and I know of no other way to be, yes. I expected you to be brusque and resistant."

"Well, I'm not."

"I can see that now, sir."

He wasn't proud of having earned such a reputation. The years had turned him hard from the inside out. Now even relative strangers thought him grim and unapproachable. Consciously easing the perpetual scowl from his brow, he made an appointment to meet with Miss Mundy at the waterfront facility. She scribbled down the day and time, and as she did so, curiosity got the better of him.

"Are you familiar with the Brolin case?" he asked.

"I am, sir. It's a privilege indeed. In fact, Dr. Vickery might elect to publish something about it."

Blue hesitated, but only for a moment. Some doctors were territorial and did not welcome input or commentary on their active cases. Vickery, on the other hand, was a teacher. Surely he would not object to one of his students being quizzed by another doctor, a colleague. "Have you come to any conclusions about the case, Miss Mundy?"

"The patient has been rendered comatose from a gunshot wound to the head."

"Yes, Miss Mundy, but what do you make of it?"

"A brain injury is an unpredictable and challenging trauma. Dr. Vickery is keenly aware of the public interest in Officer Brolin. But you know, sir, I find it curious —" She hesitated. Her eyes flickered to Blue, and he read a struggle there. "May I speak frankly, Dr. Calhoun?"

"Of course."

"There has been no surgical treatment of the injury."

"I'm aware of that."

She carefully aligned the edges of her charts and hugged them closer. Clearly she had questions about the case. He wondered why she was asking him rather than Vickery. "The operation takes place tomorrow," she said. "In the meantime, Officer Brolin is being sedated, sir. Those are Dr. Vickery's orders. I asked him if he supposed the sedative could impede the patient's regaining consciousness, and he assured me it's necessary for his recovery."

The woman was as talkative as a magpie. As different as she was from him, Blue could hear echoes of his own past in her questions. He recognized the busy speculation in her wide, clear eyes, the quest for answers that must be buzzing through her mind. She was becoming a physician in her own right, forming strong opinions but hesitant to challenge convention.

They walked together toward the lobby. Sharp smells and muffled voices drifted from the wards on either side. Nurses in wimples swished past and orderlies pushed trays and carts up and down the corridors. Miss Mundy seemed agitated. An orderly jostled her, and she dropped her charts.

"Oh, clumsy of me," she murmured and stooped to pick them up.

As he helped her, Blue's gaze slipped past the clinical notations and orders, and stuck on a name that ripped through him like a jolt of electrical current. He stood and handed the chart to Miss Mundy.

"Nathan Glasscock Skinner is your patient?" he asked.

She nodded. "He's in the war veterans' ward and failing fast, I'm afraid."

Since they'd parted ways so bitterly, Blue had seen his former army commander off and on through the years. Skinner was a chronic alcoholic with a history of violent encounters, and more than once he'd staggered into the Rescue League to be patched up, given a meal and discharged. Much as he despised the man, Blue took no satisfaction in Skinner's misery. That would have been too easy.

The fact that Skinner had wound up here neither surprised nor moved him. But it did make him curious to see the ruins of a man who'd ruined so many lives.

He made his way to the men's medical ward, feeling Miss Mundy shadowing him. Her worry hovered like a cloud. She could not know his thoughts, but perhaps sensed his mood.

They came to the end of the corridor and stepped into a long room with a high ceiling and rows of beds along two walls. The men were charity cases for the most part, and they'd brought the blight of their misfortune with them. Despite the liberal use of boric acid and lemon oil, the airy room reeked of refuse-strewn alleys, waterfront hideaways and ships' holds. At the far end of the ward, a weary intern was trying to keep a victim of narcotics poisoning on his feet, slapping him with a wet towel and marching him around the bed.

Blue was startled to see a woman in a feather-decked hat and wasp-waisted green dress, standing at the bedside of a seemingly unconscious man, reading scripture from a leather-bound book. "Clarice?" he said.

She turned in an elegant sweep. "Don't look so shocked, Theodore. I often come to minister to these poor unfortunates." She closed the book and smiled up at him. "Perhaps I've discovered a way to see more of you."

"Perhaps," he said, mystified by her presence.

"Unfortunately I must be going. I shall see

202

you soon, Theodore, at the Benevolent Aid Society Ball."

"Of course," he said, and found himself standing in a waft of her perfume as she departed. He turned to Miss Mundy. "Is it true? She visits the charity ward?"

"This is the first time I've seen her, sir."

Blue gave his attention to the man in the bed. Captain Nathan Glasscock Skinner was unrecognizable from the square-jawed military man he'd once been. To call him a ghost of his former self would be generous. He was simply a skeleton draped in dying gray flesh, jaundiced eyes glassy and staring at nothing. He lay supine beneath a thin blanket, his hands folded across his chest, thick yellowed fingernails embedded with dirt. Old beyond his years, he was the embodiment of the cautionary tales favored by fiery Temperance League sermonists.

As Blue stood at the foot of the painted iron frame of the bedstead, Skinner's eyes cleared for a second or two. "I know you. You're that doctor, down at the end of Mission."

Blue said nothing. He felt Miss Mundy beside him, waiting and worrying.

Clouds of confusion moved through Skinner's eyes, but then he said the last thing Blue expected to hear.

"You're Lieutenant Calhoun."

Lieutenant Calhoun. He remembered the

name being barked from this man's snarling mouth. The rank had been stripped from Blue upon his discharge. But in that weak and wavering voice, worn out by drink, Skinner brought back memories of the moment Blue Calhoun's soul turned to ash. . . .

It was the sort of bright, crisp fall day that made even the smallest child in the Wyoming stockade volunteer to help with the apple harvest. Women bracing themselves for the frozen darkness of the coming winter seized the opportunity for a picnic in the blessedly warm sun while the youngsters played chase, climbed trees, skipped stones across Carrington Creek.

Sancha and Lucas had set out together that day to visit their friends in the Arapaho tribe across the creek. Blue stood at the stockade gate watching them go. He would have joined them, but he'd been called away to tend to a wood gatherer who had injured himself cutting alder and poplar to dry for the winter.

It didn't bother him in the least to see Sancha and Lucas heading off to visit the Indian camp. They had done so frequently throughout the summer. To the relief of most in the stockade, the tribe was peaceable — except when some of the young braves drank whiskey. However, women and children were never involved in the noisy skirmishes, and the occasional friendship formed between the whites and the Arapaho. Like ladies at an ice-cream social, soldiers' wives and Arapaho women traded sewing tips, methods of smoking meat, child-rearing dilemmas. Only that morning, Sancha had confessed to Blue that she'd be sorry to see the tribe break camp and seek winter quarters in the lowlands, where the herds of elk went to graze.

Holding hands to steady each other as they waded across the rocky creekbed, Sancha and Lucas forded the swift-moving, shallow water. In her other hand, Sancha clutched her shoes and the hem of her skirt. She wore her hair in two shiny black braids, like a schoolgirl. Though raised in the strict manner of the Spanish aristocracy, she had never concerned herself with modesty.

Sunlight struck the water with fierce intensity, as though to deny the signs of the dying summer. Framed in turning leaves and flashing water, Sancha appeared to be surrounded by diamonds and gold. Above the rushing burble of the creek, Blue could hear her laughter and Lucas's squeals of delight as he splashed about.

The next events were cobbled together from a patchwork of accounts, none of which were particularly reliable. All became part of the official reports later.

After waving to his wife and son as they crossed the creek, Blue returned to his patient.

That day, Sancha and her friend Efrena Nightshade, an Arapaho whose education in a Christian convent had given her a strong foundation in speaking Spanish and English, intended to exchange parting gifts. Sancha's offering was a supply of corn relish and pickles and a warm knitted shawl. Efrena gave Sancha a beaded white doeskin jacket Sancha had long admired. She must have been so delighted with the gift that she had put it on, right over her shirtwaist.

She was wearing the Indian jacket when the first shots were fired.

In the stockade surgery, Blue heard the gunfire just like everyone else. A series of pops, like rocks in a campfire.

Later testimony would claim the shots were fired by brewed-up braves, but Blue had always doubted that. In the first place, the shots came from east of the fort, and the Arapaho were camped to the west, beyond the creek. They're skilled horsemen, was the explanation. They rode in stealth to the east in order to mount a sneak attack and steal the barrels of corn whiskey stored in the stockade.

When the order to return fire was given, Blue had abandoned his patient, leaving the man's wound half-stitched. In the official record, that was the first infraction — willful dereliction of duty.

Over the protests of the stockade guards

who were frantically bringing the civilians safely in from the orchard, Blue raced past the great log gates. Infraction Number Two — desertion of post.

Troops formed a horseshoe-shaped defense ring inside the stockade. The guard towers bristled with long-barreled rifles. But defending the fort was not enough for the commanding officer. Riflemen and sharpshooters had already advanced across the creek. Above the rushing water, glaring sunlight speared through thick smoke. Skinner stood at his command post, a raised bluff at the creek's edge. He had his feet firmly planted, his sword pointed in the direction of the attack. He was yelling himself hoarse, screaming at his men to fire at will.

Breathless from running, Blue told him to order a ceasefire immediately. Skinner barked at him to return to his post. Like all great cowards in a position of power, Skinner was a dangerous man.

Blue yanked out his sidearm, shoved it up against Skinner's temple and directed him to give the command to cease fire. His final and most egregious infraction — assaulting a superior officer.

Skinner had pissed himself. That detail never made it into the official record. With the fort doctor's pistol still boring a hole in his head, the commander told his bugler to sound a retreat.

The massacre had lasted only minutes. It didn't take long to slaughter unarmed women and children.

Before the smoke cleared, Blue was in the middle of the village, wading through bodies while survivors fled from him as he looked for Sancha. He would never forget the smells and sounds of that place. The stench of burning buffalo skin shelters and freshly spilled blood, the wails of women and the cries of children haunted him to this day.

By the time he found Sancha, she'd lost consciousness. She still wore the beaded jacket, a gift from her dearest friend. A freshening wind cleared the gunsmoke from the air and golden autumn sun shone down on his wife.

"Shh. Mama's sleeping," Lucas said.

Efrena explained to Blue later that when the attack began, Sancha had shielded her small son's body with her own. There was a bright smear of his mother's blood across his forehead, a look of bewilderment in his dark eyes. Then he said, "Save her, Daddy, save her."

What he'd done next became part of the official record but he hoped Lucas didn't remember. No child should ever be witness to a failed resuscitation effort, performed on a battlefield by a man half-mad with desperation.

By the end of the day, there was enough

evidence against Blue to court-martial and hang him. Nobody really thought a few drunken braves with rusty rifles posed a serious threat to a well-defended stockade. But nobody except Blue wanted to say aloud that Skinner had overreacted.

The only person prepared to speak on Blue's behalf was Delta Beasley, but her testimony was dismissed because she was a woman and a Negro. However, in light of his tragic loss, the review board was prepared to be compassionate.

The official report cited bloodthirsty braves crazed by battle frenzy and out for blood. The reality was a trio of drunken boys who could barely walk a straight line, much less discharge their weapons. The report claimed that Indians had shot the beautiful young wife of the stockade doctor. But the bullet Blue had found embedded in Sancha's chest was standard army issue.

The braves stole firearms as well as whiskey, Skinner asserted. The explanation had satisfied the army's board of inquiry. Captain Skinner had acted properly in ordering aggressive counterfire against the village across the creek.

The massacre of dozens of women and children was justified.

Blue was cashiered and told to count himself lucky for not being thrown in the brig.

He left Fort Carrington in a wagon filled

with medical supplies, a son who cried himself to sleep every night, Nurse Beasley, who had resigned over the incident and Sancha's friend Efrena Nightshade, who had no relatives or family and wanted to be with Lucas.

They buried Sancha on a bluff overlooking the creek, in the shade of three cottonwood trees whose leaves had turned to weightless golden coins. Delta warned him he'd regret leaving her there. He should seal her up good, transport her home to San Francisco. But Blue shut his eyes, pictured the alabaster effigy his wife had become and said, "That's not where she is."

Now the architect of the tragedy, this corrupt creature, clinging to life for no purpose Blue could fathom, lay dying. Blue could summon no feeling whatsoever about seeing him again. Neither rage nor compassion, hatred nor vengefulness. Certainly not forgiveness.

"They say he was a hero," Leah Mundy commented. "Did you know him in the Indian wars?"

"I did. And he was no hero. Has anyone besides Mrs. Hatcher come to see him?"

"I've seen no one else since he was brought in early last Thursday morning."

The mention of that particular day caught his attention. On that day at dawn, he'd been extracting a bullet from the mysterious Miss

Fish-Wooten. "He was admitted Thursday," he repeated.

"Yes, sir. Near dawn, it was."

He grabbed the medical record. "It says here he was brought in by police."

"He was."

"From the vicinity of East Street and the China Basin."

"Yes, sir."

The attached report listed among his belongings a boiled wool derby hat, a pair of stitched boots and an army issue Bowie knife.

"Did the police question him about the Brolin shooting?"

"I don't believe they did."

"Why not?"

"Sir, I don't know."

"One of their own was shot. He could have witnessed the incident. Surely he was questioned."

She shifted uncomfortably on her feet. "Perhaps I wasn't aware of it."

Blue thought about Rory McKnight's ballistics tests. And he thought about what he knew of Skinner's character. There was no doubt in Blue's mind that the man responsible for Sancha's death was capable of gunning down a police officer and Isabel.

Skinner mumbled something, pawed in agitation at the thin blanket covering his bony knees.

For the first time, Blue directly addressed him. "You shot a man on Thursday."

Skinner responded with a violent shake of his head. "Wasn't me, I swear. Couldn't've been me."

"What were you doing at the waterfront that night?" Blue asked.

"Sleeping. But I seen —" Skinner started to cough. The fit lasted several minutes, and in those minutes, Blue lived it all again — the massacre and the inquiry that followed, his trek to San Francisco with his tiny, confused boy. And then he relived that first morning with Isabel, remembering her anger and her agony and her courage. Now finally this bastard was dying. Yet Blue felt no satisfaction at all, no sense of justice.

He turned to Miss Mundy. "Who's in charge of his belongings?"

"I believe they're in a locker." She gestured at a row of locked metal cabinets on the wall. She was looking at him with a mixture of bafflement and suspicion.

His lips purple from coughing, Skinner lifted one shaking hand to signal that he wanted to go on.

"Nod your head yes or no," Blue directed. "You saw Officer Brolin get shot."

Yes.

"You saw the person who shot him."

Yes.

"Do you know his name?"

No. A tremulous hand reached out, wavered in the air. "But . . . th' shooter was . . . a woman."

Blue looked at Miss Mundy, then back at Skinner. "The person who shot the officer was a woman?"

Yes.

Fifteen

Isabel paused dramatically in the middle of her narrative, making certain all her listeners were fully engaged. "I actually had to attend school in order to practice the proper way to curtsy to the queen."

"Imagine that. A school for curtsying." Bernadette stood and executed a lopsided curtsy.

"It's required. And you must also practice walking backward. After being presented to the queen, one must never turn one's back. Wearing a twelve-foot train makes it a bit of a challenge." Sitting on an upholstered chair and wearing a white dressing gown, Isabel beamed at her visitors, gathered in the sunlit bedroom: Bernadette and Delta, Mrs. Li and her daughter June. Efrena Nightshade, the quiet Arapaho woman from the frontier, was painfully bashful and usually avoided these afternoon gatherings, but the others were always eager to spend time with her. Mrs. Li and June had set up a mahjong table and were teaching the game to Isabel and Delta while the others looked on. But the playing had yielded to Isabel's chatter.

"Tell us what London is like," June Li said. "I have always wanted to visit London."

Isabel fixed a rapturous expression on her face. The London she knew was a squalid hole where even the decent had to steal to survive. But she happily described the London of her imagination. She used to conjure up a better life for herself in such detail that she felt absolutely certain she'd seen the splendor of Hyde Park with its glass pleasure dome, the ancient wonders displayed in the natural history museum, the art treasures of the Queen's Gallery. She convinced even herself that she'd come of age while shooting the bridges of the Thames in famous company, that she'd attended soirees that lasted until dawn.

She used to think money and mannerly ways were the keys to perfect happiness. After escaping the workhouse, Isabel had reinvented herself entirely. Lying about her background, she'd managed to find a post as a companion for Lady Cornelia Quiller-Plowden. While in her service, she had helped herself to a number of invisible assets. Like the boldest of thieves, she'd appropriated a well-born lady's refined way of speaking and moving and holding herself, of tilting her head this way or that to indicate interest, amusement, fascination — any number of socially useful responses. She studied the customs of the gentry, imitating their speech and mannerisms until she was no longer imitating, but had adopted the habits as her own. She learned to speak, eat, ride and shoot as though to the manner born. She appropriated every subtlety of phrase and movement a young lady of status might exhibit. When she was confident of her acquired breeding, she reinvented herself. She was Isabel Fish-Wooten, lady adventurer.

Her first adventure had been a voyage to the Greek isles, and she'd been so successful in persuading her fellow travelers of her new identity that she had simply gone on from there, aboard trains and boats and coaches, visiting places most people only ever read about. She traveled so far and for so long that often she forgot her shameful roots and the deception she constantly practiced.

What a jolly lot these women were, truly interested in anything Isabel had to say, and guileless enough to believe her. Oh, she was enjoying her stay here. Often she grew restless after a week or two in one location, but she had not the slightest inclination to leave this place. After all, it wasn't every day she had the opportunity to live in a mansion with people who wore shoes and spoke properly. She had not had such excellent accommodations or such merry company in ages.

The last time was the previous summer, soon after her arrival in America. She'd stayed at legendary Moon Lake Lodge in the Hudson Valley. She could have remained there indefinitely, but the women who ran the place did not seem interested in becoming millionaires, and that was the goal Isabel had set for herself.

"A millionaire, is it?" said Bernadette, clearly taking Isabel's goal seriously. "Like Mr. Carnegie or that poor Mr. Hepler with his railroad fortune. He built a castle by the sea for his wife, though the poor creature died without ever seeing it finished."

"I don't imagine I'll be building anything," said Isabel. "I never stay in one place long enough." But what would it be like, she wondered, to be the kind of woman a man would build a castle for?

"Why not?" Delta asked.

"I've always had a strict personal rule — I never stay in a place longer than one season."

"Faith, and why would you have a rule like that?" Bernadette asked.

She hesitated, then settled for a partial truth. "There's too much of the world to see. How could I be content to stay in one place when I've not seen it all?"

"You can never see it all," Mrs. Li pointed out. "No one can."

Isabel acknowledged this with a nod. "Perhaps one day I'll find a place to settle. I've heard that Honolulu is a paradise beyond imagining. And the season never changes there, so perhaps I'd never feel compelled to leave." She frowned and shifted in her chair. Delta said the itchiness of her wound was a normal stage of healing. "But then again, perhaps I'll move on from there. I don't know how a person can tell whether or not she's found her proper home."

"I'm not going anywhere," Delta declared stoutly. "I done enough traveling to last me a lifetime."

"Delta used to be a slave on a cotton plantation, long ago," said June Li.

Isabel studied Delta's broad, ageless face, the capable hands that could change a bandage with deftness and delicacy. She tried to picture her bent over in a field, working beneath the watchful eye of a man armed with a vicious lash. Surely there was no hell worse than being owned. "How awful for you." She hesitated, remembering Daisy, a former slave who lived at Moon Lake Lodge. She was a deeply sorrowful but powerful woman. "I confess I'm ablaze with curiosity."

"Sure you are, honey. I tell anybody who'll listen, so folks don't ever forget." Delta studied the mahjong board in front of her, but a certain distance glazed her dark eyes with memories the others could only guess at. "I was born at a place called Royal Oaks in Natchez, Mississippi. Prettiest house you ever did see, tall white columns, trees all draped in moss, flower gardens everywhere. Fact was, the Beasleys didn't beat us or starve us. But no matter how folks treat you, you don't have your own self, and that's the only thing a body ever really needs in this life. Your own self. I knew that from first I can remember. It was like I was holding my breath for fifteen years."

"And after fifteen years?"

"My mama died birthing a baby. I was there, along with the granny woman. We worked a day and a night to save them, but they both died." She spoke in a low, solemn voice, yet nothing could soften the heartbreak she must have felt, a young girl losing her mother in such a terrible manner.

"Soon as we buried my mama and little sister," said Delta, "I waited until everyone was asleep. Then I just plain walked away."

"Did no one try to stop you?"

She offered a taut smile. "Honey, everyone tried to stop me — the overseer, the blood-hounds, the neighbors on horseback, the local militia, bounty hunters and slave catchers who swore they'd bring me back alive."

"There was even a song about her," Bernadette said. " 'The Ballad of Delta Beasley.' That's how the story was passed among slaves everywhere. Shall I sing it for you?"

"Maybe another time." Isabel wanted to hear the actual story, not the legend. She was fascinated.

"The real reason they didn't find me is I became a soldier in the Union Army. Joined the Seventeenth Flying Ambulance Unit, and that's where I learned nursing. By the time they figured out I was a woman, they needed me too bad to let me go."

"So you met Dr. Calhoun in the army." Isabel was enjoying this immensely. She wanted to know everything about Dr. Calhoun, the people he cared about, the past that lived inside him. And she was coming to understand that Delta Beasley was an important part of that past.

"I did, but he wasn't a doctor yet. Just a scared young soldier bleeding to death on a muddy battlefield."

"So you saved him."

"The Lord Almighty himself gets the praise for that. But I nursed that boy through a bullet wound and an infection, and he never forgot it. When the war ended, he married his sweetheart and became a doctor. Hired me on as his nurse and we've been together ever since. We set up a fine practice right here, but he was restless, even after the baby came. We did another turn in the army together, out on the frontier." She winced at an unspoken memory.

An intriguing notion occurred to Isabel. "So you knew him before —" She stopped. There was no delicate way to put it.

She studied the other women gathered

around the gaming table and realized she didn't have to finish. They all understood what she meant. Blue Calhoun's life was divided into two segments, before and after. Everyone knew what the dividing line was.

"Yes, honey, that's a fact," said Delta, lining up her next tile with surgical precision. "I did know him before."

So Isabel wasn't the only one who had noticed. She probably wasn't the only one half in love with him, either. "How did it happen?" she asked. "How did she die?"

"He took a post at a fort in Wyoming," Delta said, her face softening with memories. "Most folks think Indians mean nothing but trouble, but out at Fort Carrington, we hardly had any trouble at all. Except that once." The softness in her face turned to grief. "Miz Calhoun and Lucas were visiting the tribe and something went wrong. Efrena could tell you more, if she had a mind to talk about it."

"Efrena was there?"

"Uh-huh. I was inside the fort. Heard the gunfire. Next thing I heard, Miz Calhoun was shot."

Isabel remembered her terror the night of the shooting. She could only imagine what Sancha Calhoun had felt in the midst of a battle. "Heavens," she said. "And Lucas was there?"

"He wasn't but five years old. Pray to Jesus

he doesn't remember the incident."

It was entirely possible to remember an event from that age. Isabel had a clear memory of being abandoned at a workhouse when she was tiny. But she said nothing.

"Turns out she was killed by a U.S. Army bullet," Delta said. "We worked for hours to save her but . . ." She didn't finish. "Anyway. He wasn't always like this."

When he appeared in the doorway and walked into the room, his coattails wafting out behind him with the swiftness of his stride, Isabel wondered how much he'd heard.

"Like what?" he demanded, his gaze thundering at Delta.

"Like a bear that ain't had a bite to eat in three seasons," Delta said, unfazed by his temper as she discarded a tile.

Bernadette swallowed a giggle, ducking her head as she pushed away from the table and stood up.

Dr. Calhoun glared at her. "You ladies will have to excuse us. Miss Fish-Wooten is far too weak to be playing at parlor games."

June Li swept the tiles and racks into their bamboo box.

"I was winning," Isabel informed him, trying to read his expression as he sent the five of them scuttling like hens. "I had four Kongs and a pair. I believe that's called Heavenly Joy."

He didn't respond, but waited in icy silence until the door shut. She had never seen him quite like this. There was a new edge to his anger. Something deep in his eyes. A flicker of hurt, she thought.

This business of being in love was new and not altogether pleasant, she decided. It bothered her to see him hurting and angry, and to know somehow, even before he spoke, that she was the cause.

"Tell me one more time you didn't shoot Officer Brolin."

"I didn't shoot Officer Brolin."

"Now tell me why I should believe you."

"Tell me why you don't."

"There was a witness after all. He claims that the person who shot the officer was a woman."

She relaxed gingerly on the bank of pillows propped against the back of her chair. "Well, that's a relief. Now you know it wasn't me."

"Weren't you listening?"

"Weren't you thinking? Perhaps you've forgotten, but I certainly haven't. I was dressed as a boy that night. You thought I was a lad right up until you tore my shirt off."

She tried not to smirk as he paused to consider this. His face changed, the edges easing just the slightest bit.

"Who is this sterling witness?" she asked.

"A former army officer."

"That's what he formerly was. What is he

now?" She held up a hand. "You needn't explain. There is really only one type of war veteran who can be found lurking around the Barbary Coast at that time of night." She leveled a steady glare at him. "I am not your shooter, Doctor. You know that. You know that better than ever now."

Sixteen

Blue cursed himself for forgetting her disguise. He'd have to question Skinner again. Had he known the person in old trousers and battered jacket was a female?

Stone-cold sober, Blue had not recognized her as a woman. Stirred from drunken slumber, Skinner wouldn't have, either. He had seen something — someone — else. Blue was surprised by how much he wanted for that to be the case. He made up his mind to seek Rory's opinion on the situation, and to get his friend to test Skinner's weapon. But in the meantime, Blue was still stuck with his unwanted houseguest.

"Why were you abroad at that hour, impersonating a man?" he demanded.

"Because it's entirely improper for a lady to go abroad at that hour."

He glared down at Miss Fish-Wooten. She still glowed with an elevated temperature, but he could tell by looking at her that she was not burning with the lethal brightness that signaled an infection at its peak. As usual, the combs he'd given her ornamented her hair. The dark brown curls gleamed almost as luminously as her eyes. Her lips were wide and moist, and he caught himself bending closer, drawn by a force he was trying not to acknowledge.

He caught himself just in time and did the only thing he could think to do. Taking out his stethoscope, he listened to her heart and lungs, finding her pulse normal and her lungs clear.

She smelled of floral soap. He wasn't supposed to notice that. Her wrist was slender, her skin as fragile and soft as gossamer. He wasn't supposed to notice that, either.

He dropped her wrist and scowled at her. "You're doing much better."

"And you're so very happy about that."

"It means I'm doing my job."

"As am I. Why don't you like me, Dr. Calhoun?"

He barked out a rusty laugh. "Oh, let me count the ways."

"I'm not the gunman, and well you know it."

"According to your story, you are an innocent victim who happened to be in the wrong place at the wrong time, dressed as a boy and armed to the teeth."

She clasped her hands. "Exactly. It's about time you got your facts correct."

"Even if you were not a part of the mayhem, Miss Fish-Wooten, you are most definitely hiding something. I neither like nor trust you, and I shall use all my skill as a doctor to insure a fast recovery so you can leave. For good."

"Believe me, Miss Fish-Wooten," said a familiar, teasing and wholly unwelcome voice from the doorway, "my brother is not always this charming. Sometimes he's even more obnoxious."

Suppressing an inward groan, Blue put away his stethoscope and turned to greet his sister. "Belinda. Still sneaking around, listening at doorways."

As imposing as an anointed queen, she sailed past him in a silken swish of skirts. Blue's sister could never be called a great beauty, but her presence was so commanding, her wit so sharp, that no one seemed to notice that she was not absolutely stunning.

"How do you do?" she said to Isabel. "I am Belinda Calhoun, this disagreeable man's spinster sister."

Though she liked to call herself a spinster, Belinda hardly resembled the prune-on-the-shelf the designation suggested. The fact was, although she was well past marrying age, her dramatic presence was matched only by her fiercely independent streak. Over the years, dozens of suitors had learned it was a terrible mistake to declare one's feelings, for she scorned them all.

Blue could think of only one man who had

not succumbed entirely to his sister. But Rory McKnight would suffer savage torture before calling himself her suitor.

"How do you do? I am Isabel Fish-Wooten. Also a spinster." They beamed at one another, friends already. "How completely interesting," she added, "to find that the good doctor has a sister."

"Sisters," Belinda corrected. "You'll meet Amanda later." She strode about the room, clearly intrigued by the fact that Blue's uninvited guest occupied Sancha's domain. "My family has long since despaired of seeing me married off," Belinda confessed. "Have yours given up on you?"

Blue waited for her answer, listening while pretending not to.

"Oh, yes," she assured Belinda. "They gave up on me long, *long* ago."

Belinda aimed a teasing look at Blue. "Men are such dull creatures, are they not? I'd sooner watch moss grow on a barn roof as endure a courtship."

Miss Fish-Wooten laughed. "I think we're going to be fast friends."

Belinda said, "I think so, too. What a pity we can only stay a short while. We've come to the city for the annual Benevolent Aid Society Ball. It's a charity event to raise funds for the Rescue League. Then I must go home to Cielito while the rest of my family sets out on a voyage with my uncle Ryan and aunt Dora."

"A voyage," said Miss Fish-Wooten, clasping her hands together.

Blue had never known a woman whose eyes shone quite so brightly. He turned away, pretending to ignore the conversation.

"How lucky you are," said Miss Fish-Wooten. "I adore travel."

"I don't," said Belinda. "It's just as well, anyway. Someone has to look after the family business while the rest are away." She leaned toward the mirror over Sancha's vanity table and patted her yellow hair. "We're all staying at the Excelsior Hotel, but I'm certain we'll spend plenty of time right here with my dear brother. Beginning with supper tonight. I understand you've suffered an injury, but I hope you'll feel well enough to come to supper with the entire Calhoun family."

Blue was horrified. "Absolutely not."

"I'd love to," said Miss Fish-Wooten, ignoring him. "I've been confined to this room for days on end, taking my meals on a tray. I should be honored to join you."

"It's a perfect fit. I just knew it would be." Belinda beamed like a fairy godmother. She and her younger half sister, Amanda, had helped Isabel to dress in a somewhat outdated gown of a plain but good-quality blue serge, a chemise of white batiste and a petticoat with a satin hem. They'd brought in June Li to make the necessary alterations, and the girl's flashing needle and clever eye for design had tailored the dress into a proper gown for dinner.

"This belonged to his late wife, didn't it?" Isabel said, feeling a now-familiar tingle of apprehension as Amanda fastened a row of sleeve buttons from elbow to wrist.

"She won't be needing it, will she?" said Belinda with a merry wink. Then she sobered. "I really am terrible, aren't I?"

"I've been telling you so for years," said Amanda. She finished buttoning Isabel's sleeve. "Just ask Blue. Our sister has always behaved badly."

"Why is he called Blue?" asked Isabel, turning her wrist this way and that to admire the onyx buttons. His late wife had enjoyed expensive things.

"I gave him the name when we were children," Belinda said. "For one thing, his middle name is Bluett, after our maternal grandmother. And for another, Little Boy Blue was my favorite nursery rhyme, and it was infinitely simpler to pronounce than Theodore. I'm told I was quite insistent about keeping the name, and in those days, I got everything I wanted instantly. Ah, the days of my youth —"

"Growing ever dimmer," Amanda said with a dramatic flourish.

"No pesky little sister bedeviling me," Belinda pointed out. "Borrowing my things and forgetting to return them." She snatched a hair ribbon from Amanda, who snatched it back.

Belinda set a pair of kid leather slippers in front of Isabel. "Try these on."

She obliged, studying the Calhoun women as she did so. The two sisters were completely different, but each utterly delightful in her own way. Fair-haired, big-boned and bossy, Belinda had a way of dominating a room with the sheer force and energy of her personality. Yet she was so good-humored and kindhearted that no one minded. Amanda was much younger, perhaps eighteen. Small and dark and quick, with flashing eyes and a fleeting smile, she struck Isabel as being a watchful observer. She didn't seem timid, but quiet and thoughtful. A subtle air of mystery surrounded her.

"You don't look like sisters," Isabel remarked.

"We're half sisters," Amanda said. "I'm the good half, she's the evil half."

Belinda sniffed. "So you say." To Isabel, she explained, "Blue and I lost our mother when we were very small. Our father married Eliza, and they gave us another brother and sister."

So, thought Isabel. Blue Calhoun's father, Hunter, apparently had a "before" and "after" of his own.

"Hank is a completely charming rapscallion,"

Belinda continued, "and Amanda is the un-disputed spoiled baby of the family."

Amanda made a face. "*I* dispute that. I'm not the least bit spoiled. How could I be, with you tormenting me?"

"Someone has to keep you in your place."

Isabel felt a rare ache of longing as she observed the sisters together. They knew each other so well and were so comfortable together. She wondered what it would be like to have a sister, or even a brother for that matter. Someone to give her a nickname, to tease her, to regard her with fondness or even love. To have someone who shared common roots would have been extraordinary. Perhaps her life would have unfolded in an entirely different fashion. There was safety in having a sister, even one who pestered and borrowed things and forgot to return them.

Belinda led Isabel to an oval mirror hanging over the dressing table. "Are you comfortable? Is your injury going to be all right? Did we leave the corset loose enough?"

Isabel nodded, studying her reflection. Several days ago, Bernadette had repaired her terrible haircut, shaping the dark brown locks into soft curls that looked unconventionally short, but somehow fashionable. Isabel insisted on wearing the combs Dr. Calhoun had given her. No one could know what those combs meant. Just as no one could ever know the reason she had declared a birthday for herself.

Her brush with death had reminded her of all she'd failed to do with her life. It didn't matter that she would never know her exact age or date of birth. She'd simply wanted to know what it was like to celebrate a birthday. It had been more wonderful than she'd imagined. There was magic in hearing people wish you well. It made her think that wishes could come true.

Now Isabel looked perfectly groomed and was starting to feel like her old self again, ready for adventure. She met Belinda's eyes in the mirror. In a way, she thought, there was greater adventure in getting to know a new person than in traveling to a new land. "I'm sorry about your mother," she said. "I lost mine as well, when I was very small." More she would not say. She had indeed lost her mother, though not to death.

Belinda fluffed at Isabel's hair in artful fashion. "I scarcely remember our mother, but Blue took her death quite hard. They say he didn't speak for two years after she died."

"A brother who never speaks." Amanda sighed. "I often dreamed of such a thing when Hank and I were small."

Isabel turned the information over and over in her mind. What an amazing and heart-breaking boyhood he'd had. Blue Calhoun was an undiscovered country. Getting to know him through the people who loved him was a fascinating process. Each bit of information revealed a new facet of him, and this one was important. He had lost the two most important women in his life. That explained his caution, then, at least in part. The heart was such a fragile organ. Giving it into someone's keeping was a risky business indeed. She had never dared to take that risk herself . . . until now. Unfortunately, she had chosen unwisely. Blue Calhoun had built a wall around himself, and trying to reach that well-protected heart was probably futile.

Finally Amanda asked the expected question. "How did you get shot?"

Isabel saw no reason to lie. "For an experienced traveler, I showed a remarkable lack of judgment. Just a few days after my arrival in San Francisco, I was swindled out of my entire fortune. When I tried to reclaim it, I found myself in a very bad spot, indeed."

Unlike their brother, they seemed satisfied with the explanation. She went downstairs with the sisters, who presented her as an honored guest in the drawing room adjacent to the grand dining room.

Within minutes, Isabel could tell a number of things about the large, talkative Calhoun family. They deeply loved and worried about Blue, and he deeply loved and was annoyed by them.

Eliza Calhoun, the matriarch of the clan, was a compelling woman with dark hair, pale skin and a magnetic manner that commanded attention. Belinda said she had a magical way with both horses and children, driving fear from a frightened animal or drawing out the most timid child. Hunter was a quiet man with a honeyed Virginia accent and a slow, indulgent smile. At a glance, Isabel could tell he was the source of Blue's tawny-colored hair, massive height and broad shoulders.

Bernadette had whispered that Hunter Calhoun hailed from the most venerable old-money family in Tidewater Virginia. According to below stairs gossip, he'd left behind a vast plantation in order to found a horse ranch in California with Eliza, who was the subject of some scandal no one seemed willing to speak of.

Judging by the clothes and jewels, the obvious refinement and education of the Calhouns, Isabel guessed that they had made a fine success of their enterprise.

They had come to the city, explained Eliza, for the annual charity gala. The proceeds would benefit the Rescue League. "I do hope you'll be well enough to attend," she said to Isabel.

"I shall do my best to mend," Isabel said without sparing so much as a glance at Blue. She already knew he'd be appalled by this further intrusion into his life. "The Rescue League is the worthiest of causes." She used her most charming and refined manner of speaking, having stolen the cultured nuances and cadences from the daughter of a nobleman. It had been a revelation to Isabel to discover the many ways a clever woman could manipulate the world around her. She employed the techniques often and discovered they almost always worked. A judicious sigh of discontent, a well-timed tear, a favorable smile — all were weapons in a lady's subtle arsenal. Blue Calhoun, she had discovered, was one of the few men who seemed impervious to her. He disliked her regardless of the role she played.

Unfazed, she beamed at the handsome family gathered in the formal drawing room, determined to amuse herself despite her dour host. "I owe my life to Dr. Calhoun," she said. "I'm sure there are many who make that claim."

"We're so proud of the work he does," said Eliza. "We always have been."

The flattery earned her nothing but a flat look from Blue.

Rory McKnight arrived, greeting everyone with obvious pleasure. "You Calhoun women slay me with your beauty," he said, bending over each one's hand, staggering and clutching his heart when he reached Amanda, who blushed and giggled. To Isabel, he said, "You fit right in with the lot. Beautiful and, I think, rather naughty."

Belinda and Amanda each exchanged a

glance. "Did he just call us naughty?" asked Amanda.

"I believe he did," said Belinda.

"Then I misspoke," Rory said, keeping hold of Belinda's hand. "For you, naughty is too mild a term. You are evil."

Amanda touched Isabel's arm with her fan. "Didn't I tell you?"

Belinda aimed a devastating smile at Rory. "You're just saying that because I don't swoon at the very thought of you like all your other women."

"Which proves you have no taste." He cocked out his arm to accompany her to the supper table. "And how would you know about all my other women?"

"Ha. You just admitted it by asking the question." The two of them squabbled all the way to the lavishly set dinner table.

"Allow me," said Hank Calhoun, offering his arm to Isabel.

She sent him a warm smile and was gratified by his reaction. Like all the Calhoun men, he was uncommonly handsome, perhaps too much so; he could almost be described as beautiful. He had a wealth of wavy dark locks, a physique that was whipcord lean and athletic. His intelligent, penetrating eyes hinted at a gratifying sense of humor. His sisters had told her earlier that he was a university student. He had manners, charm and political ambitions, and was a distant cousin to Mr. Jamie Calhoun, Speaker of the House in Washington, D.C.

As he held a chair for her, Hank said to his brother, "By God, Blue, it seems we're going to be leaving you just as your life is finally getting interesting again."

"She's not staying." Blue stood behind his chair at the head of the table. With his massively built father at the other end of the table, the blond giants dominated the room.

"And so polite," Eliza said tartly. She turned an apologetic smile to Isabel. "I taught him better. Truly I did. Now I wonder if I should postpone my trip, stay around and beat some sense into him."

"We'll postpone nothing," said Amanda. "You promised we would finally go."

"Where exactly are you going?" Isabel asked.

Eliza beamed. "On a dream voyage. After the charity gala is over, we're actually going to be sailing around the world."

"It sounds like a wonderful trip. What is the shipping line?"

"There's no affiliation," Hunter explained. "It's the last command of my brother, Ryan. He's a ship's captain and this is his final voyage before he retires."

There was some elusive quality to his elongated drawl that prodded a vague memory in Isabel. She studied him discreetly, wondering if there was some way she could have encountered him in her travels.

"Can you imagine, months and months at sea?" said Hank. "We shall only pass over-land at the Isthmus of Panama."

In fact, Isabel could imagine such a voyage, for she had made quite a few on her own. The trouble was, she could imagine it so well that it didn't seem new or fresh to her.

"It's so exciting." Amanda opened her napkin with a flourish. "Hank and I have never been anywhere, and now we are going everywhere."

"It's something we've always meant to do," Eliza explained. "My late father was a sea-faring man."

"Not all of us are partial to sea voyages," said Hunter.

Eliza smiled wickedly at him. "But you are partial to your wife and so you're going." They exchanged a private look that spoke volumes.

Isabel felt a lurch of yearning and she won-dered what it would be like to travel in the company of loved ones, to have someone to talk to or just while away the hours in com-panionable silence. She always traveled alone, of course, and often that meant weeks of solitude. Listening to their talk of faraway places, she kept waiting for her old, familiar wanderlust to strike. But surprisingly, she felt nothing other than benign interest.

"Blue refuses to leave his practice," Amanda

said. She aimed an accusatory glare at him. "I can't believe you won't come with us."

"I have patients who need me. I can't turn my back on them for months on end," he stated.

"That's what partners are for," Hunter pointed out. "Have you considered taking on a partner?"

"Many times. But most promising young doctors are put off by the nature of my practice."

"They expect to be paid for their work," Hank explained to Isabel.

"Oh, you never go anywhere, you huge stick-in-the-mud," said Amanda. She turned to Isabel. "He never goes anywhere, ever. Once a year at Christmas, he brings Lucas to Cielito. Other than that, he never leaves San Francisco. He hasn't left since he got back from the Indian wars."

"Our ship is called the *Intrepid*," Eliza said, speaking quickly as though to switch the subject. "It's one of the Easterbrook fleet out of Boston. . . ."

"I shall expect a letter each week," said Belinda, also eager to deflect the topic. "I'll be all by myself, looking after the ranch."

"No one could abide the idea of a lengthy sea voyage with her," Rory said.

"Did you hear something?" Belinda frowned. "I think it was the buzzing of a gnat. Someone slap it."

"Have you a large family?" asked Hank, gazing earnestly across the table at Isabel. He seemed so young to her. So innocent and sincere. She caught herself wondering what would end his innocence for him. A betrayal? A broken heart? Failure? Disillusionment?

"No, I . . ." She paused, trying to decide which story would forestall further questions.

She was spared from answering by Lucas. The boy arrived only seconds before the soup was served. He was out of breath, his hair hastily plastered down by a handful of water, his cravat crooked and his waistcoat half buttoned. "Sorry I'm late," he said. "I was working at the church." He went directly to Eliza and bowed. "Grandmama, hello."

She favored him with the fondest of smiles, then turned her cheek up for a kiss. "Goodness, you're tall as a redwood tree. You must be starving after all that hard work."

Lucas's manners as he greeted everyone else were impeccable, and Isabel noticed a secret gleam of pride in Blue's eyes as he watched his son. He was a man whose pleasures in life were few but, despite his troubles with his son, Lucas was a source of quiet joy.

After the soup, there was a delicate sea bass with saffron rice, deliciously prepared by Mrs. Li and served by June, who blushed every time she caught Lucas's eye. The talk was lively and cordial, and despite her status

241

as an unwanted houseguest, she was suffused with a curious feeling of belonging. How wonderful they all were, she thought. How affectionate and caring.

What must it be like to belong in a family like this? she wondered. Even Lucas, though rebellious, found comfort and safety with his father and relatives. And Blue, with his unrelieved grief over a loss that would never heal, relaxed into the invisible cocoon of their affection.

Isabel had never known that. Ever. What was it like to know there was someone there to cushion every fall? It must be like a miracle.

She glanced at Rory and recognized the expression of need on his face. She remembered what June had told her about him. We are orphans, both of us, she thought. Our lives are defined by the fact that we don't have families.

Rory, beside her, touched her hand under the table. "They're always like this," he said, answering the question she didn't know how to ask. She listened to the laughter and murmurs of conversation, the warm and civilized sounds of a deeply bonded family. It hit her then like a blow. After a lifetime of moving from place to place, she had finally found a spot she never wanted to leave.

Part Two

Rescue

Whoever rescues a single life earns as much merit as though he had rescued the entire world.

— The Talmud

Seventeen

"How did you know I was restless?" Isabel asked Lucas as they walked through the arbor behind the house. It was a perfect summer day, and from the hill, she could see the shipping traffic traversing the bay. All the gardens in the elegant neighborhood were in full bloom, and she filled her lungs with the sweet, clear air. What a lovely place to live, she thought. In her mind, she made a picture of a younger, happier Dr. Calhoun with his beautiful wife and small son, enjoying the gardens here in summer. And then, without warning, the image of the wife changed to an image of Isabel herself.

No, she thought. *Don't.*

Lucas headed for a walkway leading down to the carriage house. "I thought I could show you our horses."

"I don't know anything about horses."

"You don't?" He looked incredulous, his eyes wide and his Adam's apple bobbing. "We've always kept horses," he said, striding down the hill. After a few steps, he hesitated and turned to her. "Sorry," he said, offering his arm.

She took it graciously and pretended not to notice the fiery blush that colored his entire face. They entered the dim, hot carriage house. "Efrena lives in the quarters upstairs," Lucas said. He showed her the horses, Ferdinand, Gonzalo and Trinculo. "Those are names from *The Tempest* by William Shakespeare," he explained. "All horses from Cielito are named after characters in the play. It's a tradition my grandmother started."

Family traditions were so foreign to Isabel. She wondered — if she had a family, what traditions would she start? "Your horses are beautiful," she said, "so sleek and healthy."

"Efrena and I look after them." He drew his hand down the bay's broad neck. "Father and I used to exercise them at Laguna Park or down at the shore."

"Used to?"

He shrugged his shoulders. "He's busy with his practice. I usually ride alone now. I sometimes wonder who'll keep them fit when I leave."

Isabel hesitated. She was not part of this. But she had come to care so much for Lucas. "You have plans, then," she prompted.

He picked up a currycomb and idly stroked the horse. "I do. The trouble is, they're a bit different from my father's plans. He wants me to finish my education here in the city and become a doctor."

246

"And what do you want?"

He stopped combing and looked up, as though the question startled him. "I want to win an appointment to the Military Academy at West Point. Senator Stanford has said he'd give me a nomination."

"That's an admirable ambition. What does your father think of this plan?"

The comb started moving again, making furrows along the horse's flank. "I haven't told him."

"You told a United States senator, but you didn't tell your father?"

"He won't approve. He doesn't approve of anything I do." He put the comb away and checked the horses' feed and water.

Isabel watched him thoughtfully. The urge to get involved with Lucas and his father was overwhelming. She'd never felt anything quite like this before. She hurt for them, but she didn't know how to fix this. So she said nothing as he held the door for her. Instead, she smiled at him. "Thank you for showing me the horses."

"Maybe you could learn to ride one day."

"I'd like that. It would be quite an adventure." She took his arm and they started back toward the house. "Life is filled with adventures I haven't had yet," she told him. "Do you know, I've never seen a whale?"

"You'll see them in the winter, when they migrate from the north," he said.

She stayed silent, knowing she wouldn't be here for the event.

"Blue, you must come, and hurry." On a sunny Sunday afternoon, Belinda found him in his study, conferring with Rory about the finances of the Rescue League. When she spied Rory sitting in a wing chair by the hearth, she wrinkled her nose. "Oh. I suppose you'd better come, too."

"With an invitation like that, how can I refuse?" said Rory.

Blue was already striding to the door. "What's the matter?" he asked his sister.

"It's awful," she said. "Truly awful. You see, Isabel —"

"What's happened to Isabel?" he demanded. Even as he spoke, two things struck him. First, even the suggestion of danger to her had the power to knock him over. And second, he had stopped thinking of her as "Miss Fish-Wooten." She was Isabel, and she had become a permanent fixture in his thoughts, no matter how he resisted.

"This way," she said. "My driver's waiting."

"Confound it, Belinda. Just tell me what's wrong. Do I need my surgical kit?"

"It's not a matter of life or death, if that's what you're asking." She stood and stared pointedly at Rory until he handed her up into the buggy, then sat down beside her.

"Then what is it?" Blue climbed up, and

the buggy rolled forward even before he took a seat.

"You'll see." She focused her attention on the roadway, but failed to conceal a gleam in her eye.

"She's a nightmare," Rory said, edging away from her on the seat in mock horror. "She's kidnapped us."

"You only wish that were true," she stated, thrusting up her chin at a haughty angle.

They turned into Laguna Park, crowded with strolling couples. Women in dresses like white blossoms studded the croquet green, and in the distant hills, golfers enjoyed a late-afternoon round. Belinda directed the driver to the far side of the park, past the mirrorlike lagoon, to the riding arena. Even from a distance, Blue recognized Gonzalo, his best horse, tethered in the shade beside the paddock fence.

"Damn it, Belinda —"

"Oh, don't get all huffy with me. You weren't using him." As soon as the buggy stopped, she thanked the driver and gave Rory a shove. "Hurry. Help me down."

"So what's the calamity you keep promising me?" Blue demanded, stalking after his sister.

"It's Isabel. Oh, it's awful." Belinda led the way to the horses. In the shade of a eucalyptus grove, Amanda, Hank, Lucas and Isabel were seated, drinking lemonade. The sight of her, calm and quite healthy, made

Blue's gut lurch with relief.

"What's awful?" Rory asked, as frustrated as Blue now.

"She doesn't know how to ride. Can you imagine that? The poor woman has no idea how to ride a horse."

Blue swore under his breath. "You dragged us out here to tell us that?"

"No." Belinda waved to Isabel, summoning her over. "I dragged you out here to *do* something about it."

Isabel had the sort of smile, Blue realized, that wrapped around his heart. It was all he could do not to smile back.

"Thank you so much for offering to teach me," she said. She wore a light gray riding habit. He thought it might have belonged to Sancha, but in truth, Sancha had owned so many gowns, he couldn't remember them all.

"I offered nothing of the sort. My sister coerced me into coming here."

"But now that you're here, you might as well stay." Putting on her bowler hat, Isabel slipped her arm into his. "I've always wanted to learn, but I've never had a chance."

He glared at his younger brother and sister, and then at Lucas. The boy lay back against the tree trunk, his eyes lazy slits, watching Blue with frank amusement.

"Any one of you could teach her," he said to them.

"We certainly could," Amanda agreed. She

beamed at him and Isabel. "Everyone who bears the Calhoun name learns to ride before walking. But Blue must be the one to teach you." She turned away to pour more lemonade for Lucas and Hank.

"Why would anyone want to learn to ride a horse?" Rory muttered. "I can't stand horses."

"I adore them," Belinda declared. "And if you know what's good for you, you'll learn to adore them, too."

"I grew up around horses," Rory reminded her. "Nebraska farm plugs. A horse was nearly the death of me. I'm going to drink lemonade with Amanda."

Isabel walked over to the paddock and opened the gate. If she truly didn't know horses, she could get in trouble. Blue hastened to catch up with her and put his hand on the gate. "How is it that you never learned to ride?" he asked.

"Perhaps I was waiting for the right teacher to come along." She brushed past him and went straight to Gonzalo's side. "Or the right horse. He's lovely, isn't he?"

"He's my best horse."

"Well, I'm flattered that you chose him for me to learn on."

"I didn't — Watch that," he said, grabbing her hand. "You don't want to startle him. You've got to approach a horse from this angle, and let him know what you intend."

251

"And what do I intend?"

"To ride him." Blue could only marvel at the turn the day had taken. He supposed he could have flatly refused to go along with the scheme. Then he realized that he wanted to be here, out in the open air on a summer day, teaching someone to ride a horse. Once he surrendered, the rest was easy. He helped her to mount, using a more-than-willing Hank as the mounting block.

Between Blue's hands, her waist felt slender and fragile. "Are you sure you're well enough?" he asked.

"More than well enough," she stated. "Convalescence is so tedious."

Gonzalo hadn't worn a ladies' saddle in years, but seemed unperturbed by the two-horned contraption as Isabel took her seat. "Oh, my," she said. "A horse is a very tall animal, isn't he?"

"You aren't mounted properly," said Blue, ignoring Hank's snicker as his brother sauntered away.

"What do you mean?" She clutched Gonzalo's mane.

"Your legs aren't situated right. You want the right one hooked over the first horn —" He gave up trying to explain. "It's like this." He knew he was breaking every rule of polite society, but he cared even less than she did. Reaching up, he placed one hand on her calf, the other on her thigh. Through the layers of clothing, he could feel the firmness of her muscles. Even more gratifying, he heard her sharp, swift intake of breath.

"Dr. Calhoun —"

"Do you want to learn this or not?" He shed his jacket and waistcoat, and rolled back first one sleeve, then the other.

"Yes," she said, touching her tongue to her lower lip as her gaze swept over him. "I do."

Eighteen

"Perhaps it was a good idea to get you out into the fresh air," Dr. Calhoun told Isabel two mornings later. "Your recovery is remarkable."

"That's quite a relief," she said, folding her hands atop the counterpane. She could hardly believe this was the same man who had taught her to ride a horse, who had handled and teased her with careless affection.

Today he was all business and seemed intent on reminding her of her status as an unwanted intruder. "You're a fast healer."

"I always have been. However, I've never been shot before. I might have a relapse."

He regarded her, stony-faced and inscrutable. Honestly, she didn't know why she liked this man. He mistrusted every hair on her head and clearly wanted her out of his life. Almost as much as she wanted to stay in it.

"Very well," she said, "you needn't trouble yourself over me a moment longer."

"Fine," he said, putting away his stethoscope.

"Fine," she said, swinging back the bedclothes. With a twinge of satisfaction, she saw him glance at her bare legs and feet before averting his gaze.

Perhaps he was remembering the way he'd held her and touched her during the riding lesson. She certainly was. There was something happening between them, no matter how steadfast he was in his refusal to acknowledge it. A powerful current of energy, invisible but undeniable, hummed between them. This was both new and surprising to her. She had been in the company of many men, often against her will, yet she had never felt this heat and yearning.

Perhaps he hadn't, either. Perhaps that was why he wanted to get rid of her.

Some people were reluctant to embrace things that were new. He probably felt an aversion to the unfamiliar. Then again, she conceded, maybe his aversion was specific to her.

She went to the doorway of the adjacent dressing room and paused. "I'll be needing my belongings back, please."

He regarded her with narrowed eyes. "Your clothing was ruined. You may help yourself to anything you find here."

"I already have."

"I've noticed."

That was something, at least, to know he was aware of more than her pulse rate and temperature. But she knew he wouldn't be so agreeable about the next issue. "What have you done with my guns, Doctor?"

"I don't allow firearms of any sort in my house."

"You didn't answer my question."

"If you must know, McKnight has them."

So that was it. Now she knew that despite the evidence furnished by Rory McKnight, despite the fact that an eyewitness claimed the shooter wore skirts, Blue Calhoun didn't trust her and didn't believe in her innocence. The only way to prove her claim and banish his doubts was to find the culprit who had shot both her and the patrolman that night. Then again, she thought, her guilt or innocence would cease to matter if she simply left, as he seemed so eager for her to do.

And she must, Isabel realized. Staying was impossible, no matter what her heart wanted. She didn't belong in his world and never would.

A knock came at the door. "You are not setting this poor woman adrift," said Eliza, entering the room.

"I'm discharging her." He made a great show of reorganizing his surgical kit.

"It's all right, really," said Isabel. "I must be on my way, as well."

"Where will you go?"

"I've been reading Mr. Robert Louis Stevenson's essays of the south seas. I've always wanted to see paradise for myself."

"Then you should do so as soon as possible," said Blue.

Eliza smacked him on the arm. "That's no way to treat a guest."

Blue glared at Isabel. "She's not a guest. She's a patient. Now that she's better, she's free to go." Without another word, he walked out of the room.

Eliza stared at the empty doorway, the clean lines of her profile sharp with concern. "I must apologize for —"

"No, you mustn't." It occurred to Isabel that as harsh as he was, he'd shown her more kindness than any other man ever had. She'd come to him, wounded and bleeding. And he had healed her. Not another person in the world had done that for her. Yet that didn't lessen the pain of his dismissal.

Looking at Eliza, she wondered how much of herself to reveal to this kind, dignified woman who had known Blue Calhoun for so much of his life. Eliza had seen him as a child so devastated by the loss of his mother that he couldn't speak. She'd known him as a young soldier, a doctor, the bridegroom of an aristocrat. And somehow, for reasons Isabel could not fathom, she seemed to expect something from Isabel.

"I need no apology," she reiterated. "I cannot even afford to pay his fee."

"Money has never been important to Blue."

Because he's never gone without, she thought. She crossed the room and picked up a porcelain oval frame with a miniature painting of Sancha Montgomery Calhoun. "Delta told me how she was killed. And Belinda told me about their mother."

"Then you know the ghosts that haunt him. Sometimes I fear his grief gets worse, not better."

"He thinks he should have saved her," Isabel said.

"Yes."

"He's been trying to save people ever since."

Eliza smiled briefly. "You noticed." She took the small picture from Isabel and carefully set it down. "His father was a widower when we met. Hunter took the death of his wife hard, too. But he finally found a way to make peace with the past. In his case, he changed nearly every aspect of his life. He left behind a plantation in Virginia and married me . . . eventually."

Isabel was surprised and touched that this woman would share such a personal story with her. She thought about Hunter Calhoun, who seemed so quietly contented in the company of his family. Yet despite that contentment, she sensed a sadness in him, a peaceful melancholy. People with tragic pasts went forward in spite of things.

"If Dr. Cal— Blue wishes to change, it's

up to him, I suppose," said Isabel.

"Yes, and no."

"I don't understand."

"It's entirely up to him. But if he's going to change his life, he needs a reason." Eliza reached out and adjusted one of the combs in Isabel's hair.

Isabel flinched at the look on the older woman's face. "You think I could be that reason."

"What I think isn't important. What do you think?"

"That you want him to marry again and be happy." Isabel nearly laughed with the irony of it. "You probably say that about every woman he meets."

"I think you know better than that. You do love him. I can tell."

The certainty in Eliza's voice caught at Isabel's heart. She was shocked at the tug of yearning she felt. "I'm the last person in the world who could be Blue Calhoun's reason for living."

"Why do you say that?"

"We're from entirely different worlds. It's simply impossible."

"I'm surprised to hear an independent woman like you declaring anything impossible. Now. What is this nonsense about you leaving?"

"It's time for me to go."

"The gala is coming up. You promised my

259

daughters you'd attend."

Isabel adored balls and social events. She felt torn, and the longing must have shown in her face. "I made no promises, and as I said, it's impossible. We're too different. He can't leave this place, and I can't stay."

Eliza hesitated, perhaps deliberating whether or not to reveal more of herself. She clasped her hands in front of her and regarded Isabel steadily. "Would it surprise you to know my mother was a Negro freewoman from Kingston, Jamaica?"

Isabel studied the pale, porcelain face, the delicate features, the perfectly coiffed hair. "I suppose it's not the first thing that occurred to me when I met you."

"Would it surprise you to know that my husband is the son of the slave owner?"

Isabel's jaw dropped.

Eliza smiled. "You see, there are differences that matter and differences that do not. So I suppose you need to decide whether or not the differences between you and Blue matter."

"Mrs. Calhoun —"

"Eliza."

"Eliza. You've only just met me. You don't know anything about me. Yet you seem rather keen on matchmaking. Forgive me for asking, but why?"

"Because I know my stepson. Something new is happening to him because of you.

Something good. My dear, when I see the way he looks at you, I know all I need to know. I won't lie to you and say he's an easy man to love. But then again, what man is?"

Nineteen

Blue and Rory emerged from the Excelsior Hotel, with its lush court and abundant atrium gardens, out onto the noise and dust of New Montgomery Street. They had just finished a luncheon with Blue's family, who were staying there.

"Your mother is a wonder," Rory said, flipping the domed top of his pocket watch to check the time. "She gave me her pledge to raise at least twenty percent of the Rescue League's annual budget."

"She'll do it, too."

"I used to despise charity balls, but I find I like them when *my* charity is the beneficiary." He tucked away the watch. "How about you?"

Blue ran his index finger around his stiff, boiled collar. The morning fog had yielded to glaring sunshine. "You know how I feel about dances and galas, regardless of the cause."

"It's different this time."

"How so?"

"I can tell you that in three words. Isabel Fish-Wooten." He counted off the syllables on his fingers. "Don't pretend you don't understand what I mean. I'm happy for you, Blue. I'm glad you met her."

"Damn it, she's a patient —"

"Who happens to occupy your wife's bed-room."

"That was not my choice."

"I realize that. Lucas put her there. Surely you won't ignore the underlying intent there."

"She's too old for Lucas." *And too young for me.*

"Idiot. The boy wants a mother, not a mistress."

Lengthening his strides, Blue headed across the road, dodging a horse car trundling through the intersection. He didn't want to think about charity balls or Isabel today. Or ever.

"Where are we going?" Rory asked.

"To Mercy Heights Hospital. According to the news reports of Officer Brolin's shooting, there were no witnesses to the event."

"And?"

"And there's someone I want you to meet." Blue explained about Nathan Glasscock Skinner, who claimed to have seen the incident but also swore he hadn't been questioned by the police. "Why do you think that is?"

"We both know how careless the police can be."

"Even when it involves an attack on one of their own?"

Inside the hospital, the heat of the day mingled with oppressive humidity and the ever-present atmosphere of sickness. The nurses' wimples sagged, leeched of starch by the damp air.

"You said he was a hopeless drunk." Rory exhibited that annoying lawyerly skepticism and challenge. "Perhaps he was making up a tale."

"Perhaps." Blue thought of the jaundiced, half-mad man in the veterans' ward. "But why would he do that?"

"Why does a drunk do anything?" Rory wrinkled his nose at the sharp smells that permeated the arched corridor.

In the dim, quiet ward, they encountered Leah Mundy, the young medical student from Philadelphia. True to her word, she was now working regularly at the Rescue League, proving herself to be fearless and practical as she ministered to the cast-off detritus of the city's underworld. Today, Miss Mundy looked smaller and more schoolgirlish than ever as she sat atop a white enameled cabinet, scribbling notes. The bed Skinner had occupied was empty, stripped down to its stained, striped mattress.

When she spied Blue and Rory, she quickly dropped to her feet and smoothed her hands down her smock. She still regarded Blue with a mixture of awe and fear.

He couldn't be bothered to allay her nervousness at the moment. He glanced at the empty bed and then back at Miss Mundy. "When?"

"Last night, or rather in the early hours of the morning. He was discovered by the orderly on duty."

"And the cause?"

"Heart failure."

Blue turned to Rory. "So much for questioning Skinner." He headed for the door, sparing Miss Mundy only the briefest of nods.

"Doctor, wait," she said.

"Yes?"

"I have a question about the patient. I noticed — that is, when they came to transport him to the morgue, I observed that, well, that his tongue was thickened and . . . discolored."

A fine chill crept over Blue. "And?"

"And I observed broken vessels in the eyes."

He caught Rory's eye and saw the questions there. Miss Mundy looked at Blue, then Rory, then Blue again.

"Rory McKnight," said Blue, "and even though he's a lawyer, I can vouch for his character. You may speak freely in front of him."

"Sir, according to my research —" she indicated her notes and her *Materia Medica* "—those are symptoms of asphyxiation." She spoke very low, the word a haunting sigh in the hot, soundless room.

"Where is Skinner now?" Rory asked.

"He had no next of kin to contact, so he's been transported to Lime Kiln Point."

"So quickly?" asked Rory.

She swallowed delicately. "At this time of year, they tend not to linger over such things."

"Thank you, Miss Mundy. And how is Officer Brolin today?"

"I'm afraid there's no change, sir."

As they left the hospital, Rory asked, "What do you make of that?"

"I can't be sure. Either the old bastard managed to smother himself . . ."

"Or someone wanted him dead."

Twenty

Lucas insisted on driving home from the waterfront, where they had gone one damp evening to retrieve a shipment of supplies. The packet was delayed due to fog, and the usual crew of stevedores had melted into the evening before it docked. Blue and Lucas had found themselves laboring alongside the few lingering dockworkers, loading crates into their carriage.

It was dark by the time they finished and Lucas took up the reins. Blue had schooled his son in driving and horsemanship, and the boy was a capable driver, even in the steep and congested streets of the city.

They exited Pacific Mail dock gate at the junction of First and Brannan Streets and Mission Bay, making their way through a heavy fog that held the meaty odor of sewage gas. Lamplighters had already come down the hill on their nightly rounds, and the street-lamps cast pools of white mist along the roadway. Blue glanced at Lucas to see him breathing through his mouth and sitting very straight on the seat as he kept control of the reins. A jolt of affection inundated Blue, a sensation so sweet he nearly forgot the miasma of the city's filthiest district. But then the open carriage picked up speed, and instantly concern dominated Blue's thoughts. Too often, the boy drove with a reckless edge.

"You took that last turn too fast," Blue said. "We were all but screaming around the corner on two wheels."

"No, I didn't," Lucas stated, navigating swiftly through the traffic, which thickened around the beer saloons and chop houses of the commercial district. "Didn't you say you were in a rush to sign for the medical supplies?"

Blue couldn't dispute it. Due to the number of patients he served, he was always running low on bandages, lancets and imported medications. He was down to his last stock of smallpox vaccine. "I was, but there's no need to hurry now. It's late, and we've long since missed supper. By the time we get home, they'll all have gone to bed."

"I don't see why I had to come," Lucas said with a smart snap of the reins. "It's after hours anyway. We should have waited until morning."

"A physician's duties extend around the clock," Blue reminded him.

"I'm not a physician."

"But one day —"

"One day I'll make up my own mind about my future," Lucas said quickly, then hunched his shoulders to indicate he was concentrating on his driving. They passed alleys strewn with refuse, where shadows darted, quick as secrets. Crimps loitered in front of the Sailor's Home, ready to pounce on the hapless greenhorns who mysteriously found themselves unable to pay their tariff. Lucas drove by a noisy saloon crammed to the curb with ne'er-do-wells and dockworkers, laughing and arguing under a sign advertising steam beer for five cents a pint. "Are you thirsty?" Lucas asked.

Blue couldn't quite keep from smiling. "Keep driving."

Misty globes of gaslight floated in the fog. The brick clock tower at the intersection of Geary, Kearney and Market Streets formed a black monolith that loomed over them as they passed. Pedestrians and lightly-sprung driving traps made way for the imposing Calhoun vehicle. With an air of noblesse oblige he could only have inherited from his mother, Lucas occupied the middle of the road until a large cartload of ice blocks forced him to give way.

Blue literally bit his tongue to keep from saying something critical. It never helped, even when he was right. If it was raining straight down on his head, Lucas would argue that it was dry, and if Blue pointed out that it was daylight, Lucas would insist it was dark. In the matter of Lucas's future, he knew his own aspirations didn't necessarily match those of his son. He wanted Lucas to study medicine and made no secret of that fact. The lad was uncommonly bright, and when he didn't think his father was watching, tended to show compassion to others.

Except while driving. Setting his jaw, Blue braced one arm against the upholstered side of the carriage and hoped that when they toppled over, they would not take any pedestrians with them. The damp, brick-paved streets raced past as Lucas aimed the rig uphill, away from the swamplike atmosphere of the waterfront.

"I wish you wouldn't drive so fast," Blue said, unable to hold his tongue any longer. Then, catching the look on his son's face, he added, "You've a fine hand with the horses."

Even in San Francisco, where gorgeous rigs and matched teams were a common sight, passersby stared in admiration at the glossy carriage and nimble horses. Impressing people had never been all that important to Blue, but appearances had always mattered greatly to Sancha. Perhaps that was where Lucas got his self-consciousness.

Lucas applied the buggy whip lightly to urge the team up Canby Hill.

Slow down, Blue wanted to say. What's your hurry?

He used to be in a hurry when he was young. He'd hurried off to war, only to see horrors that never left. He'd hurried to marry, only to lose his young wife to an act of brutality that proved the world made no sense. Life was a string of tragedies. Why rush from one to the next?

"Regardless of your future profession," he said, "I've given a great deal of thought to your education. I've sent a letter to my colleagues on the board of Milton."

"I'm not going to Milton."

"Not today, at any rate." Blue tried to keep the annoyance from his voice.

"Not ever," said Lucas. "Sir."

"Why the devil not? There are young men who yearn for such an opportunity. It's a first-rate institution, it's close to home —"

"It's not my dream."

"Your dream."

"Yes, sir. My dream."

"You're nearly grown. You can't be chasing dreams."

Lucas gave a bark of laughter. "I'm nearly grown. This is the perfect time for dreaming."

Gathering patience, Blue said, "So. What do you dream of?"

He hesitated, then said, "Not Milton College."

Blue forced himself to say no more, because he knew where this type of conversation always went. They would wind up quarreling, then armoring themselves in angry silence. In this now-familiar argument, both of them lost. He didn't quite know what to do about it. Day by day, Lucas was slipping away from him. The harder he tried to hold the boy in check, the harder Lucas strained to be free.

Blue understood that his son was destined to make a life of his own. He wanted that for him. But letting him go felt like a devastating loss. He wondered if other fathers experienced this and what they did about it.

"Your grandparents have offered you a berth on their cruise," he reminded Lucas.

"Several times," Lucas said. "They made you the same offer."

"Several times." Blue had no trouble declining the invitation. He wondered why people like Isabel constantly craved the change and upheaval of travel. She claimed she was seeking adventure, but sometimes, when secrets shadowed her eyes, he suspected she was hurrying away from something.

"You never leave the city," Lucas said. "Why not?"

Blue was surprised; his son had never asked such a thing before. "I'm needed here. My life and work are here."

"And they'll still be waiting here if you take a holiday."

Blue waved away the notion. "I've seen enough of the world."

"I haven't."

"Then perhaps you should join them."

"Sailing around the world with Grandpa, Grandmama, my aunt and uncle?" Lucas shook his head. "No, thank you."

Blue wanted to feel gratified, but he knew better. Lucas wanted to stay where his friends were, even though those very same friends were the ones who landed him in trouble, time and time again. He was probably thinking of June Li, too, though he would never say so to his father. Their friendship was showing signs of blossoming into romance, a situation that would eventually break both their hearts. Not for the first time, Blue wished with painful intensity that Sancha was more than a memory. These were matters one discussed with a wife. Women had a way of understanding such things.

Isabel Fish-Wooten was hardly a motherly type, yet she had developed an easy rapport with Lucas. Did he confess his dreams to her? Blue wondered.

Halfway up the hill, they emerged from the thick mist of fog into an area of gaslit residential streets, boxy wooden houses and blocky mansions surrounded by sloping grounds. Lucas steered the team to the service alley. Efrena must have heard them arrive, for she waited with a glowing lamp. Blue shooed her off to bed and instructed Lucas to take charge of the team.

While Blue unloaded the shipment, Lucas pointed out that one of the horses was cowhocked in its hind legs and needed attention from the farrier. Like all Calhouns, Lucas was good with horses. It was something in their blood and bone, perhaps. He himself used to ride like the wind, far beyond the reaches of Cielito, just for the sheer pleasure of the speed. But that was long ago. He could scarcely remember the person he'd been when he was Lucas's age. Had he defied his father? Made mischief just to prove his independence? Argued with his parents? He honestly could not remember.

They entered the house through the back. The kitchen was dark and spotlessly clean, the way Mrs. Li left it at the end of each day. Lucas helped himself to a jar of sugared peaches and half a loaf of bread, as if he had not just consumed a pound of boiled peanuts at the waterfront only an hour before. The front hall and parlor lay in darkness as well. Blue turned up the gas jets to light the wide, curving staircase. Its ornamental rail threw a giant skeleton of shadow across the opposite wall. The woodwork gleamed with a polishing of beeswax, diligently applied by Bernadette.

"I'd best check on Miss Fish-Wooten," said Blue. "Then I'll be in my study."

His mouth stuffed with bread, Lucas nodded. To Blue's surprise, he followed him up the stairs. When Lucas was small, he used to follow his father everywhere, like a tiny apparition. Now he rarely voluntarily went anywhere with Blue. But like everyone else who encountered Isabel Fish-Wooten, Lucas had fallen under her spell.

As he made his way to her room, Blue felt annoyed at himself. When had he begun thinking of it as her room? Nothing in this house belonged to her. She was a temporary wayfarer, nothing more.

No light leaked from around the door, which was unusual. She had a voracious appetite for reading, as though she wanted to devour every book in the world. Often she stayed awake late into the night, poring over borrowed volumes of poetry and recipes and travelogues. She showed no particular preference. She read novels and memoirs and medical tracts with equal interest, sometimes as many as two per day.

Blue tapped at the door, then frowned when he heard no answer, no rustle of bed-clothes as she stirred in her sleep. The idea of seeing her asleep in bed was deeply — disturbingly — appealing to him. After a moment he pushed the door open and turned up the wall sconces by the door.

Behind him, Lucas gulped down the mouthful of food he was chewing and stated the obvious. "She's gone."

Blue surveyed the room, which was not simply vacant but which held a curious air of being undisturbed. There was no trace of her left here, no hint that she had ever inhabited these quarters. The bed was made, the carpet swept, the drapes drawn and hanging motionless, as though made of stone. It was hard to imagine that only a few hours earlier, she had filled the room with her laughter and blithe talk, the aroma of raspberries as she ate them from a bowl. This room was as empty as it had been after Sancha died.

He felt something unexpected and not altogether pleasant — regret. Quickly shaking it off, he turned to Lucas. "Yes. Well, she was feeling better and no doubt eager to be on her way."

To his surprise, fury flared in Lucas's dark eyes. "That's not true, and you know it. She didn't want to leave. She was happy here."

"She was a stranger. How would we know whether she was happy or not?"

"You drove her away," Lucas said. "You always ruin everything."

"Don't be absurd. She was a patient. Clearly she felt well enough to be up and about and on her way. That is the entire goal of the healing art, is it not?"

"You wanted her gone," he said, dismissing Blue's rationale with an angry swipe of his hand. "You hated having her in my mother's room. You hated it that she was alive while my mother —" He stopped, but Blue heard

276

the rest of it anyway. With no further explanation, Lucas stormed away, stomping up to his third-floor chamber and slamming the door.

Blue stood alone in the empty room. Sancha's room. But he couldn't picture Sancha here anymore. Instead, he saw Isabel everywhere — pale and slight as she lay against a bank of white pillows, watching her opponent across the gaming table with a gamin look in her eye, unexpectedly studious as she sat reading, oddly vulnerable as she stood before the tall oval mirror, studying her reflection, adjusting the hair combs he had given her.

In the short time she'd been here, Isabel had made this room her own. Now she was gone, and he told himself he ought to be relieved. She was like any other patient, giving him a glimpse of her life but never the whole picture, and then moving on entirely when she had no further need of him. That was the nature of his profession.

Yet even as he labored to let go of her, he kept thinking about where she might go, whom she might meet. She was secretive about herself and her past, but any woman who carried two guns was likely headed for trouble.

And then there was the mysterious matter of Nathan Skinner. Perhaps he'd drunk himself to death, or perhaps he'd died because he saw something he shouldn't have on the night of the shooting.

The thought jolted Blue into action. He didn't walk swiftly back to the carriage house. He ran.

Twenty-One

Blue Calhoun's late wife had exquisite taste and a budget to match, thought Isabel, picking her way through the busy network of streets and alleys leading to the waterfront. She lifted the hem of the indigo cotton traveling skirt above a gutter overflowing with refuse. She had no qualms about appropriating a suit of clothes from Sancha's dressing room.

The tailored gown, with its matching cropped jacket and hat, were years out-of-date, she conceded, but only the most discriminating arbiter of fashion would notice. Besides, it couldn't be helped. She had been swindled out of all her scraped-together savings and could ill afford a proper set of traveling clothes.

As she had dressed herself and made her brief, hurried preparations, it had occurred to her that she might help herself to something more than clothing. As quickly as the notion occurred, she dismissed it. There had been times in her life when she wasn't above stealing in order to survive, but this was not one of those times. Even though the stately Calhoun house offered any number of fenceable goods, from silverware to jewelry, Dr. Calhoun had done enough for her. She would not add insult to injury by stealing from him.

There was another reason, one she would scarcely admit to herself. She wanted him to think well of her, or at least not judge her too harshly. His opinion mattered. This was a new and unsettling concept for Isabel. Ordinarily she cared nothing for the good opinions of people she left behind. But this latest sojourn was anything but ordinary.

However, it was over. Right up to the last moment, she'd harbored a private hope that he would ask her to stay — not because she was injured or ill, but because he wanted her around. But his dismissal of her, right in front of Eliza, had pointed to only one option for Isabel. Her mission now was to resume her travels, all on her own.

The prospect of an imminent departure used to gladden her. There was nothing quite like the sharp anticipation of embarking on a voyage to a new place. Yet something had changed her here in San Francisco. A part of her yearned to sink deep into this place, to take root and make herself a part of it. For the first time, she understood that home was much more than a place to live.

The deep ache that pressed at her heart

was a new and unwelcome surprise. How silly of her to get attached. It wasn't like her at all. Worse, she had developed friendships with Lucas and Delta, Mrs. Li and June. She already missed them.

It didn't pay to give your heart. She had always known that. Now she was living proof of it. But it seemed her heart was a fickle organ that didn't always listen to her head.

"You are Isabel Fish-Wooten, lady adventurer," she whispered to herself to shore up her determination. It was a role that had come easily to her, fitting like a comfortable dancing slipper. As far as anyone knew, she was an aristocrat so mysterious and sophisticated that she created a stir wherever she went. There was only one drawback to maintaining the illusion, however. She could never stay anyplace for long. Invariably the questions became more probing, the pretense more strained. A prolonged sojourn was far too risky. It meant unmasking herself and revealing the despised and terrified creature she had once been.

Stopping at the broad plaza in front of the commercial wharves, she tried to shake herself free of regrets and focus on the task at hand. She'd been foolish enough to allow herself to be swindled. Now she had to be smart enough to get her money back.

Certainly it would behoove her to be smarter than she had been upon her initial arrival in the city. Flush from a successful shooting tournament at a Wild West Show in Denver, she traveled in high style to California. Her first night in San Francisco, she immediately sought out a ticket agent to book her passage to the magical isles of Hawaii. Mr. Henry Leland of the Great Pacific Line had been most accommodating, promising her a first-class berth on a modern steamship that would make the crossing in just seven days. He was polite and efficient, and occupied a respectable office in Ecker Street, right next to Underwriters Fire Patrol. There was nothing about him to tip her off, which in itself should have roused her suspicions. She couldn't think why it hadn't.

She even inspected his vessel before purchasing the berth. Moored at Central Wharf, the Hawaiian steamer *St. Ives* was modern and sleek, its staterooms gorgeously appointed, its purser gracious and accommodating. Leland had taken her money as well as the steamer trunk packed with all her belongings, promising that the porters of the shipping line would see to everything. He told her to report to the *St. Ives*, advising her that the ship would leave from the Market Street Wharf. She should have questioned him about the change of moorage, but she had been almost giddy with excitement, imagining flower-scented tropical breezes, the cry of exotic birds, the heady sensation of surf-riding in crystal waters.

She'd arrived at the designated wharf to find a garbage scow moored at the pier.

Even now, she felt dull echoes of her hollow sense of disbelief. Her sinking, sickening disappointment. She tried to tell herself that no, she must've got it wrong. But she couldn't deny the dread certainty that curdled in her gut. She'd been swindled.

She wasn't sure what had been stronger — shame or anger. She of all people should know better. She should have seen through the setup. But now she knew something valuable about Leland. He was good. Better than good. Better than her. If he'd fooled her, that meant he was one of the best.

Immediately upon realizing she'd been bilked, Isabel took action. Though she knew the probable outcome, she tried to lodge a complaint with the authorities. The local police wearily informed her of the six dozen swindles they were currently investigating, and told her they would get six dozen more complaints the following day. She'd find no help there.

On her own, she traced Leland to a suite of warehouse offices. A brass plaque on the brickwork identified the firm as the Far East Tea Company. With haughty insistence, she demanded restitution of her money and belongings. He claimed to know nothing of her or her allegation.

She had reached into her reticule for her gun, but someone else had arrived, foiling her. Some official, whose role related to cargo inspection. He had come to sign off on a shipment. At first, she was mystified. Why would an official of the health department have to sign off on a shipment of tea?

Isabel remembered waiting in the shadows, either forgotten or ignored by Leland as he spoke with the unseen official in the next office. Within moments, their conversation told her what she should have realized from the start. The tea warehouse was a front for the opium trade.

She remembered wondering why opium traders would waste their time swindling someone like her. Because a thief was a thief, and an opportunist didn't confine himself to one swindle only.

She fled the office empty-handed, though lucky to escape with her life. But Isabel was no ordinary gull. She refused to be outfoxed. Late that night, she raided one of the hundreds of laundries of Chinatown, disguised herself as a boy, loaded her guns and headed back to the Far East Tea Company to reclaim her fortune.

The last thing she'd expected was to find herself in the middle of a crime in progress. The last thing she wanted to witness was the shooting of a police officer. Yet that was where she'd found herself that night, to her everlasting regret. In nightmares, and even when she was wide-awake, she relived the horror of seeing a man gunned down — the powder flash and the sound of his body hitting the pavement, her instant impulse to draw fire away from him and, finally, the terror of knowing the gun was turned on her.

Tonight, she was determined to conclude her business in this darkly beautiful city. She had to leave before she lost her heart. Unlike her fortune, it could not be recouped or repaired. Or replaced.

She plucked a handkerchief from her sleeve and pressed the wisp of fabric briefly to her nose to give herself some small relief from the stench of the waterfront. At the same time, she studied the crowd moving like ghostly swimmers in and out of the thick fog. Cutpurses darted past gamblers in dusters and frockcoats or sailors prowling for adventure. Molls of all ages, shapes and sizes lingered in dimly lit doorways. A pair of men held a protesting boy by the arms; they were probably delivering him to an outbound ship. Chinese tong members strode about in their brocaded robes, and on every corner children begged for pennies. She thought about Blue as she waited. He cared so much about this city and its people; he dedicated himself to making this a better place. It seemed so noble to Isabel, who had never contributed to the betterment of any place or anyone other than herself. A part of her wished she had the courage to stay and learn to care like that.

A crew of strolling sailors caught her eye. In their wide-legged duck trousers and open-necked shirts, they swaggered across the plaza, laughing raucously and no doubt trolling for a lively bar or bawdy house. Like many sailors, they spoke in a foreign tongue and were regarded as trouble on the hoof. While most pedestrians gave the men a wide berth, Isabel tucked away her handkerchief and squared her shoulders, preparing to approach them.

It was risky, of course, particularly since the well-meaning but naive Blue Calhoun had relieved her of her weapons. She had no defenses other than her wits. But she intended to reclaim her fortune. This time, she would do so with half a dozen burly sailors in tow.

Their laughter and joshing settled into silent admiration as she stepped into their path. "Good evening, gentlemen," she said in her most refined manner.

They jostled each other as they greeted her, some attempting clumsy bows.

The eldest of the group, a man with a grizzled beard and a gnawed-off ear, pushed his way to the front of the group. "Fine lady like you ought not to be abroad in these parts," he said.

"How kind of you to concern yourself, sir." She smiled demurely. These men were ever so predictable. She'd counted on rousing their protective instincts. "And you are right, of course, but I've got pressing business in the area." She took a quick breath, feeling a twinge in the region of her wound. She felt a flash of concern. Though no longer infected, the wound was still incompletely healed. But she had never shied from risk. Perhaps she would luck into a swift departure. The best ships and steamers all had surgeons on board. If need be, she would consult one of them.

Smiling despite her pain, she said, "Perhaps you gentlemen can help me."

"Yes, ma'am." A younger man stepped up, this one distinguished by his towering height and terrible teeth. "What can we do for you?"

"I have an unfortunate dispute with the Far East Tea Company. Are you familiar with the firm?"

"I know of it," said the man with one ear. "It's down at the end of Mission Bay."

Isabel explained her dilemma. Unlike the police, the sailors listened with utter credulity and dawning outrage. For good measure, she offered a generous reward in exchange for their help.

"What are we waiting for, lads?" said the old sailor. "Let's carry on."

They made their way past the jumbled crates and steam-powered lifts. Then they entered a maze of alleys filled with drunkards and whores. They passed deadfalls and dives, rickety boardinghouses and dimly-lit cribs. Isabel took a dread fascination in the scene and was glad to be in the company of several large men. The sailors, with their jutting jaws and rolling gaits, made an odd parade, but everyone in the vicinity was odd, so no one paid them undue notice. Outside a raucous dance hall, a burly Ranger stood on the boardwalk, fondling a blank-eyed nymphe du pave. Another man, reeking of rough whiskey, staggered toward Isabel, but one of the sailors thrust him aside with a brusque, "Shove off, mate."

Concert saloons and gambling shacks gave way to even lower establishments — the whorehouses and opium dens of the Barbary Coast. No melodeon music or rowdy singing issued from the barred windows or closely-guarded doors. From the street, Isabel caught only glimpses of the blurred chaos within. The occasional sweet burn of Shanghai smoke or the dreamy stench of cigarritos made of tobacco and opium drifted from low doorways.

She had but a limited experience with opium. On long sea voyages, even the most strait-laced matron took it as a curative, and a good many mothers used it to quiet their fretful babes. Shipboard acquaintances who termed it a pleasant diversion had offered it to Isabel.

She'd accepted, of course, in her customary spirit of adventure. Its effect on her was remarkable. She fell into a strange, haunting lethargy, a waking dream. Even after the effects had abated, she'd felt sharp cravings she was hard-pressed to restrain even now. But Isabel's keen instinct for self-preservation steered her away from opium. Her way of life depended on keeping control, not surrendering it to a mysterious substance.

On some of the boardwalks lay anonymous heaps of the drug's drowsy victims, some of them possibly breathing their last. These were the people Blue Calhoun lived to save. She could not imagine taking on such an enormous, insurmountable task.

She knew by the thick tarry odor of the wharves that they were nearing the vicinity of the Far East Company. Tea, indeed. Only the most willfully blind idiot would believe that.

Her companions spoke to one another in a patois of English and Dutch as they traveled through the streets. They were large and awful-looking, but were they large and awful-looking enough to intimidate Leland into handing over her fortune?

Perhaps she'd get lucky. Perhaps Mr. Leland would simply concede defeat and she'd be on her way.

A shiver passed through her as they approached the finished section of the Embarcadero, where the wharves jutted out like teeth in a comb. Even at this hour, the area was cluttered with vehicles, crates, puncheons, shadowy warehouses, the occasional accounting office with lights still burning. She gestured the sailors toward the windowless brick edifice where so-called tea brokers conducted their affairs as though they were legitimate men of business rather than greedy opportunists building a fortune by spreading misery disguised as euphoria.

Outside the warehouse, a coach waited, its leather window blinds shut. As they crossed the apron of stone pavers leading from the wharves to the warehouses, a shout rang out, followed by a loud crack.

Isabel gasped and threw herself to the ground, barely aware of the filthy pavement beneath her.

"Here now." A sailor's strong hand gripped her arm and pulled her to her feet. "It was only a falling beam from one of the steam lifts. Did you hurt yourself, then?" As he helped her brush herself off, his hands roved unapologetically, outlining the curve of her hips, squeezing her breasts.

She stepped quickly away. "I must have tripped," she said. She could feel an icy trickle of sweat on her brow and upper lip. Inside the borrowed gloves, the palms of her hands were damp. She kept hearing echoes of the snapping sound in her head. As though it were happening all over again, she felt the unholy burn of a bullet hitting her, felt the struggle to breathe after her lungs had been emptied by the impact.

Disoriented, she hugged herself and struggled to remain calm. "We should conclude our business," she said, marshaling her courage. She had been doing this all her life, getting in and out of scrapes, dusting herself off, forging ahead. Why did it seem so impossible lately?

She headed for the brick building. Just as she reached the warehouse, the door burst open and Isabel fell back. The passageway was too narrow to accommodate more than one person at a time. Now she realized that this was no accident, but design.

"Mrs. Hatcher, please, I beg you," called a nervous voice from within. "I promise you, the shipment —"

"Your promises are no better than the cheap wine you serve, Mr. Leland." A tall woman in grand attire and a huge, veiled hat sailed past and approached the waiting coach. "Next week, no later." The driver handed her up, shut the door with a definitive thud, then climbed up on the box and clicked his tongue.

Isabel watched the vehicle pull away and disappear up one of the streets leading away from the waterfront. She waited for Leland to retreat to the office, then motioned for her companions to follow her to the door. They opened it to reveal a narrow, unlit hallway with another door at the end. She led the sailors in a line and rapped sharply at the door to get Leland's attention.

He pulled it open and light spilled from the room. "Mrs. Hatcher, I —" The color drained from his face.

Isabel smiled, though she was cold inside with fear. "I see you remember me. Perhaps you also remember that you have something of mine."

"I don't recall anything of the sort," he said, visibly gathering his wits about him.

"In that case, maybe my friends will refresh your memory." She stepped aside to reveal a half-dozen snarling sailors, and they pushed into the doorway. Oh, they were adept at snarling, with drawn-back lips and balled fists and all the attendant threatening noises.

Leland made a little squeaking sound of surrender. "I want no trouble, now," he said, scuttling to his desk.

"Keep your hands where we can see them," Isabel said, and it struck her that she disliked playing this role sometimes.

Leland headed to the rear of the office, where a blocky safe was bolted to the floor. He appeared to be cooperating, but still, Isabel felt a nasty chill of suspicion. Leland took an inordinate amount of time fiddling with the dial on the safe. The sailors shifted and muttered with impatience.

At the back of the office, a second door burst open. Out of the shadows came a small army of men wielding cudgels and stout, shiny blackjacks. Isabel leaped toward the exit.

"Run," she yelled at the sailors. "Get away while you can!"

She heard the sickening thud of a blackjack striking flesh, followed by a bellow of pain. The howling sailors surged out into the street. The tea company men started after them.

Isabel raced after them. "Stop," she said sharply. "Let them go. They had nothing to do with this." She turned to Leland, who had followed her out to the street. Along with a keen edge of panic, Isabel felt a flash of self-hatred. She was a danger to everyone she met, even seasoned sailors. No wonder she spent her life wandering alone. "I swear, they were just passing by, and I asked them for help."

"They weren't very helpful," said Leland.

"Call back your men. Unless you prefer to be undefended."

She could see her point sink home. He summoned the men back with a whistle.

Isabel had no time to feel relieved. "I'll just be on my way, then." She raced down the street, nimbly ducking under the arm of one of the men who was returning to Leland like a trained dog. She prayed the shroud of fog would help her disappear quickly.

Leland yelled an order, but she kept running, skirts bunched in her hand, feet flying over the wet pavement. She had but a few moments' advantage, and no real hope of outrunning them. She could not evade them for long. She headed for the open door of an establishment, hoping to find sanctuary there. But when he saw her coming with a herd of armed men in pursuit, the proprietor slammed the door.

Ordinarily she was adept at vanishing. She had a particular talent for slipping into small spaces like a rabbit down a hole. But tonight she felt winded and clumsy, not at all herself. She tripped over a garbage-strewn curb and lurched into a crowd of people who fell back and dispersed. Frantic, she veered into the street again, blindly running for safety. But safety had never been there for her. She knew better than that.

She headed for the Rescue League. It was the only place she could think of. Her hat flew off, and she threw a shoe like a panicked mare. Leland's men meant business. She could hear one of them breathing heavily, closing in on her.

Around a deserted street corner, gaslight glinted off the polished side of a vehicle. It was an open carriage, as shiny and out of place here as a new penny in a mud puddle. It probably belonged to one of the well-heeled opium traders, but she was in no position to be fussy. She headed for the carriage.

Someone grabbed at her skirt from behind. At the same moment, a hand reached for her, bunching into her sleeve. She felt two powerful arms grasping her, lifting her up. She landed with a jarring thud. The vehicle lurched forward again, heading up the hill, away from the waterfront.

She struggled to catch her breath and looked up at her rescuer. Relief and astonishment poured through her. "How did you find me?"

Blue Calhoun pulled at her arm, setting her upright on the upholstered seat. "I just went where the trouble was."

Twenty-Two

Blue drove home at a rapid clip, following a line of lighted gas lamps up the hill. It did not escape him that this was the second time he'd been down to the waterfront tonight. But this time, he was the one driving.

And his hands were shaking like leaves in a strong wind. He pressed his wrists into his knees and concentrated on his driving, holding the reins soft between his fingers. The fear that gripped him was a physical force, strangling him, leaving a harsh, metallic taste in his mouth. Though indifferent to his own safety, he hated feeling afraid for other people. This was exactly what he'd spent the past decade trying to avoid. He'd been successful up until now, keeping himself walled off from caring. But Isabel Fish-Wooten had dropped without warning into his life, and everything was changing despite his best efforts to keep everything the same.

"This truly makes no sense," she said, correctly reading the fury in his scowl. "You wanted me gone, so I left."

"I never said I wanted you gone."

"I may be many things, but I'm not stupid. I did you the favor of disappearing. I thought you'd be grateful. Besides, I don't need rescuing."

"You were doing so well on your own."

"You kept saying I was better. I felt fine."

"That doesn't mean you're well enough to go chasing around the Barbary Coast."

"I didn't plan that."

"Then what the hell were you planning, Miss Fish-Wooten? A tea party? The waterfront's a thieves' paradise and worse. You know that. Why did you go back there?"

"I had business to take care of."

God, she frustrated him. Business to take care of. At the Barbary Coast. "The only people who have business down there at night are smugglers and wh—" He stopped, nearly losing his grip on the reins. He looked over at her, a small shadow with waves of light passing over her from the glowing lamps that lit the roadway.

She gave a bitter laugh. "You wouldn't be the first to believe I'm the sort of woman who would trade my flesh for money."

"I didn't think —"

"Of course you thought it."

Had he? It would be so much easier to dislike her if that was the case. And it occurred to him that, once again, she had skirted a key issue with him. He reached the stables and put up the horse and rig. As he worked, he realized that she'd managed to avoid explaining herself. "You still haven't told me what you were doing down there."

"If you must know, I was trying to get my money and belongings back from someone who swindled me." She waved her gloved hand in impatience.

He watered the horses, then held the door for her. As she stepped past, he was assailed by her — the smell of her hair, her skin. Even disheveled, having lost her hat and one shoe, she was wildly attractive to him. In the glow of the occasional street lamp, she looked ethereal. The delicate sweep of her cheekbones and the mysterious wells of her eyes seemed to beckon him to a place he'd never been before, not even with Sancha. This was insane, he thought.

"Who swindled you?"

"A ticket agent — at least, that's who I thought he was. He called himself Mr. Leland, and he sold me a very expensive first class billet aboard a ship bound for Honolulu."

"Let me guess. You reported to the pier listed on the ticket only to find a sand barge moored there."

"Worse," she admitted. "It was a garbage scow."

He fought the slightest twinge of humor, but she seemed to sense the battle in him. "All right, I deserve to be laughed at. You might as well. There's certainly no point in crying over it."

"Have you attempted to get your money back before?" As soon as he asked the question, realization dawned on him. "Ah. That's what you were doing the night you were shot." Her silence confirmed it. He stepped aside and motioned her through the stable door, rolling it shut behind her. "If you were swindled, you should have gone to the police."

"I did, but it was fruitless, of course," she said. "We both know that when one's fortune goes missing in a place like that, the police aren't likely to be of any help."

"Why didn't you tell me?"

"I'm accustomed to solving my own problems."

Exasperated, he led the way up the service alley and along the concrete walkway to the house. She stumbled a little in the dark, and he slipped his arm around her waist to steady her. She exhaled a small exclamation, then leaned gently against him. She was just a wisp of a thing; her power over him wasn't derived from physical strength. Despite her evening at the waterfront, she smelled of floral soap and some unnamable essence that drove straight through him. Beneath his guiding hand, she felt curiously fragile.

He wasn't prepared for such an abundance of sentiment, particularly in relation to this woman. Yet caution didn't seem to matter when it came to Isabel Fish-Wooten. The very air between them felt charged with invisible energy. His senses were filled with her — the dainty press of her slight weight against him, that luxurious scent, the softness of her hair.

In his mind, he enumerated all the reasons he should not want her. They came from different worlds. She believed life was an endless journey, while he wanted only to settle and stay in one place. She was mysterious about her background, a sign that she harbored secrets he would not like. Though she talked far too much, she disclosed little about herself. Her explanation of shady dealings at the waterfront was probably only a small part of a sordid story. She was wholly inappropriate.

Yet as they walked together toward the house, his arm stayed around her and she pressed even closer. All those well-thought-out reasons evaporated. Worse, his heart was tangling into a knot over her. He simply couldn't understand it. He was the type of man who planned his days and marched through them according to schedule. This was not supposed to be happening to him.

A faint glow from the parlor window cast a pale fan of light over the lawn. The thick perfume of Ligustrum and mimosa filled the air. In the distance, a foghorn blasted into the night. He felt Isabel hesitate and slow her steps.

"Are you all right?" he asked, holding out his hand in case she needed to steady herself. "Do you feel faint?"

She placed her hand in his. "It's all so beautiful."

He scanned the yard and the view of the city and the bay far below, a necklace of misty lights strung along the waterfront. "I suppose it is."

"Not just the city," she said. "Your home and your son . . . Your whole life."

How could anyone look at his life and see something beautiful? He wished he could view himself, his world, through her eyes.

She glanced from their joined hands to his face and back again. Boldly, deliberately, she moved his hand to her waist. As she tipped back her head to look up at him, light and shadow flickered across her face. "You live in a world of blessings, yet you're not a happy man."

Her statement seared him deep enough to hurt. But instead of letting go, he slipped his other arm around her and pulled her closer. No one, not even his family, had ever dared to say such things to him before.

"How could my happiness — or lack thereof — possibly matter to you?" he asked.

She rested her hands on his arms, perched them there like a pair of doves poised to fly away without warning. "I think you should tell me about your wife."

"Between Delta and my family, you've heard all you need to know."

"That's not so. It's your story to tell."

"For God's sake —"

"You're a physician. You make it your business to understand the nature of wounds and healing. Has it never occurred to you to liken such a terrible loss to an injury?"

She was watching him expectantly, and he was stunned to feel a singular urge to share his heart with her. But he said, "I never speak of what happened to Sancha."

"Perhaps you should."

"What would it serve?"

"What would it hurt?"

Blue tore his gaze away from her. Behind her, the house loomed like a fortress, an imposing presence he had never fully appreciated. He had been indifferent to luxury and style, but not to his wife.

"Words are easy," he said, resisting the idea of sharing his heart with this woman. "They're nothing but noisy air. They won't change a thing."

But then he remembered a time when words had been impossible. When he was very small, his mother had died and he'd simply stopped speaking. He recalled his elation and utter relief when he'd finally been persuaded to speak again.

He gazed down at Isabel Fish-Wooten, and a voice that didn't even seem like his own said, "We lived together in this house for five years. Lucas was born here. Sancha lavished love and attention on this house as though it was a second child. We were —" He paused. "Happy doesn't begin to describe it. But I was less content with my medical practice."

"You didn't like being a doctor?"

"It's the only thing I ever wanted to be. But my practice . . . It was the one source of friction between us. Sancha wanted me to confine my work to the Hill, and I tried that for a while. Well-heeled gentlemen sought treatment for gout and ladies consulted me about discreet but curable female ailments." He squeezed his eyes shut, remembering, regretting. The practice had flourished, but so had a pervasive restlessness. Years later, he could see himself clearly, a selfish young man, enamored of the heroics of his profession, blind to his wife's need for security and contentment. He had not ignored Sancha's desires. He simply had not paused to consider that they might not match his own. Certainly he'd never thought to ask her.

"Let me guess," said Isabel. "You wanted your work to matter more. To help more people."

"I wish my intentions had been that selfless. The fact is, I craved the excitement of saving lives and performing critical procedures. When the army offered an opportunity to practice medicine at a remote frontier fort, I leaped at it."

"You were called to duty. You can't hold yourself responsible for that," said Isabel.

Anger snapped through him. "My wife was shot by a U.S. Army bullet. She died with our five-year-old son in her arms. If you can see a way to remedy that, Miss Fish-Wooten, then you've more talent as a healer than I." The stark anger in the revelation startled even him. He watched her reaction — not pity but understanding. She couldn't know the first thing about his suffering. And yet she did.

Unfazed by his hostility, she touched his cheek briefly, and he felt the gentle caress all through him. Then, too soon, she lowered her hand. "I wish you'd call me Isabel," she whispered.

It was uniquely unsettling, the way she stared at him, seeing deep, perhaps seeing the things he tried to keep hidden. Why was it so hard to resist her, or better still, dismiss her? He was tired, that was all. It had been an unusually busy summer, juggling his work and his son, his visiting family and his duties at the Rescue League.

"We should go inside." But something was the matter. He couldn't seem to let go of her, couldn't escape the softness of her, the scent of her hair and skin, the probing tenderness of her gaze.

"No, we should continue to discuss this."

"What the devil is the point?" he demanded. "It changes nothing."

"It's true that there's no remedy," she conceded, still holding him captive with a touch as light as mist. "Nothing can change the terrible thing that happened. But there is such goodness in your life. In your work and family and your fine son. You simply need to give yourself over to the joy in that."

"I forfeited joy, Miss Fish-Wooten, when I took my wife to a fort in the wilderness."

"You can spend the rest of your life atoning for that decision," Isabel told him. "I suppose it wouldn't matter if you were the only one affected. But you force Lucas to live with a father who has forbidden himself life's joys, all because of a terrible accident that happened a decade ago."

His confession to Isabel had drained him. Emptied out, he could not reply, could only hold on to her, even though the proper thing to do would be to set her aside, draw back into himself. Perhaps she was the only one to view him as a damaged man. Or perhaps she was the only one dauntless enough to put it quite so bluntly. And she didn't seem inclined to stop now. She pressed her thumbs into his arms as though probing for wounds. "I'm so sorry you lost her. But ending your grief doesn't mean ending the way you felt about her. It simply means embracing the

things I imagine were important to her —
your son, your family."

How did this woman, utterly alone in the
world, with no one to care that she'd been
shot in the back, possess such knowledge?
Who had taught her these things? "You presume to know a lot about my late wife."

She lifted her chin a half inch. "Tell me
I'm wrong."

He couldn't, God help him, because she
was absolutely right. Sancha had lived to love
him and Lucas, to take delight in each day.

He hadn't thought about that aspect of
Sancha in many years. But it was the truest
thing he knew about her, and the reminder
brought a fleeting, phantom warmth into his
soul.

And now, for reasons that completely
eluded him, he looked into a woman's eyes
and felt a small flicker of possibility. Just
that, nothing more. But for the moment, it
was enough.

He leaned down and kissed her lightly, lips
brushing, as though taking the smallest sip
from a goblet of wine. The kiss seemed to
surprise her as much as it did him. She responded with a quick intake of breath,
though she didn't pull away. And Blue, God
help him, could not have let her go in that
instant if she'd held a gun to him.

Her fists tightened into the fabric of his
sleeves, not in protest but in supplication. He

pressed his mouth deeper, hungry now and incautious with wanting. The wild need she sparked in him was a compelling force, equal parts lust, tenderness and a host of nearly-forgotten sentiments he refused to name.

Yet despite the demands clamoring inside him, he drew back. He let go and stepped out of the circle of light cast through the window. No, he told himself. *No.* An adventure of any sort with her would be ill-advised. She was not the kind of woman who could be brought out and put away like the good china when the occasion warranted it. Isabel Fish-Wooten was the type who would infuse each moment, waking or sleeping, with her presence.

"We should go in," he said again, this time in a brusque voice he barely recognized.

She touched the fingertips of her gloved hand to her lips as if to hold his kiss there, and the expression on her face nearly undid his composure once again. She dropped her hand, opened her mouth as though to argue, then shut it and walked toward the door.

Twenty-Three

As though to atone for her escapade, Isabel stayed alone with her thoughts all through the next day, suffering silent daggers of censure from Delta when she came to change the dressing.

"What's the matter with you?" asked Isabel, seated sullenly at the edge of the bed.

"Not a blessed thing. I was wondering the same about you."

"The wound broke open again," Isabel confessed, though she knew Delta could see that for herself. "It made for a bad night."

"Wouldn't be surprised if you came down with another infection," Delta scolded. "I swear, you don't have the sense God gave a mushroom."

"I did nothing wrong."

"Only went down to the waterfront at night, got chased by hooligans and nearly caught, too. I can't abide a fool who takes risks."

"Ah. And you didn't take a risk running away from Royal Oaks plantation?" Isabel said.

"Some things are worth the risk."

"And who gets to decide?"

"Somebody with a lick of sense. Hold still now. I swear, this'll never heal up right, you keep running around getting yourself into trouble. You rest today, hear me?"

"I'm bored with resting."

"Then do something useful, 'stead of getting yourself chased by bad company."

"And what do you consider useful?"

"You could help out at the Rescue League," Delta suggested. "They always need help there."

Isabel suspected an ulterior motive to Delta's suggestion, but she didn't question her.

"I'm on my way down there just as soon as I finish with you," Delta continued. "We're inoculating for smallpox."

"I don't know much about that, except that you wound people and then infect the wound with the pox."

"And it works, just like a plain miracle. Once you're feeling better, you come on and help out."

"I haven't the first idea of how to inoculate someone."

" 'Course you don't. There's plenty of other work to be done. I reckon you'd find something to do with yourself."

After Delta left, Isabel drew her knees up to her chest and passed her hand over a long-healed scar on the inside of her lower arm. Along with learning to read the scripture, smallpox inoculation was one of her few useful acquisitions from the workhouse. The masters didn't protect the inmates out of any particular compassion, but out of fear that the disease might deprive them of their stock-in-trade — cheap child labor for the looms and mines of England's underclass. At any rate, inoculation was a remarkable concept, thought Isabel. A deadly virus was applied to a small wound in the arm, and in fighting off the infection, the body armed itself forever against contracting the disease.

She wondered if it was possible to fall just a little bit in love with someone, then heal from that and move on, never vulnerable to the affliction again. Her mind drifted dreamily to the previous night, and she relived the surprise and delight of his kiss. His soft lips and gentle touch had made her giddy with wanting more, and she'd nearly wept when he let her go. Now all she could think about was seeing him again, touching and tasting him again. She'd never be immune, she realized. Try as she might, she could not pull back or turn away from him. Each moment, even when he wasn't around, she felt herself falling a little deeper into the startling adventure of loving him. That, more than anything else, was why she'd run. And ultimately, it was why she'd come back.

Something had happened between them last night. Something had changed. Whether he meant to or not, he had cracked open a door. She knew she should not go in. But oh, how she wanted to. She wanted to see what awaited there, what kind of man Blue was. Yet she knew forcing the door to open wider could change both their lives in ways they weren't ready for. She thought she knew herself rather well, but she wasn't sure she was willing to risk her most private self. Or what she expected in return if she dared.

Maintaining her best behavior, she finished every bite of the luncheon provided by Mrs. Li. She even tried to take a nap afterward, but her mind wouldn't rest. The encounter the previous night only proved that her instincts were sound. It was time to move on. But for now, she would have to stay here, getting her heart entangled with a man who had very little of his own heart to share.

"I'm not even fooling myself," she murmured peevishly. "I don't have to stay here. I *want* to." Abandoning sleep, she decided to get dressed and do something — *anything* — with herself. Perhaps Delta was right. She should serve her fellow man at the Rescue League. Side by side with Dr. Calhoun.

Seeking a distraction, she searched the dressing room for further clues about Sancha Montgomery Calhoun, as though secrets lingered in the outmoded gowns and scarves

311

and hats stored there. Oh, Sancha, she thought, trying on an oyster-colored velvet glove. I wish you could explain his heart to me. I wish you could tell me what it's like to be loved the way he loved you.

She had taken to carrying on the occasional internal dialogue with his dead wife, finding an odd comfort in sharing bits of Sancha's former life. What was it about her that had made Blue love her enough to mourn her for a decade? What was the source of her hold on his heart?

Restless with unanswerable questions, she flung aside the glove, fled the dressing room and stood in front of a tall bookshelf. Despite the things she had in common with Sancha Montgomery Calhoun, she definitely didn't share her taste in reading matter. *Winthrop's Ladies Annual. The Virtuous Heart. Canon of the Saints.* Morality tales and religious tracts. "I'm too old to learn those lessons now," Isabel said as she hurried downstairs. Mrs. Li had gone to the joss house she frequented in Chinatown and Bernadette was outside beating the rugs. Isabel had the house to herself.

She knew she'd have better luck finding something to read in the downstairs library. She stood in the middle of the overtly masculine room, inhaling the evocative smells of leather and ink, running her finger along the spines of the shelved books. Blue's interests ranged from Gray's *Anatomy* to the works of Mark Twain to several editions of Shakespeare's *The Tempest*. She took an unexpected pleasure in thumbing through the volumes, wondering if his hands had touched where she touched, if his eyes fell on the same phrases she was seeing now.

Dear heaven, she thought. This is getting desperate. Handling his books excites me.

In her perusal, she came to a broken-spined volume, creased in one spot. Curious, she took down the book. In gold lettering pressed into the calfskin binding was the title *The Reawakening* by Henry Monmouth, Esq. It was an imaginary tale of a virtuous woman put to death by an evil king. Aided by some magical alchemy, the hero brought her back to life, but sacrificed himself in the process.

Filled with growing melancholy, Isabel imagined this book in Blue Calhoun's hands as he read the story over and over again, filled with regrets and wishing he could change history and bring a woman back to life, even if it cost him his own.

In the hall, she heard a commotion of voices and nearly dropped the book. She quickly stuck it back on the shelf and went to investigate. She followed the sound of voices to the parlor.

It was the prettiest room in the house, but also the least used. It had a fine upright piano and was filled with antique furnishings, its windows framed by a fall of velvet drapes. The longest wall was dominated by a handsome marble fireplace, over which hung a large bridal portrait of Sancha Calhoun. She had a round, solemn face of surpassing beauty, and wore a dress erupting with ornate lace. In her smooth hands she held a white-bound Bible and a strand of pearl rosary beads. Under the portrait, on the mantel shelf and side shelves, were many more portraits, mostly photographs, of his late wife. He was in some of the pictures as well, laughing and carefree, an entirely different person from the man Isabel knew.

Ignoring the pictorial shrine, Lucas and two other young men stood by the piano, arguing in good-natured fashion. Isabel lingered outside the door, unnoticed and bemused, watching them.

"You should have paid attention in class," said the taller boy. "The mazy dance always starts off with the right foot stepping sideways."

"No, you step forward," said the stocky one. "Look, I'll show you." He stumbled a bit on the edge of the carpet.

Sensing someone behind her, Isabel turned to find June Li approaching with a tray of refreshments. "They're going to the charity dance," the girl explained, "and they're worried about disgracing themselves."

"As well they should be," said Isabel, eyeing the stumbling boys.

They noticed her then, their faces turning various shades of red. Even so, Lucas wore a grin of sheer delight. Unlike his father, he had no conflicted feelings about her presence in this house.

"Hello," she said.

"It's good to see you, Miss Isabel. I was afraid you'd left."

"Why would that make you afraid?"

His ears deepened a shade. "Not *afraid*. I was worried that you might not be well enough to be up and about. I feared you might hurt yourself again."

He was much more his father's son than he realized, she thought. "You should never worry about me."

"Why not?"

She bit her lip, trying to think of an amusing remark to dismiss the question. "I've never known worry to be of use to anyone, least of all the worrier." She smiled at the two gape-mouthed visitors. "Hello."

"Miss Fish-Wooten," Lucas said, "please allow me to introduce Frank Jackson and Andrew Haas."

She greeted them while June set down the tray of lemonade. "It appears you're practicing your ballroom dancing," she said.

"Yes, ma'am." Frank and Andrew were as endearingly awkward as only adolescent boys could be. Frank was short and Andrew tall. Both seemed intrigued by her, and she wondered what Lucas had told them. That she was an uninvited guest? An outlaw on the run? A lady adventurer?

"You're in luck, gentlemen," she informed them. "It just so happens I am an expert when it comes to dancing." This, at least, was the truth. She made it a point to learn all the popular fashions, from card games to the latest dances. Looking from one hopeful face to the next, she said, "I trust one of you ne'er-do-wells can give us a little accompaniment."

Andrew shuffled over to the piano and folded his long frame onto the fringed stool. His big gangling hands hammered the keys with no art, but he pounded out a recognizable rendition of "In a Sylvan Glade." Isabel positioned herself in front of a still-blushing Frank and partnered Lucas with June, pretending it was a random pairing. She tried not to smile at the way they gazed at one another.

For the next hour, she helped them stumble and then step their way through three separate dances — the mazy, the waltz and a simple schottische. Like all young people, they were quick to learn and quicker to laugh. How fresh the world must look through their eyes, she thought, a place of endless possibilities and limitless pleasure.

For Isabel, there had never been a time when life had looked as sweet as it did to these youngsters. They reminded her that there was a better world than the one she'd come from. What a delight it was to be with them. Her current partner, Frank, had sweaty palms and adoring eyes filled with wonder that a lady would show him how to dance. Lucas held June Li as though she were a butterfly cupped between his hands.

She worked with each boy, having them take turns at the piano. She urged them to practice again and again until the proper steps seemed — well, if not as easy as walking, then nearly so. Over the course of the lesson, the lads slowly transformed them-selves from clumsy adolescents to confident young men who could adequately — if not artfully — navigate the dance floor.

"You see," she said to them, "dancing is easy. Anything is easy if you believe yourself capable." And bless them, they believed her, practicing their moves with increasing skill.

She couldn't pinpoint the precise moment Blue walked into the room, but as she was showing Frank an advanced move, she turned, and there he was. She relinquished Frank's hand and stepped away. Instantly she felt a warm rush of sentiment. Surely this was a first for her — to be overcome by the simple act of a man walking into a room.

Behind her, Lucas and June stopped and

separated, turning their blushing faces away from each other. Andrew's hands fell still on the piano keyboard.

Blue's expression was difficult to read. He disclosed nothing of himself, no acknowledgment that last night had even happened. Ignoring the pounding of her heart, she smiled invitingly. "How are your dancing skills, Doctor? Are you in need of lessons, too?"

"I don't dance," he said.

"Perhaps you should. It might improve your disposition."

The faintest of snickers came from one of the boys.

"My disposition is fine," Blue snapped, and the snickering stopped.

She could feel the young people watching them like spectators at a sporting match. They seemed half-fascinated, half-frightened by the tall, severe, scowling Dr. Calhoun.

"Then think how much finer it would be if you knew how to dance," she said.

"I didn't say I could not dance. I said I don't."

"Really? And what type of dancing do you not do? The galop? The polka? Heavens, say you know the mazurka. I've been trying to show them that one, but it's difficult." She brightened, waving June toward the piano. "We'll need the Chopin piece you played us earlier — you did such a beautiful job, love." The girl sat on the cushioned stool, but held her hands frozen above the keys. Isabel took Blue's hand and placed his other one at her waist. "Here, help me demonstrate."

He tried to extricate himself from her grip, but she held fast. She did not know how much longer she would stay, but while she was here, she was determined to explore the terrible, wonderful feelings he stirred in her.

He glared down at her white-knuckled hold on him. "You mustn't overexert yourself, Miss Fish-Wooten."

"I feel perfectly safe under your care." She sent him a dazzling smile, then looked over her shoulder. "June, the mazurka, if you please."

With far better skill than Andrew or Frank, June struck up a smooth rendition of the dance melody. Isabel took a step back, bringing Blue with her until he had no choice but to go along. True to her hunch, he knew exactly what he was doing. And despite his stated reluctance, he was an outstanding dancer, smooth and strong and sure of himself. Dancing with him was like gliding on ice.

For a rare few minutes, she was actually rendered speechless. It was a rare experience for Isabel. When he took her in his arms, even for the impersonal purpose of a dance demonstration, she felt a flash of reaction all the way down to her toes. Isabel got the feeling she had only to surrender to him, and he would sweep her away to a place unlike any other she had visited. For a few moments, the world consisted only of the music and this man. Nothing else. She nearly forgot the youngsters watching them. She nearly forgot that, last night notwithstanding, this man disliked her and resented having her under his roof.

In fact, he seemed to forget it, too. He held her as though she were precious to him and danced with her as though making love. The intimate press of his hand into the small of her back, the movement of his thighs against hers were entirely proper on the dance floor yet felt as wicked and delicious as a private caress.

Every detail of last night's kiss came rushing back to her. Although he would not believe it about her, she had never kissed a man just for the pure, sensual joy of it. Until last night. Until then, she hadn't even realized the power in a kiss. It seemed such a simple, somewhat superfluous gesture. Yet he had turned it into something else, something quite profound. She hungered again for the taste and firm softness of his mouth, even now in a room full of nosy adolescents.

She was spellbound, carried away, and she nearly wept when the mazurka ended. Blue took over the dancing lesson then, insisting on making certain the youngsters had paid attention. Like a drill sergeant, he marched the lads and even June Li through the steps.

All of them — perhaps Lucas most particularly — seemed startled by his involvement.

Finally, he poured lemonade for everyone, serving June first.

She looked terrified and took a step back. "Oh, sir, I couldn't —"

"Nonsense. You risked bodily injury by dancing with these clods. The least we can do is give you something to drink."

Though he didn't see it, Isabel noticed admiration and appreciation blooming on Lucas's face.

Blue went to the doorway and stood to one side, demonstrating the proper way to allow a lady to precede a gentleman. Then, when they reached the dining room, he showed them the intricacies and subtleties of escorting a lady to dinner.

Isabel had been escorted to dinner by steamship captains, scoundrels and noblemen. But never had a man's controlling hand at the small of her back felt so wickedly compelling to her. Never had she felt tingles racing over her skin. Never had she wanted to linger close to a man, to let his warmth surround her. And the places he wasn't touching her tingled even more insistently than the places he was.

Struggling to look composed and sophisticated, Isabel played her part while Blue held out her chair. She kept her eyes locked to his and a gracious smile in place as she seated herself, allowing him to slide the chair in. Then she thanked him with refined and earnest gratitude.

The lads watched, then took turns escorting June to the table. The poor girl's face looked fiery with embarrassment, but pleasure danced in her eyes, too. But by far the most delightful aspect of the afternoon was the change in Lucas. Isabel could tell from the expression on his face that he was seeing an entirely new image of his father.

The happy camaraderie of the afternoon struck Isabel in a tender, unprotected spot. She caught herself daydreaming of family life, the safety and contentment it offered. It had to do with helping people, she thought, and remembered Delta's suggestion about the Rescue League. She might not be able to protect people from a deadly virus, but she could certainly teach them to dance.

Twenty-Four

Blue and Hunter Calhoun stepped into the Parker Block building, which housed the facility of the Mission Rescue League. It was the first time Blue's father had seen the new facility, and Blue was startled to feel a quick sting of nervousness. One never quite outgrew the need to please one's parents, he reflected as he led his father through the reception area, greeting workers and clients along the way. Willie Bean, his orderly, handed him two papers to sign — a death certificate and a birth certificate. In the wee hours of the morning, yet another woman intoxicated with opium had given birth to a drowsy, undersized infant. The mother's heart had stopped at approximately the same moment her son had taken his first breath.

He hurriedly scribbled his signature and handed the forms back to Willie. After the orderly departed, Blue told his father about the woman.

"I'm proud of you, son," Hunter murmured.

Blue frowned. It was the last thing he'd expected to hear. "A woman died in my care. How can you be proud?"

"You saved the life of an innocent baby. He would have died if his mother hadn't come to you."

"He'll grow up without a mother," Blue said. "What sort of life is that?"

"The one he's been given, thanks to you. Blue, I see what you're doing here and it's admirable, but the burdens will crush you if you let them."

The words lingered in Blue's mind as he headed up the stairs to the gallery overlooking the main areas of the facility. He knew of no way to explain his sense of mission to his father, nor did he believe it possible to shrug off the burdens of it. But he let the subject go. "Our new quarters have a lying-in ward and separate offices for Rory and me. We've added classrooms, and there's a small garden in the back."

Hunter's gaze traveled from the vaulted ceiling to the skylit side rooms that were virtual beehives of activity. A chorus of voices spoke English in a variety of accents, Chinese and Spanish and Norse. The Rescue League had been at this address for less than a year, but already the place was filled to the rafters. In the main office, the chief administrator interviewed a pair of bashful immigrant women in dark smocks and kerchiefs. "She'll try to find them positions as domestic help,"

Blue said. "Mrs. Swansea is a wizard at that."

"No need to convince me," said Hunter. "Over the years, she's sent a dozen workers to the ranch."

The entire Calhoun family supported Blue's work. Eliza had founded the Benevolent Aid Society in order to raise funds for the league. "I'm grateful for that," he told his father. It was not what he really wanted to say, but neither he nor Hunter even spoke directly of their bond. It was the Calhoun way, Blue supposed, to hold in the words, letting the actions speak instead. Lucas was cautious with his heart as well — that was becoming more and more apparent.

"Through those double doors is the clinic and surgery," he said, pointing. "I've taken on a young medical student. She's seeing patients on her own now."

"She?" Hunter raised an eyebrow.

"Her name is Leah Mundy."

"Another of your damsels in distress?" Hunter asked quietly.

Blue felt a twinge of defensiveness. "What do you mean?"

"You know what I mean."

There were some things, Blue reflected, about a father and son that would never change. "We employ anyone willing to work, even female medical students. There's plenty to be done."

Hunter nodded, clearly aware that Blue didn't care for the topic at hand. "Your cause is good, son. I've always believed that."

"Sometimes even Lucas helps, but his heart's not in it. He's not interested in my work here."

Hunter set his hands at his waist and rocked back on his heels. "Are you surprised?"

"No. Lately he makes it his chief occupation to contradict me. In fact, I should forbid him to set foot in the building. Then he'd be here every day." Blue caught himself thinking of the unexpected moment of connection he'd felt with Lucas during Miss Fish-Wooten's impromptu dancing lesson. Startled to see his father dancing, Lucas had regarded him with, if not affection, then admiration and surprise, at least. Blue savored that moment. It seemed so simple, but he knew it would never have happened if Isabel hadn't forced him into the awkward position of teaching the boys to dance.

"When you were his age, I did everything in my power to get you to stay at Cielito and carry on the family business," Hunter reminded him.

Blue recalled the heated quarrels, chilly silences, seething resentment that had characterized his adolescent years. Yet somehow, he didn't consider himself a contrary son. "That was different," he said. "I had a clear call to duty."

"All I saw was a young hothead who thought going to war was a way to cure boredom."

Blue took in a quick breath, startled to feel an echo of the old fight between them. "It wasn't boredom."

"You were just fifteen, the same age Lucas is now."

"I knew what I was doing. The war had been going on for four years. I'd seen veterans coming back, missing arms or legs. I knew families whose loved ones never did return. You knew them, too. So don't tell me I didn't know what I was in for." He hadn't, of course. What man who had not seen the face of battle could truly understand the meaning of war?

"You nearly quarreled me into an early grave," said his father, "and in the end, you went anyway." A distant look misted his eyes. "Hardest thing I ever had to do was take you to the train station that day."

Blue regarded his father's craggy face, his strong hands gripping the gallery rail. He'd had no idea that his departure had such an impact. The fact that Hunter had concealed his feelings spoke volumes about his strength and forbearance. Blue wondered if he could do the same when the time came for Lucas to go out into the world.

"It's different between Lucas and me," he said. "The boy's a dreamer. He doesn't know what he wants. He's nothing like I was at that age."

"I know." His father was smiling and not so distant now. "He's just like I was."

"What makes you say that?" He knew his father as a strong and focused man, devoted to his family, driven to succeed in building his dream — a horse ranch where he and Eliza could make a life of their own, far from the restrictive and insular society of Tidewater Virginia.

"I had a life before you were born. Granted, it was a haphazard, misspent life for the most part, and sometimes there was more drinking than dreaming, but it was my life nonetheless. After your mother passed, well, I only drank more and cared less. There was a wildness in me. I did some things I'm not proud of, I freely admit that."

Blue could not reconcile the sober, successful man before him with the wild Virginia youth Hunter described. He had only the vaguest memories of the murky years of his early childhood. Sometimes, in the hour between dark and dawn, he saw subtle, fleeting images of his fragile mother; his father was often gone. Then his mother had died in a fire, and a silent shadow of grief had shrouded the plantation. Until Eliza came into their lives.

Hunter was watching him with a bemused expression. "I reckon about now you're hoping I'll make my point."

"Actually, you already have."

Hunter started walking toward the opposite end of the gallery. They spoke of other things as they toured the facility together. His father appreciated the well-laid-out rooms, the efficient workers, the sense that the people who came here deserved dignity. Some of the church rescue leagues provided outstanding aid for indigents, but the benefits came along with thunderous, fire-and-brimstone lectures and fear-driven conversions. Here, the only requirement was a desire for a better life.

Watching his father's inspection, Blue could not deny a surge of pride. My first audience, he thought, eyeing the tall, vigorous man who had watched him grow from timid boy to bold youth to mature man. Hunter was the first to watch him, to care about what he did, to encourage him in his endeavors, to worry about him even when he didn't want to be worried about. It was, Blue realized, what made a man a father.

He wondered if Lucas regarded him in that way. He wondered how a man could tell whether or not he was doing a good job with his son. Isabel told him repeatedly that Lucas was a wonderful boy, and she gave Blue credit for that. She was good for him in that way, at least.

They descended another stairwell at the far end of the gallery and passed the open door of a classroom. Inside stood a portly man with a walrus mustache, speaking with a group of women who sat on benches set in rows like church pews.

"This meat is putrid," the man yelled.

"This meat is putrid," the women yelled back.

"English lessons," Blue said. "We hold class every morning, and —" A small streak burst in through the double doors leading to the courtyard, nearly barreling into Blue. He moved out of the way and the streak darted down the hall toward the washroom.

"Each woman comes with at least one child," Blue said. "Usually more. We get our fair share of orphans as well, and end up sending them to Mount St. Joseph Infant Shelter. From time to time, I considered adopting, but . . ."

"But?"

"Why would I bring a child into a home with no mother?"

He realized as soon as the words were out of his mouth that he was a sitting duck.

Hunter leaped at the opportunity. "Then marry again."

"Not interested."

"You were a good husband to Sancha. You could —"

"Please. I get enough pressure from Eliza and my sisters."

"I know. I've held my tongue for years,

waiting for you to sort things out. But now you've got a prospect. We all think Isabel is charming."

"Oh, she is charming, all right. But I'd hardly call her motherly. She travels the world alone, and I doubt she'd know the first thing to do with a child."

"Really?" Hunter was watching through the double doors, which stood open to the courtyard. Under a spreading Pacific oak, an elderly nun sat cradling a baby and watching a group of children laughing and racing after a ball. They were all shapes and sizes and colors, unified by their singular pursuit across the dusty yard. And in their midst, playing and laughing as hard as any child, was Isabel Fish-Wooten.

Only a week or so had passed since she'd made her ill-fated foray down to the waterfront, but she appeared to have recovered nicely. She sparkled. There was no other word for it. There was a special, maybe magical energy in the way her face flushed and her small, compact body moved as she captured the ball from a nimble boy.

She was entirely at ease with the youngsters, charging toward a makeshift goal. Wispy dark curls escaped her hairpins, and laughter spilled from her lips. When she was a few steps from the goal, she seized the tiniest boy and handed off the ball to him. Triumphant, he barreled across the goal line.

A cheer went up, and someone hoisted the child high. Isabel threw back her head and flung her arms around the children nearest her. She looked supremely, undeniably happy in the company of children.

Blue was thunderstruck. Here was a side to Isabel he hadn't seen before. Getting to know her was like paddling unfamiliar waters and coming across an undiscovered country. Or more likely, coming around a bend and encountering a waterfall.

Still oblivious to being watched, she led her noisy crew over to the cistern for a drink of water.

"She seems fine with children to me," Hunter murmured beside him.

"So does Sister Maria Jesus," Blue said, indicating the nun with the mustache, rocking the baby. "But I don't want her for a wife, either."

Hunter's gaze tracked Isabel as she dipped water for a talkative, breathless boy. "She's not beautiful," he said.

"No, she's not," Blue agreed readily, unable to take his eyes off her.

"But there's something about her."

Blue gritted his teeth. "She's indecently young."

"Maybe that's what it is."

"You're a lecherous old thing," Blue said. "I should warn Eliza."

"Oh, she knows about my lechery," Hunter

assured him. "It's one of her favorite things about me."

Blue didn't even want to think about that. "Look, I'm not planning to marry again. After ten years, I'm accustomed to living on my own. That's the way it's going to stay. And if I was going to marry, Isabel Fish-Wooten would be the last woman on my list."

While he spoke, she had gathered the little ones around her in the shade of the tree beside the nun. Taking a length of string, she gave a demonstration of Jacob's ladder. A girl tugged on her sleeve. "I wish you would come every day, Miss Isabel. I wish you would stay for ever."

Isabel's smile dipped at the corners. "I couldn't do that. I can only stay until the season changes."

Blue looked at his father. "I rest my case."

Waving his hand in impatience, Hunter strode outside. "What do you mean by that?" he asked her.

At the sight of Blue and Hunter, the children scrambled to attention. Isabel remained seated, her skirts spread around her like the petals of a flower. Perhaps it was the angle of light, but the color in her cheeks seemed to deepen. "Well, I was actually addressing the children, but if you must know, I never stay in one place longer than a single season." She beamed up at Blue, and her smile took hold of him. "Hello. Are you surprised to see me here?"

"You'll slow down your recovery if you keep racing about, exerting yourself."

She tilted her head to one side. "Is this the same Dr. Calhoun who declared me well and ordered me to leave? Perhaps I'll relapse and stay another week. That should please your father."

"Stay, stay," said the children.

"Out of the mouths of babes," Hunter said. "I hope you know you're expected to attend the charity ball."

She aimed a look directly at Blue. "I'd be honored."

"Take the baby, Isabel," said Sister Maria Jesus, holding out the swaddled bundle. "I've got to bring this lot in for their lunch."

"But I've never looked after such a tiny baby." Panic flickered in her eyes as the infant was settled in her arms.

"Then you are in for a treat." The nun brushed off her skirts and herded the children inside.

Isabel held the quiet, wakeful baby at arms' length, as though the child were a stick of dynamite on the verge of exploding. She looked so discomfited that Blue took pity on her and stepped forward to help. But his father put his hand on his arm. "Wait," he whispered.

The courtyard was quiet after the children

left. Faint strains of the English lesson drifted through the open window, and a breeze shimmered in the leaves.

Isabel stared at the baby, who stared back. Finally, she drew the child into her lap. Her skirt formed a sling for the small body. The baby raised a tiny hand, flailing it until Isabel held out a finger. The little fist instantly closed around it. Isabel's posture softened, and she inhaled deeply, the way people instinctively did, to catch an infant's scent. "Oh, my," she whispered. "Oh, aren't you a fine little lad."

She seemed overcome as she settled the child in the crook of one arm, wrapped the other around him and held him next to her heart. When she looked up at Blue, her cheeks gleamed wet with tears.

He was astounded. He had seen her shot by a deadly bullet, yet it took an infant to make her weep.

She wiped her face with a corner of the baby's shawl. "Forgive me," she said in a soft, wondering voice. "It's just that I've never held a baby before."

Twenty-Five

The Calhoun women insisted that Isabel come to their suite at the Excelsior Hotel to get ready for the charity ball. Initially, she hadn't planned to attend at all. She'd expected to be somewhere out in the blue Pacific, with San Francisco a misty memory behind her. But now she conceded that her stolen fortune was a lost cause, and she would have to make a new plan to repair her finances.

That was yet another nice thing about money. For someone with a bit of talent and huge amounts of determination, it was relatively easy to acquire.

She did regret the loss of her valise, though. It contained one irreplaceable item, carefully preserved in a leather folio, that had meaning only to her. It was the key to her true identity, and she kept it to remind her that the only way to escape that person was to keep moving. Now the last vestige of her past had vanished, and she had come to a place she wished she could belong.

June Li accompanied her to the hotel to

help with the costume. She felt a pleasant surge of excitement as they entered the Excelsior. She looked forward to the chatter and gossip, the perfume and primping.

As she crossed the lobby of the city's grandest hotel and passed beneath the massive skylight seven storeys up, she felt a keen sense of anticipation. This was where she thrived, this place of artifice, with arched halls and potted palms, cherubs painted on vaulted ceilings and bellboys scurrying around with luggage, flower deliveries or fussed-over small dogs on jeweled leashes. Over the years, making herself a part of this glittering, transient world had brought her no end of pleasure.

Now, as she and June rode a hydraulic elevator encased in gilded bars, she felt a sense of frustration that was new to her. This was not her world. It was her stage. She could no more be a part of it than an actor could be part of the fictional family in a burlesque review.

This subtle distinction had never bothered her before. She knew why it did now.

As she stood outside the door to the Calhoun suite, hearing the intimate murmurs and trills of laughter, she understood that she'd never truly belong anywhere. Because of the way she'd chosen to live her life, she would never be surrounded by people who knew her, who loved her, who cared what happened to her. In the past, she considered that to be a liberating asset, but lately she found herself assailed by foolish and futile yearnings.

Shaking off the mawkish notions as best she could, she decided that perhaps being shot had addled her wits. Then she squared her shoulders, stepped back and waited while the bell captain knocked and the door opened.

Beside Isabel, June took in a soft gasp of admiration. The spacious and beautiful suite of rooms was grand enough to be termed an apartment. Hand-painted wallpaper, soaring French windows draped in lush velvet and gleaming antique furnishings created a sense of luxury that surpassed even the Calhoun house.

"Good afternoon, Isabel, and welcome," said Eliza. "To you, too, June. We're so glad you're here." Taking Isabel's hand, Eliza drew her into a bedroom that exploded with feminine finery. She picked her way through a clutter of petticoats, powder puffs, sashes and flounces enough for a dozen women. A maid was busy steaming the wrinkles out of silk, and another heated curling irons on a corner stove.

"Oh, good, you're here," said Belinda. "We were a little afraid you'd changed your mind."

Isabel flushed, though she offered a self-deprecating smile. She wasn't sure whether or not the Calhouns had been informed of her failed attempt to flee. She hoped they didn't take it personally. "I can't tell you how much I appreciate being included. You're terribly generous."

"I wish you had let us find you something to wear," said Belinda.

"We know how challenging it is to keep one's gowns in order while traveling," Eliza added diplomatically.

Isabel enjoyed a moment of anticipation. "It was so kind of you to offer. But you mustn't worry. I've found just the thing." She and June unzipped the muslin garment bag. "We took the theme seriously," she explained, and pulled out a pair of Turkish trousers made of deep blue-green silk with gold piping. There was a matching gold-beaded cropped waistcoat with gauzy split sleeves and a veil to match.

"It's gorgeous," Belinda said.

"She's right. It's simply luminous," Amanda said.

"Thank you," Isabel replied. "But I take no credit at all for this. The first credit goes to Sancha Montgomery Calhoun — this was made from a dress from her collection. The dressmaking prodigy is June Li. This is her creation."

The girl blushed so deeply that Isabel made her sit down.

"You're a genius," Belinda declared, giving June's hand a squeeze. "I believe Blue mentioned that you were clever with needle and thread, but we had no idea."

"I wish we were going to be here long enough for me to order my entire wardrobe for the cruise from you," said Amanda. "When we return from our trip, I must order some gowns."

"I would be honored to sew for you," said June. Then they got down to the serious business of dressing, a process that would take a delightfully long time. Isabel surrendered her hat and gloves to June and stepped behind a folding upholstered privacy screen.

"What do you think of this jade and crystal pendant?" Belinda asked, holding a lovely piece on a black velvet ribbon over the top of the screen. "I think it will be perfect with your costume."

June helped her with the myriad fastenings of the costume. Once the ocean-colored veil was pinned in place to trail down her back, she stepped out for the final primping, preening and perfuming.

"Wicked," said Amanda.

"Is it too much?" asked Isabel.

"Heavens, too much what?" Belinda demanded. "You'll be brilliant tonight."

"The goal is to raise money for the Benevolent Aid Society," Eliza pointed out.

Isabel twirled, loving the feel of the sheer

silk swirling around her. "In that case, disguising myself as Scheherazade is bound to be useful. I will do my level best to get every hideously wealthy man present to pledge a huge amount."

"Scheherazade," said Amanda. "Isn't she the one who kept herself alive by making up stories?"

Then I should be a master at it, thought Isabel. "You've all been so good to me," she said. "I don't know how to thank you."

"We have an ulterior motive," Belinda told her.

"Do you?" Isabel offered June a shrug of bafflement.

"We want you to marry Blue," Amanda stated as matter-of-factly as one might speak of the weather.

Isabel let loose with a blithe laugh, although deep inside, she was on fire. "Do you, now? Then I shall do so right away. Is tomorrow soon enough?" She was determined to make light of the outrageous notion.

They smiled at her pleasantly enough but were clearly not going to let her off the hook. "I realize you haven't known him long," said Eliza, "but we're hoping you will take the time to learn who he is."

The futility of their mission was so clear to Isabel that she couldn't decide whether to laugh or cry. "Do you do this often?"

Amanda, who was as guileless as a spring

lamb, puckered her brow in a frown. "Do what?"

"Hunt down unattached women and parade them in front of your brother?"

"Why, no," said Belinda. "Of course not. You're the first."

"Then I suppose I should feel honored, but the truth is, I'm simply not interested in marrying anyone."

June Li crouched down to tie the trousers into soft gathers at her ankles. The girl was obviously memorizing every word of this absurd conversation and would no doubt share it with the entire household. Eventually it would get back to Blue himself. He would undoubtedly find it as preposterous as she did.

The Calhoun women watched her with compassion and hope in their eyes.

"Ladies," she said, feeling slightly desperate, "I admire your loyalty to Blue — Dr. Calhoun — but I'm afraid I can't be . . . what you want me to be." She was surprised to feel how close her feelings edged to fear. Dear God, *fear*. That was it. That was why she lashed out. It scared her, how much she wanted to do exactly as they suggested. "Perhaps I had better leave."

"I wish you wouldn't," said Eliza. "Please." Her quiet maturity, along with a gentle hand on the shoulder, had a calming effect on Isabel.

She resisted the kindness she saw in those eyes. "Please. I know you love him. I know you want him to move beyond the tragedies he's endured. But I have my own life to live. My own path to travel. I can't make him get over the past."

"It's not so much a matter of getting over the past as needing someone now," Amanda said with a wisdom beyond her years. "Look how he is with you, Isabel. He's a different person when he's taking care of you."

"If you think he needs someone to look after, get him a puppy."

"Don't you think if that was the answer, we would have thought of it years ago?" Belinda paced in agitation. Blond and queenly, she showed a temper that matched or even surpassed Isabel's. "You have to understand, you're the first."

"The first what? The first woman to be shot in the back and rescued by him?"

"Heavens, no," said Amanda. "Women adore him, whether or not they get shot. He could have a different lover each season if he chose."

"But you're different from most women," Belinda explained, clasping the ribbon with the jade pendant around Isabel's neck.

"How do you mean?"

"You don't need him as much as he doesn't need you."

The twisted logic nearly made her laugh,

except that she didn't feel like laughing. The truth was, she didn't need anyone. She never had. She was certainly not about to begin now. Yet the terrible regrets that crept through her made her wish that love was within her reach.

"Well, that's very interesting," she said. "You seem to know a lot about me."

"One senses these things," said Eliza.

"We've seen, over and over, how simply being needed is not the answer," Belinda said. "It's a prison, needing someone. Being needed. That's not the answer for my brother."

Isabel was fascinated. "You mean I'm different because he doesn't need me?"

"Exactly." Belinda clapped her hands. "He doesn't even like you. That's why you're so perfect for him."

"So he neither needs me nor likes me, and that's why you think we're perfect together?"

"Indeed. Because that means he wants you. He can't help himself. Oh, it's so wonderful when that happens."

"Oh, for heaven's sake. Why?"

"Because it's a sure sign of true love. When you want someone in spite of yourself, when you want him even though you know he's all wrong for you and you know he will change your life, then it must mean love."

"Or stupidity," Amanda said.

Eliza looked sharply at Belinda. "Are you

talking about Isabel or yourself?"

Belinda blushed even as she lifted her chin in regal disdain. "Isabel, of course. She has a perfect life of travel and adventure. Loving Blue could change all that forever, and that frightens her. And being scared makes her angry and defensive."

"But it doesn't make her want him less." Amanda touched Isabel's hand. "Nevertheless, I feel I owe you an apology. I was rude and presumptuous to tell you we want you to marry Blue."

"We just want you to have a wonderful time tonight." Eliza smiled at Isabel with such warmth that it felt like an embrace.

"I think I can manage that," said Isabel. "About the other . . ."

"About loving Blue?"

She flushed. "I really don't think I can do much about that." After being with him and feeling for the first time in her life that her heart could be touched, she was starting to doubt herself. Initially, she thought she had finally discovered what love meant. But now, observing his family and seeing the far-reaching, all-consuming expectations in the eyes of these women, Isabel knew she was only at the beginning of her discoveries.

Love was not simple. It was not just one uncomplicated matter. It was a whole huge, unseen world unto itself. She had sailed the seven seas, had traveled across the vast continents, had seen wonders of both nature and man, had kissed the ring of a bishop and had broken bread with Wild Bill Hickcock. But she had never realized that another universe existed, invisible to some people yet wholly real to those who knew what it was to love and be loved by another.

Seeing nature's marvels was as simple as boarding a steamship or train. Seeing the world inhabited by those who understood the meaning of love from the inside out was a different matter altogether. It was a puzzle whose secrets she had not yet unlocked: dark, mysterious, forbidding in some aspects.

Meeting Blue and Lucas, and now the rest of the Calhoun family, had given her a glimpse into that life, but just a glimpse. It was frustrating, because she saw it in flashes she couldn't control, a beautiful dream that evaporates upon waking.

"I think there's plenty you can do about the situation between you and my brother," Belinda said. "You just have to decide to do it."

The weight of their expectations sat like a rock on her chest. They didn't care about her, she thought resentfully. They only cared about Blue, so much that they would do anything, go to any lengths to assure his happiness.

And that, she supposed, forgiving them before she even accused them, was what love did to people.

She conceded the battle, thankful for their friendship, however fleeting. She stood up and turned in a slow circle. "How do I look?"

Twenty-Six

In the gilded ballroom of the Excelsior Hotel, Blue dropped his drink on the floor. His companion, Clarice Hatcher, gave a little shriek and stepped back.

"Theodore," she snapped, "how clumsy of you. You've spilled whiskey all over the hem of my dress."

"Sorry," he muttered. It took an almost physical effort to tear his gaze from the arched doorway, where Isabel stood. She was an exotic vision in blue-green silk, a translucent veil obscuring the lower half of her face, bangles clinking lightly from her ankles and wrists, a shocking hint of bare skin showing at her waist. He summoned a waiter to clean up the spilled drink, but his mind was filled with images of her. Her arrival had been heralded by a general hush in the crowded room, followed by a hectic buzz of conversation. "You'll want to call for your maid," he said to Clarice.

"No need," she said, shedding her temper and slipping her arm through his, suddenly companionable again. "The damage is minimal. The carpet absorbed the spill."

"Indeed, but you should check to see if it ruined your dancing slippers."

She laughed, the sound like a brass bell. "You don't dance anyway, Theodore, so I needn't miss a moment of the party for the sake of my slippers."

He barely heard. He could no longer pretend to pay attention to her. Though he fought it, his gaze was drawn to Isabel.

There was something different about her. It was not just the costume of silken veils; nor was it the way she wore her hair. Her appeal had little to do with the lavish costume. No, it was deeper than that. It was the charm in the way she held herself — the tilt of her head and the rhythm of her slow descent down the stairs, the gemstone brilliance of her shining eyes as she greeted people, the genuine warmth in her voice when she spoke.

Here again was an Isabel he hadn't seen before, not the secretive outlaw barging into his life nor the charming guest making friends with his hired help, nor the compassionate woman looking after children at the Rescue League. This Isabel was simply mesmerizing.

Eliza and his sisters had been interfering again, he thought, watching Isabel unhook her veil in order to sip from a glass of champagne. He recognized the jewel she wore on a ribbon around her throat. Clearly they had been working on her.

"Who is that strange woman you're staring at, Theodore?" Clarice asked, jarring him.

"A . . . former patient," he said. It felt odd to have to define her. She was so much more, so much he didn't want to admit. And she was walking directly toward him, a dazzling smile on her face.

God, she knew, he thought. She was aware of how she looked tonight. She had been transformed into a glistening vision out of a dream, and she seemed intent on using her powers to the fullest.

He was not the only man in the room to notice the way she shone. As she moved across the room, they gravitated toward her. Clarice's hand pressed into his arm. "I wasn't aware you'd adopted a habit of bringing your ailing patients to private social functions. Good lord, I hope she's not contagious."

"I didn't bring her, and she's no longer ailing, as you can see."

The dainty hand pressed harder. "We can all see that, Theodore. Well, since you're acquainted with the creature, it would only be polite to introduce me to her."

"Of course."

They skirted the periphery of the ballroom, making way for dancing couples and groups of patrons posturing for each other. His stepmother and sisters had outdone themselves this year in planning the event. The huge room had been transformed into a Persian

Kingdom, the walls hung with silken swags, the orchestra conductor garbed in a robe and burnoose, the buffet tables laden with Middle Eastern delights — dates stuffed with pistachios, small triangular tarts filled with spiced meat, lemons preserved in salt.

Most of the ladies had entered into the spirit of the event, wearing stylized veils and Turkish trousers, bells around their ankles and slippers turned up at the toes. Clarice wore a voluminous costume in white and royal blue, but her garb lacked the graceful gleam of Isabel's turquoise silks.

Isabel turned toward him, as though sensing his presence like an invisible electrical current in the air. Her gaze took him in with a grand sweep. The smile that lit her face made him forget to exhale.

"Dr. Calhoun," she said, closing the distance between them.

He let out his breath in a rush, feeling a prickle of irritation. "Miss Fish-Wooten, I'd like you to meet Mrs. Clarice Hatcher," he heard himself say.

"How do you do, Mrs. Hatcher?" said Isabel with a gracious curtsy. When she looked up at the tall woman, she held her head tilted to one side. "I beg your pardon, but have we met? Your name sounds familiar to me."

"My late husband was famous for his collection of rare wines and antique weapons," said Clarice. "Perhaps you heard his name in that capacity."

"No." Isabel pursed her lips. "That's not it." Her eyebrows shot up. "Tell me, do you do business with the Far East Tea Company?"

Clarice tilted her head to one side and regarded her with a slightly patronizing smile. "I have never heard of the outfit. And I certainly don't do business of any sort. I am a widow. A respectable widow. But I take it you are a woman of commerce?" She made it sound like a social disease.

As always, Isabel evaded any question that would require her to disclose personal information. "That's odd," she commented, "I have a good memory for names, and I would swear I've heard yours before."

Blue was half amused, half alarmed. The two women circled each other with the wary dislike of rival hens.

"I'm sure you've confused me with someone else."

"Oh, I rarely confuse such things. For example, I'm certain I didn't see your name on the Patrons' list. Have you pledged a donation yet, Mrs. Hatcher?"

"As a matter of fact, I plan to make a generous one. Enough to buy my way out of trouble with Theodore." She tapped him playfully on the arm, then gestured at the arched entryway of the ballroom. "Oh, look,

Theodore, it's Lydia Stanford and her new beau. We should go and greet them. I haven't seen Lydia since the benefit for Mercy Heights. And will we be seeing Dr. and Mrs. Vickery tonight?"

"They've sent their regrets. Mrs. Vickery is unwell."

"A pity. Then we must surely visit with the Coopers, too. Mrs. Cooper is one of my dearest friends, so I'm sure Miss Fish-Wooten will excuse us."

Blue watched Isabel, who watched Clarice with amused tolerance. "How fortunate that you're acquainted with all the city's finest people," said Isabel. "Why, it reminds me of a conversation I had last year with Prince Rupert. He pointed out that it's a blessing indeed to be provincial enough to meet one's neighbors."

"Prince Rupert?" Clarice's eyebrows arched in skepticism.

"Regent of Prussia. I met him in Saratoga Springs, and he's desperately lonely. He would find your local social scene quite enviable, I'm sure. It's like living in a tiny provincial town."

"I'd hardly call San Francisco provincial," Clarice said, her smile tightening at the edges.

Across the room, Blue caught Rory's eye and sent him a look of desperation. As one of the few men game enough to wear a costume, Rory looked absurd in sheik's robes

353

and burnoose, yet women couldn't seem to get enough of him.

Rory detached himself from a group of admirers and strolled to the rescue. "Clarice," he said, bending gallantly over her hand. "Charming as ever, I see." He did the same to Isabel and added, "May I steal you away for a dance?"

Isabel sent Blue a triumphant look. "I'd be honored." She and Rory walked together to the dance floor.

". . . can't imagine how she made the acquaintance of a prince, for goodness sake." Clarice was bristling as she offered all sorts of speculation about Miss Fish-Wooten.

But Blue had already drifted miles away, although he still felt her hand on his arm, heard her voice in his ear. He couldn't manage to shake loose of the things his father had said to him that day at the Rescue League. It had been an extraordinary and unwelcome conversation. What was it about Isabel that made Hunter Calhoun feel compelled to advise his son on matters of the heart? Why her, of all the infernal women?

"Shall we dance?" he suggested, suddenly eager to do something with the restless energy surging through him.

Clarice all but dropped her jaw on the floor. "You don't dance."

He forced a grin. "Then maybe it's time I started."

He wasn't sure what he was doing. Why dance with her at all? Because, he told himself, she was a familiar, substantial woman who would anchor him firmly to reality. And reality for him was work that never ended, a son who was a stranger, a life that was the same, year after year.

As they danced a waltz together, he saw Lucas at the end of the ballroom, working the gaming table for a group of overdressed women.

"Your son looks frightfully bored," said Clarice.

"I agree." But Blue refused to feel guilty for imposing the sentence on Lucas.

"He'll be leaving for university in the fall, will he not? That's good. Then you'll be free to have a life of your own." She gazed up at him with frank expectancy.

"My life has always been my own," he replied, deliberately misunderstanding her.

After a turn around the dance floor, he escaped from Clarice. Standing in the white glare of an electrical wall sconce, he noticed that Isabel had switched partners. She did so for dance after dance, each time the music changed. The men she danced with were among the wealthiest and best known patrons in the city — Mr. Ghirardelli's dashing son, and Mr. Langley, whose fortune was in vineyards, and Simon Haight, who danced like a master.

Good for her, thought Blue. Maybe she actually would find herself a millionaire. The sooner, the better. Yet deep down, he knew she wouldn't marry for money, no matter how she joked about it. He caught himself thinking about the way he'd felt when he discovered Isabel was gone. She'd left a hole in his life. Then he thought about why he went after her that night and remembered the kiss they'd shared later. The memory sent him straight for the bar.

Eliza found him knocking back a glass of whiskey. He recognized the firm set of his stepmother's chin and the determination in her eyes.

"Not you, too," he muttered, bending to place an affectionate kiss on her cheek.

"So distrustful," she said, setting down a plate of boiled prawns. "I simply came over to let you know we've officially doubled the amount of donations since last year."

"You're remarkable," he said. A long-held tension inside him uncoiled; no longer did he have to wonder where he would come up with the money to pay for the latest shipment of imported medicines.

"I didn't do it alone," Eliza said. "Belinda was in charge this year. You owe a debt of thanks to your sister for expanding the guest list. And to Isabel, of course."

"Why her? She's done nothing but dance with every grossly wealthy man in the room, batting her eyelashes and then moving on to the next victim."

Eliza laughed. "Heavens, what do you think she's been doing all evening?"

Dancing with everyone but me, he thought.

"Do you think she's entertaining herself, waltzing around the room with seventy-year-old lechers?"

He spied Isabel on the dance floor just as she tipped back her head and laughed in delight at her spellbound, gray-bearded partner. "Apparently so."

"Don't be a clod, Blue. She's soliciting donations in larger amounts than we'd ever dreamed. She has persuaded each of her dance partners to increase his pledge."

He nearly choked with surprise. This was the last thing he'd expected — Isabel Fish-Wooten working on behalf of the poor. He felt a twinge of shame for thinking the worst of her. "I'll be certain to thank her."

"Don't look so flabbergasted," Eliza chided him.

"Everything she does surprises me," he admitted.

"You say that as though it's a problem." Eliza handed him a peeled prawn, which he ate while watching Isabel waltz with the chairman of the Wells Fargo Company.

"I don't like surprises." He sounded more gruff than he'd intended. "Look, Eliza. I appreciate your concern. I always have. But after so many years, I don't understand why you've suddenly taken it into your head to embark on a campaign to marry me off."

"Well, up until now, you hadn't met the right person. Isabel has changed all that. Life is filled with many loves, Blue. Those who claim to love but once are being willfully blind."

"As I explained to my father, she's entirely inappropriate."

"Nonsense. When did you turn into such a snob, Blue?"

"It's not a question of being snobbish. We don't suit. It's as simple as that. She's completely impossible. Lord only knows if she actually is who she says she is. She hides more than she surrenders."

Eliza offered him another prawn. "She's in love with you."

He gave a harsh laugh. "That's preposterous."

"Let me tell you something, Theodore Bluett Calhoun."

"Don't you have guests to attend to?"

"This is more important. I've never said this to you before but it's time someone explained certain fundamental facts. And the fact is, you and Sancha were an easy match. Perhaps too easy."

He bit the prawn in half. "What the devil do you mean by that?"

"You grew up side-by-side at neighboring

ranches by the sea. Both families were friends. The Montgomerys adored you. Sancha was stunningly beautiful, and she wanted nothing more out of life than to love you and to be your wife."

Eliza's statement brought back memories so sweet he nearly winced from the sharpness. "Yet according to you, it was a mistake," he observed.

"I never said that. Never think I don't honor the years you had with Sancha. I simply said it was easy. She was easy to love. She was gentle and uncomplicated and had no ambitions beyond pleasing you. Loving her came as easily to you as breathing. Your first marriage was a blessing, Blue. Truly it was a gift. But you never learned how to fight for love. And that has kept you frozen, unable to move on. In a curious way, it left you crippled."

He grabbed another prawn and ripped its head off. "Crippled."

"I don't mean to be unflattering, but you came away from that marriage with a distorted sense of what love is. Your time with Sancha gave you the impression that it is, and always should be, an easy prospect."

"Of course it's easy, once you find the right person."

"That's not so. Look at your father and me." She offered a slightly mysterious smile. "You probably don't recall how different we were when we first met, how desperately we fought to keep from falling in love."

He didn't recall a struggle. But then, he'd been a lad with troubles of his own and had taken little interest in his father's life.

"He was the son of the most important plantation owner in the county. I was an orphan living on a barrier island. We barely spoke the same language. Love wasn't easy for us. It was — to use your word — impossible. But when we finally found a way to be together, our bond was that much more powerful for having been tested."

She took the prawn from him. "That's quite enough."

"I do appreciate your concern, but I don't see the point of loving someone as inconstant and unpredictable as Isabel," he said. "She's determined to leave."

"Then go with her."

"You realize you're the only person in the known world who is allowed to talk to me like this."

She touched his hand. "Dear Blue. You've never intentionally hurt a single creature in your life. But seeing you like this, so lost and lonely, for so long, hurts everyone who loves you. And now something wonderful has happened. A person has walked into your life who could change everything. But she's not going to make it easy. You might have to fight for her, Blue. And the hardest fight of all is going to be with yourself." She gave his hand a squeeze, then stepped back. "Heavens, look at me. I've made myself cry."

He handed her his handkerchief. "I can't make any promises. But in the matter of Isabel . . . I'll think about what you said."

"I have a better idea. Don't think. Just follow your heart."

Even if that led to perdition? he wondered. He didn't quite feel like himself as he crossed the crowded dance floor. A piece had just ended, and people were milling about in search of partners for the next number. He encountered Clarice, who regarded him curiously. "Have you lost something, Theodore?"

My common sense, he thought, sending her a cordial smile. "I'm fine, thank you," he said, giving her a gentle shove in the direction of the gentleman partnering her. Then he moved on.

Isabel was like some exotic flower blooming in a formal garden. Slender and supple, she moved like a blossom in a breeze as she conversed with a dignified couple Blue didn't recognize. With her shining eyes and lovely smile, she drew in her listeners as she told one of her improbable stories. She spun tales out of thin air and people believed the things she said.

That was part of her mystery, he thought. Part of her allure.

"Miss Fish-Wooten," he said, bowing. "May I have this dance?"

She stared at him in astonishment. "No. I've already promised it to Mr. Florian. He's right here on my dance card."

"To hell with the dance card." The orchestra played the opening strains of a waltz. Blue felt hot. His pulse was accelerated, his head light. From the corner of his eye, he saw Anthony Florian, the portly owner of a prosperous bottling company, approaching them.

"She's taken," he said in a low voice.

"By me," Florian said, trying to shoulder past Blue.

"I don't think so."

Florian must have recognized the threat in his voice and stance. He stepped back, palms out. "I'm not looking to quarrel with anyone tonight."

"Then you'll excuse yourself now."

As Florian walked away, Blue turned to Isabel.

"You just did yourself out of a five-hundred-dollar donation," she said.

"I don't care."

"Such an impressive display of male aggression," she said, her eyes laughing at him. "Tell me, is that only the beginning of the evening's entertainment?" She was heaven in his arms, sturdy and soft all at once.

"Would you rather be dancing with him?"

"Truthfully, no. But I'm curious. You claim you never dance. I practically had to force you when we were giving lessons to Lucas. What changed your mind?"

"I wanted to hold you again," he said simply, and nearly laughed at her astonished expression.

Twenty-Seven

Sarah Jean Swansea had the world's sweatiest hands. Or so it seemed to Lucas as he partnered her in a dance he privately termed "the waltz that never ends." She also had a fantastically big bosom, which had attracted his attention in the first place. Unfortunately, she kept her best feature well-armored in ruffles and lace, and probably a lot of fancy underpinnings of steel and whalebone. When they were younger, he and Frank used to sneak into his mother's dressing room and study the mysterious trappings of female undergarments, which were almost medieval in construction. At any rate, holding Sarah Jean during the waltz was not nearly as interesting as he'd hoped it might be.

It was only slightly more interesting than working the gaming tables with old ladies who wore too much perfume. He'd escaped after an hour of that, but he hadn't been quick enough to elude Sarah Jean.

"Gladys Portman said you've been working at St. Mary's this summer." Sarah Jean seemed determined to make conversation. She resembled a handmade doll, with plump cheeks and pink lips, curly yellow hair and round eyes the color of Delft china.

"Oh. Um, yes, that's true."

"I think that's ever so admirable." She smiled at him, and her bosom pushed a little closer for a moment.

"Don't admire me for it," Lucas blurted out. "I was caught stealing communion wine and sentenced to labor for Father Jock."

"Goodness." She blinked as though she had something stuck in her eye. "Well, then, I can admire you for accepting the penance. Not every man is big enough to do that."

Not only were her hands clammy, Lucas realized, they were cold.

This was a bad idea, he thought, stretching his lips into a smile. Attending his grandparents' charity ball had seemed a grown-up, sophisticated thing to do, but the actual event was a disappointment.

He scanned the ballroom for his friends, Andrew and Frank. Andrew was sampling the rum punch again and swaying a little on his feet. Frank was dancing with Lizzie Mae Watkins, who was even blonder and plumper than Sarah Jean. They caught each other's eye, and Frank grinned, clearly happier with the situation than Lucas was.

"Who is that woman dancing with your father?" Sarah Jean asked him.

Still unused to the novelty of seeing his

father dancing, Lucas craned his neck around to see. He felt a funny lurch in his gut when he saw them together, his father and Miss Isabel. It was like opening a door in a familiar house and seeing a whole new room he didn't know existed.

His father — driven, difficult, impossible to please . . . beloved. Lucas was always confused when it came to his father. When he was younger, he'd seen it as his mission to keep Father happy. Somewhere along the way, he realized he had no power to do so. That was when he had stopped trying.

"Her name is Miss Isabel Fish-Wooten," he said to Sarah Jean. "She's from England."

"She is quite dashing. And your father's so taken with her."

"How do you know that?"

She giggled, and her bosoms shuddered against him. "It's obvious, silly. He can't take his eyes off her."

Sarah Jean was right. He had never seen his father look like this. He was almost . . . happy. And finally, with that observation, Lucas understood what the feeling in his gut was. Hope. He wanted this for his father. He wanted this for himself. He wanted the happiness back.

His father thought Lucas couldn't remember the time before his mother had died, but Lucas could. He knew he saw it through the distorted filter of a small child's vision, but the memories of his mother were vivid and real to him. He remembered the way they had been as a family. He remembered the sound of laughter and the comforting satisfaction of shared pleasures. He remembered the way his father used to gather both Lucas and his mother in his arms. He would roar like a bear and squeeze hard until Mama laughed and Lucas shrieked with delight. After Mama died, his father still hugged him sometimes, but he never roared and he never squeezed hard. Instead, he held his son carefully, as though Lucas were made of glass.

Now that Isabel had come into their lives, Lucas saw glimpses of happiness in his father, like flashes of light in a mirror or like shooting stars. If you blinked, you missed them.

But Sarah Jean's remark meant that he wasn't the only one who had noticed the change. Just for making that observation, Lucas liked her — a little.

"She's rather young, isn't she?" asked Sarah Jean.

Lucas's esteem for her slipped. "I wouldn't know."

"Well, if she snags your father, she'll have succeeded where half the women of San Francisco have failed."

He suddenly didn't want to be talking about his father. He didn't want to be dancing with Sarah Jean Swansea, with her clammy hands and blue button eyes. Playing a game with himself, he decided to hold his breath until the end of the waltz, just to see if he could.

He fixed a bland smile on his face and stopped breathing. Sarah Jean kept talking, but he could only hear the pounding of blood in his ears, like the sound of the waves over rocks on the beach at Cielito. Sarah Jean tipped back her head and laughed as though he'd just said something enormously clever.

But he said nothing, didn't allow himself to breathe. The thought of his mother's death had a familiar effect on him — a mixture of confusion and guilt and grief. He could not recall the exact moment of her death. What had he been doing? Where had he been? He'd asked about the incident many times, but Father would say only that in the confusion of the skirmish, no one could be certain who was where. Delta and Efrena always said the same thing, too. Yet he had such vivid images racing through his head. As if he were a small boy again, he could hear an angry whine followed by a wet slap. He remembered the smells of burning and blood and, incongruously, pickles. Screams grinding in his ears. And pressing on top of him, a blanket of softly tanned leather. He had been in the thick of battle. He was sure of it. But Father would never explain that day to him.

It was taking longer than he thought for the dance to end. He could feel his pulse in the tips of his fingers and behind his eyes, and the breath trapped in his lungs clamored to get out. Determinedly, and for no good reason other than sheer stubbornness, he continued to hold his breath.

His gaze wandered to the lower gallery, where servants, maids and footmen milled about, listening for their coded summonses from the bells mounted on the wall. From the corner of his eye, he caught a glimpse of raven hair, a yellow gown. June Li.

The breath exploded from him in a roar.

Sarah Jean Swansea gave a little shriek and jumped back, slamming into the gentleman behind her. Nearby dancers skittered away like water drops on a hot skillet.

"Are you all right?" Sarah Jean asked.

"Yes." His gaze searched the crowd like a hunter through overgrown weeds. There. She'd moved to the gallery rail to watch the dancing. "Will you excuse me?" Without waiting for an answer, he led her to the fringed and upholstered benches lining the wall and left her with Andrew. He hoped his haste to leave her was neither apparent nor insulting. But actually, he didn't much care.

He headed straight for the crowded servants' gallery. They stepped aside with a deference that made him feel like an interloper. June stood like a dark flower among all the maids and footmen. Her mouth formed a little O of surprise when she saw him, but she didn't say a word as he grabbed her hand. Ignoring the curious glances, he led her out a side door to a colonnaded loggia that ran the length of the building.

A row of torches along the figured concrete railing burned in the summer night. The golden flames illuminated a formal garden and a view of Telegraph Hill, where an observatory had just been built. In the distance, the bay glistened under the stars.

Lucas looked left and right to be certain they were alone. A hot feeling prickled across his skin, and he felt the way he always felt around her — like the emperor of the entire world, like a tongue-tied idiot.

"Someone might see us," she whispered, craning her neck to see toward the door.

She was right. They were seen. Mrs. Hatcher's footman, a lean Irishman nearly seven feet tall, sauntered into the pathway. His companion, a Chinese man with a long, thin mustache, leaned over and whispered something to him.

A subtle chill of warning stung Lucas. "Ignore them," he said. "Just keep walking."

No such luck, of course. The Irish giant blocked the way. "Where are you going with the China girl?" he asked in a rough brogue.

"That's none of your business," said Lucas. "But I'll make it mine, if you want."

June put her hand on his arm. "Don't provoke them. I beg you."

Lucas glared at the Irishman, who towered a full head taller. Size was no object. If the son of a bitch bothered June, Lucas would flatten him. "Excuse us," he said.

The Irishman grinned and grabbed a fistful of Lucas's shirt, just under his chin. "What's that, little man?"

June spoke up in Chinese, sounding calm but speaking rapidly. The man with the mustache stepped between them, prying Lucas's shirt out of the Irishman's hand and pushing the two of them apart.

"You shoulda said you were a Calhoun," the giant said. "Don't always do things the hard way, little man." He and the Chinese man headed back inside.

Lucas's heart hammered in his chest. June touched his hand. He wanted to hold her close, to whisper that everything was all right. Instead, he squeezed her hand. "Do you know that fellow?"

"A little. I've seen him at the joss house."

"Did they scare you?"

"Yes. Bullies always scare me."

Her honesty touched him. "I'm sorry that happened, June. I wish I could have stopped it."

"You did stop it."

"No, I didn't. The fact that I'm a Calhoun stopped it. That's not good enough, June.

371

What good is a world that won't let us be to-gether?"

"It's the only world we know," she pointed out gently.

"It's not right," he said. "After I finish at West Point and serve in the army, I'll run for office and change things."

She smiled at him, admiration glowing in her eyes. "I believe you'll change the world, Lucas."

He felt like hugging her, but couldn't figure out how. "I will," he said. "I swear I will."

"Have you told your father about West Point yet?"

He didn't even want to think about that, so he didn't answer. He took her hand and led her to the shadowed garden adjacent to the hotel property, which was terraced into the side of the hill behind the massive building. Unlike Sarah Jean, June had soft, warm hands that weren't clammy at all. The garden pavers became their dance floor, and he boldly took her in his arms.

"Lucas!"

"It's just a dance," he said. "Remember, the way we learned from Miss Isabel." They danced until the music stopped, and he wanted to laugh with the joy of holding her.

He brought her to a curved garden bench set beneath the blooming hedge. From here, they had an even better view of the bay.

Ships too many to count outlined the wharves or lay anchored out in the water. Their lights twinkled like water-borne stars.

He turned to her on the bench, feeling more nervous and happy than ever. "I didn't know you would be here," he said.

She offered her special smile, the one that was both bashful and wise, the one he saw when he closed his eyes and thought of her. "Miss Isabel brought me along to help with her costume." He thought she was probably blushing, but he couldn't be certain because of the darkness. "She says I have a special talent with the needle."

"Of course you do."

She laughed softly, a bird warbling. "You wouldn't know."

"But Miss Isabel would."

"She says I am a fine seamstress, but I would be an even better designer. She believes I should learn the art of dressmaking."

"She's the first woman my father has danced with since my mother died," he admitted. June had that effect on him. She made him feel he could say anything.

"I hope she will make him a happy man," said June.

"I hope so, too." He realized that he meant it. He really did. Finally someone had come along who was seeking out the dark places inside his father, the places Lucas was forbidden to go. He could tell Father was trying

373

to keep her away, but she was fearless and persistent. He admired her tenacity.

"Your aunts and grandmother think she should marry your father."

Lucas's eyes bugged out. "They do?"

"That's what they said."

His father. Married to Isabel. It was too amazing to contemplate.

"Lucas? Would that upset you?"

"I think it would be perfect." His answer was swift and sure.

"I sometimes wish my mother would marry, too. But she never will."

"Don't be too sure of it. Look at my father. You never can tell."

They sat quietly together, listening to strains of music from the ballroom.

"The party is a big success, yes?" June said after a while.

"According to my grandfather, it is." He inhaled the phantom scent of flowers and inched closer to her on the bench. "But I'd rather be out here, with you."

She turned slightly, and her knees bumped his. He studied every aspect of her. He could not take his eyes off her. "June Li —"

"Yes?"

"I'm trying to find the right way to tell you something, but I'm afraid the words will come out wrong."

"Then just tell the truth." She tipped her head to one side. Her straight black hair fell in a glossy curtain, inches from his shoulder.

He couldn't help himself. He ran his fingers through her hair. Like silk. Thick black silk.

She made a startled sound but didn't pull away.

"June Li," he said, fumbling for words. "You are so beautiful. You're the prettiest thing I've ever seen."

She shut her eyes. The smile that suffused her face showed him how inadequate his words were.

He captured her hands in his. "I think about you all the time," he said.

With slow deliberation, she opened her eyes. "And what is it that you think?"

"Everything. I think of everything about you. The sound of your laughter. The way your hair smells. Your soft skin." Feeling reckless, he slipped his arm behind her and pulled her close. She gasped, but didn't pull away. In fact, maybe she leaned a little closer to him.

Bolder than ever, he said, "I think about how your lips would taste. I think about that all the time."

She made a funny sound that came from her chest or throat. He had never heard the sound before but the sentiment it expressed was completely familiar to him. He recognized the yearning and frustration and, finally, the surrender.

Before he lost his nerve, he leaned forward and kissed her. Their noses bumped clumsily and their lips failed to come together in exactly the right place. A familiar disappointment sank down through him.

But then something happened. He stopped thinking about doing it right. He stopped thinking about anything at all. He simply kissed her. He cupped her face, her beautiful flower of a face, between his hands and gently pressed his lips to hers, tasting and feeling everything.

Heated explosions went off inside him. He nearly shook to keep himself from smothering her with all of his wanting. Holding her was like holding a moonbeam. She was that beautiful and that mysterious. She tasted like spice, like a flower, like dreams.

Twenty-Eight

"Be careful, Dr. Calhoun," said Isabel, following him outside to the loggia with two cups of champagne punch. "Someone might mistake that expression on your face for a smile."

He turned to her, and her heart lifted. Heavens, but he was the handsomest of men. His broad shoulders were outlined against the backdrop of the glittering city, his hair slightly mussed by the breeze, his cravat loose, his collar lying open to the summer heat. And she had not been imagining the slight smile. It belonged more to his eyes than to his lips; in the torchlit facets of his eyes she detected slivers of amusement and quiet delight.

She knew him well enough to know those were rare commodities in Blue Calhoun. Rarer still was the notion that she had something to do with his mood. That was far more intoxicating than champagne punch.

"So tell me why you're looking so happy after offending one of the richest men in the city," she said, handing him a cup.

Keeping his eyes on her, he touched the rim of his glass to hers. The soft clink punctuated a moment of connection so intense that she forgot the question she'd just asked.

"We don't need Florian's donation. We've raised enough money to cover our operating budget for the year," he said, then lifted the cup to his lips.

Though he was in many ways still a stranger to her, she understood this man. Sometimes, like now, the things he didn't say held greater significance than the things he said aloud. She took a drink, finding the punch pleasant but a bit too sweet. "Congratulations."

"It's my family's doing."

"They did it for you."

"The benefit is for the Rescue League."

"They did it to make you happy. You see, I don't believe you allow yourself to be happy simply as a matter of course. You always seem to need a plausible excuse for happiness."

"Ah. You've been reading Dr. Freud again."

" 'What we call happiness in the strictest sense comes from the satisfaction of needs which have been dammed up to a high degree,' " she quoted. "Yes, I've been raiding your library. Sometimes he makes perfect sense."

"But not always?"

"Heavens, no. His thoughts about women are simply preposterous. He really has no understanding at all of our sex," she said. "No wonder there are so few truly happy wives."

Repressed laughter gleamed in his eyes. "So tell me, Dr. Fish-Wooten, what makes a wife happy?"

She gazed up at him, charmed but a little skeptical. Could he be flirting with her? Blue Calhoun? She touched her tongue briefly to her bottom lip, tasting a lingering drop of too-sweet punch and remembering the time he'd kissed her. She wondered if he could see the memory of that kiss in her eyes.

"To be honest, I am no expert on women," she whispered, still watching him. They weren't touching, yet she could feel a peculiar warmth thrumming invisibly between them. "I can only speak for myself."

"Then do."

She watched the way the night wind toyed with a lock of his hair. "I forgot the question."

"It's the one that has puzzled even the most brilliant minds for centuries. What pleases women? What pleases *you?*"

"In general, or right now?"

"Both."

She broke the stare holding them spellbound and turned away. She went to the balustrade and stood looking out at the black-

and-gold night world of the city, the sea and the stars. Above her head, a torch flame snapped in the breeze. "If I told you that, my air of mystery would be gone."

"That's the idea," he said.

She felt him come up behind her. He didn't touch her or even press close, but she felt that phantom warmth again, that burn of anticipation. She turned, drew a breath with an audible gasp. He took a step closer, all but trapping her between the railing and his tall form.

She kept thinking about dancing with him earlier and how it had been much more than a dance.

And this, she realized with a warm shiver, was much more than a conversation.

A low murmur of voices and laughter drifted from the opposite end of the long, colonnaded porch, reminding her that they were not quite alone. She slipped away from him, catching her breath as her full skirts whispered across his legs. He was not even touching her, yet his nearness felt as scandalous and evocative as an intimate caress.

Turning her back on him, she felt an unexpected attack of confusion. She had spent years transforming herself into a woman of sophistication. Urbane, well-traveled, impervious to inconvenient sentiment. But it was all a masquerade, and here was proof. Inside her lived an Isabel no one saw or knew existed, a needy creature who craved the love she saw in the Calhoun family, the deep contentment that grew from bonds that lasted, not just for one brief season, but for a lifetime.

Leaning her elbows on the rail, she said, "You're crowding me."

"You like it."

"How do you know that?"

"Because you'd never tolerate something you don't like."

"How do you know that about me? You don't even know me."

"You go to great lengths to assure that."

"I most certainly do not." Isabel always had the same response when she was feeling cornered. She lied through her teeth. "My life is an open book. In fact, there happens to be a book about my family, if you care to know. The Fish-Wootens of Fakenham in Norfolk. But it's all extremely tiresome, so no one I know has ever actually read it." She quickly switched the topic. "Your family, on the other hand, is interesting in the extreme. If no one has written the Calhoun history, perhaps someone should."

"We were discussing *your* family."

"We were not. I much prefer yours. They're charming and fascinating and delightful." A smile touched her lips, but she stayed where she was, looking out at the city, safe from his penetrating gaze. She felt such ease with him when he was relaxed and not flogging himself with worries about Lucas, his patients, the Rescue League and ghosts of the past.

"I never said they weren't," he said. "And by the way, they think I should marry again."

His words dropped like stones into a deep well.

She was grateful beyond measure that her back was turned. For a fraction of a second, she considered telling him about the conversation she'd had this afternoon with his sisters and Eliza, but decided against it. Trying to keep her voice light, she asked, "Is it because they want you to marry in general or were they referring to a specific . . . target?"

"You, specifically."

She held her breath, then let it out. "Why me?"

He took her by the shoulders and gently turned her to face him. Then he grazed his knuckles under her chin so that she had no choice but to look at him. "Because," he said, "they believe you're in love with me."

Everything in her simply stopped. She didn't move a muscle, didn't breathe, didn't blink. Perhaps even her heart stopped beating. She could sense him standing close behind her, could feel the smooth painted concrete of the rail beneath her elbows. But she was very much afraid that she had lost the ability to move or speak. At the most critical moment of her life, she was frozen. Stuck. If she moved, she would fall to pieces like a cracked vase.

But she had to get past this terrible state of inertia. Of course she was in love with him. There could be no other explanation for the soaring joy she felt when she was with him, the restless sense of anticipation when she wasn't and the dreams of him that haunted her sleep. She probably started loving him the moment she'd forced him to treat her gunshot wound. Still, the last thing in the world she needed was to be found out.

Taking a deep breath, she moved her jaw from side to side, making certain she still had the ability to speak. Then, finally, she found her voice. "Well. If they expected you to marry every woman who fancied herself in love with you, then you would have been married a dozen times or more by now," she said with a laugh. She pulled back from him, although the place where he'd touched her still pulsed with his warmth, and went back to gazing over the railing.

There. Moment over. She had neither confirmed nor denied his assertion.

They were completely silent for a long time. She felt him move, repositioning himself next to her at the viewing rail. The orchestra played on. The guests laughed and talked, random phrases floating like tobacco smoke through the air.

"I love looking out at the city at night," she commented when their silence became unbearable.

"Any city?"

She thought for a moment. "All the ones that can be viewed from a vantage point like this. Prague Castle from the Charles Bridge. Paris from the steps of Montmartre. Although I must say the very worst I've visited is London. When the weather is fine, it's decently pleasant to take a picnic up to Harding Mound and look down over the rooftops, but even then, you can see coal smoke belching from every chimney pot. A dreadful layer of soot coats everything. Now, Athens." She took a peculiar pleasure in speaking about the places she'd been. Memories of her travels, she realized, meant so much more when she shared them. "Athens," she repeated. "There's a city that is beautiful to behold, particularly from the Temple of Zeus. Everything just glows. It's as though the ancient stone of the buildings absorbs light and reflects it back." She slid a glance over at him. "Before you confined yourself to this city, I don't suppose you visited Athens."

"No."

"London?"

"No. Not Paris, and not Prague. I've never been anywhere that would impress you."

"Never mind impressing me. You should go

traveling. There's so much to see in the world."

Leaning on one elbow, he turned to face her. She felt caressed by his gaze, though he wasn't even touching her. "There's plenty to see right here," he said, never taking his eyes off her. "Traveling is for people who lack imagination and are easily bored."

She laughed. "That's clever. But unfortunately, wrongheaded." She had a terrible urge to place her hand on his cheek, perhaps winnow her fingers through his hair. Lord. In all her travels, she had never seen such a man.

Oh, Sancha, she thought. You were such a lucky woman.

"In what way is it wrongheaded?" he asked, annoyance creeping into his voice.

"Let's not quarrel again."

"Why not?"

"Because we excel at it already. We certainly don't need to practice." Leaning her elbow on the railing, she cupped her chin in her hand and studied his face, shadowy and lean in the torchlight. "Besides, I like it better when you're flirting with me."

"You're easy to flirt with."

They were so close their shoulders were nearly brushing. He had a smell all his own — the expected cedary scent of macassar oil and then something else, something unique and grassy and real. She had an overwhelming urge to fall into him, to explore until she found a name for that heady scent. She wanted to feel his arms around her, lifting her up and out of her own life, pulling her off the path she traveled and into a new world.

"Do I take that as a compliment?"

"Take it," he said, straightening up and folding his arms in front of him, "as you will."

She was trying to decide how to respond. Who was this new Blue Calhoun? Who did he want her to be?

A fresh wind rippled through the night garden, carrying the scent of the city and the sea, and far-off places she suddenly had no interest in seeing. Inside, the orchestra played "The Maiden's Heart," and down in the garden a couple strolled, their meandering path winding in and out of flowering hedges. She watched the slender man and petite woman stop walking for a brief, furtive embrace. They were in a world unto themselves, it seemed. Somehow their stance conveyed a complete disregard for their surroundings. They exuded a peculiar passion that made her look away to give them their privacy.

She placed one hand over the other on the railing and clenched her fingers so she would not inadvertently reach for Blue. "I flirt all the time," she said with a nonchalant toss of her head.

"Funny," he said. "Then one would think you'd be better at it."

"I am good at it."

"I've seen no evidence of that."

"And just what are you looking for, Doctor?"

"Skilled flirting. The sort that makes me raving mad with lust. That makes me dizzy, as though I'd been hit on the head with a hammer."

"That can be arranged." Now her pride was at stake. She had failed at many things in her life, but she'd never failed to gain a man's attention by flirting.

"Now you're looking at me oddly," he said.

"I'm just trying to decide how to begin this," she said. Her voice sounded as low and soft as a secret.

"Begin what?"

She held out her arm and slowly, deliberately adjusted the edge of her glove. Her hand brushed lightly against his chest. "My flirtation," she said.

An expression she had never seen before dawned on his face. The flinty-eyed doctor was changing before her eyes, and she was filled with undeniable excitement. Maybe there was hope for them after all. Maybe.

For the first time in her life, Isabel felt a sense of destiny that was not confined to her and her alone. Before meeting him, she had thought her path was laid out as clearly as the markings on a navigator's chart. She would travel the world alone until she was very old and very rich. Then she would settle in some anonymous place by the sea where she would go for long rambles each day. In the evening, she would read books, or more likely write a memoir. *Isabel Fish-Wooten: Lady Adventurer.* She had always kept a chronicle of her life. Because she invented so much, she had to keep track of herself. It seemed important to write the truth somewhere, for her eyes only. Unfortunately, her calf-bound journal had disappeared the night of the shooting. It was a small loss, but to Isabel it felt huge. She had no one who knew her true history; that travel-worn book contained the only record.

Lately, her plans for the future had begun to seem lonely and lifeless. Now she craved a richness she could never find in her single-minded, solo journey.

She could only find that by straying from her chosen path, and here he was, standing before her, this unexpected detour into a vast new world that had been hidden from her until the moment she met him. Even lying wounded and bleeding, she had glimpsed the possibility of a different life.

"Isabel," he said, "what if I won't settle for a flirtation?"

She sensed, as she often did with Blue, the things he was not saying. She knew what he wanted, and she was terrified. She had never offered her heart. She would not be able to bear it if he refused her. And he would, of course, if she ever allowed the whole truth of herself to emerge. Giving him the answer he wanted would force her to sacrifice the life she had made for herself, and for what? So he could treat her like the other women the world had cast off, like Bernadette or Mrs. Li or any of the pathetic creatures who came to him for help?

She cleared her throat. "If you find a flirtation unsatisfactory, then what is it you want?"

A disturbance nearby broke the mood before he answered. Someone was coming. Isabel could not decide whether she was relieved or frustrated by the interruption. She stepped back and so did he. They maintained a decorous distance. Pretending nothing had happened, they resembled any other man and woman sharing a polite conversation.

Backlit by torchlight, a couple came toward them up a wide flight of flagstone steps from the hotel garden. They were holding hands and laughing, and a strand of the girl's hair had slipped loose. They were so absorbed in one another that they didn't even realize they were no longer alone.

Isabel watched them with fondness, and perhaps a twinge of wistfulness as well. The road would not be easy for these two.

She felt the moment Blue recognized them. The air around him took on a distinct chill as he stepped out of the shadows and planted himself at the top of the stairs. "Lucas," he said in a voice that was both unfailingly cordial and glazed with ice. Then he bowed slightly. "Good evening, Miss Li."

Lucas and June froze like hunted creatures unsure of whether to fight or flee. Both were flushed, their hair mussed by the wind. Their lips bore that subtle, indefinable but unmistakable look of having just been kissed.

"Good evening, Miss Fish-Wooten. Good evening, Father," Lucas said, every bit as cordial and as brittle as Blue.

"Good evening, Miss Fish-Wooten. Good evening, sir." June's voice was little more than a terrified whisper.

"You'll have to excuse us, sir," Lucas said, offering no further explanation. With bold defiance, he took June's hand and led her hastily inside.

Isabel studied Blue's face. "Don't look so shocked," she said.

"Do I look shocked?"

"Like you've just been given a death sentence."

"I suppose I was . . . startled to see them looking so . . ." His voice trailed off. He looked so helpless that she had the urge to hug him.

"So grown-up?" she suggested.

"They're children. They were practically raised together."

"Then they know each other well. They are both young and beautiful and on the verge of discovering their own world. It happens to everyone. Children grow up. They fall in love. They get their hearts broken. You can't stop it from happening. It is as inevitable as the turning of the leaves in autumn."

"This could be more than hurt," he said. "Mrs. Li is a stern mother and a proud woman."

"She also loves her daughter."

"Enough to know that Lucas would be a disaster for her. Any non-Chinese boy would. Broken hearts would be the least of their troubles."

"I don't know. A broken heart seems rather serious to me."

"Have you ever had your heart broken, Miss Fish-Wooten?"

She looked him straight in the eye. "Not yet."

Twenty-Nine

Blue awoke in the middle of the night. A thrum of prescience, honed by years of midnight disasters, resonated through him. He lay still, listening for the outside call bell or the telephone bell. Perhaps a patient needed him. Perhaps there was an emergency.

But no, the house was quiet. Yet now he was fully awake. He felt restless, agitated. Despite the cool wind blowing gently through an open window, he was hot. And despite his best efforts to dismiss Isabel Fish-Wooten from his mind, he could not stop thinking about her. It was not just thinking, either. Nor was it ordinary lust; this was nothing like the straightforward and readily dispelled urges any man experienced.

No, his thoughts of Isabel were no mere urges. She was a burning obsession, a sheer, dizzying madness. She was a fever of the blood. Moderation and common sense had no power over the way she made him feel.

Made him *feel*. This was what was so new and disturbing. She had found the frozen, lifeless places in his heart and brought them to a state of stinging awareness. When he was with her, she made him come alive — against his will and better judgment. And unlike all the other areas of his life, he had absolutely no control over what was happening to him. He could not make himself not want her. He couldn't pretend he didn't want to make love to her, night after night, and sleep with her held close in his arms.

The way he wanted her was complicated. Straightforward lust he could've understood, but there were layers to his feelings for her that defied understanding.

Muttering under his breath, he flung back the bedclothes and donned a dressing robe. He abandoned all attempts at sleep and left the room. The moon cast a bluish wash of light down the carpeted staircase. In the darkened kitchen, he poured a glass of water from a stoneware pitcher and drank it down. But his thirst still raged, coming from a place the cooling water couldn't reach. Nonetheless, he refilled the glass and prowled through the downstairs, past the shadowy landscape of beautiful antiques and tasteful furniture Sancha had taken such pleasure in choosing for their home.

Sancha. Lately, she drifted farther and farther from his thoughts. The idea that he might be forgetting her rattled him, and he stood in the formal parlor and forced himself to focus on her. Oh, he could still conjure up an image of her face, her smile. He could still hear her laughter and feel the shape of her hand in his. But she was like the antiques and art treasures in this house. Something beautiful but . . . remote. Untouchable. She wasn't warm and vital and intriguing. She wasn't sleeping in the bedroom adjacent to his.

Try as he might, he could not keep his mind on the past. He could still hear echoes of Isabel's voice. *You force Lucas to live with a father who has forbidden himself to take joy from life, all because of a terrible accident that happened a decade ago.*

That was no longer true, Blue conceded. Somehow, over the course of the summer, his heart had changed. He wanted to put the past behind him, not only for Lucas's sake but for his own.

He trudged upstairs again, knowing he shouldn't, knowing he would. At the first landing he paused, spying a thin knife-edge of light around the door to Isabel's room.

Isabel's, not Sancha's. The room belonged to a living woman once again.

He knocked softly and heard a murmured, "Come in."

She sat up in bed, an open book spread across her lap. When he stepped into the light, she surely must have recognized the stark hunger in his expression, but she said nothing. She looked like a dream, sitting there, watching him. She had a way of looking at him that was utterly unique. With uncanny insight, she saw things he'd managed to keep hidden from the world — even from himself.

He lowered the flame of the reading lamp, then set aside the book she was holding. A diffuse glow of moonlight fell over the bed, lending mystery to the topography of rumpled pillows and pale coverlet.

She sat in uncharacteristic silence, yet he was coming to understand her silences as she understood his. All words were superfluous. There was no protest, no rationalizing, no declaration of any intent. Just . . . silence. And a shared yearning that had been building a bridge between them all summer long.

Without saying a word, he leaned down and kissed her. Every precious essence in the world flavored the kiss, the mingled spices of attraction and desire and loneliness and endless longing. Passion eased through him, borne on a wave of tenderness that took him entirely by surprise.

He drew her against him, intoxicated by the warm press of her body. Scarcely able to govern his hunger, he took in all he could of her, feeling the softness of her lips, tasting the candy sweetness of her mouth. His hands slid to places he had only imagined: gently rounded shoulders and yielding breasts, the petal-like smoothness at the base of her throat. She trembled beneath his touch, yet she didn't seem fearful in the least. If she had, it would have been easy to pull away, to leave her be. But Isabel didn't make anything easy. He sensed that she never, ever would. She blushed but made no attempt to hide herself. Instead, she returned his kisses with a generosity he hadn't expected.

A woman's body should be no mystery to a physician, yet it was. And perhaps the mystery was only deepened by his knowledge of physiology. How could something so real and vital evoke an invisible storm of emotion? When he'd treated her bullet wound, he'd seen her as something broken to be fixed. Now as he held her in his arms, he saw something else entirely — an object of earthy reverence, someone he could cherish and lavish with caresses, someone who had become so important to him that he could not imagine life without her.

"I shouldn't be here," he said, making one last attempt at resistance.

"Then you should leave right now." She spoke with total control over her emotions, yet he was coming to know her. He knew, somehow, that she was struggling as much as he.

"I'm not leaving," he said.

"I didn't think you would." With that, she slipped out of her nightgown. He knew this garment, like all the others, had been borrowed from Sancha, and then he realized he didn't care. It didn't matter. He watched Isabel peeling away the layers to reveal smooth bare skin, creamy as alabaster. Her blush deepened, but she made no sound, not even taking a breath. The stubborn will with which she'd survived a bullet wound now held her modesty at bay.

She reached for him, slipping her hands up over his chest, leaving a trail of heat and need. He wanted to believe she seduced him with the practiced ease of a courtesan, but that wasn't so. She was simply frank and direct in a way that startled and excited him.

There was nothing more to say. He'd had the debate raging endlessly in his mind for days, and he knew a hundred reasons — moral, ethical, societal — why this was wrong, and yet here he was anyway. The urges of the body were a powerful force that could be resisted by steely willpower. But the urges of the heart had no antidote.

He stopped thinking and applied himself to kissing her. With a gentle thrust of his tongue, he conveyed the pulse of his desire. She answered with a shuddering sigh of surrender, opening to him like a flower, lips, arms and thighs spreading to encompass him, to invite him in, to carry him away to places that had existed only in his imagination — until now.

He used to believe he was dead to feeling; now his heart was as desperate as his body was parched. He wanted to tell her so, but he knew the words would sound hollow and inadequate. False, even. But his hands and mouth imparted the honesty and tenderness words could not. With his body, he shared deeply intimate truths that verbal declarations couldn't express. Feverish need heated and nearly burst into flame when she touched him with slow, searching caresses. For long moments, broken only by the uneven rasp of his breathing, he struggled to hold back, wanting to prolong the moment of pleasure.

He lowered his mouth to hers as he pressed his full length against her, flesh to flesh, as though to take in her vibrancy, her energy, the passion she gave with a generosity he didn't deserve. Finally, trembling with the effort of control, he braced his arms on either side of her, letting her hair spill over his fingers while he kissed his way downward, her small cries like a song in his ears. She shuddered and dug her fingers into his shoulders, and he raised himself up. A gleam of moonlight illuminated the damp path his kisses had left on her skin. She stared at him with wonder and desire in her eyes, and her trusting look nearly took him apart.

He tried again to offer her the chance to send him away, to remind him that there was no future for them together. "Tell me to stop," he said, dragging the words from a painful well of reluctance.

"Why on earth would I do that?" A tremor in her voice softened the question and he realized she was moved by him.

Then he felt her hands moving over his body. There was a curious hesitancy in her touch, yet he understood that it was not reluctance or bashfulness. She touched him with a compelling sense of discovery, and with an honesty of emotions she'd never expressed in words.

Blue forced himself to hold back, though he nearly shook with the effort. Even knowing so little about her, he had expected her to be more practiced at the art of making love. Instead of the slick skill of an experienced woman, she showed a peculiar naive wonderment as she explored his body, every part of him as though gathering flowers from a garden and taking pleasure from the simple act of touching him. He couldn't tell if he was just another of her adventures or if this was all new to her. He should ask, but he didn't want to ask, not right now. He didn't want anything right now but her.

Like a fever rising from her skin, he sensed in her the same urgency that scalded his blood. He was twenty years old again and on fire. He caressed her everywhere, discovering the moist silk of her skin, the scent of her throat, the yielding softness of her breasts.

Ten years, he thought. He had endured ten years without this heat and the flavor of a woman on his lips and the raging of his blood to every part of his body. He'd been with women for the sheer relief of it, but never like this. Never with the sense that he'd found the essence of who he was. She had come to him like a gift, dropped into the middle of his life. A sense of intimacy seared his body and stole his breath, burning away the last of his doubts. At last he sank down, feeling an astonishing jolt of emotion as he joined with her.

Isabel let out a brief, sharp sound that echoed through him — triumph and pleasure with an inexplicably dark edge, as though shadows lay beyond the blaze of their intimacy. A dizzying intensity took hold and lifted him up and far away somewhere, and they soared and then plummeted, crashing down with a violent release. When she shattered beneath him and cried out, he lost himself in her, and for a fleeting moment he saw a glimmer of . . . possibility, perhaps. Finally he lay completely still, covering her, breathing hard and feeling disoriented. Like the victim of an accident, he tried to assess what had occurred, what the damage was. He should have been emptied out by the experience. That was what being with a woman had come to mean to him — a way to drain himself of feeling, to move on with no impression left behind, just a hollow relief that never lasted.

And now Isabel. She had come out of nowhere, a mysterious stranger who challenged and confounded him, who heated his blood and made him forget his whole life. Instead of emptying out his soul, she filled him with emotions and sensations he never allowed himself to feel. He gazed at her and saw the world in her eyes, and suddenly it was not a prospect to be simply endured, but a place he truly wanted to be.

When at last he separated from her, he was still burning. He wondered if she had any notion of his thoughts, if she shared even a fraction of the intensity roaring through him. He was astounded that they had spoken so little, for a rich communication had taken place, and he would swear the look in her eyes was one of complete understanding. He felt an enormous responsibility for her, even though he knew she'd claim she could look after herself.

He cradled her face between the palms of his hands and was startled to feel the warm moisture of tears on her cheeks. He'd got it all wrong, then. "Isabel," he said. "Isabel, I'm sorry. The last thing I wanted was to dishonor you."

A broken laugh escaped her. "It's a bit soon for regrets, isn't it? And too late for apologies." She put her fingertips to his lips to keep him silent. "Believe me, I'm not the sort to cling to social conventions. Particularly those that would restrict . . . this."

He took her hand, pressed a kiss to her palm and folded his own hand around it. "Then why are you crying?"

She hesitated, then used a corner of the bedsheet to blot away the tears. "I know what you're asking, and I adore you for thinking it could be true. But I will tell you plain, my dear Dr. Calhoun. I'm no virgin and haven't been for a good many years." Sliding down beside him, she turned to fold her arms across his chest. Blue-white moonglow shaded her in mystery, outlining the curve of her bare shoulders, the delicacy of her features and creamy skin. In the shadows, her enormous eyes seemed bruised by emotion, haunted by secrets. "But no one has ever made love to me," she said. "Until now."

Her words chipped away at the barriers he'd built to protect himself from moments like this. In his studies, he had memorized the anatomy of the human heart. He'd researched its complicated and vital processes, the pathology of its diseases.

But he'd never learned why a woman's honest words had the power to fill it up, to cause it to squeeze until it hurt, to make him wonder if his heart could possibly be big enough to hold her.

Thirty

Isabel watched Blue while he slept. She brushed a wavy lock of hair from his forehead, and as she studied him, a sweep of tenderness overcame her. In slumber, he appeared young and untroubled, perhaps because his brow was smooth and unmarred by worries. She grazed her knuckles along his jawline and remembered the sensual rasp of that light stubble on her skin as he kissed her. A sigh shuddered through her. She shut her eyes and tried to relive every moment of this night, every breath she'd taken, every magical sensation his touch had evoked.

This was not supposed to happen to her. She wasn't supposed to fall in love. She was supposed to be an independent woman, bound to see the world and have adventures and move on without looking back.

Yet with Blue, with this sad, damaged man, she had found a reason to wish she could stay. There was a sweetness to their new-found love that threatened to overpower her. In books of poetry, she had read the ways love could transform a person, but she had always thought the notion whimsical and improbable.

Now, finally and unexpectedly, she was learning the truth all on her own. Loving someone was more important than life itself. It nourished the invisible but vital part of a person and changed everything about her life, her future and her dreams. Before Blue, she hadn't realized the world could look and feel this way. In her travels, she had seen wonders beyond imagining, but nothing she'd seen the world over had ever given her what she'd found here, tonight, in this man's arms.

Prickles of the old restlessness drove her from the bed. Barefoot, she slipped on a robe and paced the floor, her thoughts chasing each other and keeping her from sleep. She didn't wish to wake him, so she wandered toward the dressing room adjacent to the bedchamber, shut the door and lit the lamp. This was Sancha's deepest inner sanctum, where she kept her clothing and shoes, jewelry and hats, undergarments and stockings. According to Bernadette, none of this had been touched until Isabel had started borrowing things.

"Am I going to burn in hell for wearing your clothes?" she whispered, trailing her fingers along a line of hanging gowns. "Will you haunt me for moving into your former life?"

Isabel was not a superstitious sort; she wasn't expecting an answer. So when a hatbox fell from a shelf and spilled on the floor, she nearly screamed. With her wrist pushed against her mouth to keep from gasping aloud, she crouched down and inched toward the box. The lid had fallen off, and inside was not a hat, but a cache of letters.

Like all of Sancha's things, they were perfectly organized. These were neatly folded in packets bound with string and identified by the year.

Every last one was from Blue.

Isabel started to shake as she realized what she'd found. This was their entire love affair, written from Blue's perspective.

She couldn't help herself; she started reading. She wanted to know everything about him, including the sort of man he was when he was in love with another woman. The early letters started when they were children, and his scrawled messages were cursory, inviting her to see a new foal, or to go fishing with him, or to tell her he had a new baby sister named Amanda. As a boy soldier in the Union Army, he'd written with passion and hope, begging her to marry him when the war was over. A particular statement caught Isabel's eye. "If I die in this hospital, it will not be the end for us. Our love will survive even death."

With trembling hands, she put the letters back and turned down the lamp. He was a diamond with many facets, and she had only glimpsed a few of them. Each time she saw a new side of him, she loved him more.

Isabel knew she was in trouble. Ordinarily, in the midst of a journey, her destination became clear to her. Like a city on a map, her next stop was outlined in black and white. A new place, a new adventure.

But now she questioned herself. Her desire to see the world was nothing compared to her desire to be with Blue. She wanted to stay with him, not just for a night, but forever.

That was what her heart wanted. Her head knew better. The threat of discovery lay like a thundercloud over her. The past had a way of catching up at inconvenient moments. She knew she'd ruin her fleeting happiness with Blue by staying too long. Best to leave while things were good between them. He'd remember her with fondness rather than resentment at finding himself saddled with a woman like her. Or worse, he might pity her.

Staying here could never work. Not for much longer, anyway. She could not hide from the stark truth. With Blue, she believed she'd discovered what love was, but she was probably fooling herself. She had no understanding of love, didn't know how to sustain it or keep it safe from the things the world does to a person. Good God, if her own mother wouldn't keep her, why should she believe anyone else would? She had nothing genuine, nothing of value to give a man like Blue Calhoun. She loved him, yes. She loved his son and the women who lived here, and perhaps in their own naive way they cared for her. But they didn't know her. No one knew her. That was the very key to her survival. She was not the person she pretended to be. She pretended so much that, long ago, she had lost the person she was.

One thing she knew for certain about herself was that she was incapable of living a settled life. She was made for moving on and leaving nothing in her wake but a few soon-forgotten encounters.

As she closed the door to the dressing room, she caught a glimpse of herself in the cheval glass in the corner of the room. Washed in moonlight, she looked like a ghost, as insubstantial as fog.

She was a danger to Blue, judging by her reception at the Far East Tea Company. Staying here put everyone under this roof in peril, and the reality of that was bearing down on her. She had to leave, because she simply could not conceive of a way to stay.

She would need to go soon. Each moment she delayed, she sank a little more deeply in love with Blue Calhoun. She stopped pacing and turned back to the bed, to the sleeping man there. He lay with one arm outstretched across the pillow.

Gazing at him, Isabel faltered, and a soft

sob escaped her. She held her breath until she regained control, then slipped into the bed next to him. He sighed and wrapped his arms around her, pulling her head to his chest where she could hear the strong, steady throbbing of his heart. A tear slid down her cheek and dampened his skin. It wasn't like the tears she'd shed earlier, when the bliss of his lovemaking had felt like an exquisite agony. These tears were private, and she forced them to stop. If she didn't do something soon, she'd drown, disappear beneath the surface.

It was still dark when Blue awoke to the rich smell of brewing coffee. Isabel was gone, but her essence lingered in the sheets and pillows, on his skin . . . in his heart. The madness that had possessed him still raged in his blood — but it wasn't madness, he conceded. He knew with utter sanity that he wanted her again. Now, and always. Moving silently through the dark house, he went to find her.

The quiet noise of utensils drew him to the kitchen. When she heard him come in, she turned to him. "I couldn't sleep," she whispered.

"Are you all right?"

"Are you asking as a doctor or as my lover?"

He laughed at her directness. "I'm both, now."

"My answer is the same regardless. I'm quite well, thank you." She worked in the glow of a low-burning lamp, setting out two cups and saucers. She looked delicate and ethereal, her hair mussed and curling around her face. He almost couldn't believe that just a short time ago, he had held her next to his heart and filled himself with her.

Insulating her hand with a tea towel, she picked up the enamel coffeepot from the stove and poured two cups of coffee.

He took a sip and shut his eyes, savoring the perfect brew. "I haven't had a good cup of coffee since Mrs. Li came to work for me."

She put a lump of sugar into her cup. "Tell me about Mrs. Li. She's a perfect cook, except for the coffee. She's a strict mother. What else?"

"She was the property of a tong boss, a virtual slave. She'd lost all her children except one."

Isabel's blood chilled. "June."

He nodded, remembering the terror and desperation of Li Mei when she'd appeared in his office nine years ago with her sick child in her arms. He also remembered his own sense of resolute conviction when confronted by the tong, demanding the return of their property. He would have died protecting the young mother and child, but fortunately, it didn't come to that. "June had come down with diphtheria," he told Isabel. "While she recovered, Rory and I discussed what to do about Li Mei — Mrs. Li. If we sent her back to the city, she'd be at the mercy of the tong once again. So Rory and I figured out a way to help her."

"I suspect it wasn't as simple as you make it sound."

"We never expected it to be simple." He savored his coffee. "This is the most delicious thing I've ever tasted." Then he set down his cup and went to her, taking her hand and drawing her into his arms. "I take that back," he said just before he kissed her. "It's the second-most delicious thing."

In another part of the house, a bell clattered rudely. They broke apart, and Blue swore softly under his breath. "That's the telephone," he said, heading for the coffin-shaped instrument mounted on a wall in the front hallway. Blue used it rarely. It was generally only a means to summon him to one of his well-heeled patients.

"Can you make it stop?" she asked, following him.

He snatched down the receiving earpiece and held the bell-shaped black instrument to his ear. "Only by answering the summons."

"I was afraid that would be the case."

Thirty-One

Miss Isabel seemed restless at breakfast. Lucas noticed that she barely ate a thing, and her cup rattled in the saucer when she picked it up, as though her hand shook. Maybe she was lonely; the house seemed silent after Grandfather and the rest of the family had left on their cruise around the world. Sometimes Lucas wondered if he should have gone with them after all, but he knew he couldn't stand the idea of leaving June a moment before it was absolutely necessary.

His father had left before anyone was up, called away to tend a patient. Thinking back over the years, Lucas realized his father was gone more than he was present in this house. He seemed driven to answer more and more calls, to look after more and more patients. It was an admirable trait in a doctor, Lucas knew. When he was younger, he used to wish his father was a banker or businessman who kept regular hours, who ate breakfast with his son.

Lucas didn't miss him so much anymore. He didn't let himself.

He cut a glance at June Li, who was at the sideboard checking the low-burning flame under the coffee in the samovar. She always found a reason to come to the dining room during breakfast.

June offered that special little smile she seemed to save only for him. Just the sight of that smile lifted his heart, and for a few glorious seconds he forgot his worry about Miss Isabel.

"Would you like some coffee?" asked June.

He handed her his cup. "Yes, please." It was a bitter, vile substance; her mother was famously inept at making coffee. But if June handed him a cup of kerosene, he would have drunk it just to please her. He took a sip and was amazed to taste a rich, delicious brew. "The coffee's excellent," he said.

June made a slight bow. "Miss Isabel made it this morning."

Miss Isabel ignored them as she read the morning edition of the *Examiner*. She turned the page, and he could hear her breath catch. "Oh, my."

"What is it?" asked Lucas.

"Do you know anything about the Sand Hills Shooting Club?" she asked.

"It's a social club," he said. "Lots of people belong."

"They're sponsoring a tournament at Russ Park. Two hundred targets at unknown angles. There are some rather large purses. One thousand dollars for the top shooter."

Lucas said nothing. All his friends belonged to the gun club, and many would be taking part in the tournament. He, of course, was prohibited from joining Sand Hills or any shooting club.

But sometimes, on quiet evenings, he would ride down to Hayes Park, where he could hear the shooting in Hayes Valley, a sandy desert in the vicinity of Grove Street. Lucas would sit and watch, and listen. In his mind, he sighted down the slickly oiled gun barrel, timed each shot perfectly, shattering the clay pigeons into exploding fragments. Several times, he'd slipped in among the shooters and convinced Andrew or Frank to let him have a go.

The first time he'd hit a target, Lucas had felt it — he loved the sport of shooting. Even without constant practice, he fired with confidence and accuracy. Once, the gallery master had approached him, hurrying along the gravel track where the shooters gathered in front of the field of traphouses. Lucas had been terrified, certain he'd been found out.

Instead, the master offered a handshake, declaring that Lucas was truly gifted.

"Are you planning to enter?" Miss Isabel asked.

He was a mere breath away from admitting the truth — that his father disapproved of guns and would not allow them in the house.

That Lucas had been forbidden to learn the sport of shooting. But instead, some inner voice of rebellion said, "I'd like to."

From the corner of his eye, he could see June become still, waiting and listening.

Isabel lifted one eyebrow in that curious fashion of hers, a look that made a small measure of candor break free from Lucas.

"Unfortunately," he said, "I'm not . . . very experienced."

"And why is that?"

"I've never . . . actually, I've had no instruction in shooting. And not much experience." He hated saying that. Learning to shoot was one of those things sons did with their fathers. But not Lucas, of course.

"Then it's about time you had," she said matter-of-factly. "Especially if you hope to attend the military academy at West Point."

"My father is too busy with his practice to teach me," he said, another admission he loathed.

"He certainly is, and his patients are better off for it. So I shall teach you myself."

He regarded her in surprise. "You know how to shoot?"

"I certainly do. You'll find I'm quite an expert."

He couldn't suppress a grin. Excitement surged through him. He quickly put together a plan. While his father worked — which was all the time — he and Miss Isabel could go down to Hayes Park and practice. More and more, Lucas was convinced that rebelling against his father's rules was the only way to get what he wanted. Perhaps once he won the honors he sought at West Point, Father would finally understand.

"So," said Miss Isabel, oblivious to Lucas's thoughts, "where does your father keep his guns?"

His neck prickled. China clattered as June took away the breakfast dishes, her face tight and disapproving.

"He doesn't keep any that I know of," Lucas admitted. "But I'm certain we can borrow one." Actually, he was not certain Frank Jackson would oblige. But that was the magical thing about Miss Isabel. Even when you weren't sure of yourself she made you believe anything was possible.

"Excellent," she said, bustling toward the door. "We should get started immediately."

Thirty-Two

After early-morning rounds at the Rescue League, Blue hurried home with an eagerness that felt new to him. Since going to Isabel's bed, he'd begun to look at life with different eyes. Each night, he went to her and they made love with feverish intensity, creating a world of their own, unconnected to the outside. It was a fiercely private ecstasy; he discovered a place inside himself he didn't know existed and only Isabel was privy to, his most secret self, a place of dreams.

He knew the idyll could not last forever. They would have to decide what to do about their love affair. In a lighthearted moment, he'd declared he would make an honest woman of her. She had laughed and sworn that loving him was the most honest thing she'd ever done.

By the time he reached the house, he was burning — again. It seemed to be his natural state these days. He couldn't wait to see her, and only the fact that Bernadette was in the foyer kept him from calling out to Isabel.

He took the stairs two at a time, hoping

she had not yet dressed for the day. But the room was empty, the bed made. Her light, floral essence lingered in the empty bedroom. He went back downstairs, where Bernadette was fluffing a feather duster at a fringed lampshade.

"Where is Miss Fish-Wooten?"

The maid ducked her head, but not before he caught a glimpse of her knowing smile. "I believe she's gone somewhere with Master Lucas, sir. The two of them are thick as thieves these days." She paused in her dusting to regard him with that peculiarly womanly wisdom no man could ever attain. "Go and have something to eat, sir. It's been a long night."

He didn't begrudge the friendship that had grown between Isabel and Lucas over the summer. He'd defied convention, bringing Lucas up motherless, and he knew that was a burden on the boy. Over the years, he'd encountered any number of willing candidates, but he didn't know how to share his life without giving his heart, and he refused to give his heart.

Now Isabel had taken up residence in his heart, almost against his will. And she seemed to like Lucas immensely. Perhaps, in her way, she even loved him.

Love. It was a concept she spoke of in lighthearted tones. She'd never said she was leaving, but she hadn't promised to stay, either. He wondered what it would do to Lucas if she left. And that led to the real question — what would it do to *him* if she left?

He tried to shake off the thought as he went to the kitchen. Breakfast was over, but a fine aroma pervaded the dining room. He shut his eyes for a moment, inhaling deeply.

Coffee. Real, perfectly-brewed coffee.

In this household, such a thing used to be as rare as delivering triplets. But since Isabel had quietly but determinedly taken charge of preparing the coffee, it was a daily occurrence.

He drew himself a cup and savored it, watching the curls of steam rise up and dissipate in the sunlit room. What a simple pleasure this was, a late-morning cup of coffee in a quiet room. But he didn't linger, because his concerns about Isabel forced him to determine a plan of action.

He hurried to his chamber, and as he was getting cleaned up, he heard someone whistling. A few seconds later, he realized it was him. Whistling. He almost never whistled. He'd nearly forgotten that he could. Bending forward over the shaving basin, he felt a stirring inside him, an alien warmth, something so long buried he scarcely recognized it. Then he realized what it was. Hope. Hope for a different life, a life ruled by joy rather than duty, filled by delight rather than dread.

And he knew what it was that made him feel this way — Isabel. She had moved into his life, into his heart, and changed the way he saw the world. Since finding her, he realized that now his days were to be anticipated, even enjoyed rather than merely endured from moment to moment.

Against all expectations, he faced a startling truth. A passion beyond reason had taken hold of the cold, controlled part of him and unfurled the heart of a man who had rediscovered the world. It was time to tell her, Blue decided. Past time.

The notion was simple, so simple it was completely impossible. Here he was, a settled man in the middle of his life, with his heart pounding madly over a flibbertigibbet of a female who took pride in the fact that she never stayed in one place.

How had this happened? How had he reached this place?

He finished dressing, surprising himself again by putting on a deep blue waistcoat he almost never wore and charcoal-colored trousers normally reserved for Sunday. Then he went downstairs, rushing like a lad on his way to his first dance.

As he passed the doorway to the parlor, he paused, and the anticipation running through him slowed with a sense of duty. He stepped into the doorway, paused again, then went in. This had been Sancha's favorite room, the place where she received guests, where she played the piano in the evening. The room contained a virtual shrine to her, he realized with some discomfort. A formal bridal portrait rendered in oils dominated the mantel. There was a cabinet filled with smaller portraits and a good many photographs, the sepia shades fading with the years. He paused to study a picture showing the two of them standing in front of the house, his arm around her, his smile wide and sunny. Would he ever be that happy, that hopeful, again?

He thought about Isabel, and for the first time in years, he thought, yes.

He heard someone out in the hall and turned to see Efrena in the doorway. She eyed him curiously, and though she made no comment, she seemed intrigued by the obvious care he'd taken in dressing. "I have to send for the farrier again," she said. "Gonzalo's shoe is not right."

"That's fine," he said, then frowned. "I haven't ridden him in a week."

"Oh, then . . . perhaps it was a bad fit from the start." She ducked her head.

"Lucas took him out, didn't he?"

"The boy is allowed to go driving during the day, is he not?"

"Where did he go driving?"

"He did not say."

Blue fought to hold annoyance at bay. Isabel made him believe he could live a different life, but it wasn't so simple to change. He was so accustomed to spending his days running his practice and the Rescue League that he had forgotten how to do something just for the pleasure of it, how to take an afternoon's drive or go down to the sea and look at the waves. He felt a small flicker of envy for Lucas.

Efrena rubbed her arms as though it was cold, even though the afternoon breeze wafting in through the open window was warmed by the summer sun. "I have never liked this room," she said, looking around the parlor, her gaze alighting on the shrine of portraits. "Too many ghosts."

Her words struck him with a dull, unpleasant surprise. "She was your best friend."

"That's why I don't like this room," she explained. Her precise, convent-bred Spanish accent gave extra weight to her words. "These pictures, they only remind me of the shortness of her life. They make me want to go back to that day and put things right. Shoo her away from the camp. Don't let her put on my jacket. Keep a closer eye on the men."

The pain that pulsed in her voice touched him. He was not the only one in this household who grieved. "You couldn't have changed that. You couldn't have changed anything that happened that day."

"Neither," she stated, "could you."

The truth settled around them like a shroud. In ten years, they had never spoken of these things, not in this way. Why not? he wondered. Why in God's name had they both waited to say things that were so obvious?

The deepest wish in his heart burst free. "I want to marry Isabel."

Her dark eyes flashed at him. Other than that, her expression didn't change. "I know. Everyone knows. Except perhaps Isabel."

"Am I that transparent?"

"You're in love. It shines from you."

He studied the photographs in the glass case, looking at the man he used to be, years before. Smiling, carefree, young. He *had* shone. He'd known how to feel happiness. It radiated from him. If Efrena was right, perhaps that spark was not gone. "This is insane," he said, pacing back and forth in a panic of disbelief. "I can't marry her. In seven years' time, I'll have reached the half-century mark."

"And how old will you be in seven years' time if you do not marry her?" asked Efrena. Shaking her head in exasperation, she left the room.

He stared one last time at the portrait of Sancha. So beautiful. He'd loved her so much. So much that losing her had destroyed him. His heart had frozen. A wall of ice had protected him from ever loving that way again.

In his mind, love and fear had become entangled so that it seemed one couldn't exist without the other. Lucas had suffered from the fear and desperation that had edged Blue's love for him. Only now was he starting to realize how poisonous that was. He was so afraid the boy would get hurt — or worse — that love had twisted into something dark and joyless and controlling. Thinking back over the years, he realized that a wedge of silence separated them. There was a gaping chasm they tiptoed around and always had. It had begun the day Sancha died, the day he hoped Lucas didn't remember.

His first love smiled down at him, Madonna-like. My hair is graying at the temples, Sancha, he thought. I'm growing old and you're eternally young.

"Goodbye, Sancha," he whispered through the empty air. Then he turned away and walked out of the room to find Isabel.

Thirty-Three

From the third firing station, Isabel sighted down the length of the gun barrel, sensing the trajectory of the target well before it was launched into the sky. The shooting tournament was going well, she reflected with satisfaction. She had outscored the shooter behind her and planned to break away with this next round.

A fat purse awaited her if she succeeded. Enough to purchase a ticket to her next destination.

"Pull," she said, her voice ringing with self-confidence.

If she won today, her visit to San Francisco was over.

The thought sneaked in through an undefended entry in her mind. Unbelievably, her aim faltered. No more than an eyelash, but enough to put her shot off the mark.

She stared, flabbergasted, at her failure. The clay pigeon emitted only an indignant puff of dust as it arced out of sight and disappeared into a field of wild grass and sand dunes.

"Lost," shouted the referee, correctly calling the shot.

A ripple of speculation swept through the crowd of fashionably dressed men and women in the observation gallery. It was a railed boardwalk built along the edge of the dunes, affording a view of the shooting range and, on a fine day like today, the wide, flat bay in the distance. At the moment, the boardwalk was crammed, for this was the biggest purse of the season. Tournaments, Isabel had quickly learned, were considered a sport of gentlemen and ladies of refinement, even more so than golf or boating. It was something else to like about San Francisco, she reflected.

Being a foreigner, Isabel was not the favorite here today, but her consistency and skill had won her the respect of the onlookers. Now they were obviously surprised by her amateurish lapse in concentration.

The missed shot landed her in second place for the time being. She had thought to capture the prize with ease. Few shooters, male or female, possessed her knack for timing and accuracy. Yet now she realized that, going into the final round of the contest, she trailed behind the elegant and skilled Mrs. Clarice Hatcher. Since the charity ball, Isabel had not given the woman a thought, but here she was again, imperious and sure of herself.

Unbuttoning the wrist fastening of her shooting glove, Isabel offered Mrs. Hatcher a respectful nod as the lady passed her on the way to the refreshments stand. Mrs. Hatcher returned the greeting, her eyes dark and unreadable beneath the brim of a hat that bore the dramatic ribbon trimmings of a French designer. Isabel did not begrudge her the lead spot. She had won it fair and square, and if there was something a bit chilly in her manner, that was not Isabel's concern. She had blown her aim and lost the lead, and only the next two rounds would determine the winner in the ladies' division. Isabel conceded that if she didn't take control, she might find herself in a shoot-off with Mrs. Hatcher.

Frustrated, she decided to see how Lucas was doing in his division. Since hearing about the match, they had spent hours practicing at Hayes Park. Despite a lack of experience, Lucas possessed a marksman's eye and a good sense of timing. Though not yet in a league with champions who had been practicing their sport for years, Lucas was holding his own in the junior men's division.

She milled through the crowd of spectators and shooters. Russ Gardens was a beautiful setting of shady arbors and mossy banks. Families picnicked on its green slopes, and a band played in a distant gazebo. The Sand Hills Shooting Club was made up of the cream of society, and she was an expert at acting as though she was one of them. She smiled and murmured greetings, gliding along as gentlemen tipped their hats and ladies said, "How do you do?"

The old Isabel would have found the refined but festive atmosphere entirely delightful. Mingling with Hopkinses, Chases and Stanfords was something most San Franciscans only dreamed of doing. Yet she felt a vague nudge of discontent. These people were interesting enough, but they didn't know her. She'd crafted her entire existence around that concept. Now, thanks to Blue Calhoun, she was starting to question herself. This was skimming along the surface of life, never dipping deeply into its very essence. She realized that she could go along for years like this. She could spend the rest of her days in shallow pursuits, meeting delightful people and then promptly forgetting them. And she did not delude herself — as soon as she left, they would forget her, too. Perhaps at a dinner party they might remember the eccentric English lady with the sharp tongue and steady aim, and regale their friends with an anecdote about her. But at the end of it all, she was no more than a passing acquaintance, a ship putting out to sea and then disappearing over the horizon.

Uncomfortable with the thought, she went to find Lucas. He stood amid a group of other boys with their entry numbers tied to their upper arms. His grin widened as he shaded his eyes to study the scores on the posting board.

What a marvelous profile he had, she thought with an unexpected rush of affection. He was such a beautiful boy. He was taller than the others, black-haired and blue-eyed, with an actual cleft in his chin. Other people were watching Lucas, too, simply because he was so glorious to look at. The Swansea and Portman girls, whom she recognized from the evening at the Excelsior Hotel, strolled past Lucas, their looks of longing almost painful in their intensity. Isabel couldn't help but smile. One day, women were going to flock to him, and she hoped he would choose wisely and well.

An unfamiliar sensation jabbed at her, and it took several moments before she was able to identify the fierce emotion that grabbed her and held on tight. It was a feeling made up of love and happiness and something almost spiritual, something that transcended ordinary sentiment. *Pride*. And not just ordinary pride but something more gratifying: maternal pride. She'd never had a mother to take pride in her. She'd never had a child to take pride in. But she had seen this look on the faces of other women watching their sons at cricket matches or their daughters playing the piano.

Oh, Sancha Montgomery Calhoun, she thought. You have a magnificent son. I hope somewhere, somehow, you know that.

Isabel knew she would think of Lucas often after she was gone. She would wonder and worry. She wished she could be present to see the future unfold for this handsome youth. Who would he love, and who would love him back? What would the years bring him? She would never know for certain, but his future would be filled with laughter, tears, happiness, heartache, riches, poverty and everything in between — all the pleasures and perils of a life fully lived.

She caught herself longing to be present to witness Lucas's coming-of-age, to celebrate the happy times with him, to commiserate with him over the inevitable bad times. This was a foreign and discomfiting notion for her — to want to stay in someone's life instead of leaving all the time.

Her smile as she offered a dainty curtsy to Mr. Larkin Spivey, a shooting club official, felt strained. This was not a good time to experience such inconvenient longings. Her life consisted of travels without end, and it was foolish to change direction now.

To gather her composure, she went to the refreshments booth and helped herself to two glasses of lemonade. Then, squaring her shoulders, she marched up to Lucas.

His grin seemed a mile wide. "Miss Fish-

Wooten, look at the board. I'm third in my division."

"Of course you are," she said briskly, handing him a glass. "I expected no less."

The look in his eyes warmed. "Thank you. Maybe that's why I'm doing well," he said. "Because you expect me to."

"You say that rather pointedly. Why do I sense a rather oblique complaint against your father?"

"He expects me to fail at things. To misbehave. To . . . disappoint him." He raised and lowered his shoulders in a martyr-like shrug. "Perhaps that's why I do."

"How terribly clever of you to come up with a convenient way to blame your shortcomings on your father. I declare, you must be studying the works of Dr. Freud."

"Doctor who?"

"Never mind. He's probably wrong, anyway. When do you shoot next?"

"They say the next round will take an hour, and then I compete again. Why are you looking at me like that?" he asked.

"Tell me, Lucas," she said, "do you spend much time thinking of your mother?"

He finished his lemonade and set down the glass. "No. Why do you ask?"

"I'm curious, that's all. Life isn't easy, that's a fact. Growing up without a mother makes some things that much harder, wouldn't you think?" Isabel sounded like a stranger, even to herself. Imagine, her, offering wisdom and advice.

"I don't know if it's harder or not. I've nothing to compare it to." He stared down at the boardwalk and thought for a moment. "It's not that I don't miss her or that I didn't love her, but I just don't have . . . much of her."

"I understand. I don't remember much about the time when I was small, either." Thank goodness, she thought.

"I don't remember the day she died," he softly confessed.

"And you don't need to. That's not your job," Isabel said quickly, regretting the choice of topic. The things she'd learned about that day were disturbing enough to her, and she'd never even known the woman. She touched his hand. "We'd best get ready for the final round. Come along."

They went together to the ammunition stand adjacent to the judging platform.

"You didn't tell me you'd dropped to second place," Lucas said, studying the other side of the posting board.

"My last shot was shameful. I made the unforgivable and wholly common error of breaking my concentration. I lost out to Mrs. Clarice Hatcher."

"Oh. Her."

"You know her?"

"Not well. My father occasionally steps out with her."

She had suspected as much, based on her encounter with the woman at the ball. Even so, hearing the news from Lucas had an unpleasant effect on her, much as putting her bare hand on a hot stove. "Oh, really?"

He shrugged. "He's known her for years. When I was younger, I used to worry that she would become my mother."

"Why would that worry you? I would think you'd welcome a mother."

"Maybe. Not her, though. She's always talking about fashion and art, and gossiping about other people. I stopped worrying about her becoming my mother, though. It's not going to happen."

"You sound quite confident of that."

"I am. My grandmother and sisters have been trying to find him a match for years." Lucas turned his face to the horizon, where the sea and sky met. With a wisdom beyond his years, he said, "But he'll never remarry. Ever."

Thirty-Four

At first, Blue felt only mild concern. Isabel had been gone too long. He felt a twinge of irritation. She might at least have informed someone of her plans. The woman came and went like a hummingbird with no regard for what someone else might have to say about it. She loved her freedom and answered to no one. Perhaps that was why loving her was so risky.

He believed she loved him back. But that might not be enough to hold her.

After looking all through the house and surgery, he resorted to asking the help. No one knew where she and Lucas had gone. He decided to go down to the livery to ask Efrena for some hint as to where they were. It chagrined him that he couldn't figure it out on his own. He didn't know where Lucas went for pleasure, didn't know what he did for fun.

That was all about to change. He hurried with a spring in his step. Perhaps he'd finally found something he and his son had in common. They both loved Isabel.

He crossed the service alley and stepped into the shadowy livery, filled with the rich odor of horse. Holding Gonzalo's hoof between her knees as she inspected the underside, Efrena didn't seem surprised to see him, nor did she wait for him to ask. "They didn't say where they were going."

"I didn't ask."

"You are now." Efrena straightened up, brushing off her hands on her thick canvas farrier's apron. She faced him with her usual calm demeanor.

Blue's mild annoyance deepened. He knew them both too well — their recklessness, their habit of finding trouble. Lucas had made no secret of his admiration for Isabel's dashing ways, her sophistication. Perhaps he saw in her, if not a mother, then a mentor.

"Don't get in a temper," Efrena said.

"What makes you think I'm in a temper?" With deliberate effort, he eased the scowl from his face.

"Do not scold Lucas for entertaining a guest."

"Why are you being so damned evasive? Where the hell are they, Efrena?"

She set aside the hoof pick and studied him thoughtfully. Then she patted the big horse's neck and motioned for Blue to follow her into the tack room. She took down a notice stuck on a rusty nail in the wall and handed it to Blue. "This is where they are."

A shooting match. A damned shooting match. This was not a prank like stealing the communion wine, but real trouble. "Damn it, what the devil put that notion in his head?" Blue asked. "He knows my views on firearms."

"Perhaps he has views of his own."

"He's just a boy. He's not allowed to have views." Blue crumbled the handbill and stuffed it into his pocket.

Less than ten minutes later, he was riding hell-for-leather toward Russ Gardens. Almost, he thought. He'd almost declared himself a happy man, a man in love. How close he had come, he thought, to gambling his heart away to a woman like Isabel. She was careless — with safety, with the truth, with people's hearts.

There were some things, he thought, that love couldn't fix. He of all people should know that.

Thirty-Five

Isabel knew she should be concentrating solely on the shooting match, but Lucas's comment lingered in her mind, distracting her. "Why do you say your father will never marry?" she asked.

"Because if he hasn't in all this time, he never will." Lucas slipped his rifle into its polished leather case and tucked it under his arm. "Andrew's mother died three years ago. His father married again and already has a new baby. My father would never do that." They strolled the grounds, where local merchants and craftsmen had set out their wares for sale. Vendors offered fishcakes and sausages, chipped ice flavored with berry juice, candies wrapped in edible rice paper.

Isabel had no taste for anything, though. "You seem quite sure of yourself."

"His work is his one true love."

"He loves you," she pointed out.

A scowl darkened Lucas's brow. "He has a fine way of showing it, then."

"How would you like him to show it?"

"By letting me figure out my own life."

They walked up and down the rows of tables, some of them shaded by umbrellas. As they passed a display of antique firearms for sale, she nearly collided with a strolling couple perusing the pistols. She stepped back from the slant-topped table and studied the woman, who wore a tailored walking gown and clung to the arm of a dignified man with salt-and-pepper hair. A funny feeling that was more than curiosity darted through Isabel.

"Lucas, who are those people?" She indicated them amid the crowd of shoppers. "They look familiar to me."

He looked in the direction she was pointing. "Dr. and Mrs. Vickery," he said.

She studied them from beneath the brim of her bonnet. The name meant nothing to her, yet for no reason she could fathom, a tingle of apprehension skittered along the back of her neck. "Is he a physician, then?"

Lucas nodded. "Father knows him."

Dr. Vickery was a mild-looking man, well-groomed and dignified. His wife was a restless sort, charging about the antique gun display like a child in a candy store. Isabel realized she and Lucas weren't the only ones watching the Vickerys. She nudged him, indicating a pair of men in cheaply tailored clothes. One wore a dented hat sporting a long, variegated feather. "What do you make of those two?"

"Crimps," he said. "You see them everywhere you go in the city. They're probably looking for boys to shanghai tonight."

Isabel watched them for a moment. One wore a large flask on a shoulder strap and the other had a bulge beneath his frockcoat that was probably a gun. Yet they didn't appear to be looking for boys in the crowd. They appeared to be looking at Lucas.

"We should go," Isabel said.

At that moment, Mrs. Vickery picked up a German-made pistol and waved it around. Gasps and murmurs rose from the milling crowd. Instinctively, Isabel grabbed Lucas and shoved him behind her. The gun dealer crouched down behind his table. The suspicious-looking crimps scurried away. Dr. Vickery turned pale, reaching for the gun. His wife eluded his grasp, pointing it playfully at him.

"Bang," she said, then burst out laughing. "Oh, Fremont, you should see your face. You look as though you are facing a firing squad."

"Hand me the gun, Alma," he said. "These are not toys."

"I know that, Fremont," she snapped, her laughter evaporating. "Don't you think I know that?"

She pouted but allowed him to pry the gun from her and hand it back to the antiques dealer. "Leave that one," he said in a Southern drawl. "You don't want to cause an accident."

Leave that one. The words resonated unpleasantly through Isabel, echoing deep.

As the crowd started moving again, Vickery's gaze flickered past Isabel, then returned to her.

She pretended she hadn't noticed his stare, but he spoke up before she could grab Lucas and walk away.

"Have we met, miss?" he asked.

She felt cold all over and could not think why. The man was a doctor, a colleague of Blue's. She offered him a gracious smile. "I'm Isabel Fish-Wooten. Mr. Calhoun tells me you're Dr. and Mrs. Vickery, acquaintances of his father."

"Calhoun," said Mrs. Vickery. "Like that nice Dr. Calhoun who visits Officer Brolin in the hospital."

Vickery's polite expression didn't change. "I didn't know he was visiting Brolin."

"Yes, dear. They say he comes every day." A smile lingered about her lips as though she had forgotten it. "Come along, Fremont. I am getting a headache."

"Good day, ma'am," Lucas said.

What a strange pair, Isabel thought. "Well," she said to Lucas, "I should not like to encounter her in a dark alley at night. Or anywhere, for that matter. Even a tea party." She shuddered, and he laughed at her expression.

"They seem a little odd to me, too," Lucas said.

It was more than oddness that teased Isabel's brain. She sent Lucas off to prepare for the final round and lingered in the area of the trading fair. She was certain she'd never met the Vickerys, yet the encounter nagged at her. Dr. Vickery escorted his wife to a glossy closed carriage in the field beside the park. He handed her up, shut the door and walked to the rear of the vehicle. Then someone else joined him — Mrs. Clarice Hatcher, the leader in the shooting tournament. Isabel could tell by the furtive angle of their heads that they were having an extremely private conversation. Mrs. Hatcher handed him something, but Isabel was too far away to see what it was. Then a quick, passionate embrace told her all she needed to know about these two. Brazen as brass, with the poor, addled wife inside the coach. Dr. Vickery broke away and drove off.

Just then, Mrs. Hatcher looked across the field. Despite the distance between them, Isabel could feel the woman's eyes lock on to her. Pretending not to notice, she joined Lucas at the practice range, where she tried to shake off an unsettled feeling. They cleaned and polished and reloaded their sporting pieces, which Lucas's friend Frank had been kind enough to loan them. "I'm going to be the best marksman in San Francisco one day," Lucas declared, sighting down the barrel.

"Not today," said an angry voice behind them.

She heard Lucas swallow audibly as he turned around. Then she saw him straighten himself to his full height. "Hello, Father."

Isabel offered Blue her most dazzling smile. He looked particularly handsome today in a crisp white shirt and charcoal-colored trousers. A fine blue waistcoat reflected the color of his eyes. "Good," she said, "you've come just in time to watch the final round."

He was out of breath. She could tell he had ridden hard just to see his son compete. He'd even dressed up for the occasion. He was a wonderful father, after all, she reflected, her heart filling with affection and esteem. She glanced over at Lucas to see if the boy shared her pleasure. Instead, Lucas was gaping at his father in horror.

"I assure you, that's not my purpose in coming here," he said.

Something had happened, she realized. She'd never seen him quite like this. Oh, she had seen him angry. That was his customary state of mind. But this was different. He looked . . . intimidating, his wide-shouldered silhouette nearly blotting out the late afternoon sun. That was Blue — a great, large thundercloud of a man.

But Isabel had never been afraid of storms. "You won't be sorry. The leaders are desperately close, and —"

"Where did you get this?" he demanded, grabbing the gun from Lucas.

"Father, I need that for the next round."

With viciously efficient movements, Blue emptied the chamber. "What you *need* is to remember the way you've been raised. Firearms are not a part of our lives. They never have been. Not for sport or any other purpose."

"Those are your rules, Father," Lucas retorted. "I was never given a choice."

For a fraction of a second, a crack appeared in Blue's angry facade. "Damn it, Lucas, you know my reasons."

The boy's face turned pale and stiff. A certain tension in the jaw hinted he was close to tears. Isabel felt yet another maternal sensation — protectiveness. These two, she thought with a lurch of her heart. They loved each other so much, but that didn't seem to solve anything for them.

"I do know," Lucas said in a low growl that vibrated rage and hurt. "Sir." With that, he walked away, heading toward the dunes at the edge of the park, where the road led back to town.

"Why must you be so autocratic?" Isabel demanded, whirling around to face Blue. Her anger was tinged by another, more difficult emotion. Sadness. She cared deeply about both Blue and Lucas. She hated to see the two of them like this — resentful and hurting, willing to strike out at each other.

"I don't owe you an explanation. But I will say this. He's always resorted to manipulation in order to get his own way. Indulging his immature impulses and permitting him to experiment with dangerous behavior will only encourage him to put himself in harm's way."

"He's learning to shoot the proper way," she insisted. "Safely. I taught him myself, and I would never let him come to harm. I l— I hold Lucas in the highest esteem." Heavens, had she almost said she loved the boy?

Blue didn't seem to notice, or if he had, he seemed not to care. He sagged against the wooden rail and shoved his hand through his hair. "How long has this been going on?"

His air of bleak fatigue disturbed her far more than his anger. She would take passion in any form over indifference. "His mother was shot to death," she said, aiming straight for the mark. "I know he was there that day. And I know that you are intimately and horribly familiar with the damage gunfire can inflict. So am I. But prohibiting your son from touching a gun is not going to bring an end to violence."

His eyes glinted like chips of ice. "So now you're an expert on raising a son."

She refused to flinch. "No, you're supposed to be the expert. That's why I'm quite mystified by your unreasonableness." Good, she thought, watching the ice in his gaze turn to blue flame. At least he wasn't indifferent anymore. "Tell me, does he know how to swim?"

"Of course he does."

"Did you teach him?"

"Yes."

"Why?"

"So he won't drown if he falls in the water. And if you think I'll accept that rationalization for allowing him to shoot a gun, you're wrong."

"You shouldn't believe the worst of him," she said. "You always do that. You prepare yourself for the worst."

"That way I'm never disappointed."

"God, you are so —" She willed herself silent before she truly did slip. This man had a hard grip on her emotions. She wondered if he realized that. It felt strange, knowing he had the power to break her heart or make it whole. Taking a deep breath, she tried to turn the discussion calm and reasonable. "He's nearly grown. Soon he will be making all of his own decisions."

"Fine. He can do so when he's grown. He can defy me in any way he chooses."

"Defy you?" Isabel wanted to weep. "You're so wrong. He's not defiant at all. He's secretly worried that he can never live up to your expectations."

"You presume to know my son well," he snapped.

"Perhaps I do. In one summer, I've come

to know him in ways he only prays his own father will know him." She could see his temper deepening, but she couldn't stop herself. Apparently no one, not even his own family, had dared to stand up to him in the matter of his son. She stood on a precipice here. Their fragile new love might not stand up to a fight like this.

She had to make a choice — hold her silence in the matter of Lucas or risk her already strained bond with Blue. She made her next statement with a full awareness of what it might do to her and Blue. "If you keep imposing your strict rules on Lucas," she said, "then you won't have to worry about losing him to gun violence. He'll simply leave and never come back."

She could see the dart hit home. He stiffened and, without moving, seemed to draw away from her. "A habit with which you're intimately familiar," he said acidly. "Your constant travels used to mystify me, Isabel, but I think I finally understand why you can never stay in one place very long."

"Oh? Enlighten me, Doctor."

"You make yourself obnoxious to people and then you leave. I've never seen anything quite like it."

So he was fighting back. She felt each word like a physical blow. "How dare you?"

"How dare *you?* Without my permission, you handed my son a shotgun and tutored

445

him in shooting. You let him enter a bloody contest —"

"And who is the worse for the wear?" she demanded, fighting back tears. "Not Lucas, at least not until you humiliated him by keeping him from finishing his first match."

He glanced down at the gun in his hand and then at Isabel. He no longer looked angry, but resigned, and that look of resignation was a death knell. Whatever it was they were building between them was gone; she knew it even before he spoke. "In a perverse way, I suppose I'm grateful for what happened here today."

She was having trouble breathing. Her throat and chest hurt with an ache she had never felt before. Even though she knew the answer, she wanted to hear him say it. "Why is that?"

"Because I was about to . . . do something foolish," he said.

"Do you never do foolish things?"

"Not anymore," he said.

Thirty-Six

On her way home from the market, June Li went to the joss house she and her mother had attended ever since she could remember. Located in the Street of the Serpent in Chinatown, the building had a plain facade, unremarkable to the casual passerby. The rich interior always made June feel as though she was in the parlor car of a train. Not that she'd ever been on a train, but it was what she'd imagined it would be.

She had always liked the joss house with its paper-shaded lanterns, statuettes of bronze and gold, painted pots and brass gongs. The smell of sandalwood incense hung in the air, clinging to the fringed silk curtains that separated the rooms. June shut her eyes and sent out the same silent plea she always did. She and Lucas wanted to be together forever. It seemed such a simple notion. Why was it so complicated?

Someone stirred in the next partition. "There you are," said a voice June recognized. Mrs. Clarice Hatcher. "Simon told me it was safe to meet here."

June was about to make her presence known when a man's voice asked, "Can we speak freely?"

"Indeed we can, dear." Then Mrs. Hatcher murmured something June couldn't hear, because the blood was pounding so hard in her ears.

". . . name is Isabel Fish-Wooten," said the man called "dear." "She brazenly introduced herself to me at the match."

At the sound of Miss Isabel's name, June's heart beat even louder. She didn't move a muscle, though her knees ached on the thin cushion. Her mind whirled with indecision. Should she make a dash for the exit? Walk past and pray they didn't recognize her? Wait until they left?

They were whispering again. June willed her heart to stop thundering.

". . . name is Isabel?" Mrs. Hatcher asked, her voice like a knife. "So that's her given name, is it? I knew she was slippery the first moment I saw her."

"We should never have left her that night," the man said. "None of this would have happened."

"No matter." There was a rustling sound. "She left this behind. I imagine she'd do anything to keep her secrets. Even disappear."

"What if she doesn't?"

"Then we'll have to finish what we started that night. This transaction is too important.

If it goes smoothly, we'll never have to worry again."

". . . act tonight. I've a meeting at my club and then I'll join you."

June thought she might explode from holding her breath. Her heart hammered so loudly she was sure they could hear. There was no way to leave without being seen. Or perhaps there was. These people didn't know her. To Anglos, the Chinese all looked alike. They even had stupid pidgin names for them like China-girl.

She made plenty of noise gathering up her parcels. Then she walked past them, pretending she didn't understand English. In the dim hallway, she passed a Chinese man who glanced at her, then looked again, harder.

June recognized him from the charity ball; he'd been with the Irish giant. But maybe she'd be lucky. Maybe he wouldn't recognize her at all. She kept walking, a girl on a routine chore. She'd been doing it for years.

She started breathing again, certain she'd escaped. Then she felt someone jostle her from behind. She opened her mouth to scream, but it was too late. A hand holding a cloth was clapped over her nose and mouth. She recognized the sharp reek of chloroform on the cloth, for it was a substance Dr. Blue used in his practice. She tried not to breathe it in, but the dizzying effects of the heavy, toxic liquid overpowered June. Her legs seemed to melt into her feet. A strong arm choked her throat and she was sucked into a doorway. She didn't even feel herself hitting the brickwork floor.

Lucas sat ramrod straight on the bench seat of the buggy. Beside him sat Miss Isabel. Father was on her other side. His saddled horse plodded along, tethered behind as they all headed home.

The Shooting Club members and guests would celebrate late into the night. This was the final tournament of the season, and according to Lucas's friends, honors would be bestowed, toasts drunk and challenges made for the coming year. That, of course, was the least of Lucas's present worries. In truth, he didn't care about the celebration.

A cool wind swept up from the bay, stirring the first autumn leaves from the tree branches that arched over the roadway. Lucas considered remarking upon the weather, but decided against it. If he knew what was good for him, he'd never speak again. He'd never even breathe again.

His father didn't storm in anger or yell. He simmered quietly, a steam engine on the verge of overheating. This would not be a good time to tell his father what he'd bought at the trading fair at Russ Gardens. Revealing his new acquisition — a short barreled Angleton pistol and loop of bullets — would most assuredly not improve his father's mood.

He kept the gun concealed inside his coat, but honor compelled him to speak up. "It was all my idea. I wanted to go shooting."

"I have no doubt of that."

"He couldn't have done it without me," Isabel said with a loyalty Lucas didn't feel he deserved. "He's gifted at the sport. Had he been permitted to finish the contest, he might have taken home a prize."

"My son has better ways to spend his time." There was not one shred of pride in Father's voice. Instead, there was the promise of a lengthy lecture on trust and responsibility, and no doubt a litany of corrective activities that would make the work at St. Mary's look like a holiday.

"The members of the Shooting Club invited me to a party at the Grove Street house tonight," Miss Isabel said with determined cheerfulness. "There's quite a celebration planned."

"You're free to go," Father said in a flat voice. He stared straight ahead at the road.

Miss Isabel tossed her head and laughed. The ribbons of her bonnet fluttered in the wind. "I just might do that to celebrate my victory."

Despite Father's fury, she'd insisted on finishing her match and indeed, she'd come from behind to win the ladies' division.

Lucas admired her determination. He knew Father had upset her, but somehow she managed to focus solely on her performance and had outscored Mrs. Hatcher, the local favorite.

She patted the reticule tied at her waist. The garment used to belong to Lucas's mother, but he couldn't imagine anyone but Miss Isabel wearing it. "Money is so very useful, isn't it?" she said with a grin.

"What will you use it for?" Lucas asked, hoping to deflect the topic from the shooting match.

The long pause made him nervous. Father still kept his gaze glued to the view between the team's bobbing heads. The narrow hill leading home stretched endlessly to the sky.

"I suppose," she said after a while, "that I could buy a ticket to my next destination."

More silence, heavy with unspoken thoughts. Lucas forced himself to ask the next question. "Where will you go?"

"I'm not sure. I've been mad to see the Sandwich Islands, way out in the Pacific, but perhaps I'll simply go down to the wharves one day and see which way the wind blows." As if to underscore the comment, leaves from the pollarded birch trees along the roadway drifted down, early casualties of summer's end.

"When will you be back?" Lucas asked, then wished he hadn't. He sounded like such a child. But in the short time he'd known Miss Isabel, he'd come to like and admire her intensely.

"I never return to places I've already been."

"Never?" he couldn't help asking.

"Never."

He cast an almost desperate look at his father. Stop her, he wanted to yell. She'll stay if you ask her to.

He knew it was true. Something had happened to his father since Isabel had come into their lives, something Lucas had never seen before. His father liked her. Perhaps he even loved her. If he spoke up now, she'd stay. The special spell she cast over the entire household would last a lifetime. He was sorry he'd told her earlier that his father would never remarry.

But maybe he was right. His father simply drove onward, his gaze steady on the hill. Miss Isabel chattered away about the day's festivities. Lucas sensed an edge in her voice and a suspicious brightness in her eyes. She was working so hard to seem carefree that she was betraying herself, at least to Lucas. It was a picture of hurt he recognized too well.

Once home, he volunteered to put up the buggy and team, and his father neither protested nor thanked him. Working alone in the livery, he whistled between his teeth. Despite his father's fury, Lucas was happy with his performance today. He loved shooting. It was hard and he was good at it. He intended to do more of it, with or without his father's permission. And that was not the only change he intended to make.

It was time, past time, for him to go out and find his own life. Father would forbid it, of course. But Father's interdicts only made Lucas more eager to defy him. He was through asking permission, waiting for approval. An idea formed in his mind, abstract at first but then firming into a plan so concrete, it seemed inevitable, as though it had always been there.

He was leaving.

The rebellious thought buoyed him, and he didn't want to go up to the house just yet. He decided to think up some excuse to find June. At this hour, she'd probably be in the tiny row house where she lived with her mother, across the way from the livery in the service alley. Day maids and laborers carrying tools trudged home from the big houses on the hill, and a gang of kids were playing in the roadway. Men loitered on the stoop of one of the larger houses, and some of them didn't resemble laborers at all, but shifty characters from Barbary. Lucas ignored them as he passed, slipping through the shadows of the close-set buildings.

Mrs. Li's ground-floor flat was painstakingly neat and nondescript, like dozens of others along the row. Here lived the servants of people like his father. But Lucas was so used to thinking of June as someone in his world that he rarely imagined her in a world of her own, living a life entirely separate from his. Unlike his friends' parents, his father took a casual attitude about the hired help. Others held Celestials in suspicion and contempt, and were appalled that Dr. Calhoun treated them as any other patient when they came to him for help. He approved of including June in lessons when they were small. Lucas grinned just thinking about the fun they used to have, writing messages in code on their slates and pulling pranks on the tutors. Even though Chinese children were forbidden to attend public school, Father encouraged June to expand her education and her dreams.

When he remembered that about his father, Lucas had to work harder to keep his resentment kindled.

He knocked tentatively at the low red door to the house. There was a shuffling sound, then Mrs. Li opened the door. When she saw him, she didn't even give him a chance to fumble through some invented excuse for being here. He hadn't even decided on one yet.

"June is gone," she said. She was dressed to go out, in her smock and head scarf and tiny shoes with carved soles. Her eyes held a world of worry.

"Gone where?"

"She went to the market and joss house hours ago, and she is not back yet. She is a good girl. She never fails to come home."

Her calm voice didn't fool Lucas; she was worried. He knew only vague details of Mrs. Li's background. He knew, for example, that the "Mrs." was a courtesy and that she'd never had a husband. Once, he'd asked June about the scars on her mother's arms, but June just shook her head and refused to speak of it. Given Mrs. Li's unswerving devotion to his father, Lucas guessed that life had not always been good to her, that she'd been mistreated in ways he could scarcely imagine.

What he could imagine was the sort of trouble a girl like June Li might encounter down in the city. The waterfront was riddled with shadowy places where young girls came to harm. Chinatown was a place of mystery, where an unsuspecting victim might disappear and never come out. He was suddenly acutely aware of the gun in his inner coat pocket. It was a hard, solid, welcome weight.

"You're on your way out to look for her," he said.

"Of course."

"I'm coming, too."

She slid a glance down the block at the loitering men. "There could be trouble."

He squared his shoulders. "That's exactly why she needs me."

Thirty-Seven

Isabel paced her bedroom in agitation while holding her hand pressed to her chest. "Something's the matter with me," she said to Bernadette, who had come ostensibly to help her change out of her afternoon suit, but really to hear the gossip from the shooting match.

"What do you mean?" asked Bernadette, folding down the coverlet. "Are you ill? Shall I fetch the doctor?"

Isabel gave a despairing little laugh. "Certainly not. I believe he's the cause of it." Holding the bedpost with one hand and keeping the other against her breastbone, she sat down on the edge of the bed. So this is what heartbreak feels like, she thought. It was a special agony, something she'd never felt before — deep, intense, invisible. Impossible to ignore. Or to cure. No wonder it was the topic of so much story and song. No wonder it was called heartbreak. Something inside her had broken, and she had no idea how to put it back together.

"Oh, dear." Abandoning her task of fluffing

the pillows, Bernadette sat down beside her and spoke in a soothing tone. "You'd best tell me all that happened today."

Isabel tried to keep control. The old Isabel would have known how to protect herself. She would have turned the entire disaster into an amusing anecdote. She was supposed to take all of life as a grand adventure. Nothing was supposed to hurt her. But the old Isabel was gone, and in her place was a new person who had discovered new ways to feel, to hurt.

She looked into the housekeeper's soft, kindly eyes and the dam burst. The whole story poured from her in a flood and Bernadette absorbed it into her ample bosom, all the pain and shame and confusion of the day. The excitement of the tournament. The strange encounter with Dr. and Mrs. Vickery. The tense contest with Mrs. Hatcher. Her adoring, motherly feelings for Lucas. And then Blue's arrival, his quiet rage that penetrated to the bone.

"I've never seen anything like it," she confessed in a damp whisper. "He scarcely spoke a word all the way home, yet he managed to make me feel two feet tall."

"When you love someone the way you love him, dearie, you don't ever want to hurt him."

"He wasn't hurt. *I* was hurt. *Lucas* was hurt. He was —" She stopped, and wonder and horror broke over her in equal measures. That was the special quality that gave his anger its power, she realized. It was fury borne of hurt. "Bernadette. Heavens, you're right. I betrayed him."

"Ah, no."

"I introduced the person he loves most in the world to the sport he despises most in the world."

"Did you know how he felt about guns and shooting?"

"I do now."

"But when you went shooting with Lucas, you didn't know."

"That doesn't matter. A responsible person would have asked."

"Look on the bright side. It's a sure sign he loves you." She offered Isabel a folded white handkerchief.

Dabbing at her cheeks, Isabel said, "That makes no sense at all."

"Sure it does, dearie. If he didn't love you, he couldn't possibly be hurt by you. Why do you think he's gone so many years loving no one save Lucas?"

Because he doesn't want to feel the way I'm feeling now, Isabel realized. Her mind and heart filled with the revelation, swelled and overflowed with amazement. She finished drying her face, then stood and brushed out her skirts. "Where is my reticule?"

"In the dressing room." Bernadette followed her, all but clucking like a hen. "Isabel? What's going on in that head of yours?"

She paused in the doorway to the dressing room. Now that she had a good sum of money in her possession, she saw her path clearly before her. Really, the solution was perfectly simple. Turning to Bernadette, she said, "You know."

"Ah, no." The maid tried to wedge herself into the doorway. "You'll not be leaving us."

"What would you have me do? Keep hurting him? Wait until he throws me out?"

"How about staying? When there's enough love, anything can work."

It was a fairy tale. She should know better than to believe it. But in a small, hidden corner of her heart, she did. "How do you know when there's enough?" she asked.

"You don't. And wouldn't life be a sorry prospect indeed if a body always knew what was coming next?"

Blue didn't ordinarily drink hard liquor, but at present he craved something as strong and harsh as the anger he felt at Isabel. He headed for the San Francisco club because it was close to home, yet far enough from Isabel to give him room to sort out his feelings about her.

It didn't work out that way, though. The moment he arrived at the elegant club, the doorman recognized him and hustled him inside. "Thank you for coming so quickly, Doctor," the doorman said.

Blue didn't bother explaining that all he'd come for was a drink. He sensed a hum of panic in the air. "What's the matter?"

A maidservant scurried across the lobby. "She's in the ladies' parlor, and we don't know what to do."

"Who?"

"Mrs. Vickery, sir. She collapsed."

"Where's her husband?"

"We don't know. They meet here often for supper, though. We all thought he was on his way. She was taking tea with Mrs. Hatcher —"

"Clarice was here?"

"Yes, but she left. And Mrs. Vickery seemed perfectly fine." She brought him to the parlor and then stepped back, her nervous fingers folding accordion pleats in her apron. Mrs. Vickery lay supine upon a chaise, unmoving and ghostly pale. Her lips and fingertips appeared distinctly bluish in tone. Lacking a stethoscope, he pressed his ear to her chest. After a few seconds, he said, "Help me loosen her dress and corset. For God's sake, hurry."

The maid worked swiftly to open Mrs. Vickery's dress and loosen her corset laces. "She's so cold," she said, holding Alma Vickery's hand.

"What did she have to eat? What did she drink?" Blue asked.

"As I said, sir, she took tea with Mrs. Hatcher."

"I want her head level with her heart," he ordered, shoving aside the corset and lowering his patient's shoulders. Then he looked at the maid. She was a bland little woman, had probably worked for the family for years. "Listen," he said, "she's under the influence. Trying to protect her reputation now will do far more harm than good."

"Champagne was served, but she's a member of Ladies Temperance," she said. "Perhaps she took some laudanum for her nerves."

"Whose preparation was it? A patent medicine? Where's the bottle?"

"I don't know, sir." The maid was on the verge of tears.

A commotion sounded in the hallway. Then Dr. Vickery arrived, his coat undone, his eyes wild. He was breathless from rushing. "Becca, what's the matter?" he demanded. The maid moved away, and he spied his wife. "Alma, dear God, what have you done?"

Blue thought his choice of words was odd: What have you done?

"I've only been here a few minutes," he said. "Her breathing's slow and shallow. Her pupils don't respond to the light."

"No, for the love of God, *no*." Vickery's hat bounced and rolled across the floor as he bent over his wife.

"Is it laudanum," asked Blue, "or does she eat the substance directly?" He peeled down Mrs. Vickery's dress sleeve and found what he'd expected: a small, purplish wound on the inside of her bare arm. "Oh. I see."

"Don't say it," Vickery murmured. "Damn it, man, I know."

For a moment, he and Vickery locked gazes over the poor woman. Then they took action, working for what seemed like a long time, hauling her up and moving her around the room, though she sagged like a broken doll between them. After a while, Mrs. Vickery coughed and vomited. Her eyes were slits of semiconsciousness.

With a trembling hand, Vickery bathed his wife's face and brow with a damp cloth.

"Fremont." Alma Vickery murmured her husband's name in a faint whisper. "Oh, my dear Fremont."

He set aside the handkerchief. "Ah, thank God, Alma. You're awake."

Blue counted her pulse, checked for fever. Her wispy hair was plastered to her brow with sweat. Mrs. Vickery stared at him blankly, then turned to her husband. "I feel so horribly strange, Fremont. I beg you, get me my medicine. That is all I need, and then I'll feel better."

"Let's go home, dear. I'll take you home now." He lifted her up, straining no more than he would to carry a small child.

"I want to stay at the club, Fremont," she said, her mood shifting uncannily. Her eyes glowed in the electrical light.

"Let's go home," he repeated. "I can take better care of you there." He ducked his head and didn't look at Blue as he and the maid helped her out of the room.

An unseasonable chill bit the air as Blue left the club. Was that what love did to a man? he wondered.

He was nearly home when he realized he never did get that drink.

Isabel had always considered herself a courageous woman. She'd sailed stormy seas and climbed treacherous mountains, haggled with dangerous traders in crowded foreign marketplaces and faced both sharpshooters and gambling sharks in high stakes contests.

But she had never asked anyone to love her.

The very prospect made her tremble. She stood in the darkened upstairs hallway, listening to Bernadette's sturdy tread on the stair as the housekeeper went to her quarters for the night. On the floor above, Lucas made no sound. Isabel pictured him lying on his bed or perhaps staring out the window, probably sulking about the fact that his father had forced him to give up the shooting contest.

The hour was early. She knew Blue would be in his study downstairs, where he retreated each evening, unless he was on duty at the Rescue League. Her pulse pounding, she stood in front of the polished oak door. Then she took a deep breath and knocked.

"Yes? What is it?" he asked in a distracted voice.

She resisted the urge to flee. Instead, she forced herself to go in. He wasn't at his massive rolltop desk, as she'd expected, but stood in the middle of the room as though he'd just been pacing the floor. He'd removed his jacket and waistcoat. The white shirt she'd admired earlier gaped open at the collar; the sleeves were rolled back to the elbows. His deep blue cravat lay discarded on a chair. A shock of wheat-colored hair tumbled over his brow.

"What do you want, Isabel?" he asked.

"There's something I'd like to discuss with you." Dear heavens. Was that really her voice, with that humiliating tremble of uncertainty?

He folded his arms across his chest. "Go on."

She remembered how she'd felt when those muscular arms were wrapped around her, holding her close. Yet now they formed a barrier. "Do you think perhaps we could sit down together?"

A long, unbroken alarm sounded, making her jump. The doorbell, she realized, half-relieved, half-frustrated by the interruption. Rather than waiting for Bernadette to answer the door, Blue strode to the foyer.

He opened the door, and Clarice Hatcher swept into the house. "There you are, Theodore," she said. "I was hoping you'd be at home."

"Is something the matter, Clarice?" he asked.

"It certainly —" She spied Isabel and pruned her lips into a grimace. "Miss Fish-Wooten. Or have you reinvented yourself again? Should we call you Florence Nightingale today?"

Isabel directed an imperious gaze at her, giving no indication that the taunting words and knowing look posed a threat. They were rivals for Blue's heart, and they both knew it. That was the source of Clarice's animosity. Yet she seemed to possess some inner knowledge of Isabel — or perhaps that sprang from Clarice's sharp instincts.

Isabel hid a flutter of apprehension behind a haughty look. "Hello, Mrs. Hatcher. It's so kind of you to come in person to congratulate me on winning the tournament."

"What's the matter, Clarice? Are you ill?" Blue asked again. The edge in his voice conveyed clearly that he was in no mood for a rivalry of any sort.

"I'm not ill, Theodore. But I've come to you on a matter of some urgency."

Isabel wondered what sort of "matters" Clarice and Blue had between them.

"Then you should have said so." He looked disheveled, his eyes weary and his hair tumbling over his brow.

Clarice led the way into the parlor without waiting for an invitation. "I had meant to discuss this in private, Theodore," she said, "but it involves your houseguest, so she should hear this as well, though I'm certain she'll deny it." She pinioned Isabel with a glare. "Theodore, you are harboring a dangerous criminal under your roof. I feel compelled to tell you this for your own safety. She could be stealing you blind — or worse."

Isabel laughed aloud, although her stomach clenched. "Oh, for goodness sake. Are you mad? Why would you make such an accusation?"

Something shifted in Clarice's regard — a flicker of inspiration. "Because I've found evidence to prove that you've done nothing but lie since you appeared in San Francisco, seemingly out of nowhere." She pursed her lips in superior fashion. "Isn't that right, Miss Dawkins?"

Isabel felt the blood drop from her face to the bottom of her gut.

"Who the devil is Miss Dawkins?" Blue demanded, his patience fraying at the edges.

Clarice jerked her chin at Isabel. "Ask her."

Isabel struggled to appear confused. "I don't know what you're talking about."

"Of course you do," Clarice said, each word edged in cold steel. "I'm talking about the Isabel Dawkins who grew up in a workhouse. An object of pity, of course, until she turned into a petty criminal who lied her way into an aristocratic household, learned the ways of the gentry and then stowed away on a ship to New York. That is the Isabel Dawkins I'm speaking of."

No. No. No. Isabel's pulse thundered in her ears, and she raised her voice to drown it out. "Goodness, you are quite a yarn spinner, Mrs. Hatcher." She sneaked a look at Blue, praying he'd exhibit shock and disbelief. Instead, his face was a granite mask. He wasn't surprised at all to hear this.

"I've long had my suspicions," Clarice declared. "I finally guessed the truth when I saw your handwriting on the tournament entry form." As she spoke, she retrieved a calf-bound book tied together with string. She loosed the string with a flourish. "I have the evidence right here."

Clarice opened the book to reveal pages covered with Isabel's neat handwriting. Stuck between the pages were a certificate and a creased and scarred placement card.

Isabel froze, watching through a fog of

horror. This could not be happening. It could not. If she moved, it would all be real. She felt sick. Blue didn't understand yet, but she knew exactly what he was about to learn. The book was a terrible keepsake, a record of her shameful life before she'd turned herself into someone else. Why, oh why, had she dragged it around all those years, a memento of misery, a memorial to the mother who had dumped her like an unwanted kitten in a sack?

"Let me see that." Blue grabbed the book.

"Fascinating, isn't it?" said Clarice. "This is a placement card for St. Anselm's workhouse in Fish Street in the town of Wooten, Norfolk. It's all chronicled in this book, you see."

Isabel wanted to scream a denial, but she couldn't. She was unmasked, naked before them. She watched Blue's face, but could not fathom his thoughts as he read over the evidence of her deception. She burned with humiliation, but something bigger was at stake. A different sort of horror broke over her. She grabbed the book from Blue and held it in front of her like a shield.

She stared at Clarice. This time, recognition hummed between them so palpably that she wondered if Blue sensed it. She felt ice cold with fear and suspicion. "Where did you get this, Clarice?"

"I'm certain I don't know. A servant came across it somewhere."

Isabel turned to Blue. "My belongings went missing the night of the shooting. Only someone who was there could have found them."

"Shooting?" Clarice said. "Heavens, Theodore, she's burying lies beneath lies. Really, this is all too —"

"Shut up, Clarice," Blue snapped, startling them both. "There was a shooting. A police officer and Isabel were both wounded."

"I wouldn't know the first thing about that," Clarice said, "except for what I've read in the papers."

"Then I'll need to speak with the person who found this."

"You'll do no such thing."

"Would you rather I brought in the police?"

Isabel took a chance. "I don't believe there was any servant involved."

Clarice sniffed. "So now you'll accuse *me* of the shooting."

"Are you confessing to it?"

"I'll not dignify that with a reply."

"But it's all so fascinating," Isabel said, struggling to regain her balance. She had nothing more than a hunch about Clarice, but she was desperate. "Your timing is simply uncanny. You just happened to contrive some terrible story about me because I've discovered the truth about you and Dr. Vickery." One look at Clarice's face told her the bluff was working. "Perhaps that's what we should be talking about, your association with Dr. Vickery and your ties to the Far East Tea Company." She was scraping together bits and pieces of information, pretending she knew more than she did.

Clarice turned bright red. "This is preposterous. Theodore, I came here with the best of intentions, to prevent you from being swindled. Why would I bring this out into the open if I knew it was so closely connected to a horrid crime?"

"That's an interesting question, Clarice." Blue spoke with calm conviction. "I imagine it's because you believe you have enough money to buy your way out of trouble. Isn't that what you always say?"

"I refuse to listen to this another moment," said Clarice with a queenly sniff. She left in a swirl of silk skirts and indignation.

"Are you just going to let her go?" asked Isabel.

"Would you like her to stay? The two of you were getting along so well."

Isabel held the book tight against her. "She attacked because she's cornered. Couldn't you see that? She was part of what happened to me that night. But not all of it. I didn't bring up Dr. Vickery by accident. I saw them together today at the shooting match, and I assure you, they're more than passing acquaintances. They were both there that night,

Blue. The sound of his voice brought it all back. No matter what you think of me now, you must believe that. One of them shot two people." She held her breath, willing him to believe her.

"You're asking me to point the finger at a fellow physician and a woman I've known for ten years."

She wanted to dissolve into tears, but forced herself to stand still, to regard him without flinching. "Yes."

He hesitated only a second. "Get your cloak. We're going to see Rory. He has more experience separating lies from truth than I have."

Thirty-Eight

As a criminal lawyer, Rory would advise him as to the best way to go about this — as if there was any good way to do it at all. He had a number of unanswered questions, Clarice's presence at the hospital, for example, shortly before Nathan Skinner died, and the fact that Mrs. Vickery had collapsed after taking tea with Clarice. Then there was Vickery's secret about his wife. Those facts, coupled with Isabel's suggestion of an involvement in the opium trade, would give Rory plenty to chew on.

But in fact Blue's mind — along with his heart and every other part of him — was preoccupied with the woman beside him. Since the moment they'd gotten into the buggy, she hadn't stopped talking. He wasn't really listening, because she was remarking on Clarice's fanciful imagination and the lengths the jealous widow went to in order to discredit Isabel. Dousing a glimmer of sympathy, he reminded himself that this woman had lied to him from the first moment she'd stuck a gun in his back.

"Why are you looking at me like that?" she asked.

"You're a chameleon, Isabel. You've never lived an authentic moment in your life."

"How would you know that? You've only known me one summer."

"I haven't known you at all. I've known some self-invented fraud who calls herself a lady adventurer."

"I *am* an adventurer. I can be whoever I choose."

He turned his face away from her and concentrated on the road. "How about choosing to be yourself for once?"

She fell silent. Didn't move a muscle. He kept glancing at her, watching the lamplight slip over her in pale waves as they drove down Broadway, but she neither moved nor spoke. Finally he had found a way to stop her from talking. And that was to hurt her.

The expression on her face had an unexpected effect on him. "Isabel —"

"Are you sure that's my name?" she asked. "Why don't you go and ask Clarice what to call me?"

She's not hard to love, he thought, remembering Eliza's words the night of the charity ball. She's impossible.

Only because she's making it so, said a deeper, wiser voice inside him.

As he pulled up to the elegant building that

housed Rory's bachelor's quarters, he wondered if he would let her get away with it.

June came awake slowly, though she did not remember falling asleep. Then a terrific headache possessed her, and she reached to press her hands to her temples.

Her hands were tied.

She tried to call out, but there was a piece of cloth stuffed in her mouth. She tried to spit it out, but it was held in place by a cord tied around the back of her head. She whimpered, but it sounded like a hiccup. She wept, but the silent tears did no good, so she forced herself to stop. Whimpering and crying were not going to save her.

She was alone in the damp, dark place. No, not quite alone. The place was infested by rats — she knew that sharp reek. Artificial light leaked through the slats of a rough wooden door. The room had an earthen floor and tall ceiling, and was littered with wooden crates. She tried to puzzle out her location. She smelled old brick and dank earth and seawater. Sounds from outside confirmed it — she was at the waterfront, across from the wharves. She recognized the unmistakable creak of great vessels pulling at their moorings, and the quiet chuckle and croak of roosting birds.

She heard footsteps, quite close. Struggling to her feet, she shuffled forward across the uneven floor. Pressing her face to the door, she peered between the planks. A man stood in an alley beneath a conical beam of light spilling over an awning. He wore an old-fashioned peaked hat with a long pheasant feather stuck in the brim.

His name was Mr. Abner Punch. He and his partner, Charles Pisco, were the two most notorious crimps of the Barbary Coast. Everyone knew who they were, everyone except the hapless greenhorns they pressed into shipboard service. June was terrified, but she was also confused. She had been afraid they would sell her to a Chinese tong. But instead of being brought before a fat-cheeked tong boss, she was dragged here. This could not possibly mean anything good for her.

She sank down to the cold earthen floor and went to work. Although her hands were bound so tightly she'd lost sensation in her fingers, she managed to work her feet free. Her toes tingled painfully with the rush of blood, but she jumped up, jubilant over her small victory.

Angry voices sounded outside. She heard a woman pleading in Mandarin. *Mother.*

June hurried to the door and looked out, but could see no one. Fresh tears of fright and frustration squeezed from her eyes. Then she heard another voice — Lucas. She would know his voice anywhere, like an unforgettable song. She wanted to scream, to warn her mother and Lucas to go away and keep themselves safe, but she couldn't.

There was a commotion in the alley, the thud of a blow and a body falling, the sound of running feet. Lucas said one of his vilest swearwords, and Mr. Punch said something worse. A heavy weight slammed up against the warehouse door, and June jumped back, falling to her knees.

Then the door opened, and a tall figure stumbled into the room.

It was Lucas, looking bigger and stronger than she'd ever seen him, the gaslight behind outlining the form of a grown man, his hair and the hem of his coat swirling on the wind. Mr. Charles Pisco came in behind him and gave him a terrific shove, and Punch joined in, hammering with his fists. June could hear the breath rush out of Lucas. Then she heard sickening thuds as blow after blow rained on him. For the longest time, he didn't go down, no matter how many times they hit him. He put up a valiant fight, but it was June herself who finished him off.

She didn't mean to. She ran at the crimps, her only thought to get them to stop. One swat from a rubbery blackjack flung her down.

"June," Lucas yelled. There was an awful crunching sound and he staggered, then sank to his knees and finally pitched forward. The crimps gave him a couple of kicks for good measure. They stepped back, and the heap on the floor lay unmoving, making no sound.

Grief erupted from a black well deep inside June, but she couldn't make a sound. The only noise in the big, cavernous room was the ragged breathing of the crimps.

Something stirred. At first she thought it was the wind rushing in through the doorway. Then she realized it was Lucas.

And when he dragged himself up, like a bear standing on his two hind legs, he was holding a gun in his hand.

"Untie her hands and let her go," he said.

The crimps looked at one another, then Mr. Punch hastened to cut loose her hands. Her fingers felt useless and numb. When she spat out the cloth, she couldn't speak.

She froze when she heard Lucas swear. Peering through the shadows, she saw that he still held his gun to Pisco's head.

But Mr. Punch had a gun of his own, and he was pointing it straight at Lucas. A standoff, she realized with a sinking heart. Someone would die. That was the only certainty.

"Let the girl go." Lucas spoke in a commanding voice she scarcely recognized. "When I see her walk away free with her mother, I'll drop my gun."

Pisco said, "Let her go."

No, thought June, even as she edged toward the door.

"Go on," said Lucas in a rough voice that touched her deep inside. "I'll be all right. I promise."

"Lucas —"

"Have I ever broken a promise to you? Ever?"

Not once, she realized. Oh, she loved him so much. With every bit of her heart.

"You have ten seconds to disappear, China girl," Pisco warned her. "Don't let us see you around here again."

She could not tear her eyes from Lucas. His lips moved, though he made no sound. He didn't have to. She understood. *I love you.*

"Go," Lucas repeated. "Hurry."

Hurry. She wasn't sure what he was thinking, but she guessed it was the same thought she had. Their best chance was for her to go get help.

She scrambled for the partially-opened door. Behind her, she heard the sound of Lucas's gun dropping with a thud. She stepped outside and found her mother sitting on the ground, shaking herself awake. June sank to her knees and hugged her mother close. For a moment, the sweetness of safety overwhelmed her, but a sense of danger chased it away.

"Are you all right?" she whispered to her mother. "Can you run?"

"Like the wind." With the same strength

that had seen her through the dark years of June's earliest memories, Li Mei stood up and took her daughter's hand.

June didn't dare look back, but plunged into the damp shadows and up the fog-shrouded hill, leading the way for her mother. She ran faster than she ever thought she could, faster than the wind, than danger, than a storm. But she left her whole heart behind.

Part Three

Travels with Isabel

A lie can travel halfway around the world while the truth is putting on its shoes.
— Mark Twain

Thirty-Nine

Isabel sensed a tang of autumn in the night air. Dead leaves from the Dutch elms and blue gum trees tumbled across the roadway and collected in the gutters. How swiftly the summer had passed, she thought. And how foolish she'd been to stay too long.

The truth about the shooting was finally coming to light, but with it came a truth she had prayed would never surface. Her identity. Her shame. The reason she could never, ever stay in one place. What an idiot she was to suppose otherwise.

Rory wasn't to be found; his manservant indicated that he'd been on police business all evening. She and Blue had driven home without speaking. *Home.* Such a strange and inappropriate way to think of this place. She sneaked a look at him as he stopped the buggy under the port cochere at the side of the house. The image of him imprinted itself on her memory — strong, serious, hurting. She prayed he would remember the better times they'd shared, the brilliant summer days when they'd gone riding all the way to the Presidio, the deep, soft nights when they'd made love until dawn touched the sky. It was a futile hope, though. She was certain that he would always remember her as a woman made of no substance who could not stay in one place.

It was late, and she knew Blue would put the horse and buggy up himself rather than disturb Efrena. But first he seemed intent on ridding himself of his unwanted burden. He lashed the reins around a brass-headed post and walked to her side of the buggy. Wordlessly, he held out one hand, palm up.

"Thank you," she said, and put her hand in his. Oh, that touch. Even now, her heart responded with a surge of longing. As she rose from her seat, she held his gaze with hers. He placed his hands at her waist, and just for a moment, as she swung down, she had the sensation of dancing. She remembered dancing with him. She remembered every touch, every kiss, every caress they had shared. She remembered the way he had looked at her when he'd thought she was someone else.

What she wouldn't give for him to look at her that way again. But it was not to be. Now, his eyes were dark with anger, his face a frozen mask that hid his emotions. His retreat to the place where he buried his past was complete — and it was her doing. She'd won his trust and perhaps even his love, only to become living proof that it didn't pay to give your heart.

He set her down gently as though she might break. Then he stood looking at her for a long time. The scent of late roses and mint perfumed the misty air. A night bird warbled; the breeze picked up. For some reason, he kept hold of her. She didn't want to let go of him. For as long as he allowed, she would hold on. Later, she would treasure the memory of this final embrace.

"I wanted to love you, Isabel," he said. "You. Not some illusion you conjured out of lies."

She flinched at his tone of voice, surprised that he spoke of love now that it was out of the question. She forced herself to regard him with careless pride. "I suppose that's what you get for letting an armed gunman into your house."

"I didn't let you in. You came by force. And for what it's worth, I came to believe in your innocence."

She let a brief laugh escape. "Innocence is something I lost the year I started to bleed like a woman, but no hard facts will change your opinion of me."

She thought that would make him let her go, but instead, he tugged her closer. "Don't do my thinking for me, Isabel."

She lifted their hands, still clasped, and studied the way their fingers wove together.

"I used to fantasize that I was the daughter of a good-hearted but impoverished noble-woman, who wept upon relinquishing me and promised to come back and rescue me one day," she confessed. "But the fact is, my mother was a whore who littered the city of London with her babies, leaving them like abandoned pets for others to care for." The admission left her emptied out. She disengaged her hand from his. "I tried to leave. Remember that. I did try."

"Isabel." He seemed at a loss, wrenching her name from a well of hurt. "Why didn't you tell me who you are?"

God. He didn't understand. He would never understand. "This *is* who I am," she said, pressing her hand to her chest. "My name is Isabel Fish-Wooten." Her voice shook and she prayed he hadn't noticed. "Excuse me. I must get a few things packed." She walked toward the door.

He grabbed her upper arm and spun her around to face him. "I never told you to leave."

She refused to flinch at the hard bite of his hand on her arm. "Blue, I don't fit into your life. We've always known that. Now the entire city will know, because Clarice is not about to keep this to herself."

"Do you think that matters to me?"

She held her gaze steady on his. Then, with measured deliberation, she pried his hand from her arm. There were some things she would never be able to explain. "It matters to me," she said.

"Dr. Blue." Breathless and frantic, June Li came running up the walk. Far in the distance, her mother followed, hobbling in her wooden clogs. June's shining hair was mussed, her smock soiled around the hem, her cheeks stained with tears.

Isabel's agonized shame burned away when she recognized the terror in the girl's face. She broke away from Blue. "What's the matter?" she asked.

"Dr. Blue, you must come. They have Lucas."

Blue was already heading for the house while the girl explained. She'd overheard talk of the shooting. Mrs. Hatcher's footmen handed her over to a pair of crimps, but they released her in exchange for Lucas. Blue fired off his questions — Where were they keeping him? What was their purpose?

June sobbed out the answers as best she could. Isabel's hunch had been correct. Clarice Hatcher and Vickery had played a part in the waterfront violence. And they weren't finished yet. They had Lucas. Finally, Isabel understood what it was to love a child. Until this summer, she'd been driven by a need for money and adventure. Now she realized she would willingly give her own life, if only it would keep Lucas safe.

She also understood that she'd brought danger and corruption to this house. It used to be a safe place, but thanks to her, with her ties to the corrupt and violent underworld, they'd almost lost June Li and Lucas was missing.

She held the girl's hand tightly as they followed Blue to a storeroom in the basement. With deadly purpose, he opened a musty footlocker, yanking out an old pistol. His sidearm, she realized. According to Delta and Efrena, he had laid it to rest the day his wife was killed.

With an expertise that should not have surprised her, he oiled the chamber and loaded it, then strapped on a belt of bullets.

Isabel didn't ask him where he was going. She knew. "I'm coming with you," she said.

"No, you're not." He held up a hand to silence her. "I'll hogtie you if I have to, Isabel. I swear I will."

She didn't doubt it for a minute. "All right," she said, casting her gaze to the floor and squeezing the girl's hand. "I'll stay and look after June."

"You do that."

"You should take money," she advised.

"What?"

"There might be a ransom demand."

Swearing under his breath, he took the stairs two at a time as he went to his suite of rooms, where he kept a safe. Isabel, too, burst into action. She felt responsible for all of the day's disasters, and if there was a way for her to help, she intended to find it. She needed only two things — the pistol she'd borrowed at the tournament, and the money she'd won.

"What are you doing?" June whispered as Isabel slipped outside and headed for the buggy.

"Hoping the good doctor doesn't check his luggage rack."

Forty

───❦❦❦───

In all his years of racing through San Francisco to answer emergency calls, Blue had never gone so fast. Any other horse would have collapsed under the punishing pace, but the Calhoun-bred gelding was equal to the task. Blue's fear was as clean and cold as a naked blade. He would not falter or fail in his determination to save Lucas.

He drew the buggy to a stop in a plaza facing the waterfront and backed by dark warehouses. Even at this time of night, dock-workers and sailors were busy loading freight. The bay swarmed with skiffs and ferries.

"You're too late." Fremont Vickery's shiny shoes, clad in snow-white spats, rang on the new brickwork of the Embarcadero as he walked toward Blue. "He's already gone."

Blue flung the reins into the buggy and leaped down to the pavement. "What the devil are you up to?"

"Protecting myself."

"By kidnapping an innocent boy?" Blue slipped his hand into the pocket of his coat.

Vickery noticed, but stayed perfectly calm.

Blue watched him through new eyes. The man was uniquely dangerous, a fellow doctor and eminent colleague who lined his pockets with the glittering wealth of the opium trade, a millionaire who would go to any lengths to protect the source of his wealth.

With his hand still in his pocket, Blue closed his grip around the gun and fit his finger snug against the trigger. In ten years, he had not touched a gun, yet his hand remembered the heft of it, the chill steel against his flesh, the almost delicate feel of the trigger mechanism. "Let my son go. He has nothing to do with this. I'll take him home and leave you to go about your business."

"As you did in the matter of my private patient, Officer Brolin?" snapped Vickery. "You're a meddling fool, Calhoun. You and that woman —" A chorus of rough laughter rang out. Vickery broke off, flicking a glance over his shoulder. Like Blue, he seemed to know the waterfront denizens weren't likely to intervene.

"Why Lucas?" Blue demanded. "Your quarrel's with me."

"I believe I know how far you'd go to protect someone you love," Vickery said, and he looked away again, this time at the gleaming coach parked across the plaza.

Alma Vickery, Blue realized, following the direction of his gaze. His addict wife. Was she in the coach, awash in bliss after her husband injected a dose of morphine? Blue wondered how much she knew, how deeply she was involved. Had she shot Officer Brolin and Isabel that night? Or had Dr. Vickery done the honors?

The gun was smooth and hard in his grip. He was through trying to reason with Vickery. "Where's Lucas?"

"There was a ten-thirty tide. The bar pilots have been ferrying men out to the fleet all evening. So your boy is at sea already, Dr. Calhoun. But you needn't fear. So long as nothing happens to me or to those I care about, nothing will happen to him."

Lamps on curved poles bobbed from the gunwales of scores of Whitehall skiffs. The swift, slender crafts crossed the bay to the deep-water moorings of the brigs and tall clippers. Crews of outbound sailors sang and swore in a multitude of tongues, their hoarse voices rolling across the jammed waterway. Women stood in clusters on shore, waving and weeping and calling farewell. No one took any notice of the two tense men facing each other at the head of the wharf.

Blue imagined Lucas beaten, frightened, forced into service aboard a ship that might not return for months or even years. He wanted to roar with frustration. Vickery felt no threat at all from him. He knew Blue wouldn't harm him so long as he knew the whereabouts of Lucas. What the hell did you say to a man who wouldn't listen to reason or threats?

"This is insane," he said.

"You should have thought of that when you let a dangerous criminal into your house."

The door of Vickery's coach thumped open. "He didn't let me in. I forced him to take care of me." Moving with the lightness of a hummingbird, Isabel dropped to the pavement.

Vickery gasped. Blue, on the other hand, felt no shock at seeing her. After an entire summer of Isabel, he should have realized she would not wait patiently at home while he played the hero. She'd defied him, of course, following him down to the waterfront. His gaze slipped to the luggage rack of his buggy. It took him no time at all to figure out what she was up to. She'd stowed away, and then while he and Vickery argued, she'd slipped into the coach with Mrs. Vickery.

She turned and took Mrs. Vickery's hand, helping the older lady down. Blue could see instantly that she was under the influence. The wobbling legs, the flat, glassy eyes, the expression of childlike bliss were all too familiar to him.

She never saw Isabel's gun, but Blue and Vickery did.

"Dear God," Vickery said, staggering a little. He quickly recovered and rapped out a command: "Put that away."

"I hope to momentarily," Isabel said in her perfect accent. She sounded every bit the haughty noblewoman she pretended to be. "However, that is up to you."

"Fremont, what's happening?" Alma asked, her blurry gaze sweeping the busy wharves.

"An unfortunate situation," Isabel said.

"Oh. That seems to be a common occurrence this summer," Alma said distractedly. "It was awful the last time I had to come down here after you, Fremont, remember? You thought you'd put me on the train to Monterey, but I followed you here, you and that hussy —"

"Dear, please," Vickery said. "You're upsetting yourself."

"For the time being, that's the idea," Isabel explained with an icy calm. "Each of us harbors someone beloved of the other. Making a switch is the only way to solve this, isn't it? Lucas hasn't really been shipped out yet, has he, Alma?"

"Of course he hasn't, has he, Fremont? He's with Mr. Leland and those two gentlemen who were helping with the shipment."

Vickery's shoulders sagged. "Don't hurt her. For the love of God, don't."

"That's your decision," said Blue. He looked over at Isabel, and his heart filled so full that it hurt. "Or rather, it's up to the dangerous criminal I harbored." If that was what Vickery thought of her, so much the better.

"Fremont, I'm confused. You said we were going on a voyage tonight," Alma said. She dug in her carpet bag. "I brought everything, just as you requested."

Isabel locked eyes with Blue, just for a moment. He wished he knew what she was thinking, but there were things about her he didn't understand at all.

"Your wife and I are losing patience," she said.

Dr. Vickery put his fingers to his lips and whistled. A few moments later, Blue saw the two crimps, Punch and Pisco, crossing the waterfront plaza. Between them, Lucas stumbled, his head sagging to one side.

The sight of his son, broken and bleeding, ignited a terrible rage in Blue. At a nod from Vickery, the crimps shoved the boy at him and slipped away into a stream of stevedores and other dockworkers, disappearing into the dark. "Where are you hurt? Son, can you walk?" Blue asked Lucas.

Lucas waved away his concern. "What about June and Mrs. Li?"

"They're home," said Blue. "They're fine."

Isabel stepped away from Mrs. Vickery and shoved the pistol inside her traveling cloak. Vickery rushed to his wife, a ragged exclamation of relief on his lips.

Blue went to help Lucas into the buggy.

The boy reeked of blood and dirt. He slumped on the seat. All Blue wanted now was to get away from the chaotic corruption of the waterfront.

Then, as he turned to Isabel, he saw something flash in Fremont Vickery's hand.

A gun.

"Isabel!" The warning tore from his throat even as he drew and fired his own weapon.

Two shots rang out. White flashes and gunsmoke filled the air. People screamed and dove for cover. One of the horses panicked and trotted forward, taking the buggy. Isabel lay on the ground, unmoving. Like a flash of lightning, a remembrance of Sancha flickered through him, but then she was gone, and his entire world was filled with Isabel, only Isabel. Blue raced across the plaza and plunged to his knees beside her.

A denial jolted through his body as he took her in his arms. The still-hot gun dangled from his hand. He released it and pushed at the dark folds of her dress and cloak, searching with his eyes and hands, but also with his other senses. As though returning to the battlefield, he caught the hot cinderburn of powder, the salty-sharp tang of fresh blood. A desperate sound came from him, and he realized it was a prayer.

"I'm not hurt," she whispered, tightening her fists into his sleeves. "It just occurred to me to get out of the way when a gun appeared."

The sound of her voice was a gift too precious to imagine, one he didn't deserve.

"Where is Lucas?" she asked.

"Here," Lucas called from the buggy. He'd managed to stop it a half a block away and bring it back to the plaza. His hands trembled; his face had lost all color. This had frightened him more than the beating.

Blue looked over at Vickery, who lay on the ground. Alma staggered back against the open door of the coach and wailed. Blue glanced at his gun on the ground. A sound like the roar of a fire filled his head. His hand, his fingers — everything burned.

Slowly he released Isabel and got up, crossing the plaza to save the life of the man he'd just shot.

Rory McKnight stepped out of a hansom cab. Behind him, a police wagon rolled to a halt and two officers leaped out.

"There you are," he said to Blue. "I've been trying to find you all evening." He hunkered down beside Vickery's supine form and emitted a low whistle. "You've been busy, I see."

Blue finished Vickery's field dressing. The tibia was shattered, and he was in danger of losing the limb. He was conscious but chilled from shock. Alma held her hands wrapped around her waist, softly sobbing and rocking herself.

"Help me get them both into the carriage," Blue said to the hovering policemen. "I'm taking them to the hospital."

"You'll do no such thing," Vickery stated through chattering teeth.

Rory clucked his tongue, shaking his head. "Defiant to the end. I admired your wealth, Doctor, but that was when I thought you earned it legitimately."

"I'm afraid," Alma said, her eyes hazy with fright. "Fremont, I wish this whole night would go away." She turned to Rory. "He did that the last time. He told me I was away on the night of the shooting. That's what I was to tell everyone."

"Well, guess what, ma'am," Rory said. "Starting now, you can tell the truth." He motioned for the policemen to come forward. A number of onlookers, as well as Rory's cab, hastened away when the law arrived.

Lucas handed Vickery's pistol over to one of the officers. Rory promised a complete account would be given later. As the police took the Vickerys away to Mercy Heights, Blue turned to Lucas. "What the devil were you thinking, rushing off alone like that?"

Isabel placed her hand on Lucas's arm. "What your father means to say is that you've been helpful, and he's proud of you. Now, give me a hand into the buggy. I know you're eager to get home."

Without asking permission, Rory hoisted himself up onto the seat next to her. "Good show, my boy. Hello, Isabel, dear. What an eventful night it's been. When are you going to abandon this unpleasant physician and run away with me?"

She offered her trademark quicksilver laugh. "How soon can you be packed?"

She and Rory had far more in common than Rory knew. They'd both been abandoned, had both suffered unthinkably as children. She didn't have to speak of that time to him any more than Rory did. He simply knew. But the difference was, Rory had never felt compelled to conceal his past.

Blue headed up the hill toward home, grateful to leave the waterfront behind.

"Look at that," Isabel said, lifting her face to the dawn sky, now filled with a flurry of falling leaves. "The season's changing."

"What's going on?" Blue asked Rory, sensing that his friend was bursting with news.

"I thought you'd want to know. Officer Brolin is awake. And he told me who shot him."

Forty-One

Following a lengthy visit to the police station with Rory, Blue returned home at mid-morning. The events of the night had blown apart his life and when he put himself back together, he felt like a stranger. After ten years of sleepwalking, he had been jolted awake by an extraordinary summer, a love affair so passionate he was suddenly young again. He wondered, if he were to look in a mirror, would he recognize the man he'd become?

Hearing voices in the garden, he went around the side of the house, in time to witness Lucas and June break their embrace. The two youngsters stood side by side, their faces flushed but their eyes defiant. Lucas bore the bruises of his ordeal, and Blue realized there was no worse sight for a parent than a wounded child. Yet the boy didn't seem to be in pain. There was something piercing in the way he and June stood together, not touching yet exuding a bond not even the gods could break. Only yesterday, when he thought he knew what was best for

Lucas, Blue would have subjected his son to a lecture about propriety and responsibility. Now he suspected there were things the boy understood with far more authority than Blue had given him credit for.

"Son, I need a word with you," he said. His voice sounded the same as always — flat, authoritarian. And certainly Lucas's reaction was the same — a prideful lifting of the chin.

"Yes, sir."

Blue summoned up a smile. "June, thank you for your help last night. You were very brave."

Flustered, she dipped into a quick curtsy. "Yes, sir," she said, then mumbled something about helping her mother and scurried into the house.

Lucas set himself to raking leaves into a growing pile in the middle of the lawn.

"Am I that scary?" Blue asked.

"Always," Lucas said, concentrating on the raking.

The arrow darted into him. "Lucas, about yesterday —"

"Father, the shooting contest —"

They both spoke at once and both stopped. Then Lucas took a deep breath and set his rake in motion again. "You shot a man to save Miss Isabel's life."

"That doesn't mean I approve of firearms."

"It no longer matters to me. I've decided to stop seeking your approval. I've done so all my life, and nothing I do is ever good enough."

Blue was stunned. He wondered if lack of sleep had affected his hearing. "That's preposterous. You've always had my love and approval."

"And I was supposed to deduce that from your lectures and criticisms?"

"If I seem harsh, it's because I care so much, son. I want to protect you. To keep you safe and strong. It's what your mother would have wanted."

Lucas set aside the rake and turned to face Blue. "It always comes back to my mother. Why don't you ever speak of what happened to her that day? Why don't you let me remember it?"

"What?" Blue fought the urge to shake his head as though he had ears full of water. "There's nothing for you to remember. You were too young —"

"Was I? Then tell me why I dream of it. Tell me why, in dreams, I'm lying very still, feeling her warm blood pulsing out of her. Tell me why I still hear screams, sometimes. Why I wake up at night with the sound of crying in my head. Tell me why the smell of pickles makes me sick."

Blue scarcely dared to move. By God, the boy did have memories of that day. "I never wanted you to suffer."

His handsome face, a mirror of his

mother's, twisted in agony. "Last night, when the shooting started, I lived it all over again, just like I do in nightmares. How can you think I didn't suffer?"

"I was hoping you would never, ever have to remember. When I was just a boy, my mother died in a fire. I recall every moment of it. I watched her, son. It's part of who I am. I can no more rid myself of those memories than I can change the color of my eyes."

"I watched my own mother die, too, but you wouldn't let me speak of those memories, sir. You would have me believe they don't belong to me."

"I thought it would lessen the pain of losing her."

"Those memories weren't yours to take. Good or bad, they're mine. Look at your own life, Father. You grew up and became a doctor. You heal the sick. Save lives. Maybe what happened to you as a boy had something to do with it."

"It had everything to do with it."

"You make my point for me."

The words struck Blue like hammer blows. He remembered all the times he'd shushed the boy when Lucas brought up "the day Mama died." All the times he deliberately misunderstood Lucas's tears and rages, and later his misdeeds. He hadn't been protecting Lucas at all. "I should have known better," he said in a voice that was barely a whisper. "What happened to your mother was so terrible I wanted to wipe it from your mind. But you can't keep a memory silent. It was wrong of me to try." He held out his hand, palm up. "You're a fine son. A fine person."

Lucas dropped the rake. "God. Do you know how long I've waited to hear those words from you?" He stared up at the patch of sky over the hedgerow, and an autumn wind swept the leaves along the walkway.

"I thought you knew," Blue admitted, his chest aching. With new eyes, he regarded Lucas, so handsome and strapping, straining with readiness to take hold of his own life. There was a new maturity in his son, and it was like a gift to Blue. Here was someone not simply to worry about and raise like a prized horse. Here was someone who loved him, someone he could count on every day of his life. He needed Lucas more than he ever thought possible. It seemed the most natural thing in the world to take the big, ungainly boy into his arms, to hold him close to his heart as a bond of love enveloped them both.

Exhausted as he was, Blue knew he wouldn't rest until he saw Isabel. But when he walked into her room, he found the bed stripped to the mattress, the linens heaped in a wicker laundry basket. Bernadette Riordan, who was freeing a pillow from its slip, nodded in greeting.

"Hello, Doctor." She ducked her head, but not before he saw she'd been crying.

"Where's Isabel?"

Bernadette set down the pillow. "Gone away, sir. You know, like she said. She's a traveler. We always knew that."

The dull thud of a headache descended on Blue, throbbing with a voice of its own. Gone. Gone. Gone . . . But she filled him still. He only had to close his eyes, and he could feel her. When they made love, she let him come so deep inside her that he lost himself. When she thought he was sleeping, she whispered his name to the empty night. Had she been lying, even then?

"When?" he asked Bernadette.

"Hours ago, it's been. Said we mustn't wake Lucas on account of the terrible adventures last night. Did she never say goodbye to you, sir?"

"No," he admitted. "She never did."

Forty-Two

～⌘～

Whistling tunelessly, Willie Bean came into the Rescue League clinic, wheeling a load of folded draperies of some sort.

"What's that?" Blue asked, looking up from his inventory of herbal preparations.

Willie shuffled his feet, bashful as always. "New, um, shrouds from the Ladies Aid Guild, sir. They sent over a dozen, all hand-stitched."

"There's room in the storage closet for them," said Blue. Resignation sat heavily upon him, but it lacked the useless rage that used to bind him to the past. People would die no matter how hard he worked. It was part of the circle of life. Some would die tragically or senselessly. Now, in the months that followed Isabel's departure, he no longer filled himself with wrathful laments for the lost souls he couldn't save. He found another way of seeing his work, his strength and his limitations. He faced each tragedy with a different understanding. Instead of raging against loss, instead of reliving his own grief over and over again, he let go. He knew how to do that now. It was such a simple matter, but it had taken him a decade to learn it.

Willie put away the shrouds and Delta brought in his next patient, a little girl named Sadie, howling from an earache in the arms of her weary mother. The child had no fever, so he suspected he'd find some sort of foreign object lodged in the ear canal.

Delta did her best to soothe the hysterical child, but it took Blue, hunkering down and looking the girl in the eye, to get her attention.

"If you want it to stop hurting, you'll have to hold still for me," he said.

"You'll only make it hurt worse," sobbed Sadie.

The old Blue would have ordered Delta to hold her down, or he might have lied to her and said it wouldn't hurt a bit. Now he said, "It will hurt worse, but only for a moment."

"How long is a moment?"

"For as long as it takes you to sing 'Camptown Races,' " he said. "But you must keep perfectly still while you do so."

"Sing with me," she said in a small voice.

"I don't —" He caught Delta's glare across the table. Then he took a deep breath and sang quietly, with a smile on his face, while his patient joined in. Delta held the lamp and he worked as he sang, gently probing until he dislodged what appeared to be a dried lima bean. He held out the porcelain-clad tray.

Sadie ducked her head. "I was just playing. It was a long time ago."

"If you'd waited much longer, this would have sprouted." He put two drops of warm oil in her ear to soothe the inflamed part.

Her eyes widened, first with alarm and then surprise. "That didn't hurt," she declared, hopping down from the table. On the way out, she turned and smiled at him shyly. Her face was like a pansy open to the sun, and the whole world was in her eyes.

He was still smiling after she left, because he found himself thinking of Lucas. A child belongs to a parent only for a time, and trying to hang on too long betrayed the natural order of things. Two months ago, he helped Lucas pack a single traveling case and put him on a train bound eastward. Lucas's choice for his education had shocked everyone. He had convinced Senator Leland Stanford to nominate him to the United States Military Academy at West Point, where he would learn to be a warrior.

When Lucas first told Blue his plans, Blue had been staggered by fear and love and pride. He knew what war was, but Lucas had to find out for himself. Blue considered putting his foot down, refusing to allow Lucas to go, but he knew Lucas would escape him anyway. Finally — too late — he realized that holding on too tight was as dangerous as letting go too readily.

In this, too, Lucas showed a curiously adult wisdom. He pledged to stay loyal to June Li, but that didn't keep him from striking out into the world, confident that he'd come back a better man.

His son's absence would be a wound in his life, but he found a kind of sweetness in the pain. Lucas had finally decided on the direction of his dream.

There was no sweetness in the absence of another, however. Since the events of summer, he had a new sense of before and after. Before Isabel came tumbling into his world, and after she left.

He learned that she'd gone to Honolulu, just as she always said she would. As much as he loved her, he could still step back and see that she was the sort of woman who couldn't stay in one place. He was a man who couldn't leave the world he'd created for himself.

Isabel had left because he'd let her. Because he had not managed to convince her that the past didn't matter. Because he was furious about her recklessness and lack of commitment. And finally, the true reason emerged. How could he possibly love her enough? How could his heart be big enough to love her the way she deserved? His heart, jaded and weary with living and loss and worry and suspicion, was ruined for someone like her. She was too hungry for the right kind of love, the kind untainted by tragedy. She deserved a man with a heart filled with gladness, not darkness.

He remembered a conversation with his stepmother earlier in the summer. Love was not always convenient. At the time, he'd had no notion of what that meant. Now he understood it with a painful intensity. Sometimes love was hard. Still, it was the essence of life.

Knowing Isabel had changed him forever, but the realization had come at the cost of her love. Perhaps.

The old Blue Calhoun would have stepped aside, looked away, let the opportunity slip by. But he was a different man now.

Forty-Three

Soft chords from a ukelele shimmered across the open pavilion of the Grand Pacific Hotel of Honolulu. In the background, the cream-colored walls of the main building, an adobe made of coral, were painted pink by the setting sun. Clematis and passion flowers climbed the corner posts of the pavilion, framing a perfect view of the lush, waterfall-draped mountains cleaving down to the water.

The tropical breeze held a wealth of scents — the sea and Plumeria from the hedge along the sandbank, roasting fish crackling over the fire pit, pineapple and melon punch that flowed endlessly for the well-heeled guests of the resort.

A ship from the mainland had docked that afternoon, a huge paddle steamer with decks stacked like wedding cakes, balconies of iron lace, a towering pilot house and two jury masts. Hordes of native surfriders paddled out to welcome the guests. The islanders' sleek brown bodies, prone upon lozenge-shaped waxed boards, flashed in the lowering sun. Some of the more daring riders stood upon their boards, gliding ahead of the lip of an incoming wave. Coral fishers and canoes bristling with outriggers plied a brisk trade in the harbor.

Wagonloads of luggage jammed the roadway in front of the hotel. Native horsemen and horsewomen in leafy crowns jammed the roadway, offering wreaths of fresh flowers along with their services as sightseeing guides.

Isabel walked across the scrubby grass to the edge of the beach, where gouged rocks and sand lay bleached by the sun and wind. A wild storm that morning had left a wrack line of weeds and flowers, like a torn lei along the shore. She lifted a spyglass to her eye, but she didn't aim at the ship. Each evening at this time, people gathered to watch the migration of the whales past the magnificent promontory called Diamond Head. Their shadow-colored bodies were so huge that when they breached, it seemed like an act of defiance against nature.

This whole magical archipelago was a fairyland, a place of dreams. Anything could happen here.

Except nothing ever did.

She had always longed to see whales, and now she could look at them any time she wished. She let the boom of the surf rage in her ears, drowning out the sweet music.

Sometimes, if she lost herself deeply enough in the exotic new world she'd discovered, she could forget about the past for whole minutes at a time. But of course, memories and regrets always crept back into her heart.

What was he doing right now? Was his cravat in need of straightening? Was he eating supper, treating a patient, saying good-night to his son? Did he still make that contented, sighing sound in his throat when he settled down to sleep?

Isabel felt trapped in her own life. She couldn't go forward, couldn't go back. There was only one place she wanted to be, and she was afraid to go there.

"Will you be joining the other guests for supper, Missy *kamaina?*" asked Kai, the hotel's native host, a thickly built man in white trousers and a colorful Garibaldi shirt. He called her *kamaina* because she had been a guest for so many weeks that they no longer considered her a foreigner.

"I suppose I will," she said. The hotel guests — a mélange of wealthy planters, whaling captains, naval officers and missionaries — made for pleasant enough company. But Isabel had not been able to recapture her old sense of fun. Superficial acquaintances, which used to amuse her so much, now failed to fill the void. In fact, sometimes their transient nature only made her feel more lonely than ever.

With a courtly bow, he offered her a lei. The white blossoms matched the ones on her pau', a dress she wore for riding. She dipped her head forward to accept the wreath. The powerful perfume encircled her.

"Kai," she said, "is one of the ships in port bound for San Francisco?"

"Yes, Miss. The *Columbia* leaves in three days' time."

Her heart drummed painfully with yearning. Three days. In just three short days, she could be on her way to San Francisco, to . . . what? She would never find out if she didn't go. Her need outweighed her fear. "I should like to get a berth on it. Can you arrange that?"

"Yes, Miss. But —"

"What is it?" She felt giddy with impatience.

"A gentleman has requested permission to escort you to supper."

"Oh, I don't think —"

"I only asked out of politeness," said a voice she thought she'd never hear again, "but I won't take no for an answer."

Perhaps it was the expression on her face that made Kai scurry away; perhaps it was her complete and utter shocked stillness. The spyglass dropped from her numb fingers.

"What a shame it would have been," he said, "if you took ship for San Francisco just as I arrived." He stood beneath the trembling shadows of a banyan tree. Every inch of him was familiar to her — the bright bottle color of his eyes, the gorgeous shape of his mouth, the Viking-like height and breadth of him. Yet at the same time, he was wholly a stranger. He wore a loose shirt open at the throat, the sleeves pushed back. His hair had grown past his collar and his lean cheeks sported a day's growth of beard. This was not the Blue Calhoun she saw in dreams. This was a hundred, a thousand times better.

A baffling and shameful urge to weep filled her throat. Mortified, Isabel swallowed with painful effort. She managed somehow to force air into her lungs, to dampen her lips and find her voice. "Um, travel agrees with you."

"You always said it would. You were right."

She felt vulnerable, as though she might fall to pieces like one of the storm-shredded flowers that lay at her feet. Wrapping her arms protectively around her middle, she asked, "Lucas is well? And June Li and the others?"

"Everyone's fine. Lucas is a cadet at the United States Military Academy. Once I got over the shock, I realized how proud I am of him. My son and I did a lot of mending this summer."

"I'm glad," she said. *He loves you so much.* She didn't dare say so aloud, for she was afraid she might come apart.

Blue took a step toward her. The setting sun at his back outlined him in exquisite detail. "Everyone misses you. Isabel —"

She was afraid of what he might say, so she interrupted him. "So what of Dr. and Mrs. Vickery?"

He hesitated, then latched on to the neutral topic. "The night you were shot, he'd gone down to supervise the distribution of an opium shipment — illegally, of course. He preferred his imports to be duty free. His wife was supposed to be on a train to Monterey, but she followed him. She suspected he'd be meeting his mistress."

"Clarice Hatcher."

He nodded. "Alma took his old Confederate pistol and went after them. She probably arrived a few minutes before Brolin, who had been watching Vickery and was about to close in on him. He was, like you, very much in the wrong place at the wrong time. Alma and her husband quarreled."

"And then she shot Mr. Brolin?"

"There was a struggle for the gun. Clarice actually did the shooting. The only witness died under mysterious circumstances at Mercy Heights. Rory's looking for proof that Vickery and Clarice had something to do with it. Pisco and Punch admitted that Vickery paid them to . . . dispose of you."

"Good heavens. What's to become of them all?"

"Vickery will go to prison to serve a life sentence. His wife has been sent to a sanitarium in Calistoga. And Clarice goes on trial in three weeks. Rory tells me your testimony would be a powerful element in the proceedings."

Her heart sank. That explained it, then. That was why he'd crossed an ocean to find her. "So you intend to bring me back to testify?"

"No," he said quietly, taking a step toward her, stopping only inches away.

His tone, his proximity made her heart speed up. "Then tell me why you've come."

He touched her chin, lifted her gaze to his. "I miss your coffee."

Ah, that touch, so gentle that it took her heart apart. She pulled away, turned to face the restless ocean. "I never go back to a place I've already been."

"If you keep running in the same direction, you'll wind up back where you started from."

She could not believe how much this hurt. And how much hope was filling her up at the same time.

"Why these islands?" he asked. "Why did you come here, Isabel?"

"To find a place where the seasons never change." The answer came from her on an unplanned wave of honesty.

"A place you'll never have to leave," he said.

She nodded helplessly. After all her travels, she sought the slumbrous sameness of endless summer. He circled his arms around her from behind, and she sank back against him.

"Here is that place, Isabel," he said. "Here, next to my heart, is the place you'll never have to leave. In my bed, my life, wherever we go. It's where we both belong." He bent to nuzzle her neck, and heat sped through her.

On fire, she turned to face him again. The blood thundered in her ears with the rhythm of the waves. He was a complete and devastating dream, and his words made her want to cry.

"Why are you looking at me like that?" he asked.

"You know everything about me — and you don't despise me."

He smiled down at her. "I neither know all your secrets, nor do I despise you. You're an endless mystery to me, Isabel. And that's just one of the reasons I love you so much." He spoke so matter-of-factly that she wasn't certain she'd understood. He touched the fringed knot at the waist of her pau'. "Easily removed. I like it."

She was still reeling from his earlier comment. "How can you joke at a time like this?"

"I'm not joking. I do like a dress that is easily removed."

"Not that, you huge fool. The other. The heartfelt declaration of love."

"Oh, it was that. Heartfelt. And a declaration." His smile was positively rakish as he took out a slender golden ring set with a flashing diamond and slipped it on her finger.

Dear heaven. Love was such a revelation to her. It had the power to destroy her, yet without it, life made no sense.

"I . . . I feel as if I should make some sort of pledge or declaration to you, but I don't know what you want. I don't know if I'm able. . . ." She studied the facets of the diamond as she fumbled for the words. "I know I'm useless when it comes to being in love, but I'll do the best I can."

He brushed her lips with his. "I think we can probably muddle through."

Her chin trembled and she started to pull away, but he stopped her. "Isabel, I'll travel to the ends of the earth to be with you. If this is the life you wish for, then I shall make it my life as well. I swear my love for you will never change except to grow stronger with each passing day. You have to trust me, Isabel. Trust me as I never dared to trust you until it was nearly too late."

She struggled to smile through a veil of tears. "It's not too late, my love. It's not."

About the Author

"Your storytelling fills in the little holes in my soul," wrote a reader of **Susan Wiggs**, and this comment perfectly captures what the author hopes to achieve with her romantic novels. Wiggs, a former teacher, firmly believes that love can create a world in which all wounds are healed, and her award-winning tales of adventure and romance bear this out. Noted for their scenes of emotional truth, evoking both tears and laughter, her novels regularly appear on national bestseller lists.

Susan Wiggs lives with her family on an island in the Pacific Northwest, where she is working on her next book. Readers may write to her at P.O. Box 4469, Rollingbay WA 98061 or visit her on the Web at www.susanwiggs.com.